MONKEY KING

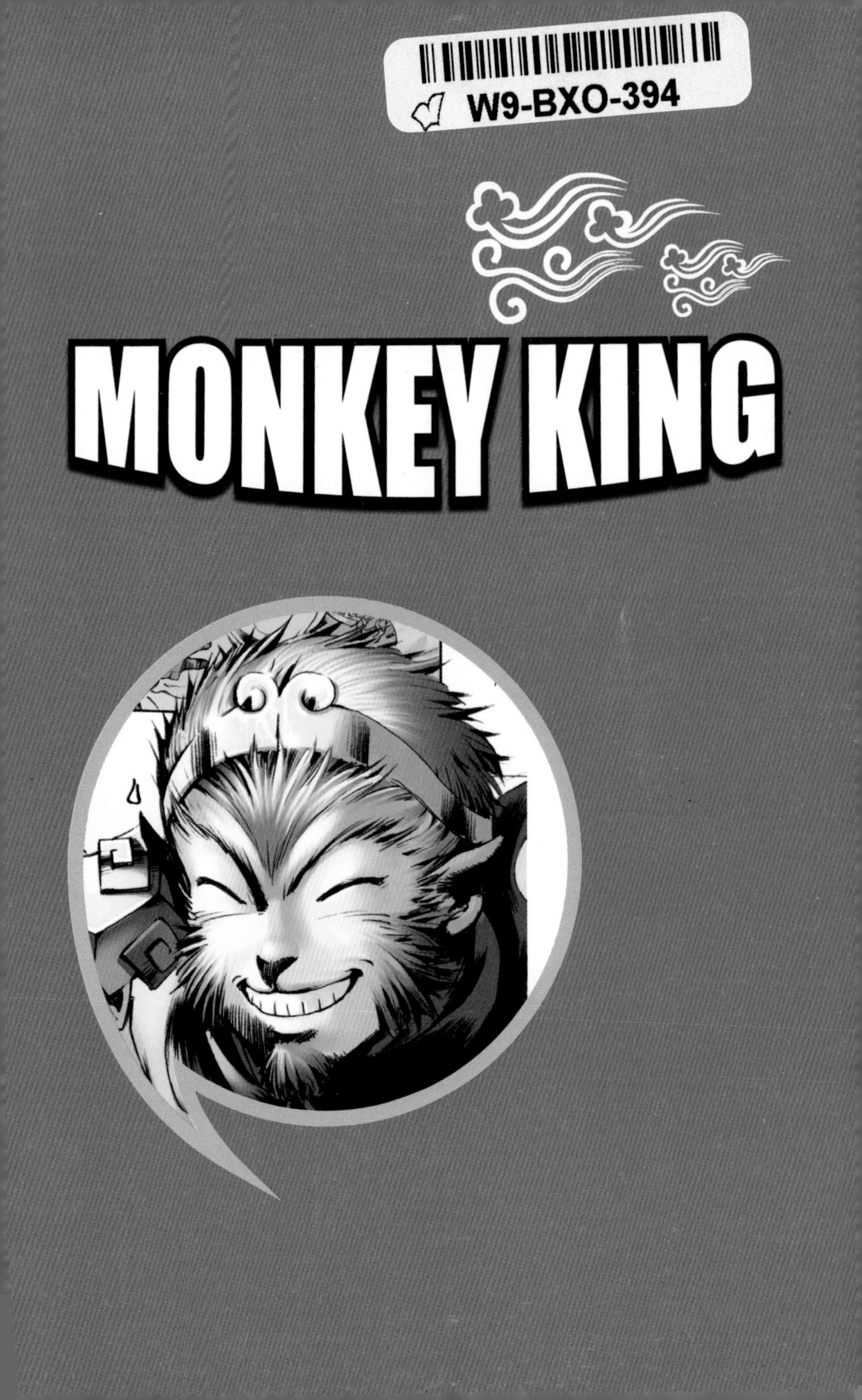

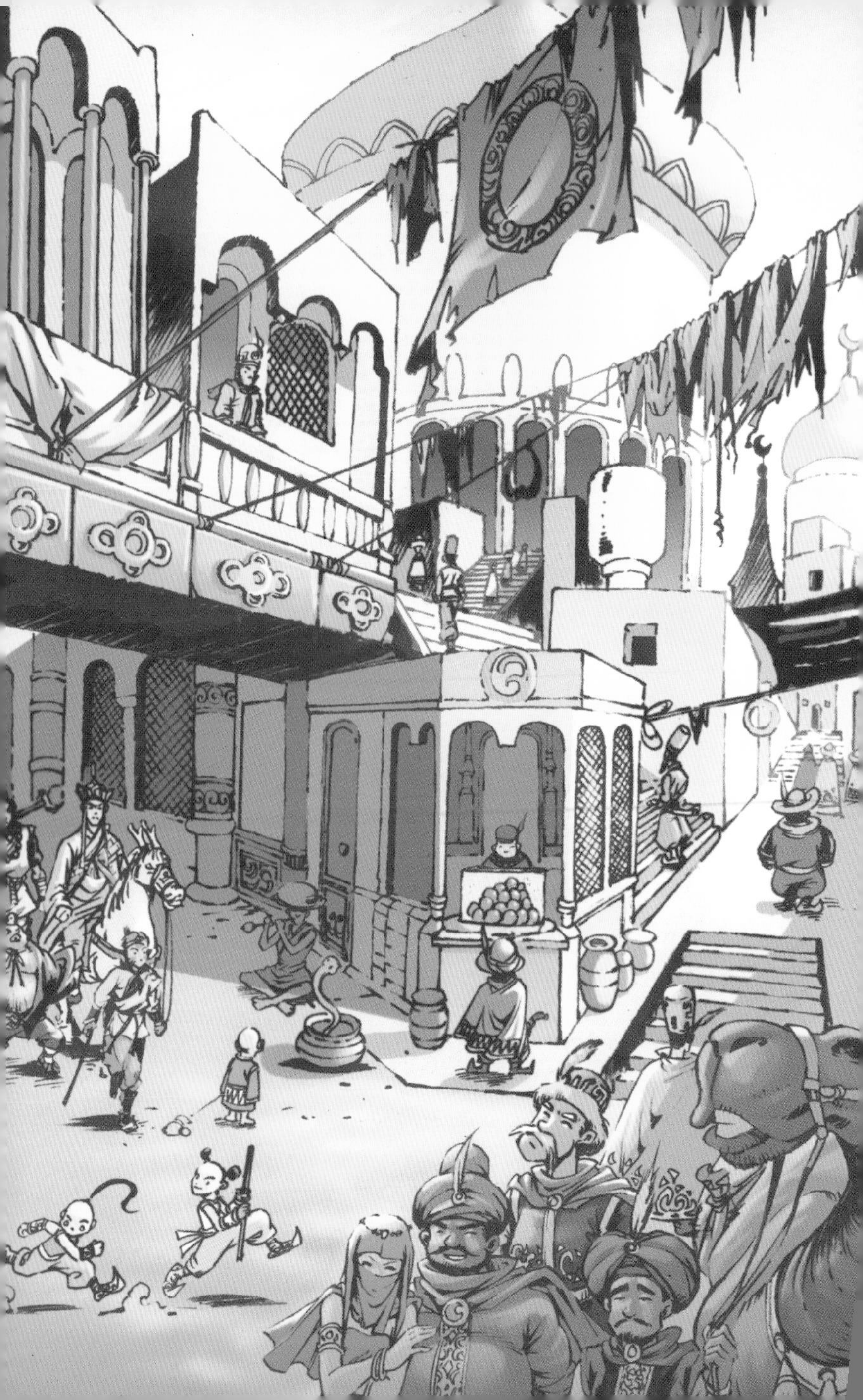

MONKEY KING

The Stolen Kingdom

Created by WEI DONG CHEN

Wei Dong Chen, a highly acclaimed and beloved artist, and an influential leader in the "New Chinese Cartoon" trend, is the founder of Creator World in Tianjin, the largest comics studio in China. Recently the Chinese government entrusted him with the role of general manager of the Beijing Book Fair, and his reputation as a pillar of Chinese comics has brought him many students. He has published more than three hundred cartoons, which have been recognized for their strong literary value not only in Korea, but in Europe and Japan, as well. Free spirited and energetic, Wei Dong Chen's positivist philosophy is reflected in the wisdom of his work. He is published serially in numerous publications while continuing to conceive projects that explore new dimensions of the form.

Illustrated by CHAO PENG

Chao Peng is considered one of Wei Dong Chen's greatest students, and is the director of cartoon at Creator World in Tianjin. One of the most highly regarded cartoonists in China today, Chao Peng's fantastic technique and expression of Chinese culture have won him the acclaim of cartoon lovers throughout China. His other works include "My Pet" and "Searching for the World of Self".

Original story

"The Journey to The West" by Wu, Cheng En

Editing & Designing

Sun Media, Design Hongs, David Teez, Jonathan Evans, YK Kim, HJ Lee, SH Lee, Qing Shao, Xiao Nan Li, Ke Hu

Original Chinese edition published by Anhui Fine Arts Publishing House.

Characters

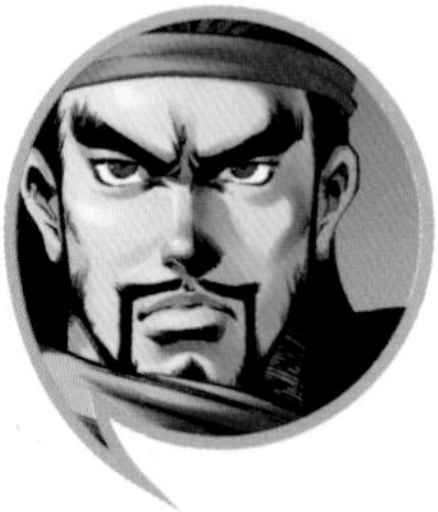

THE KING OF WUJI

The King of WuJi had reigned over a period of severe drought when he was approached by a monk seeking charity. The king was cruel to the monk and threw him into a well for three days. Shortly thereafter, the king was approached by a Taoist hermit named QuanZhen, who offered relief from the drought, but then killed the King of WuJi by throwing him down the same well. The king's ghost unwittingly appears to San Zang in a dream and asks the priest and his disciples to avenge his life and recover his kingdom.

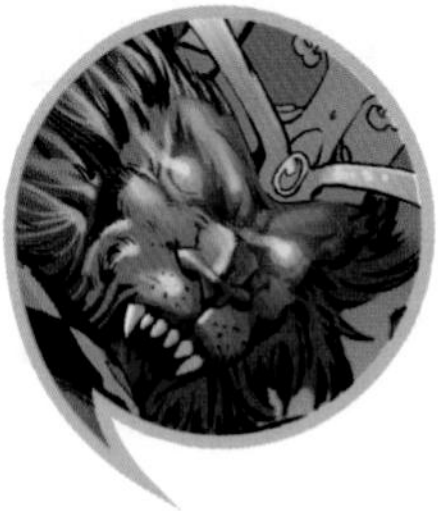

QUANZHEN

QuanZhen is the human incarnation of the Black Lion Demon, who was sent by Buddha to avenge the mistreatment of the Bodhisattva of Wisdom at the hands of the King of WuJi, who mistook the deity for a humble priest and severely mistreated him. QuanZhen killed the king by throwing him down a well, then disguised himself as the fallen king and took control of the Kingdom of WuJi.

THE CROWN PRINCE OF WUJI

The Crown Prince of WuJi is the son of the fallen king. When the king's ghost appears to San Zang in his dream, he tells the priest to seek out his son, who has been so far marginalized from the kingdom that he barely speaks to his own mother, the king's widow. The crown prince is an expert hunter and archer, which could be useful when he discovers what truly happened to his father.

THE QUEEN OF WUJI

The Queen of WuJi is the wife of the fallen king. When the crown prince, having learned from San Zang that his father was murdered and his mother is married to an imposter, confronts his mother about the possibility of treason, the queen is suspicious of the stranger's counsel. But when presented with a precious piece of white jade that belonged to her late husband, the queen knows for certain that things are not what they seem.

THE KING OF THE WELL

The King of the Well is the ruler of the water into which the King of WuJi was thrown. He has been in possession of the dead king's body for three years and considers the corpse a precious treasure. Such an attitude makes things difficult for Sun Wu Kong and Zhu Bajie, who seek to return the king to his throne.

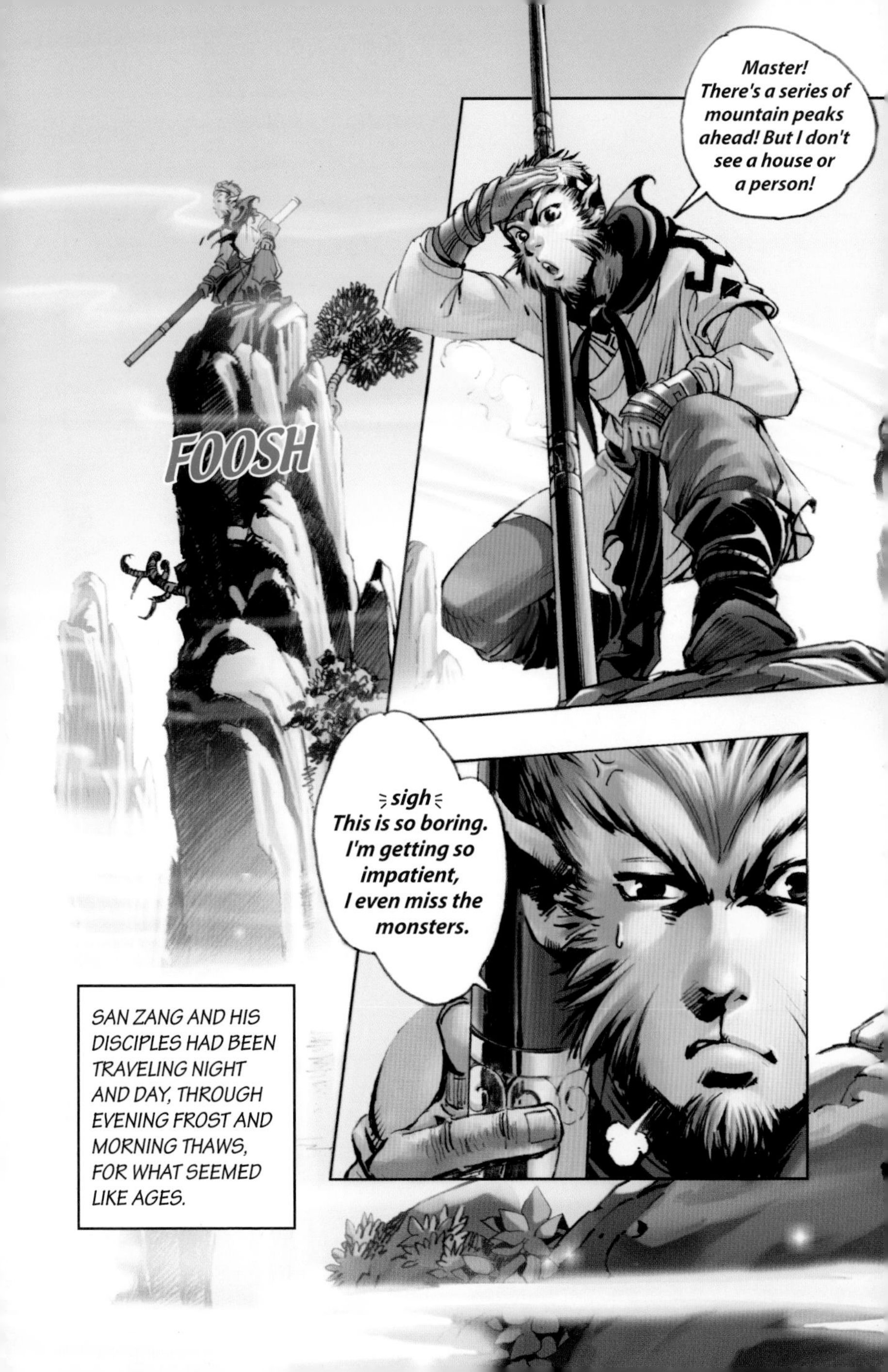
Master! There's a series of mountain peaks ahead! But I don't see a house or a person!
FOOSH
sigh This is so boring. I'm getting so impatient, I even miss the monsters.
SAN ZANG AND HIS DISCIPLES HAD BEEN TRAVELING NIGHT AND DAY, THROUGH EVENING FROST AND MORNING THAWS, FOR WHAT SEEMED LIKE AGES.

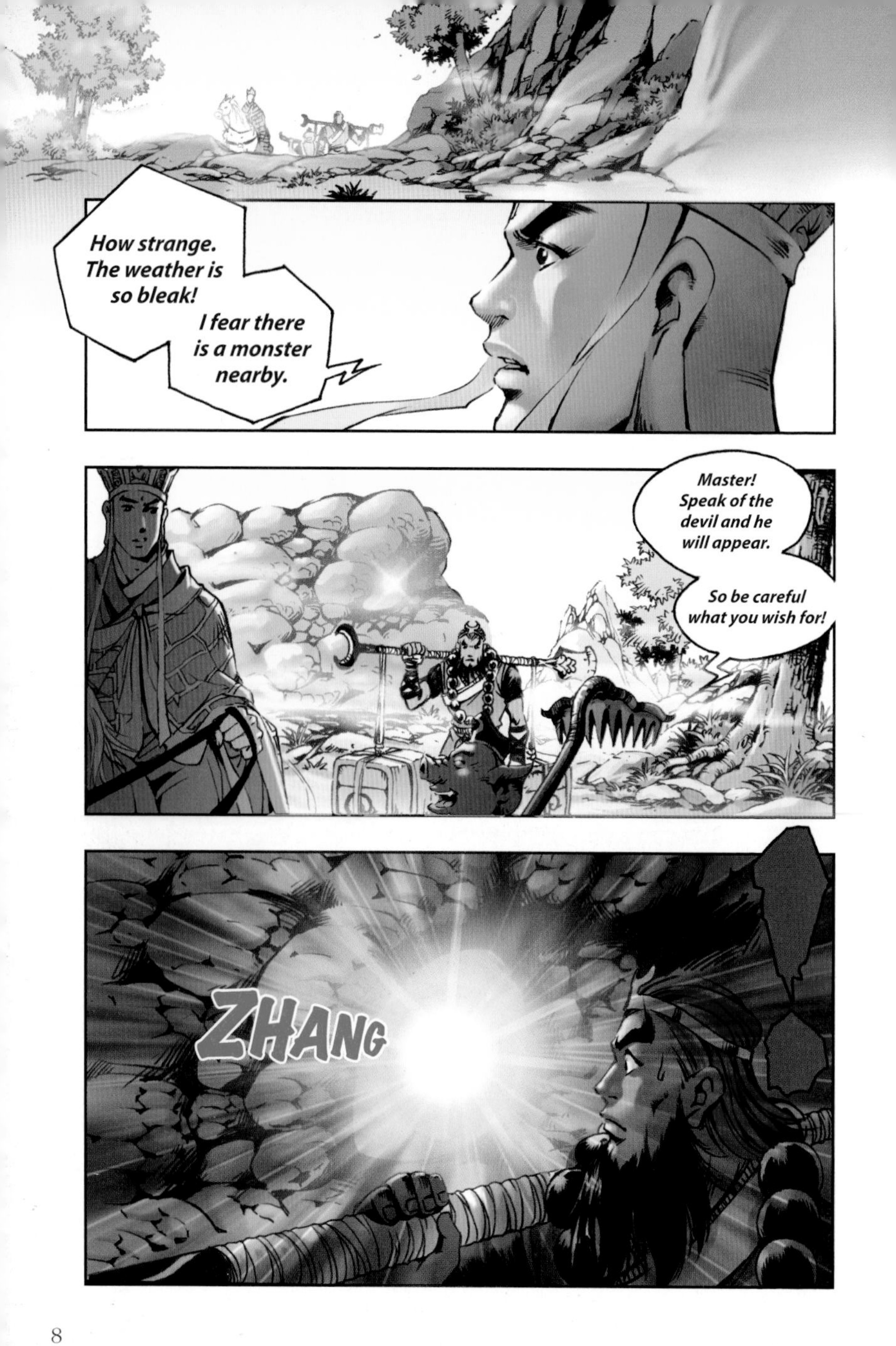
How strange. The weather is so bleak!
I fear there is a monster nearby.
Master! Speak of the devil and he will appear.
So be careful what you wish for!
ZHANG

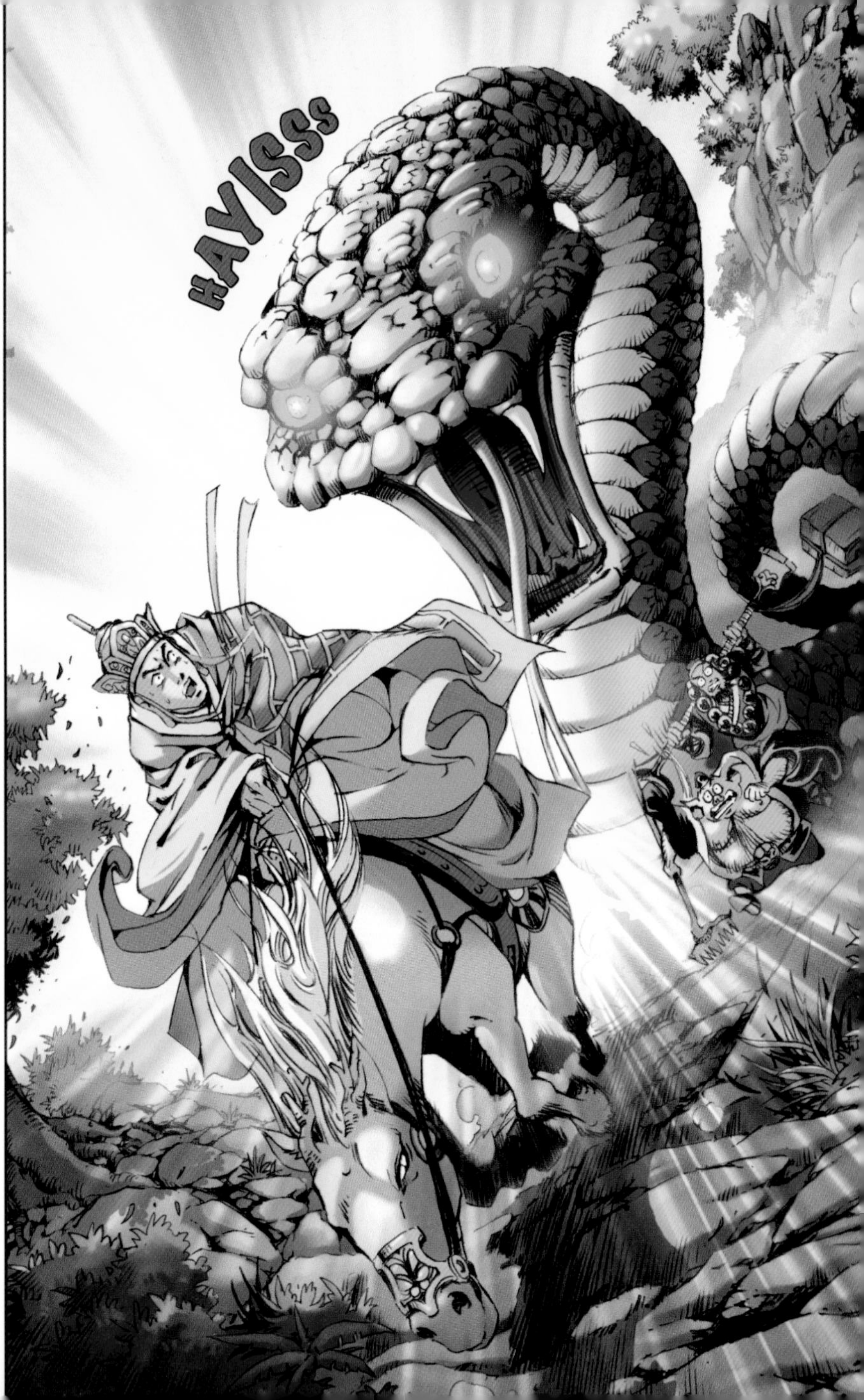
HAYISSS

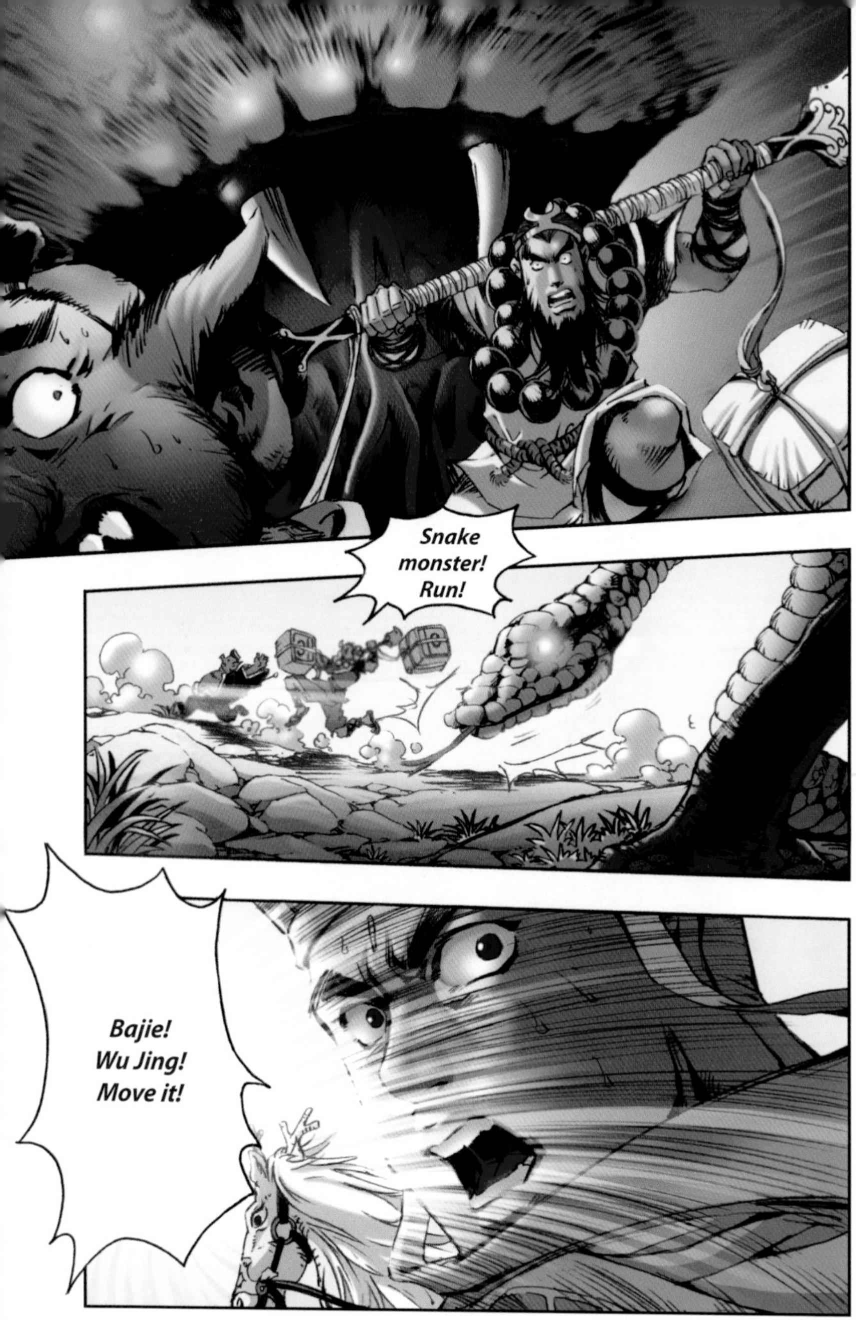
Snake monster! Run!
Bajie! Wu Jing! Move it!

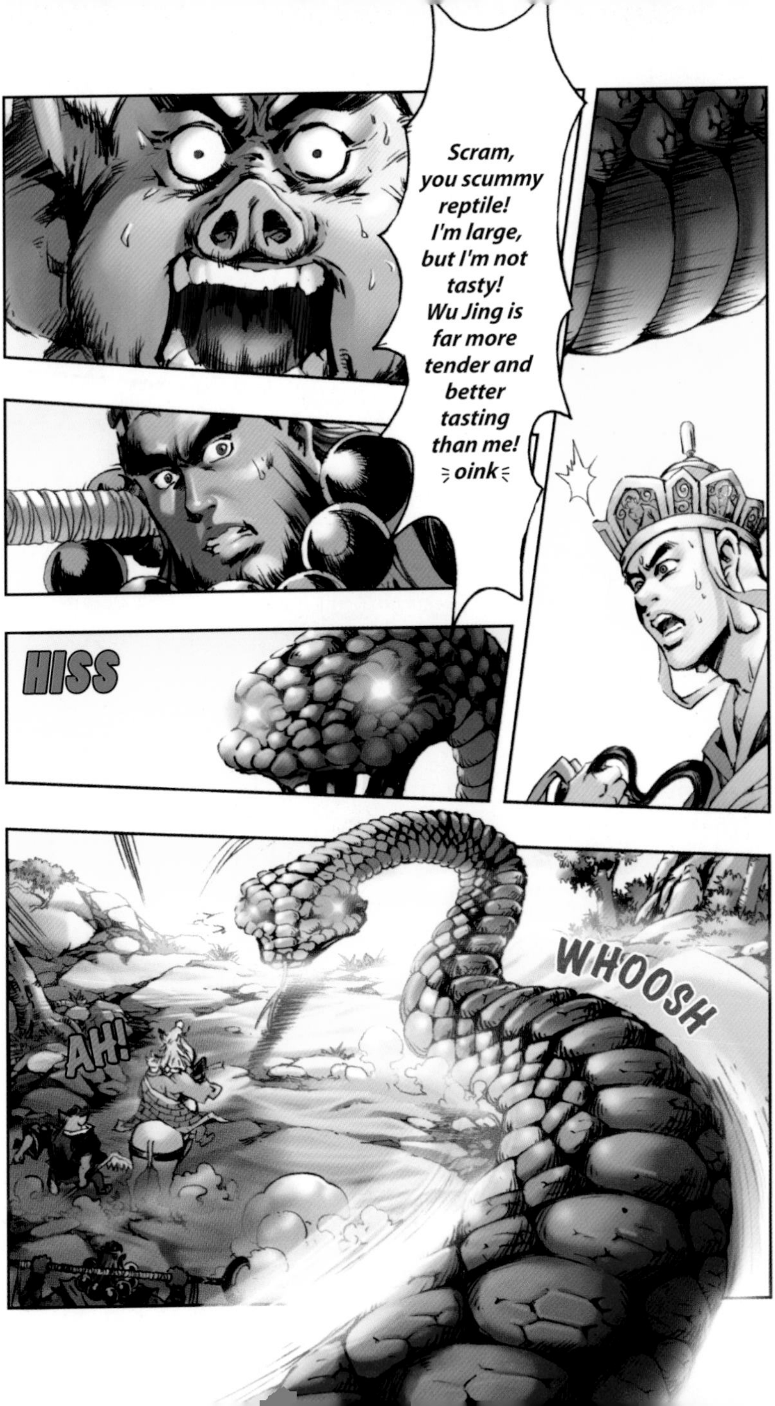
Scram, you scummy reptile! I'm large, but I'm not tasty! Wu Jing is far more tender and better tasting than me! oink
HISS
WHOOSH
AH!

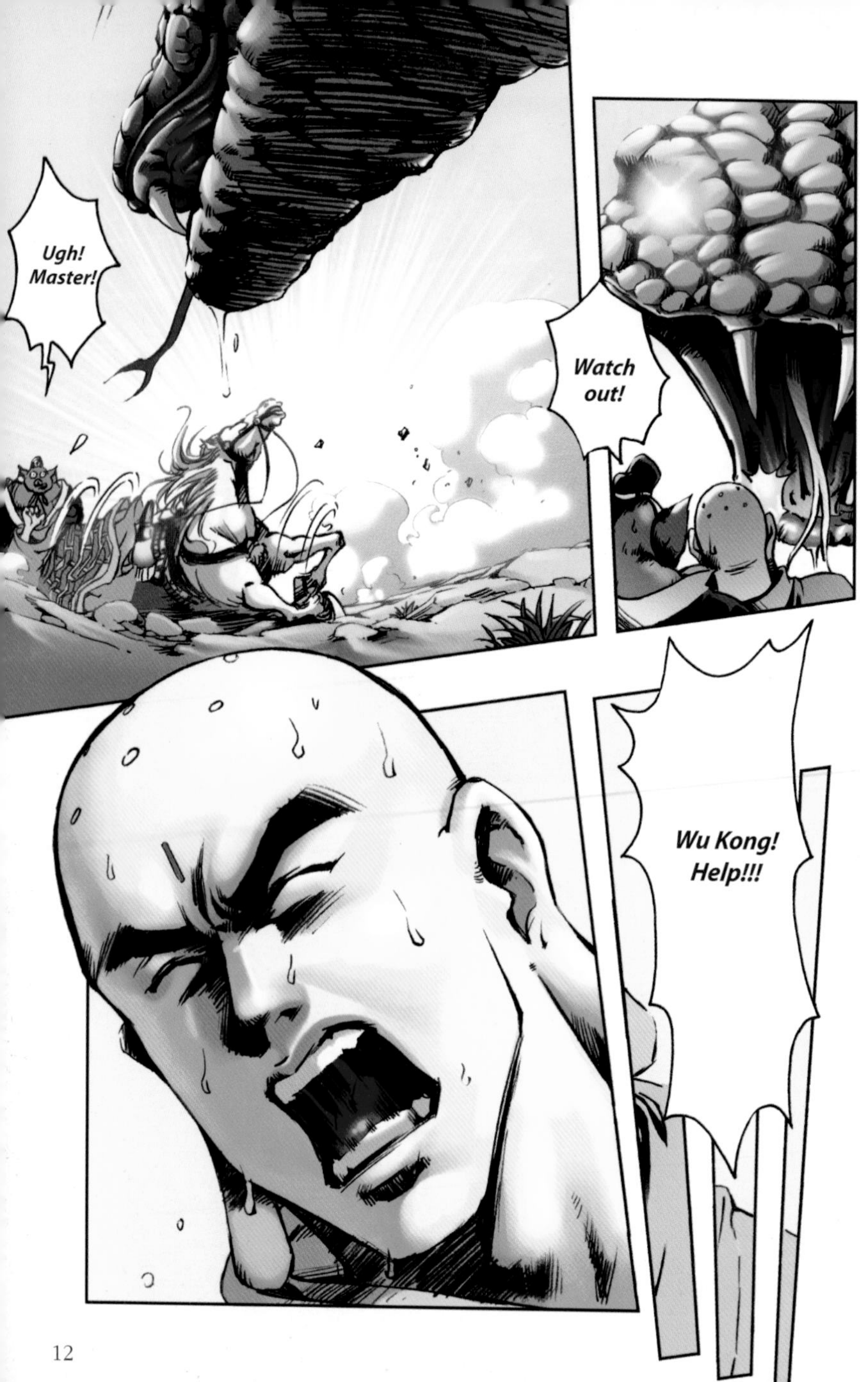
Ugh! Master!
Watch out!
Wu Kong! Help!!!

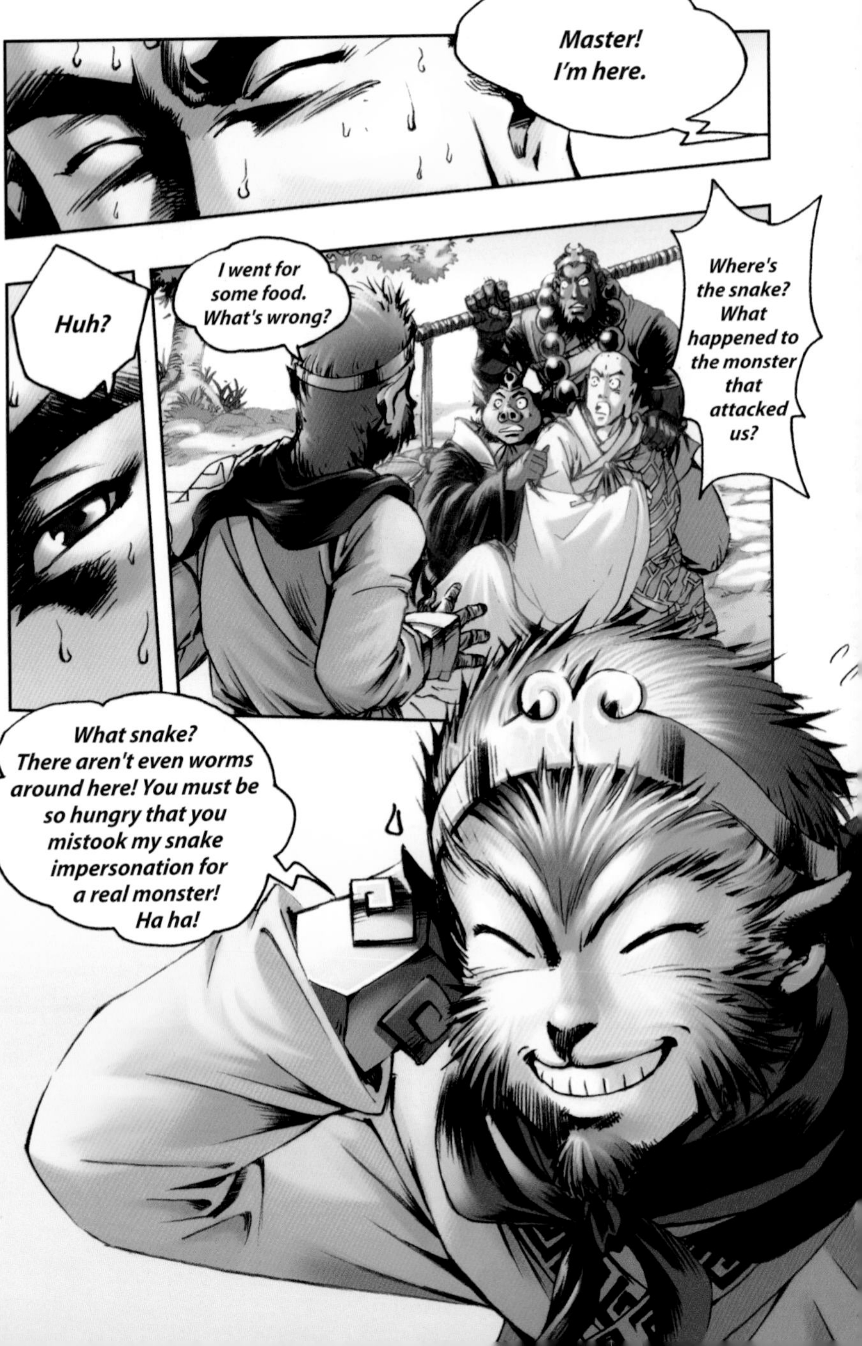

Master!
I'm here.
Huh?
I went for some food. What's wrong?
Where's the snake? What happened to the monster that attacked us?
What snake? There aren't even worms around here! You must be so hungry that you mistook my snake impersonation for a real monster! Ha ha!

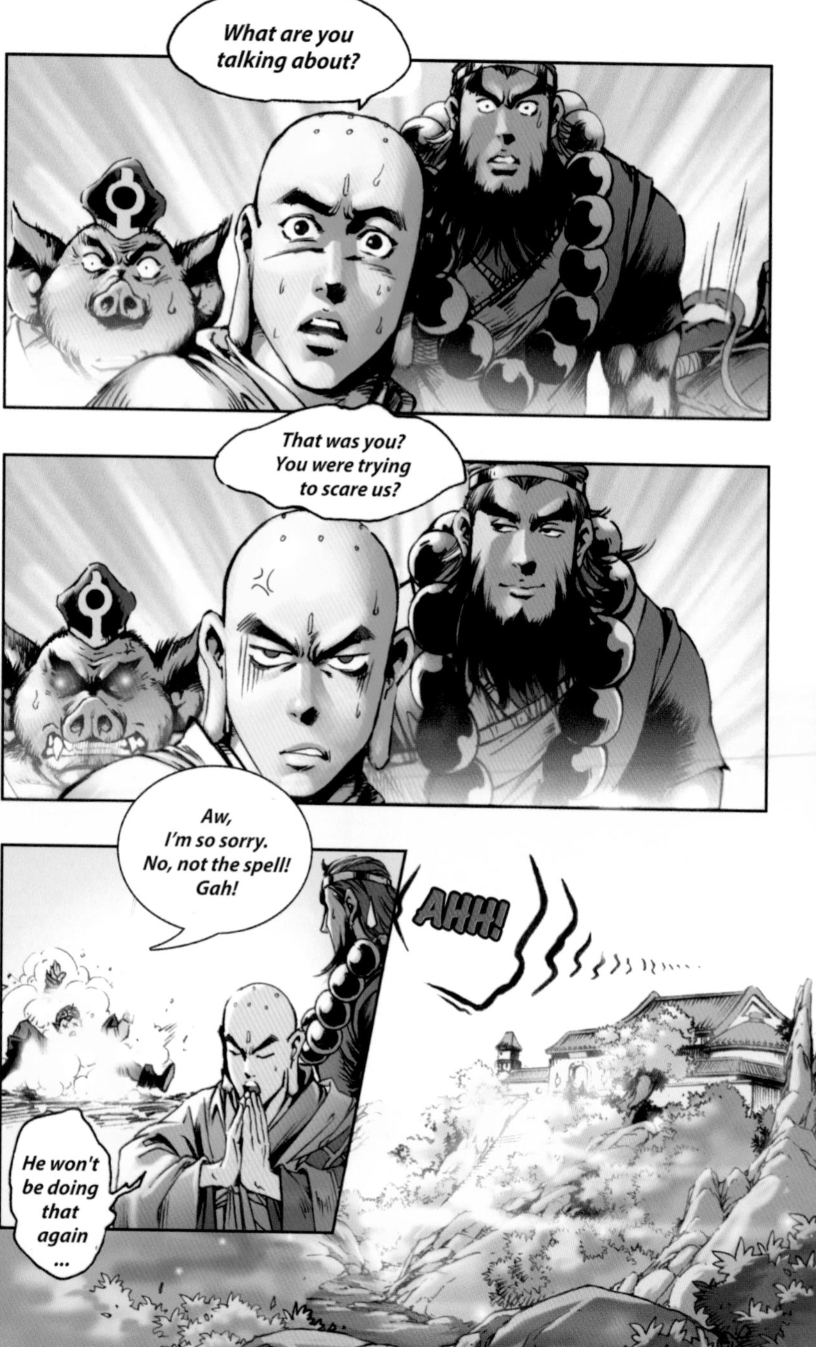
What are you talking about?
That was you? You were trying to scare us?
Aw, I'm so sorry. No, not the spell! Gah!
AHH!
He won't be doing that again ...

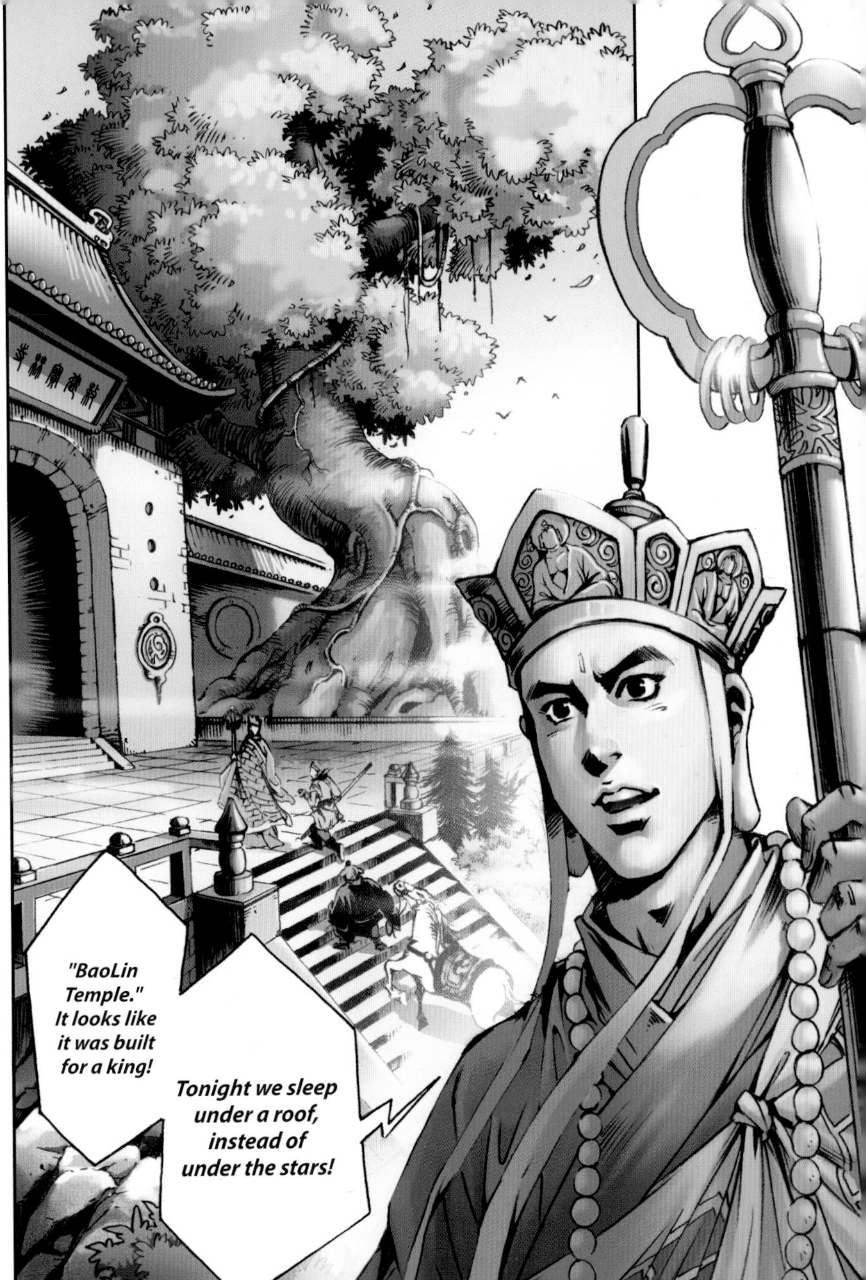
"BaoLin Temple." It looks like it was built for a king!
Tonight we sleep under a roof, instead of under the stars!

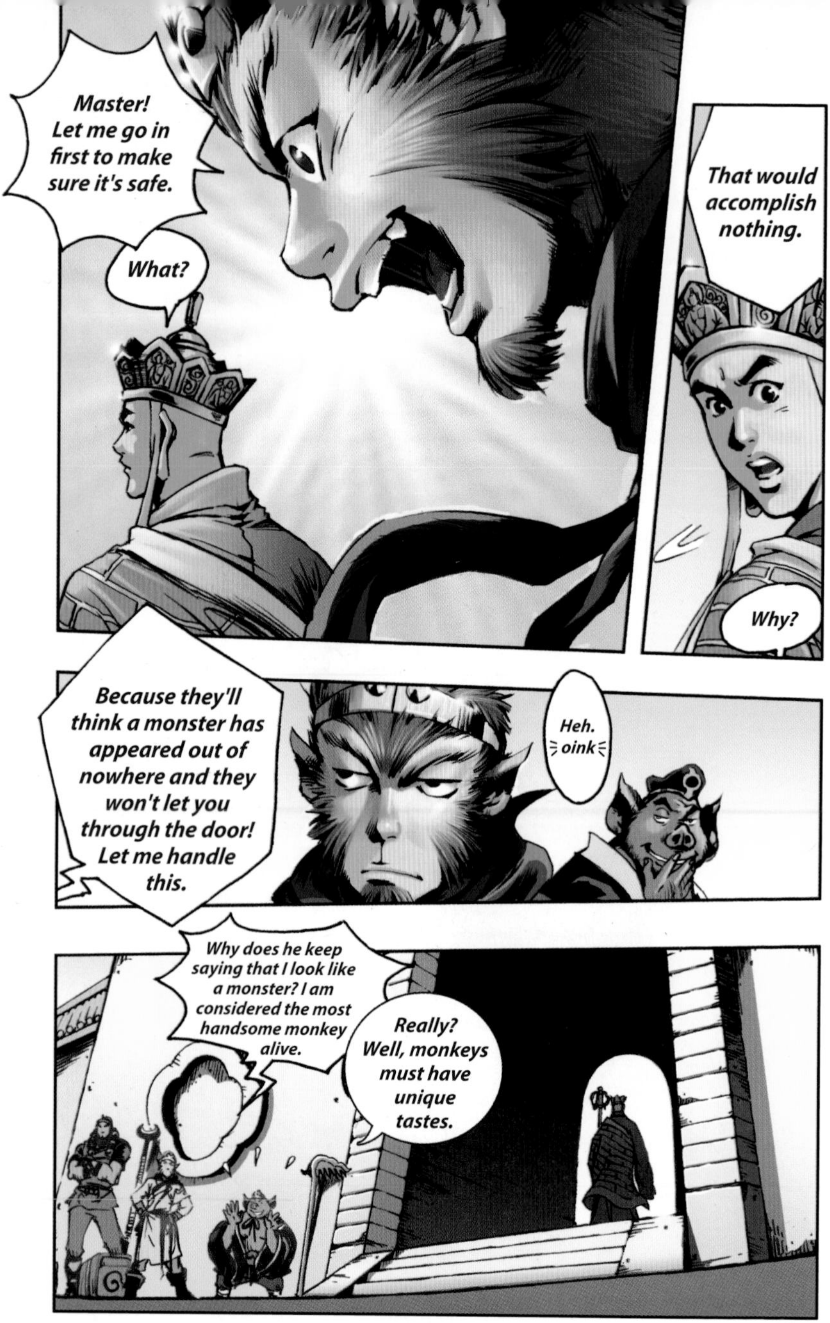
Master! Let me go in first to make sure it's safe.
What?
That would accomplish nothing.
Why?
Because they'll think a monster has appeared out of nowhere and they won't let you through the door! Let me handle this.
Heh. oink
Why does he keep saying that I look like a monster? I am considered the most handsome monkey alive.
Really? Well, monkeys must have unique tastes.

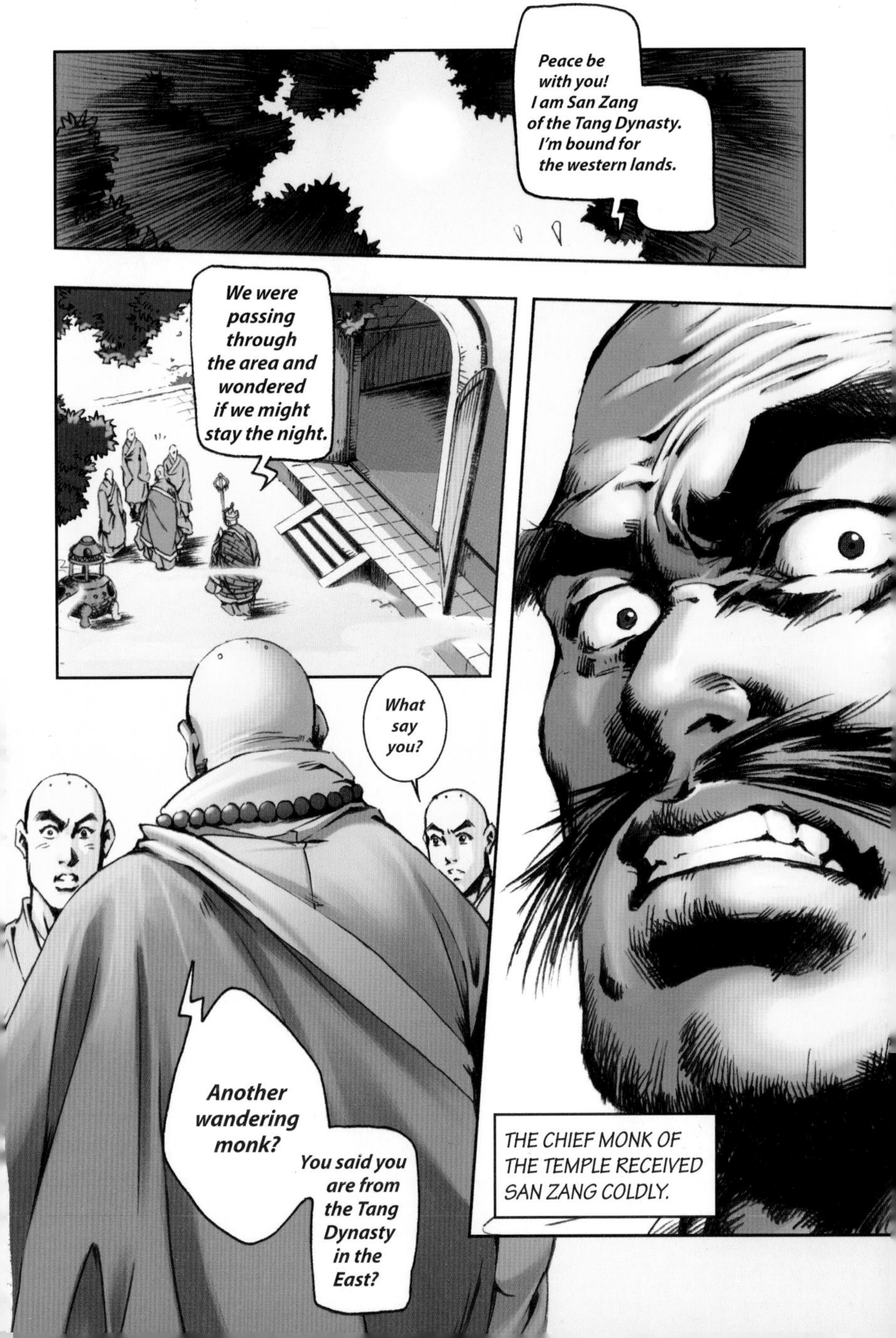
Peace be with you! I am San Zang of the Tang Dynasty. I'm bound for the western lands.
We were passing through the area and wondered if we might stay the night.
What say you?
Another wandering monk?
You said you are from the Tang Dynasty in the East?
THE CHIEF MONK OF THE TEMPLE RECEIVED SAN ZANG COLDLY.

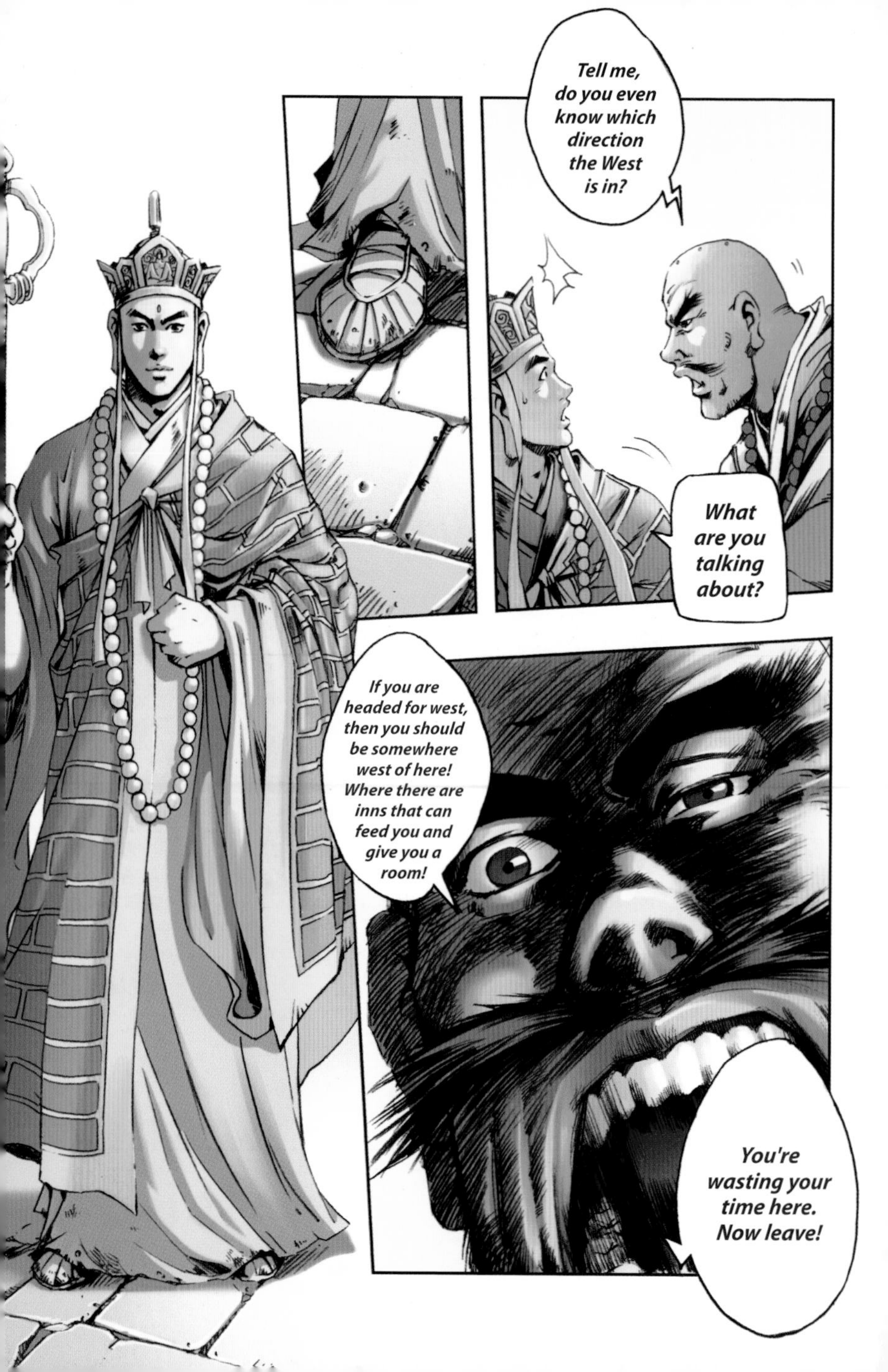
Tell me, do you even know which direction the West is in?
What are you talking about?
If you are headed for west, then you should be somewhere west of here! Where there are inns that can feed you and give you a room!
You're wasting your time here. Now leave!

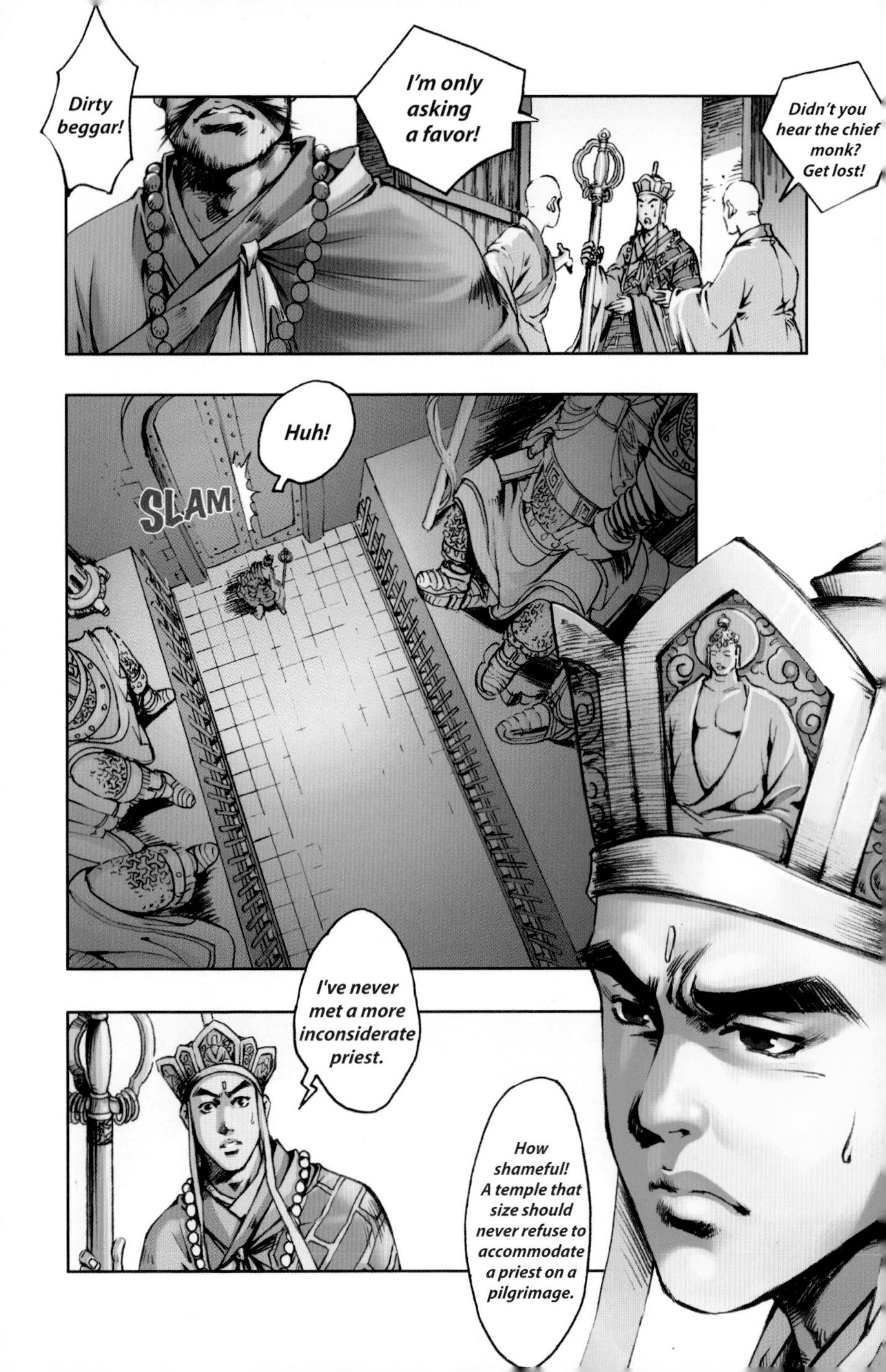
Dirty beggar!
I'm only asking a favor!
Didn't you hear the chief monk? Get lost!
Huh!
SLAM
I've never met a more inconsiderate priest.
How shameful! A temple that size should never refuse to accommodate a priest on a pilgrimage.

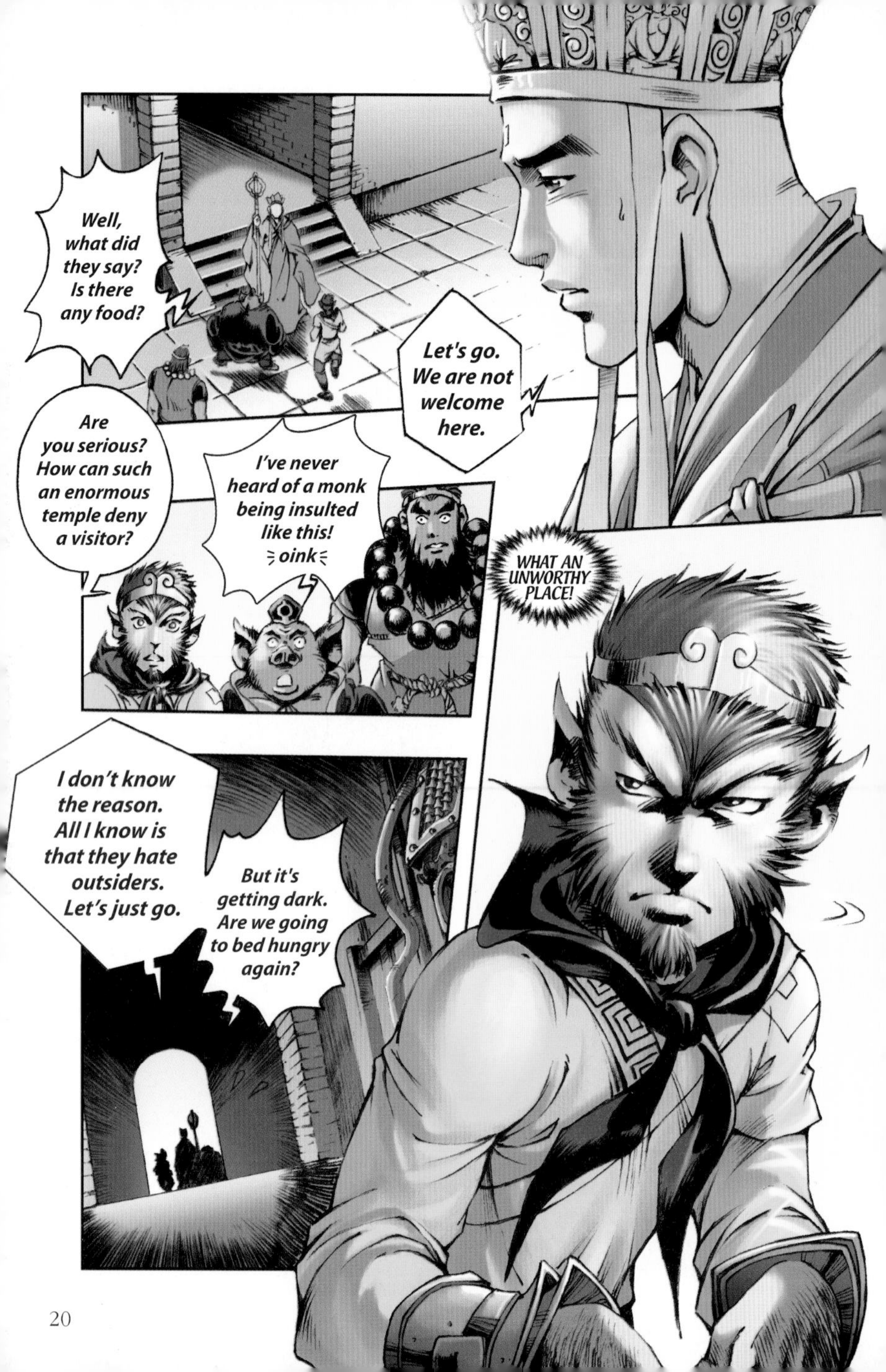
Well, what did they say? Is there any food?
Let's go. We are not welcome here.
Are you serious? How can such an enormous temple deny a visitor?
I've never heard of a monk being insulted like this! oink
WHAT AN UNWORTHY PLACE!
I don't know the reason. All I know is that they hate outsiders. Let's just go.
But it's getting dark. Are we going to bed hungry again?

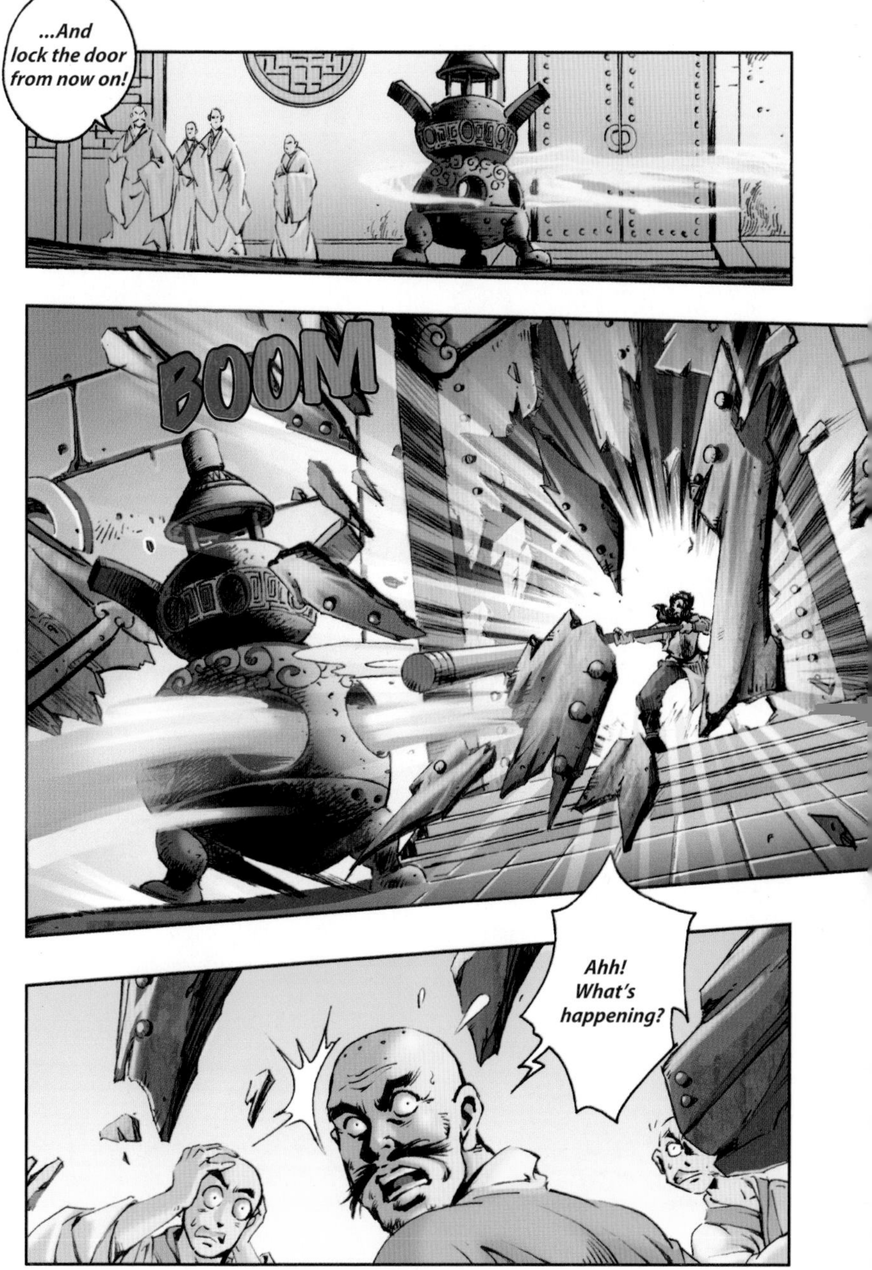
...And lock the door from now on!
BOOM
Ahh! What's happening?

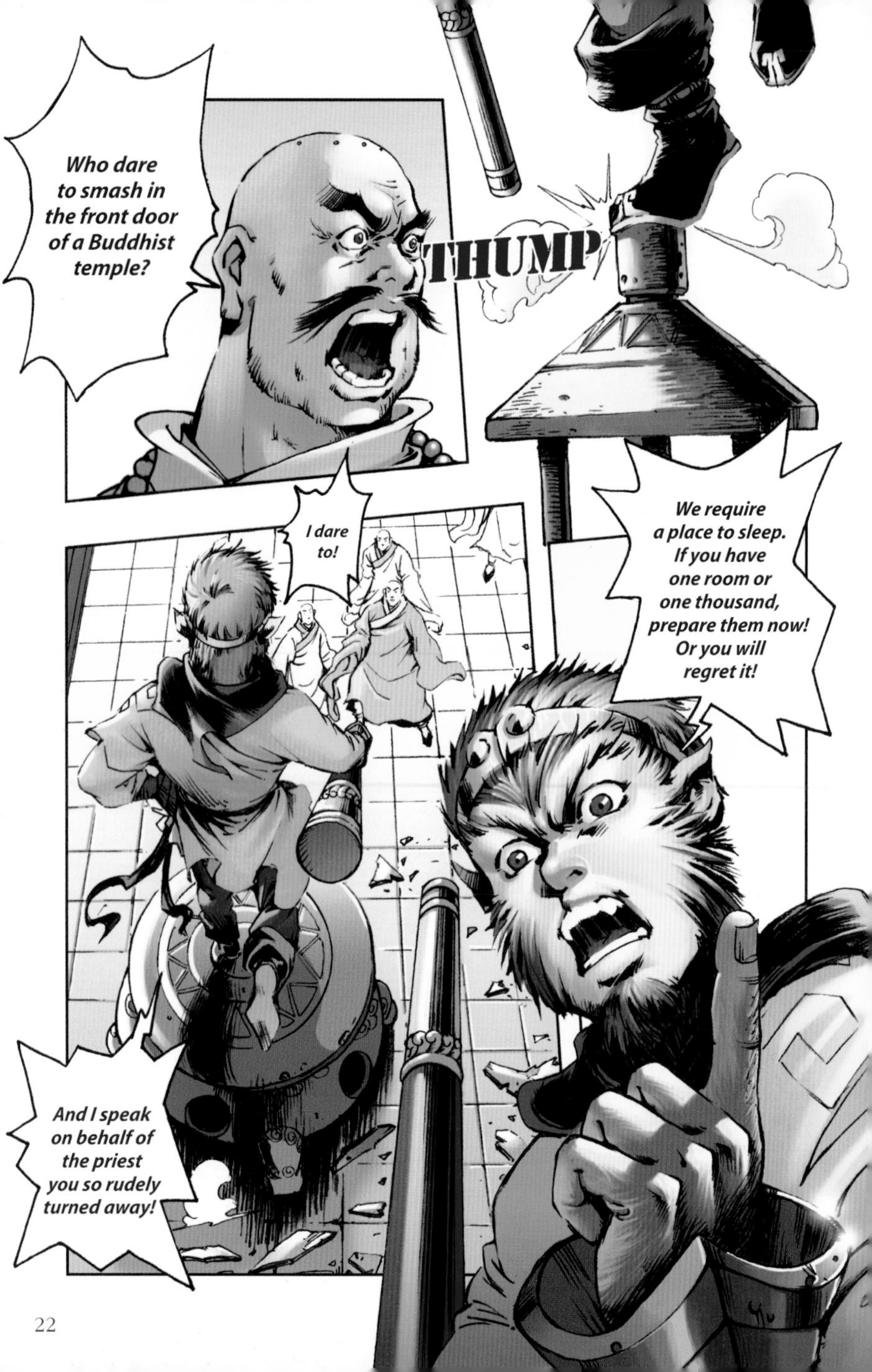
Who dare to smash in the front door of a Buddhist temple?
THUMP
I dare to!
We require a place to sleep. If you have one room or one thousand, prepare them now! Or you will regret it!
And I speak on behalf of the priest you so rudely turned away!

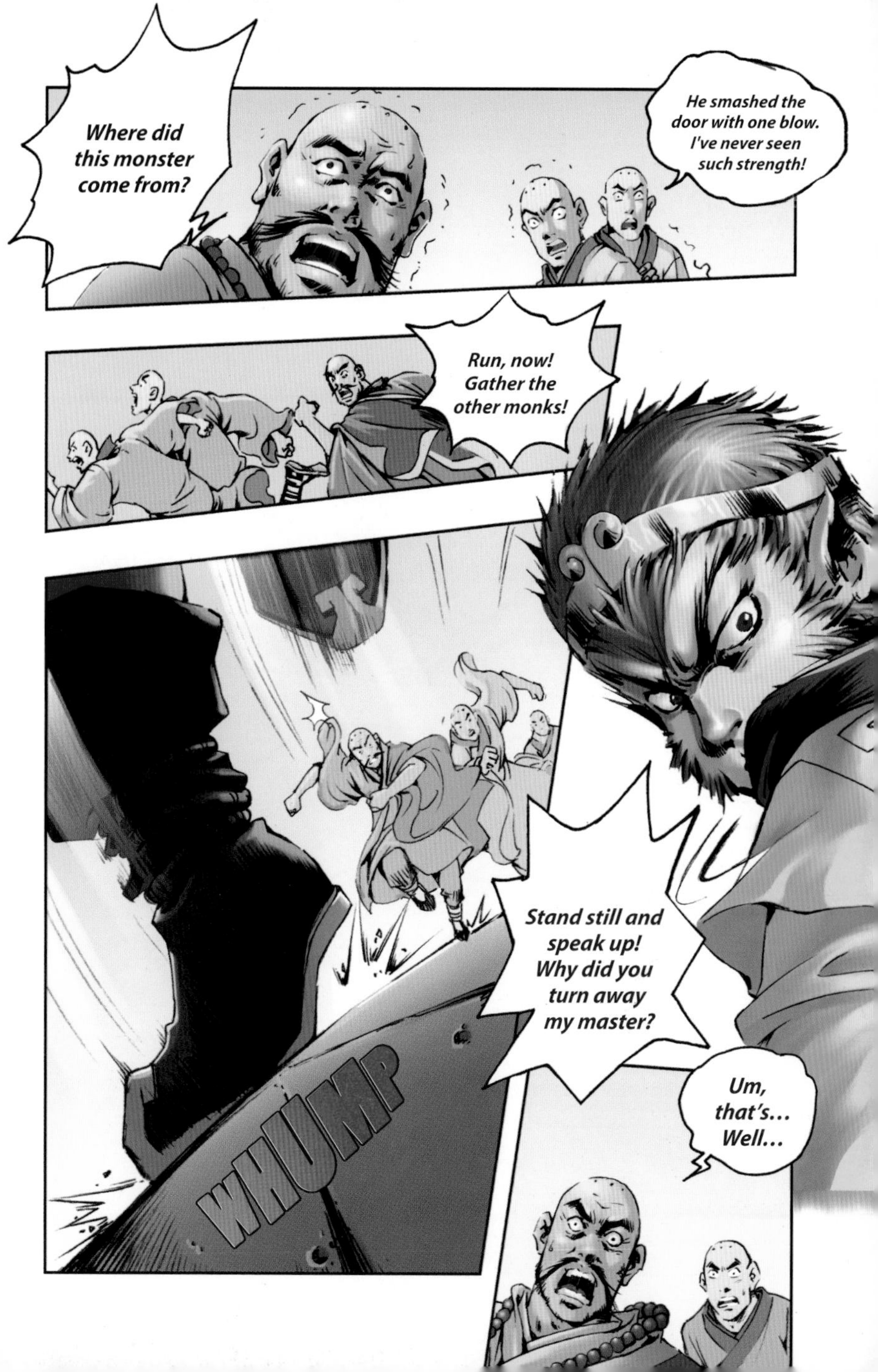
Where did this monster come from?
He smashed the door with one blow. I've never seen such strength!
Run, now! Gather the other monks!
WHUMP
Stand still and speak up! Why did you turn away my master?
Um, that's... Well...

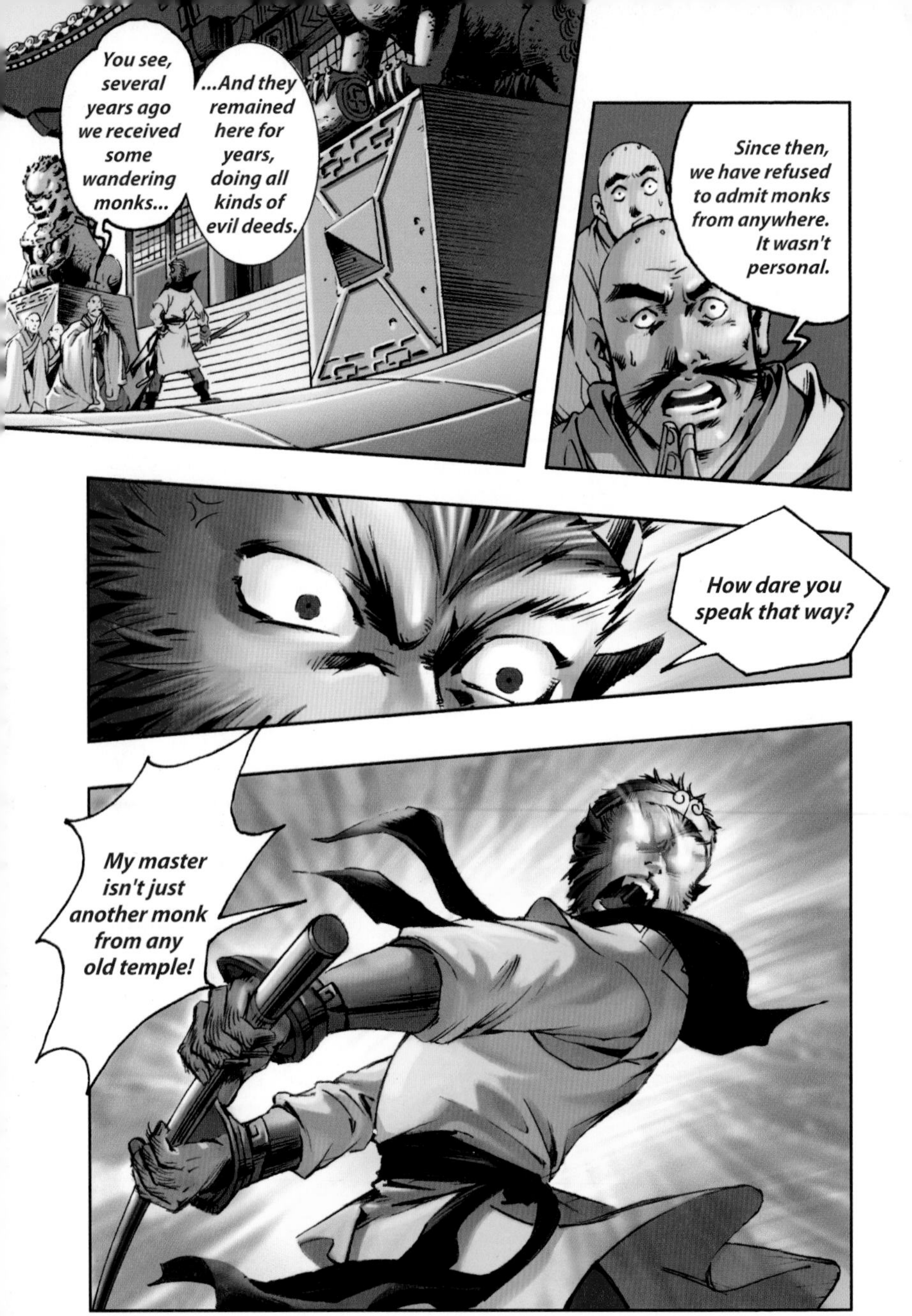

You see, several years ago we received some wandering monks...
...And they remained here for years, doing all kinds of evil deeds.
Since then, we have refused to admit monks from anywhere. It wasn't personal.
How dare you speak that way?
My master isn't just another monk from any old temple!

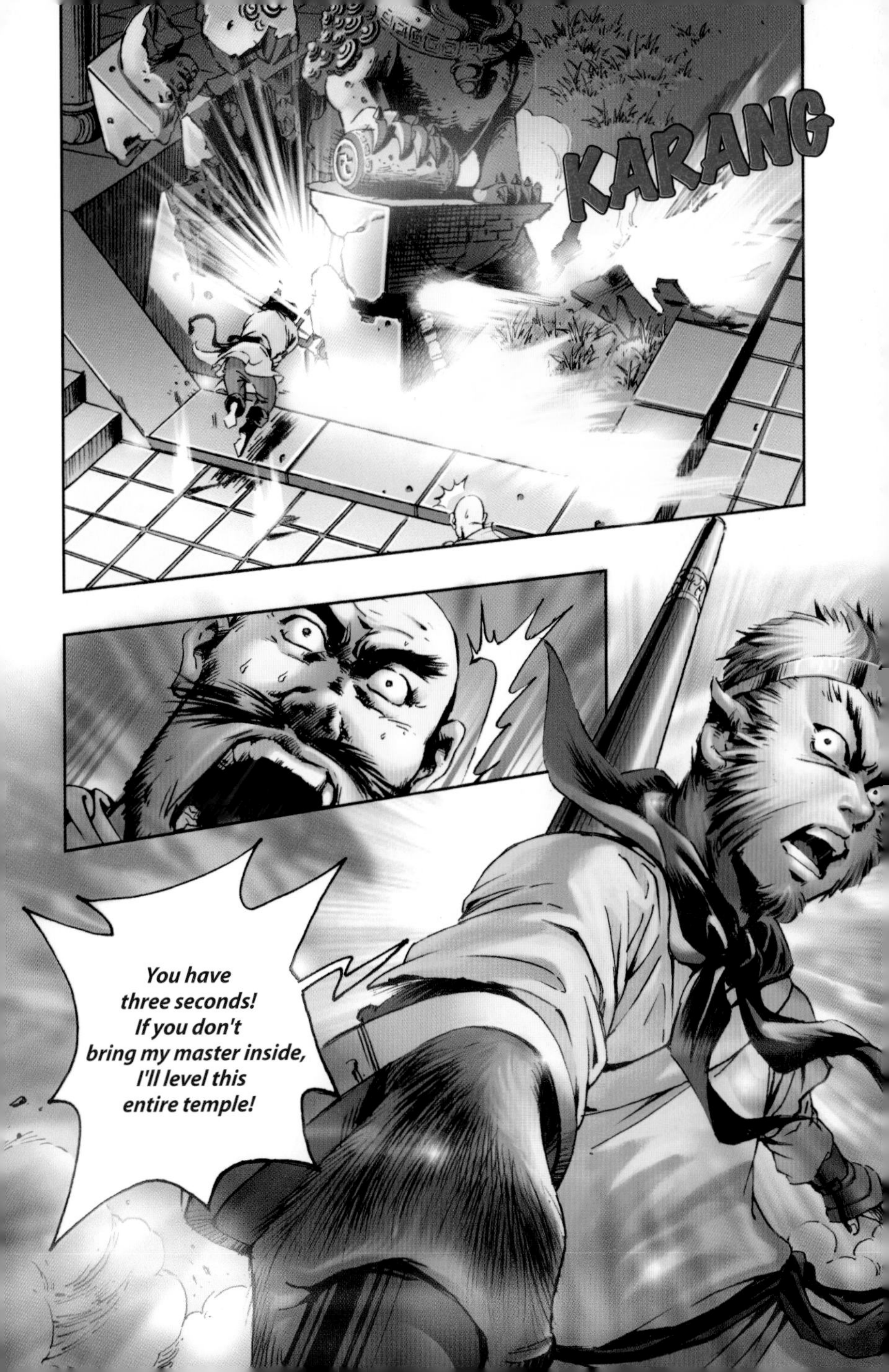
KARANG
You have three seconds! If you don't bring my master inside, I'll level this entire temple!

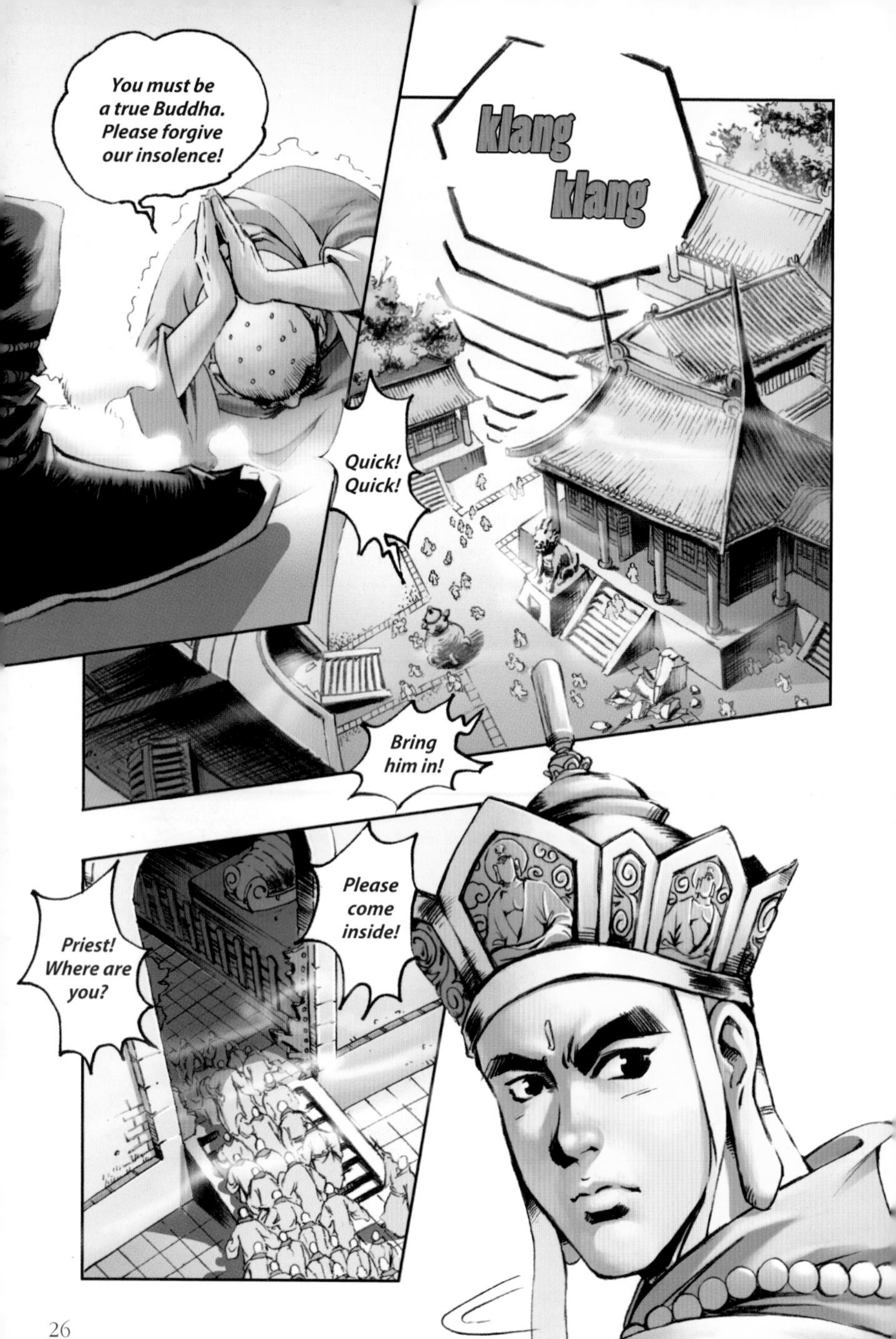
klang
klang
You must be a true Buddha. Please forgive our insolence!
Quick! Quick!
Bring him in!
Please come inside!
Priest! Where are you?

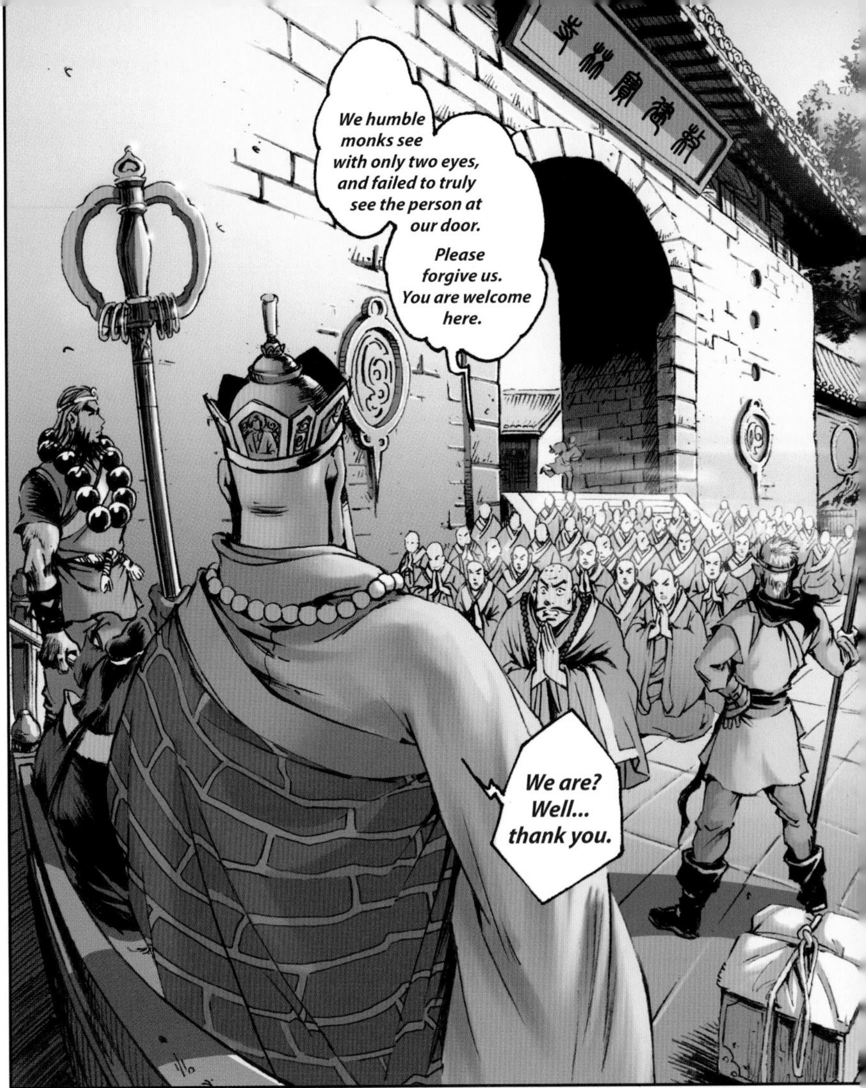
We humble monks see with only two eyes, and failed to truly see the person at our door.
Please forgive us. You are welcome here.
We are? Well... thank you.

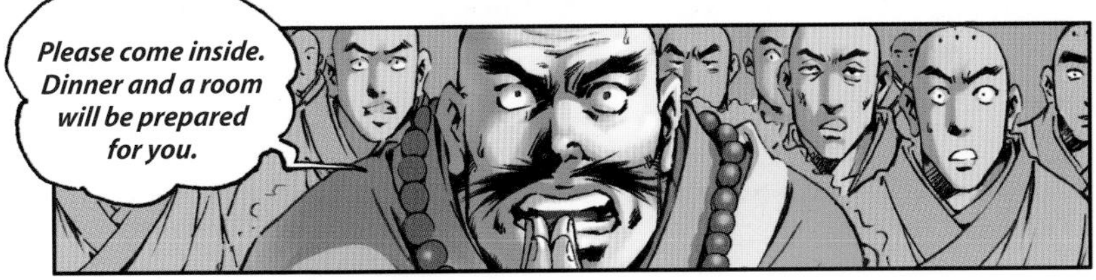
Please come inside. Dinner and a room will be prepared for you.

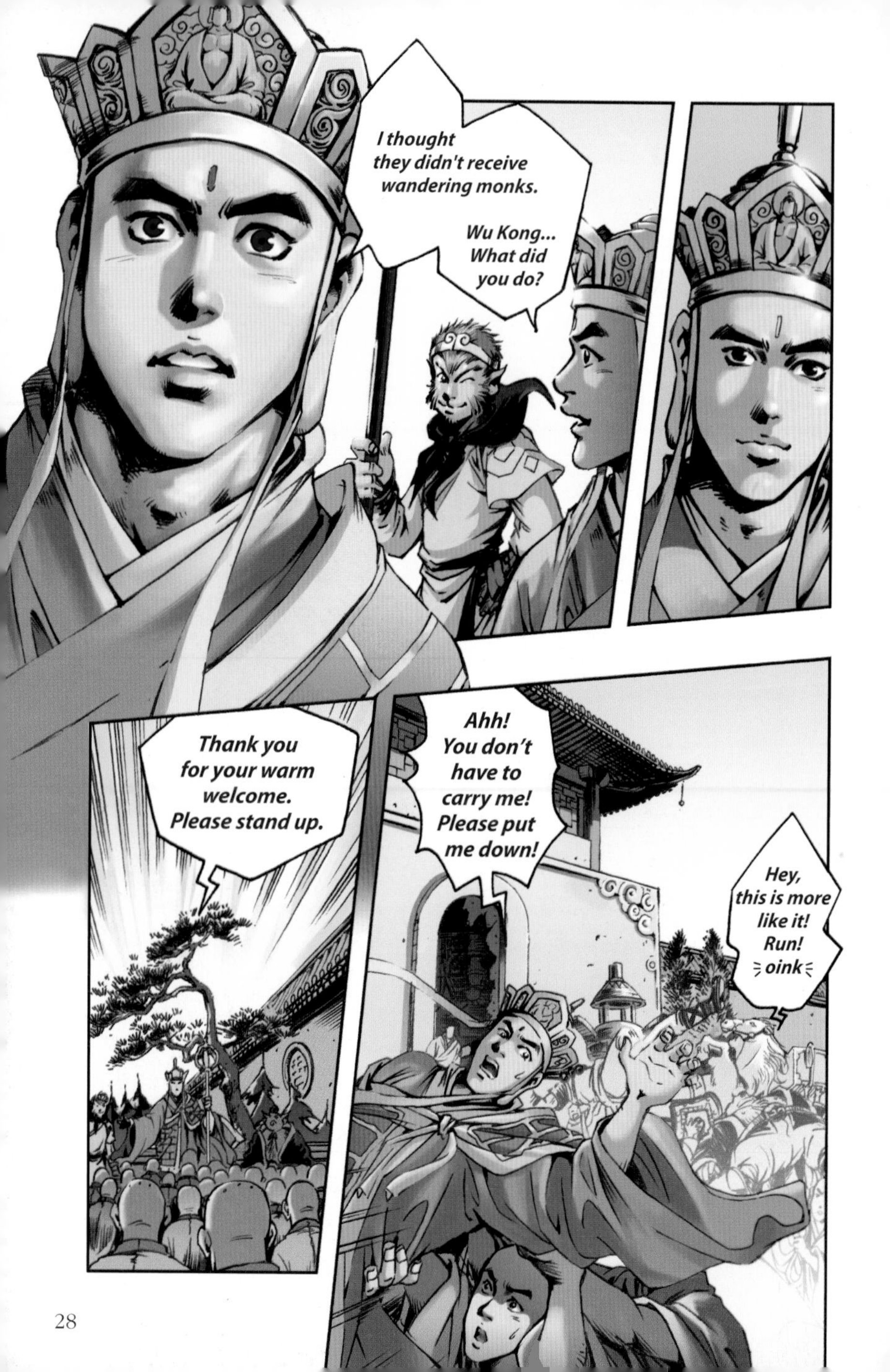
I thought they didn't receive wandering monks.
Wu Kong... What did you do?
Thank you for your warm welcome. Please stand up.
Ahh! You don't have to carry me! Please put me down!
Hey, this is more like it! Run! oink

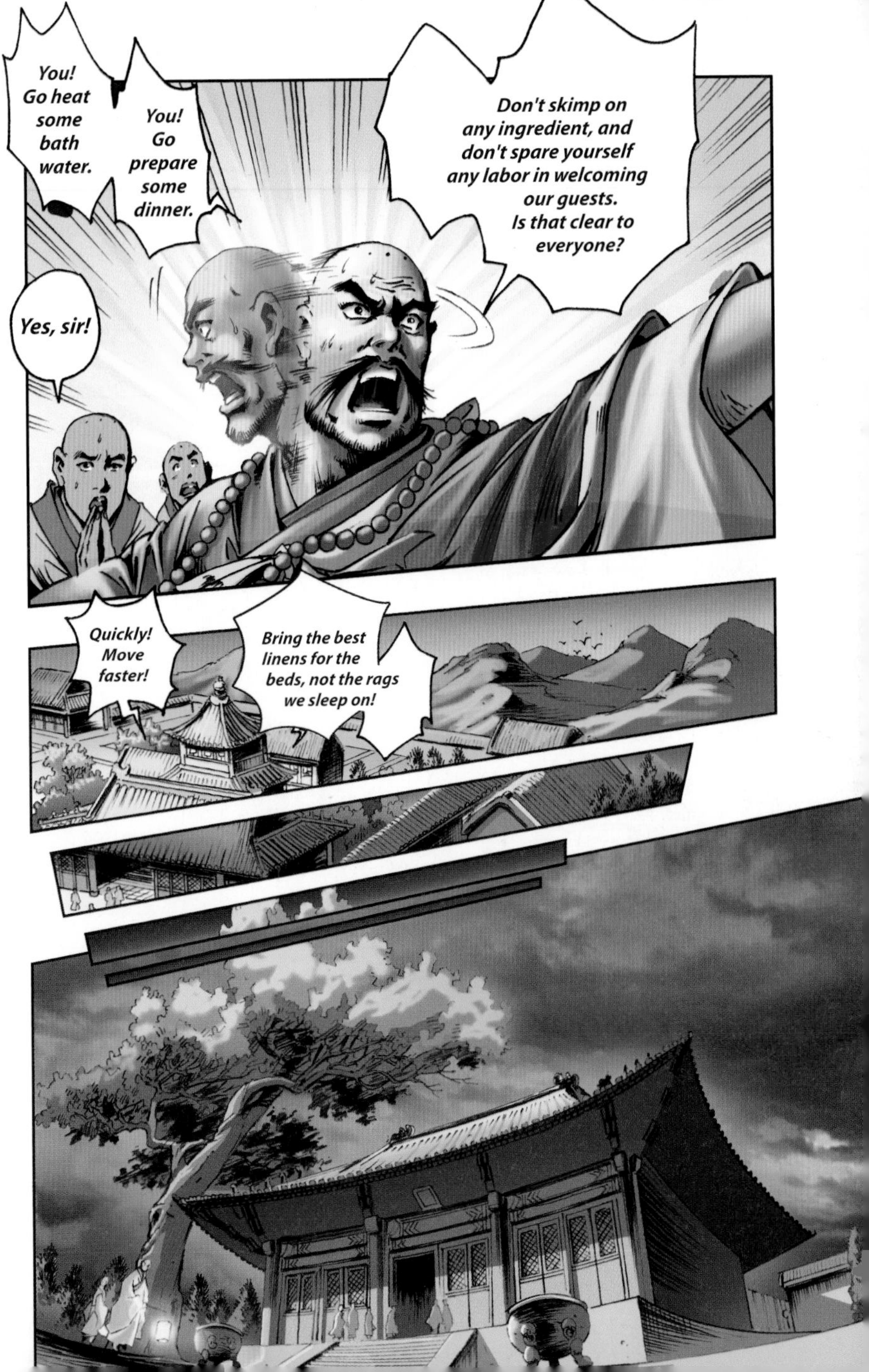
You! Go heat some bath water.
You! Go prepare some dinner.
Don't skimp on any ingredient, and don't spare yourself any labor in welcoming our guests. Is that clear to everyone?
Yes, sir!
Quickly! Move faster!
Bring the best linens for the beds, not the rags we sleep on!

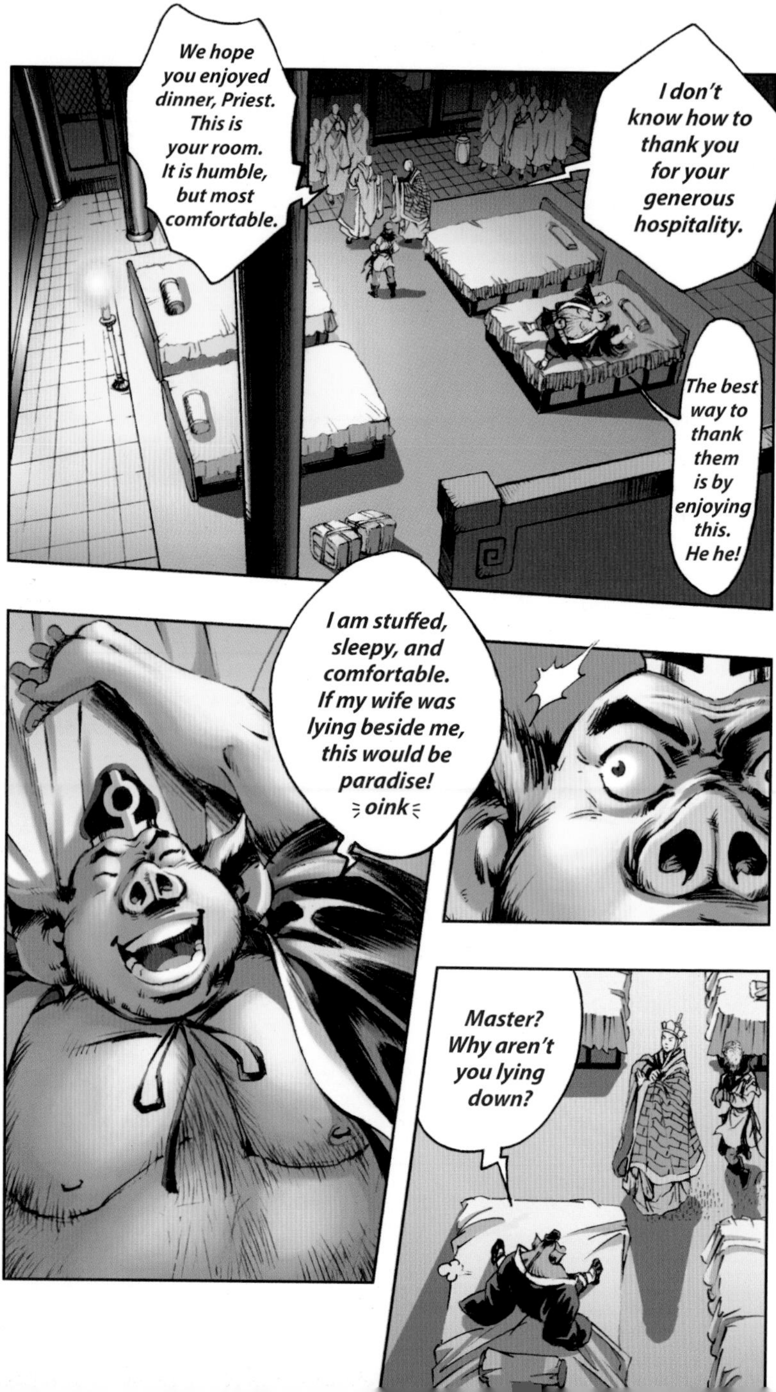
We hope you enjoyed dinner, Priest. This is your room. It is humble, but most comfortable.
I don't know how to thank you for your generous hospitality.
The best way to thank them is by enjoying this. He he!
I am stuffed, sleepy, and comfortable. If my wife was lying beside me, this would be paradise! oink
Master? Why aren't you lying down?

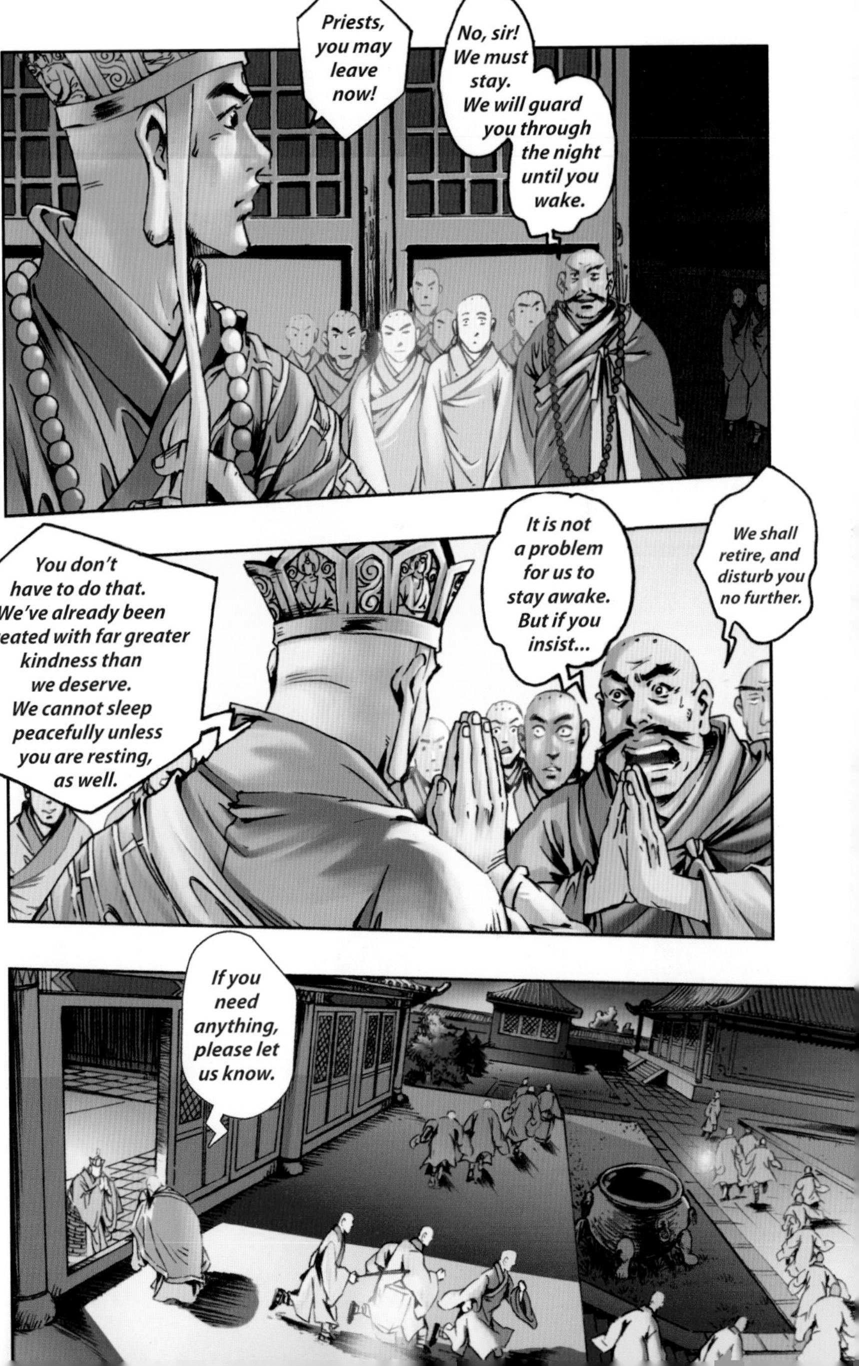
Priests, you may leave now!
No, sir! We must stay. We will guard you through the night until you wake.
You don't have to do that. We've already been treated with far greater kindness than we deserve. We cannot sleep peacefully unless you are resting, as well.
It is not a problem for us to stay awake. But if you insist...
We shall retire, and disturb you no further.
If you need anything, please let us know.

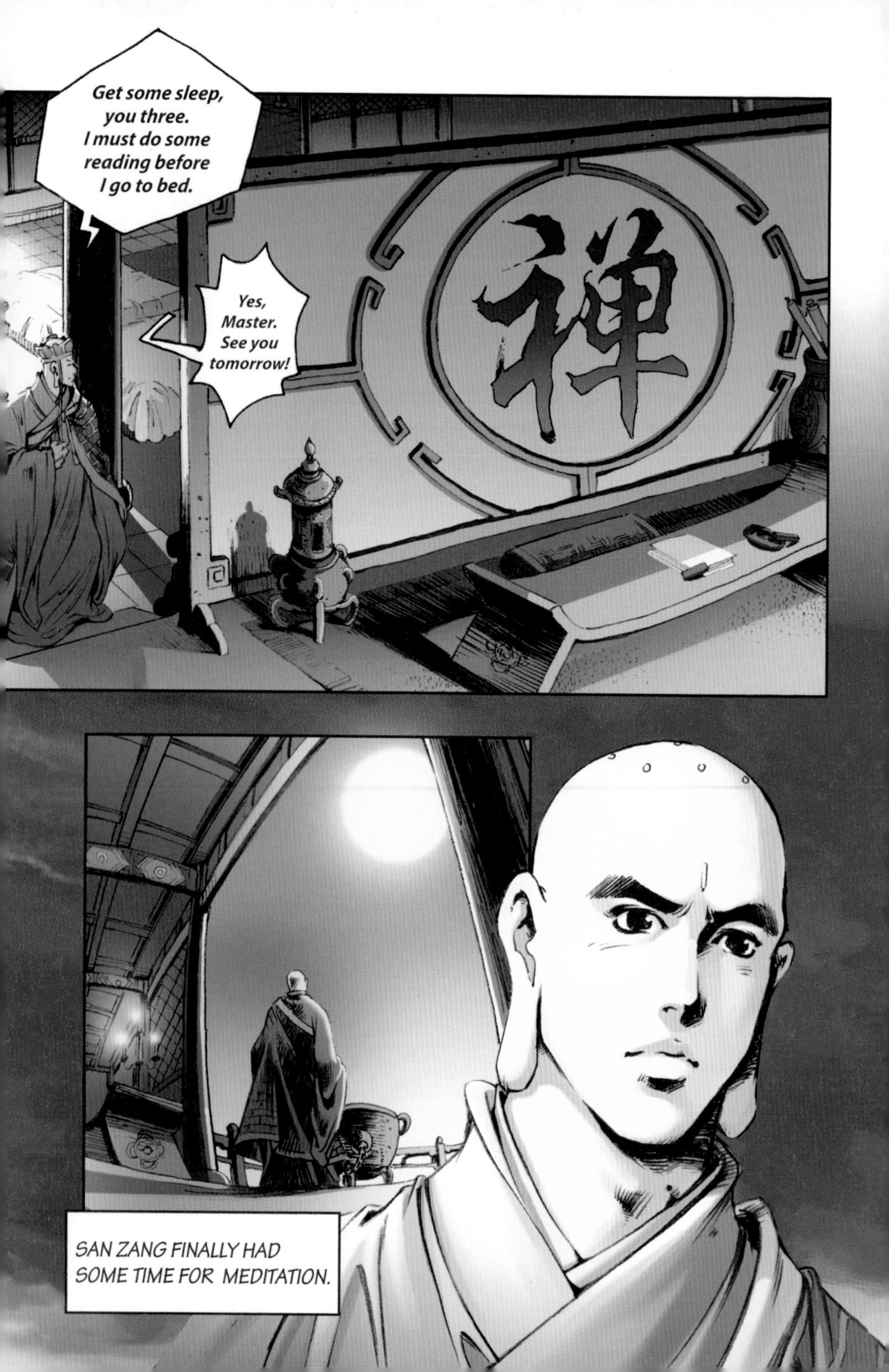
Get some sleep, you three. I must do some reading before I go to bed.
Yes, Master. See you tomorrow!
SAN ZANG FINALLY HAD SOME TIME FOR MEDITATION.

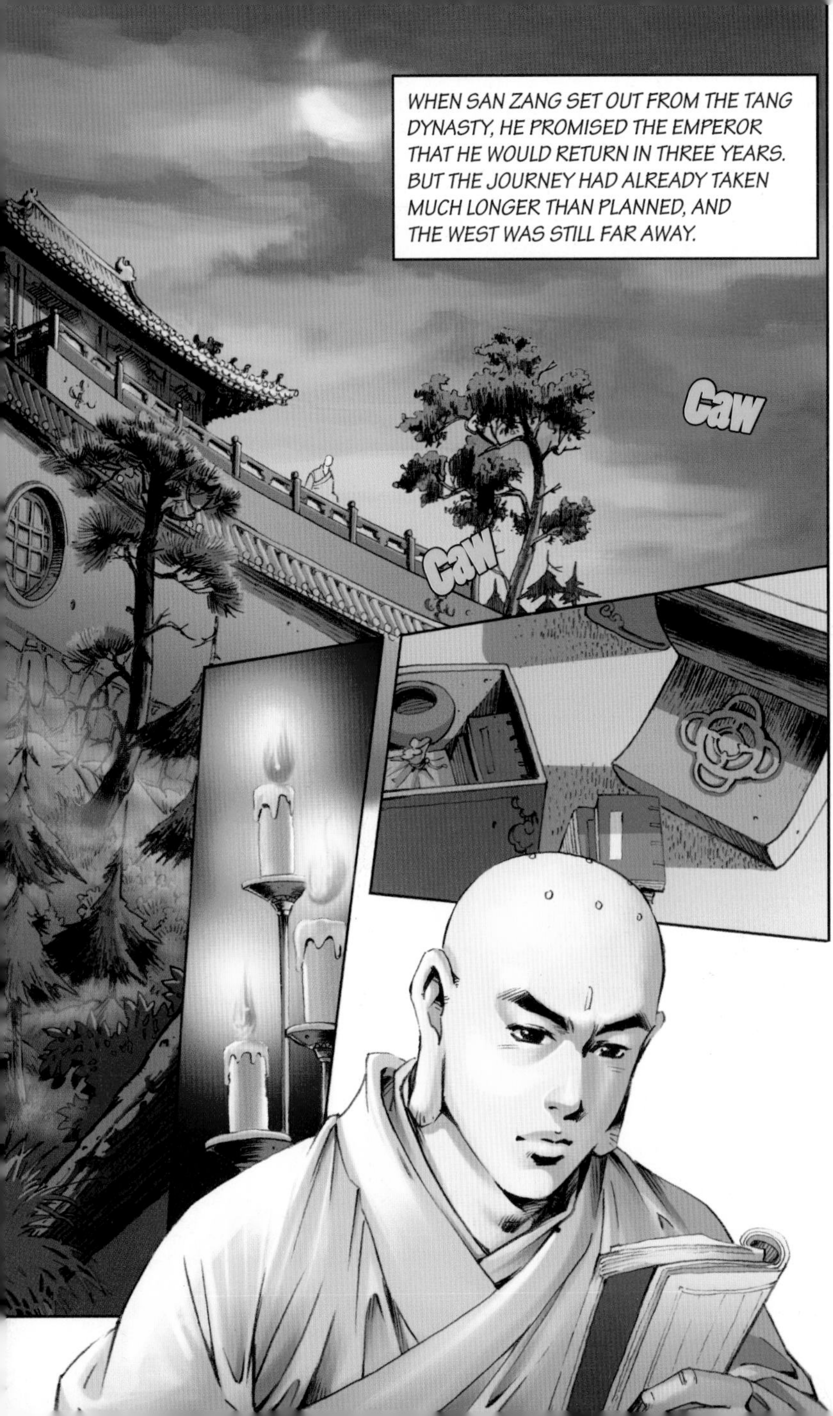
WHEN SAN ZANG SET OUT FROM THE TANG DYNASTY, HE PROMISED THE EMPEROR THAT HE WOULD RETURN IN THREE YEARS. BUT THE JOURNEY HAD ALREADY TAKEN MUCH LONGER THAN PLANNED, AND THE WEST WAS STILL FAR AWAY.
Caw
Caw

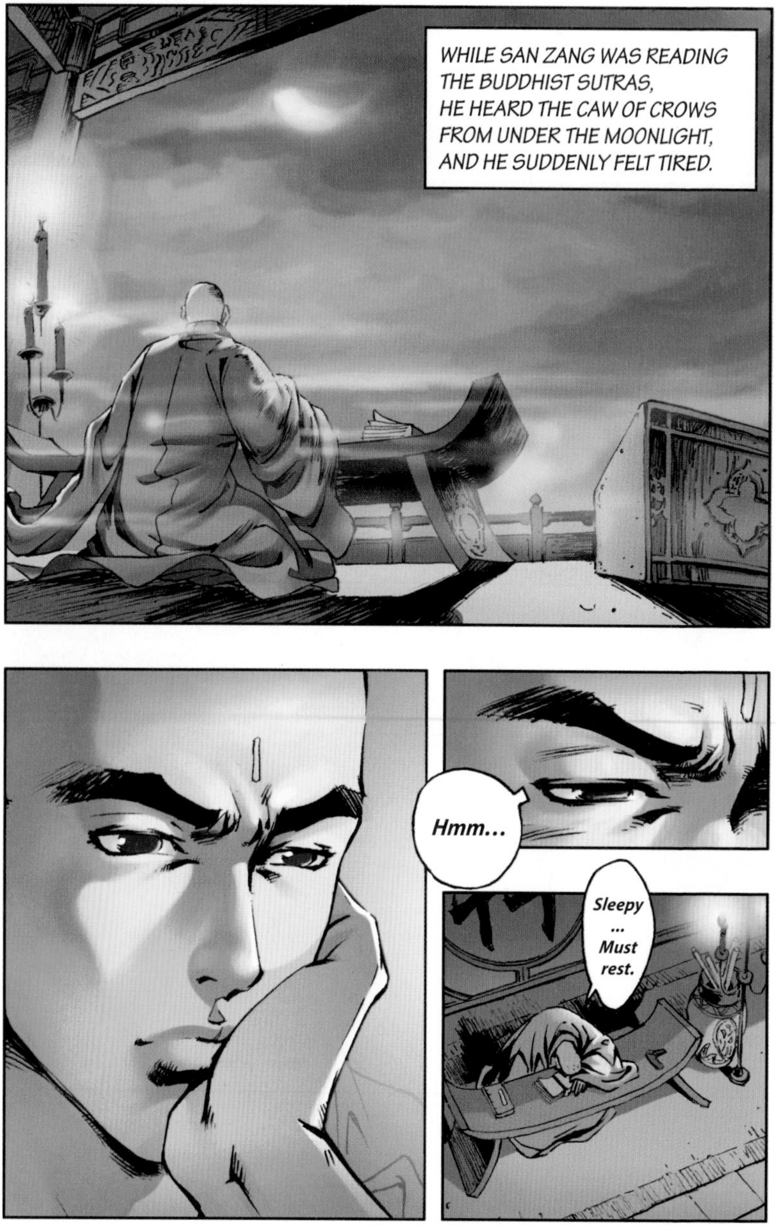
WHILE SAN ZANG WAS READING THE BUDDHIST SUTRAS, HE HEARD THE CAW OF CROWS FROM UNDER THE MOONLIGHT, AND HE SUDDENLY FELT TIRED.
Hmm...
Sleepy ... Must rest.

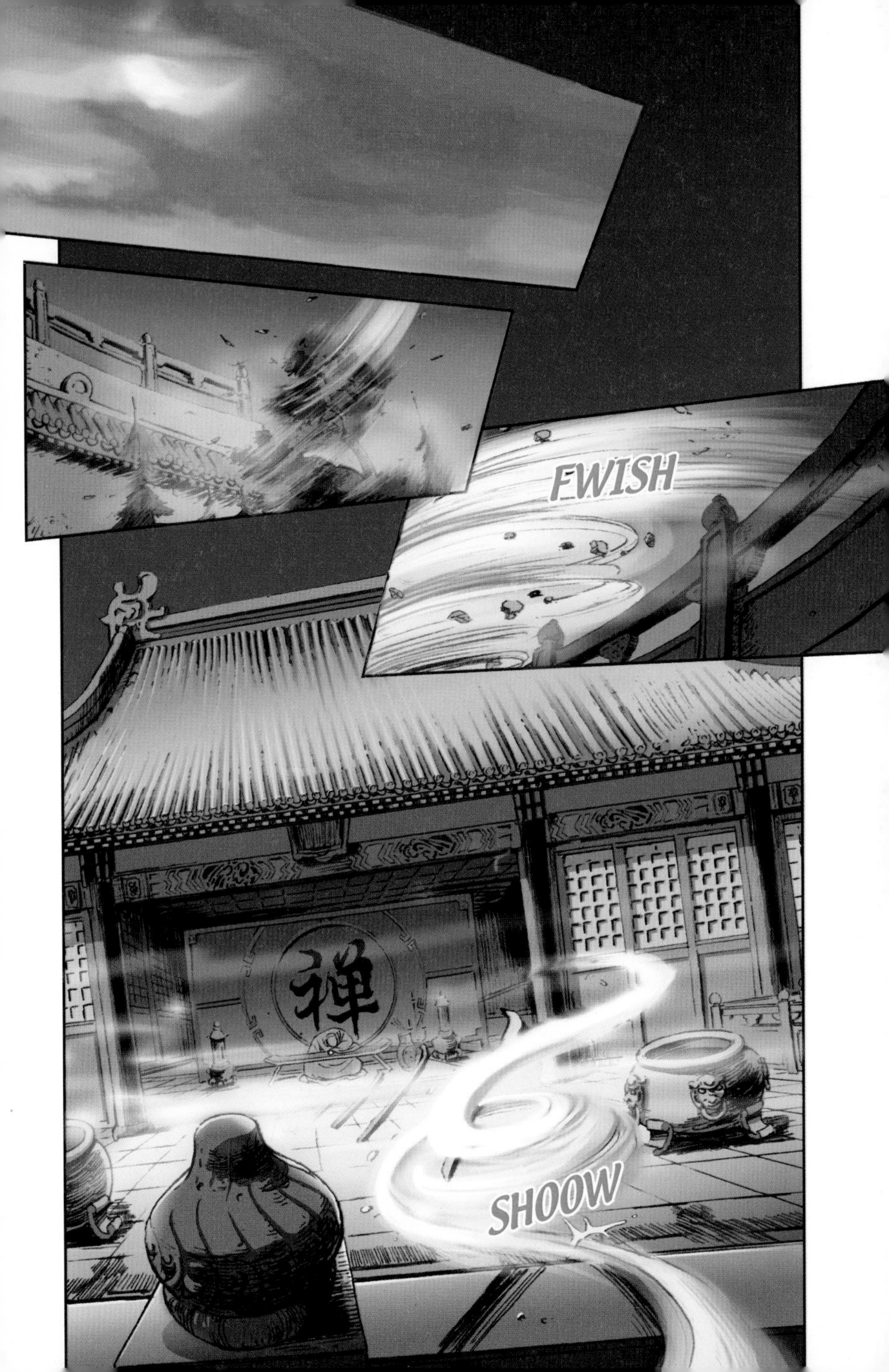
FWISH
禅
SHOOW

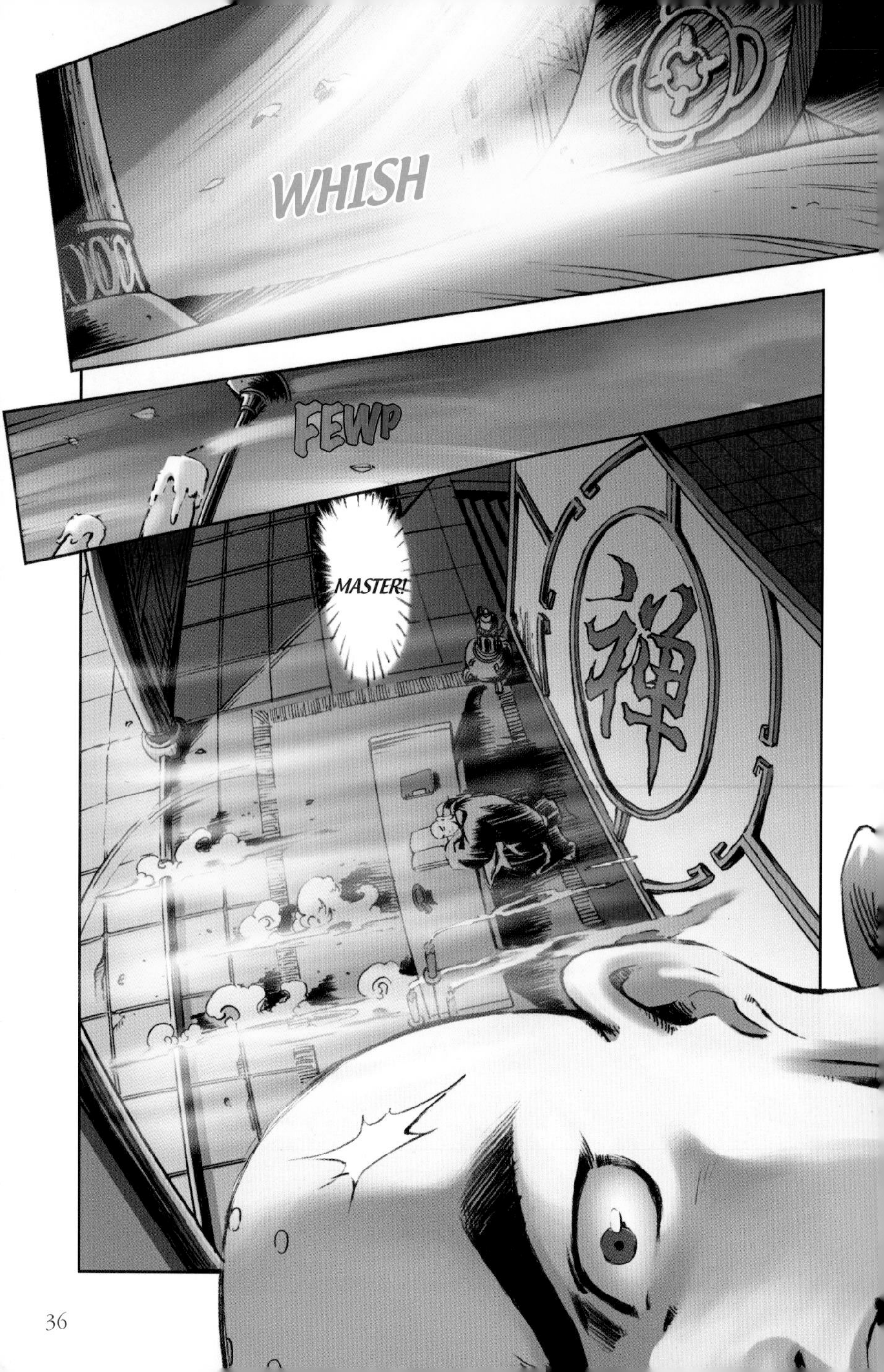
WHISH
FEWP
MASTER!
禅

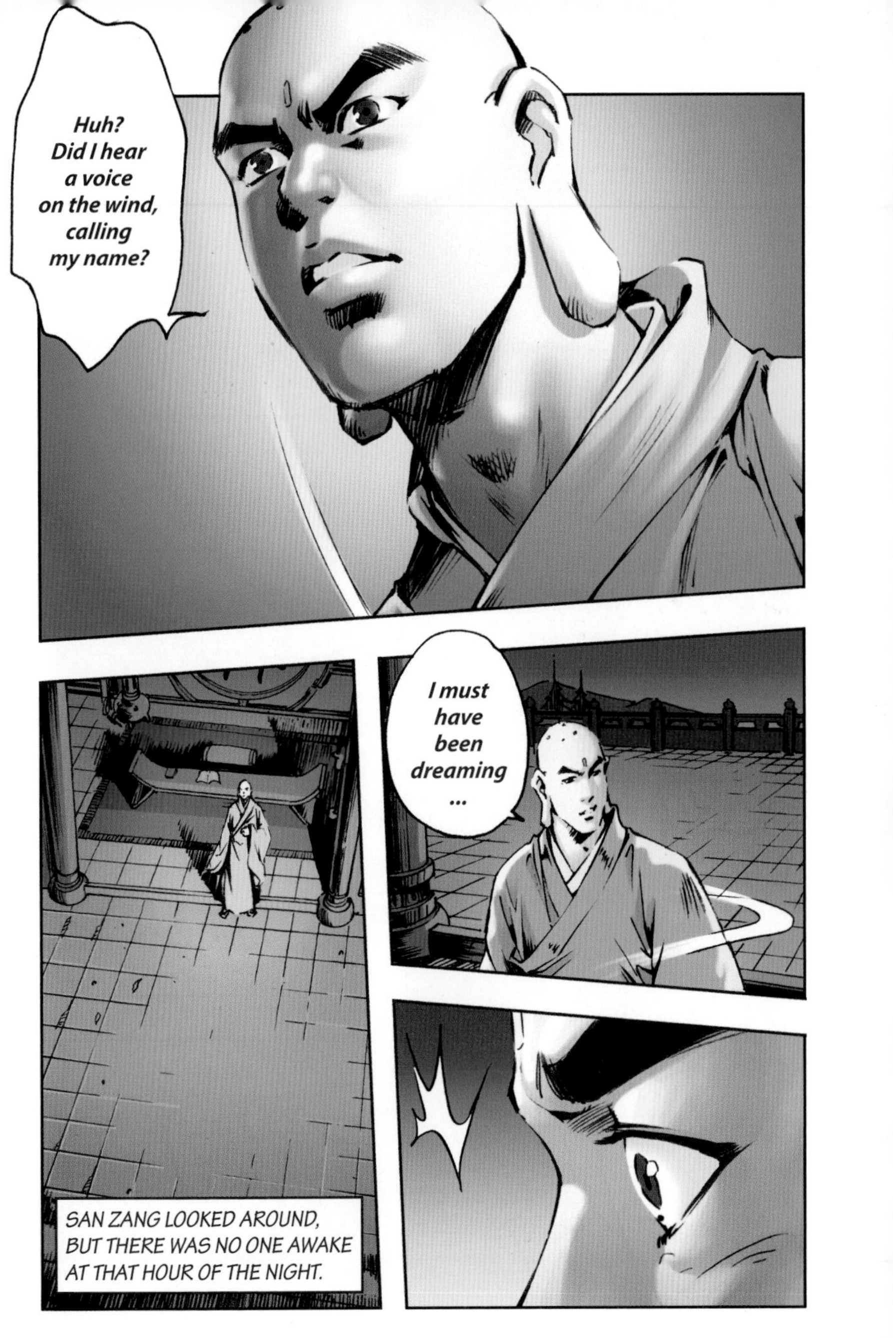
Huh? Did I hear a voice on the wind, calling my name?
I must have been dreaming ...
SAN ZANG LOOKED AROUND, BUT THERE WAS NO ONE AWAKE AT THAT HOUR OF THE NIGHT.

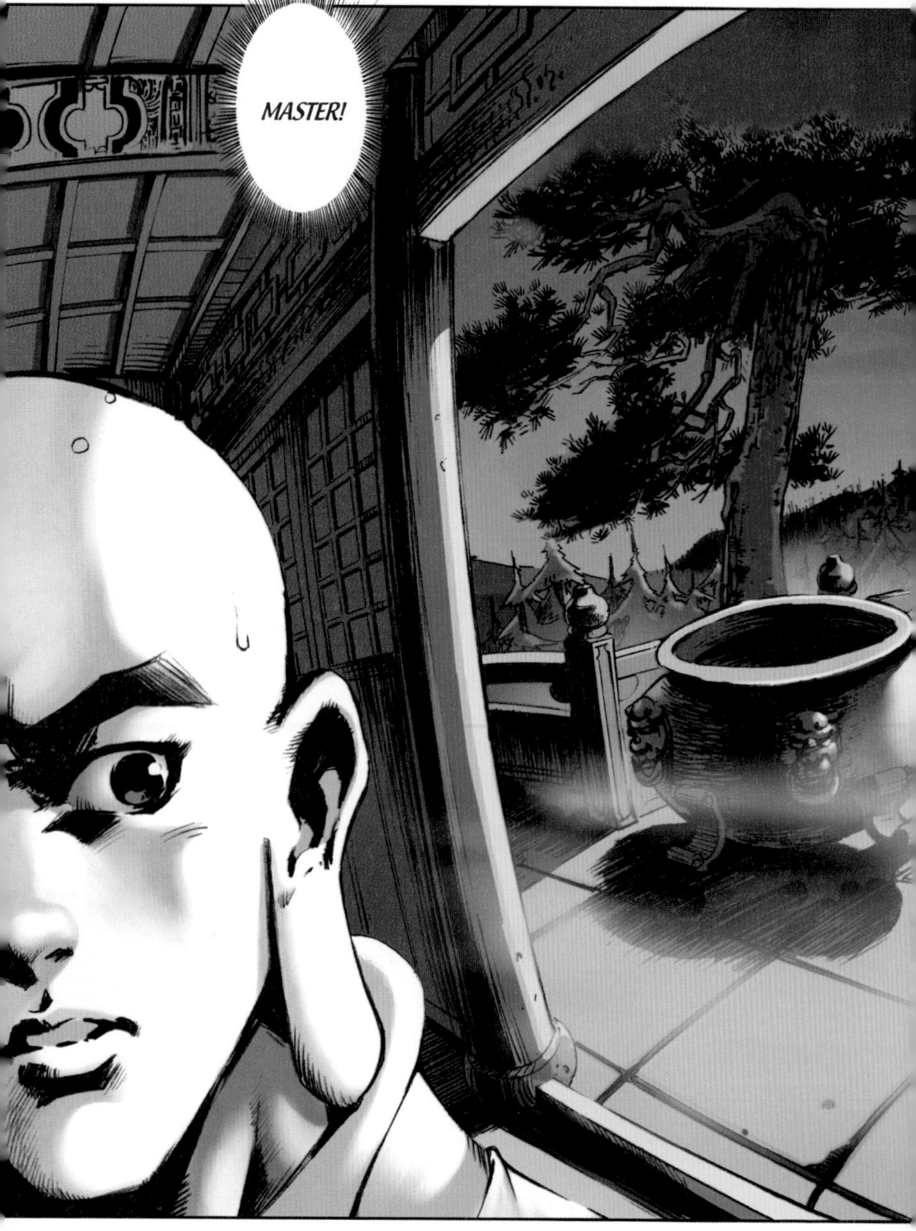
MASTER!

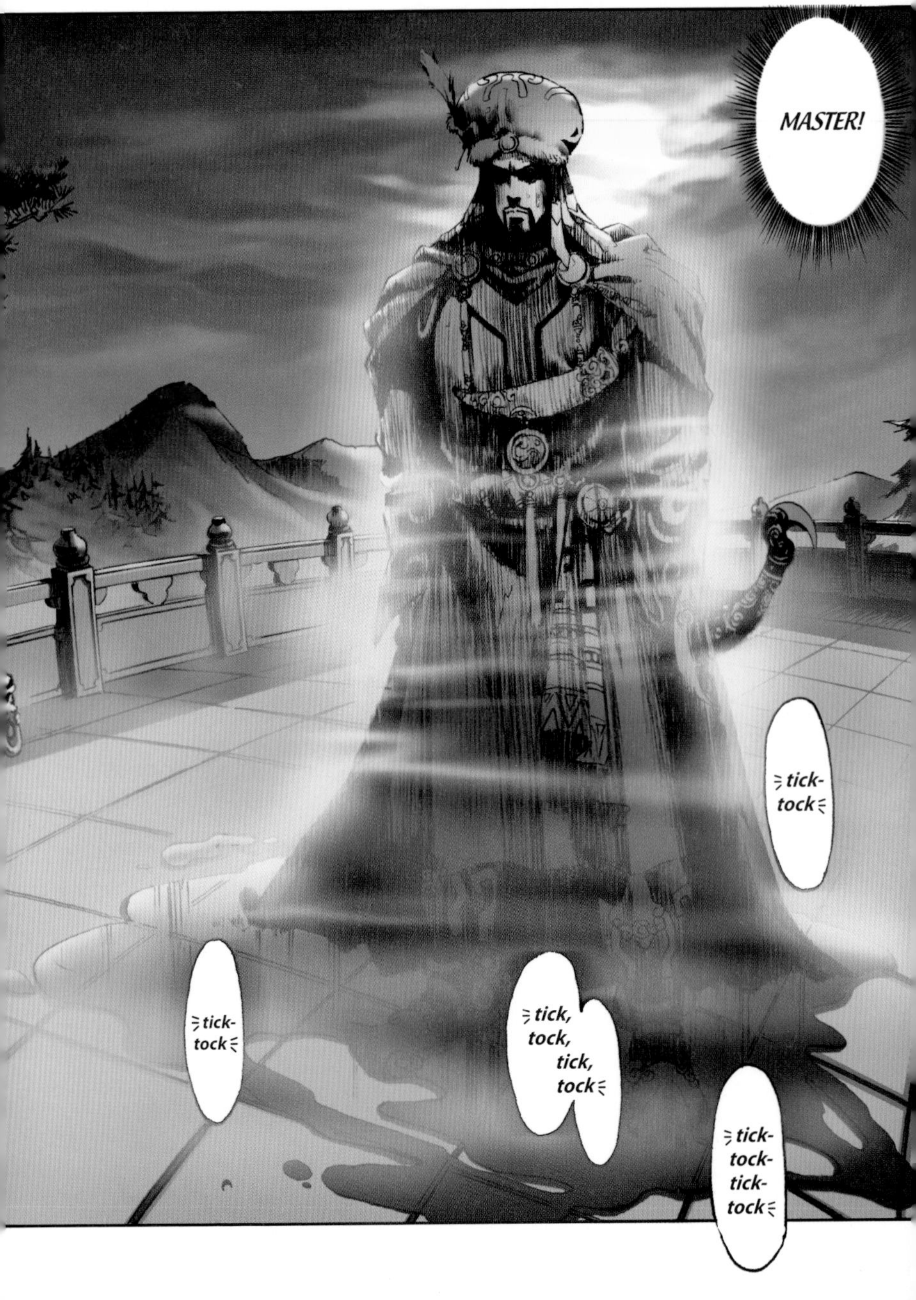
MASTER!
tick-tock
tick-tock
tick, tock, tick, tock
tick-tock-tick-tock

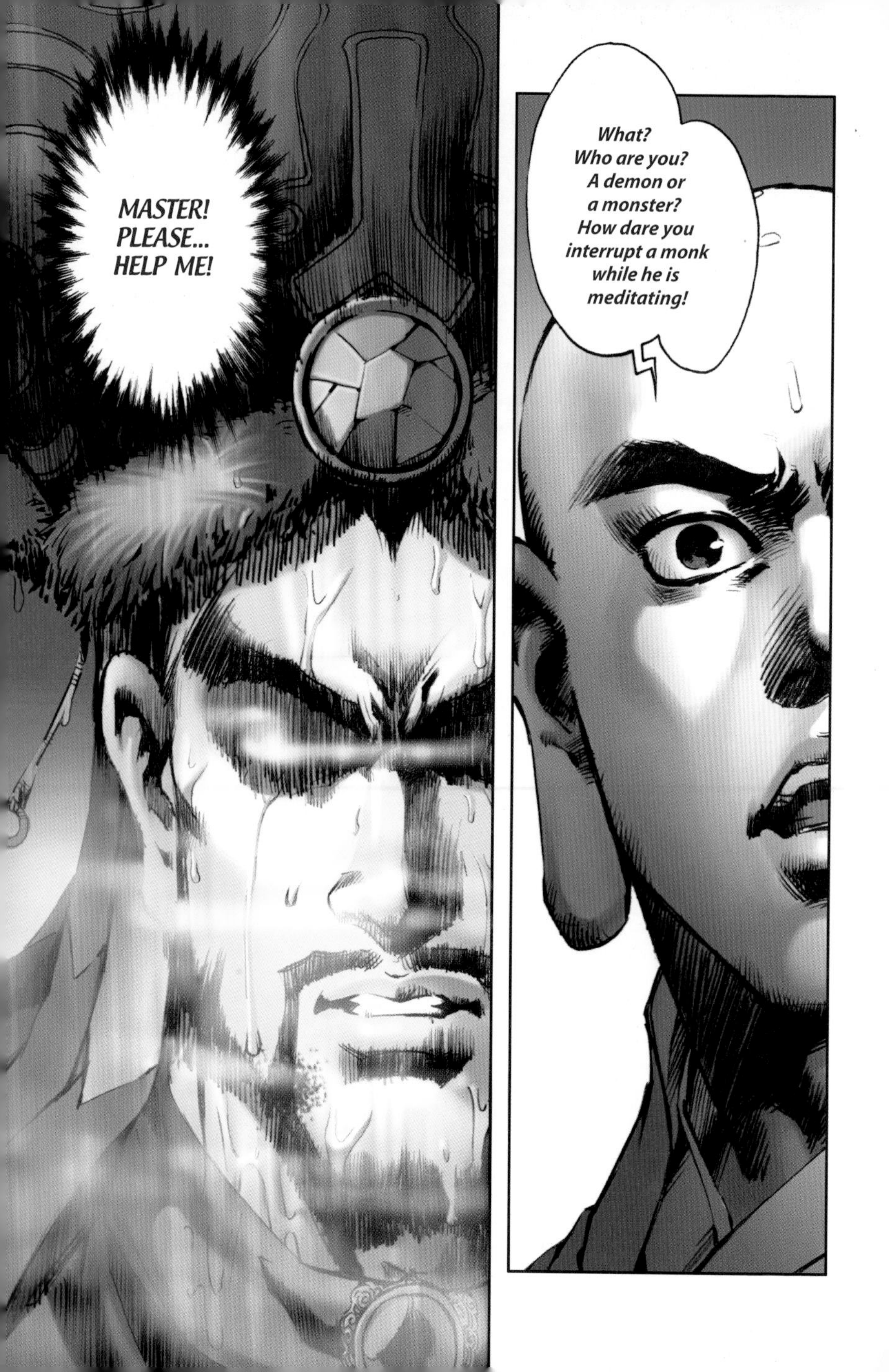
What? Who are you? A demon or a monster? How dare you interrupt a monk while he is meditating!
MASTER! PLEASE... HELP ME!

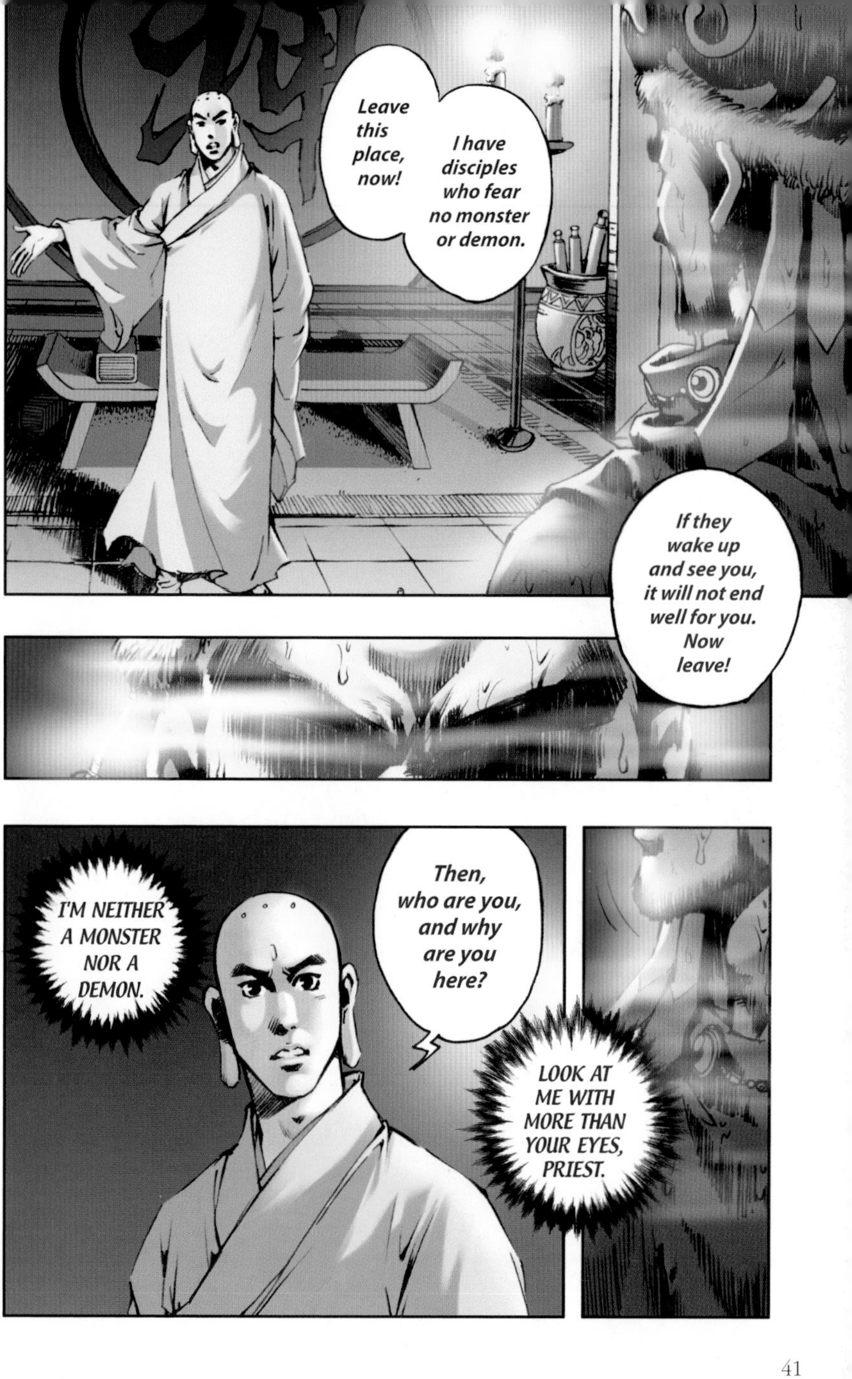
Leave this place, now!
I have disciples who fear no monster or demon.
If they wake up and see you, it will not end well for you. Now leave!
I'M NEITHER A MONSTER NOR A DEMON.
Then, who are you, and why are you here?
LOOK AT ME WITH MORE THAN YOUR EYES, PRIEST.

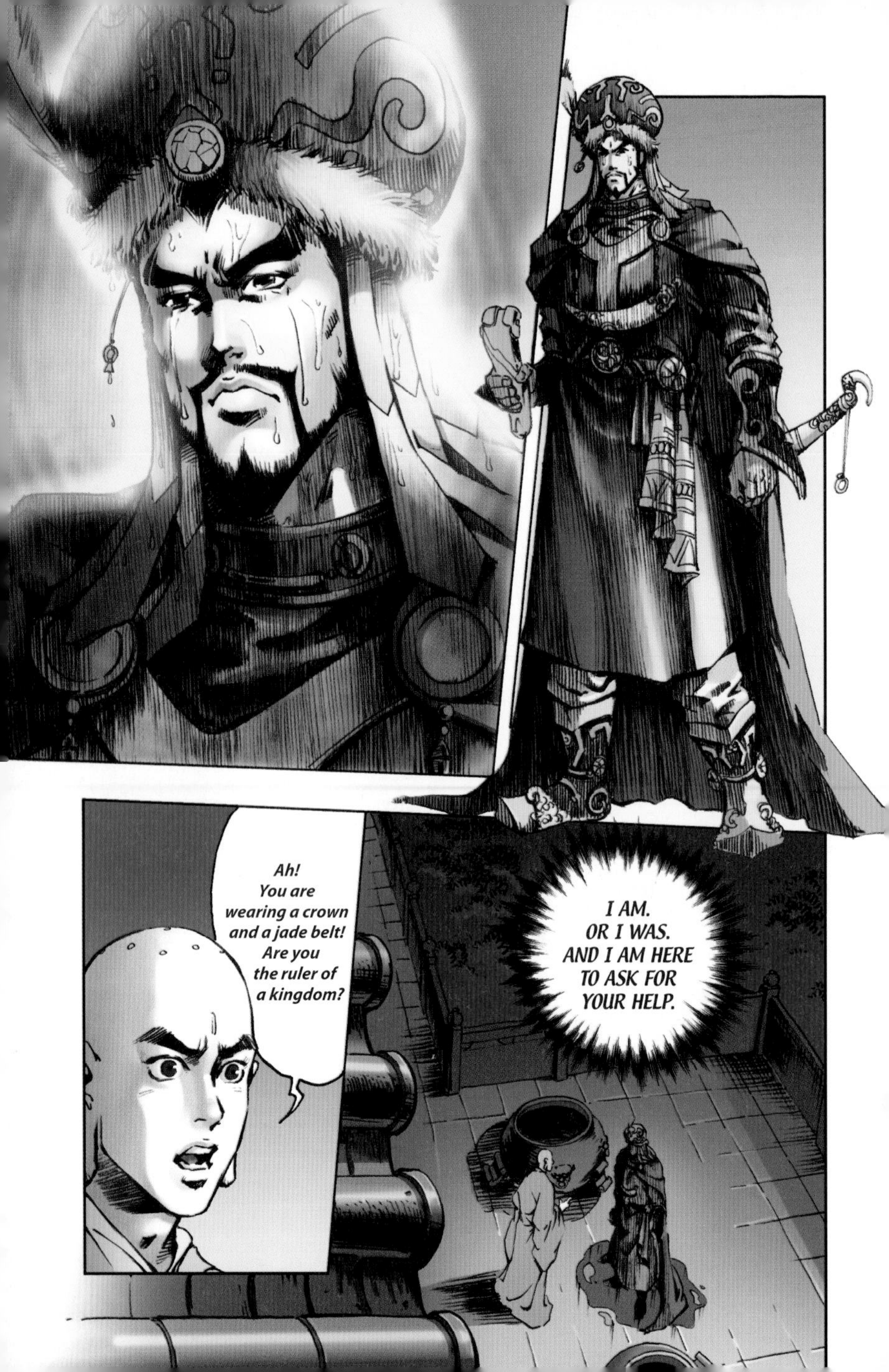
Ah! You are wearing a crown and a jade belt! Are you the ruler of a kingdom?
I AM. OR I WAS. AND I AM HERE TO ASK FOR YOUR HELP.

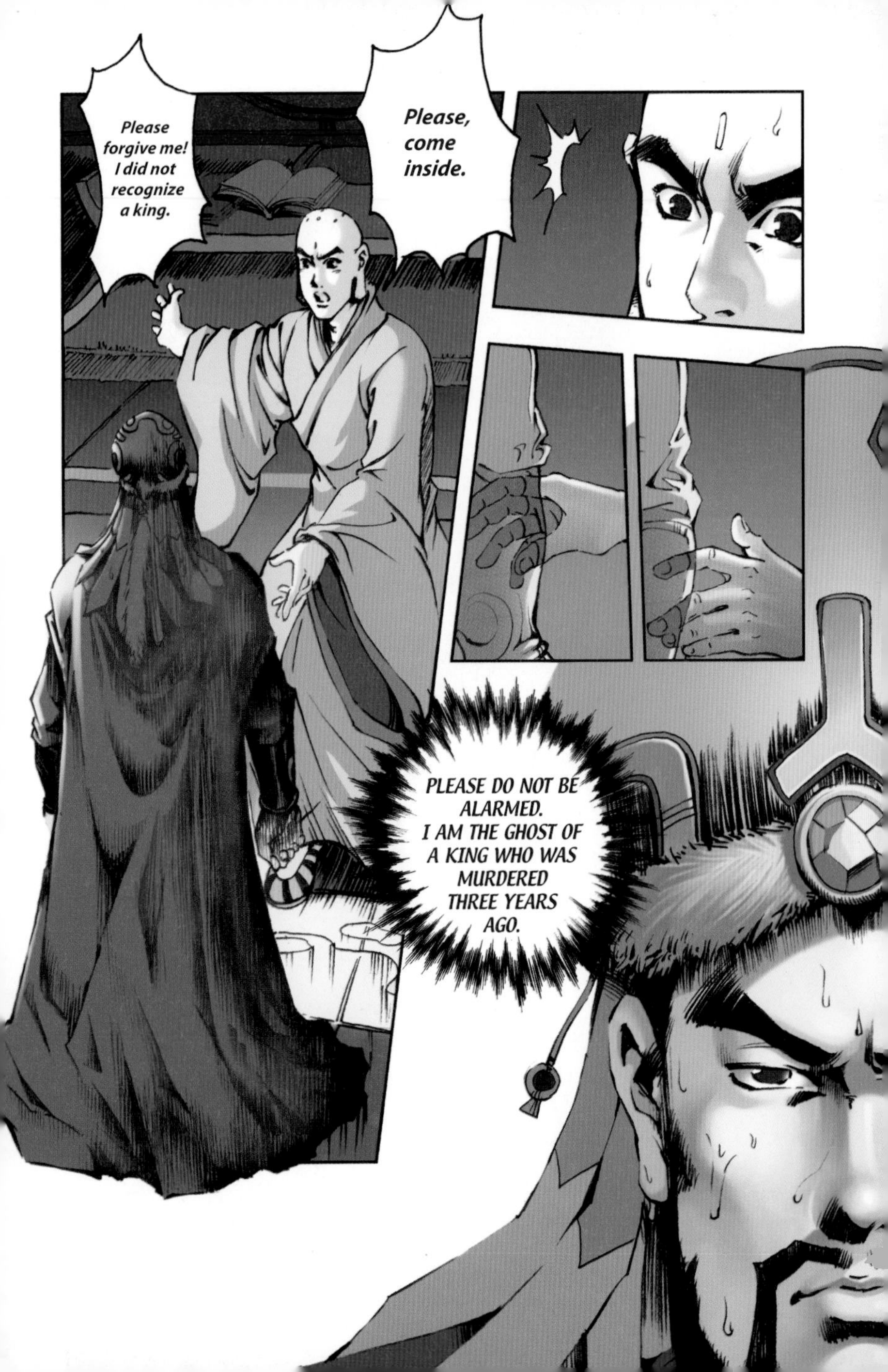
Please forgive me! I did not recognize a king.
Please, come inside.
PLEASE DO NOT BE ALARMED. I AM THE GHOST OF A KING WHO WAS MURDERED THREE YEARS AGO.

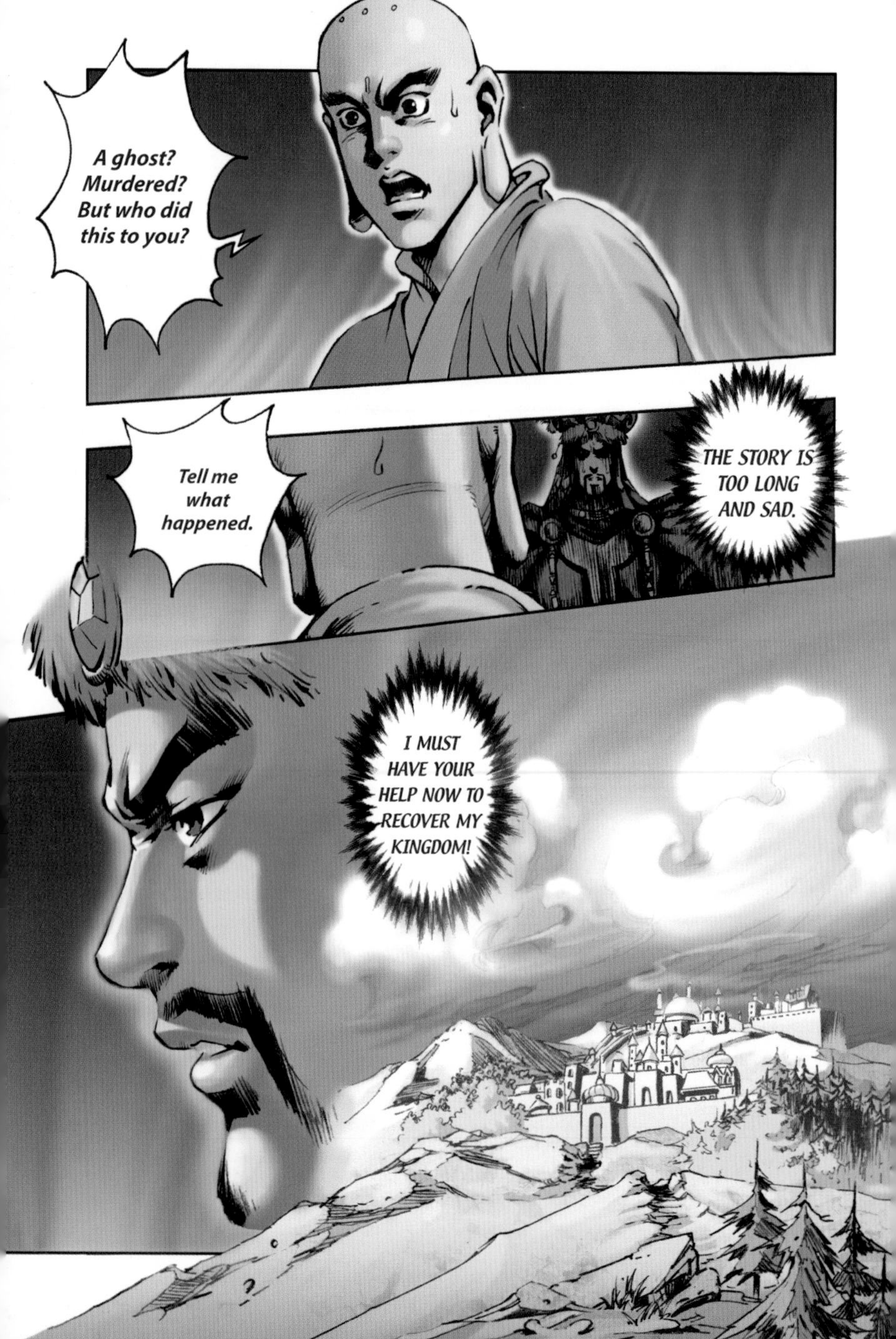
A ghost? Murdered? But who did this to you?
Tell me what happened.
THE STORY IS TOO LONG AND SAD.
I MUST HAVE YOUR HELP NOW TO RECOVER MY KINGDOM!

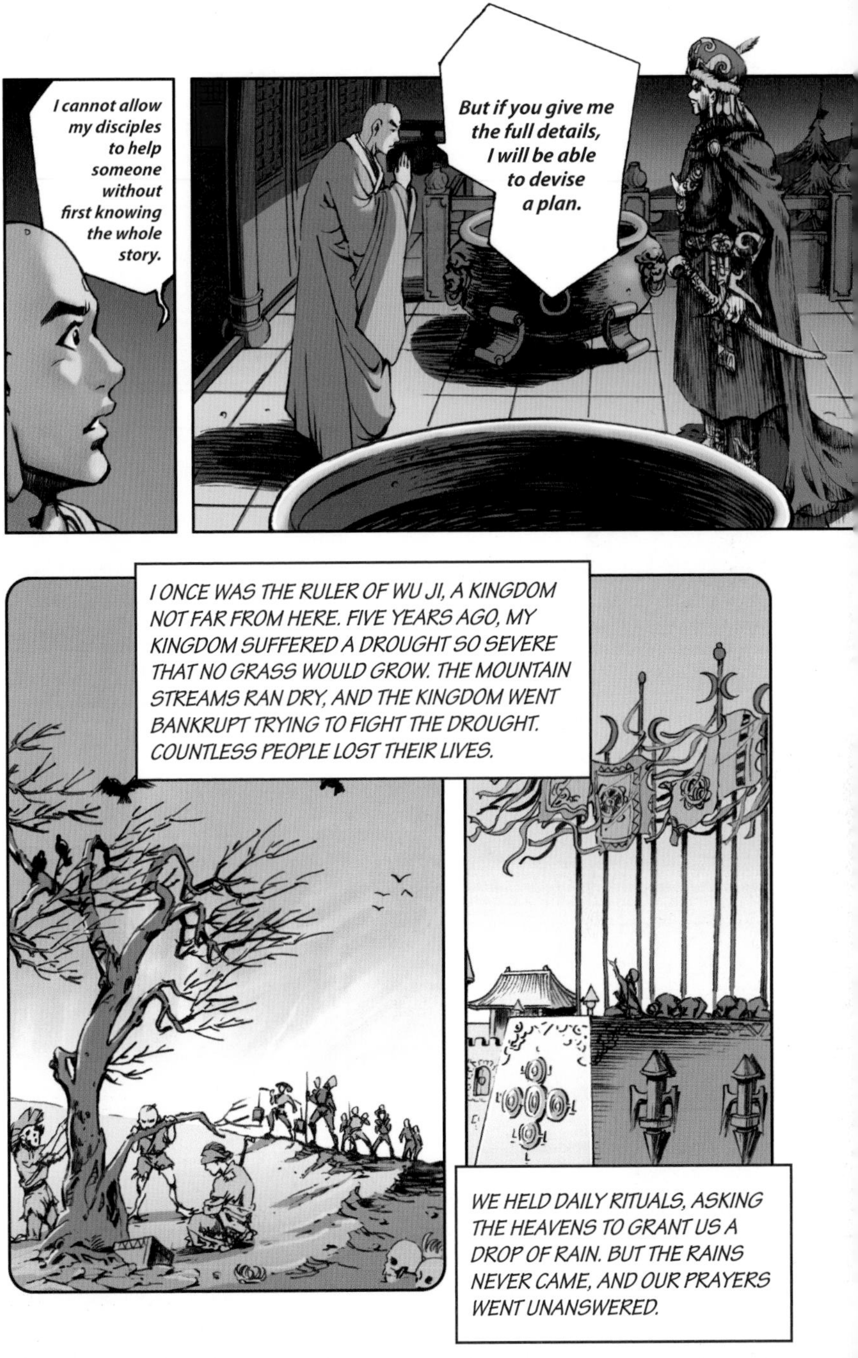
I cannot allow my disciples to help someone without first knowing the whole story.
But if you give me the full details, I will be able to devise a plan.
I ONCE WAS THE RULER OF WU JI, A KINGDOM NOT FAR FROM HERE. FIVE YEARS AGO, MY KINGDOM SUFFERED A DROUGHT SO SEVERE THAT NO GRASS WOULD GROW. THE MOUNTAIN STREAMS RAN DRY, AND THE KINGDOM WENT BANKRUPT TRYING TO FIGHT THE DROUGHT. COUNTLESS PEOPLE LOST THEIR LIVES.
WE HELD DAILY RITUALS, ASKING THE HEAVENS TO GRANT US A DROP OF RAIN. BUT THE RAINS NEVER CAME, AND OUR PRAYERS WENT UNANSWERED.

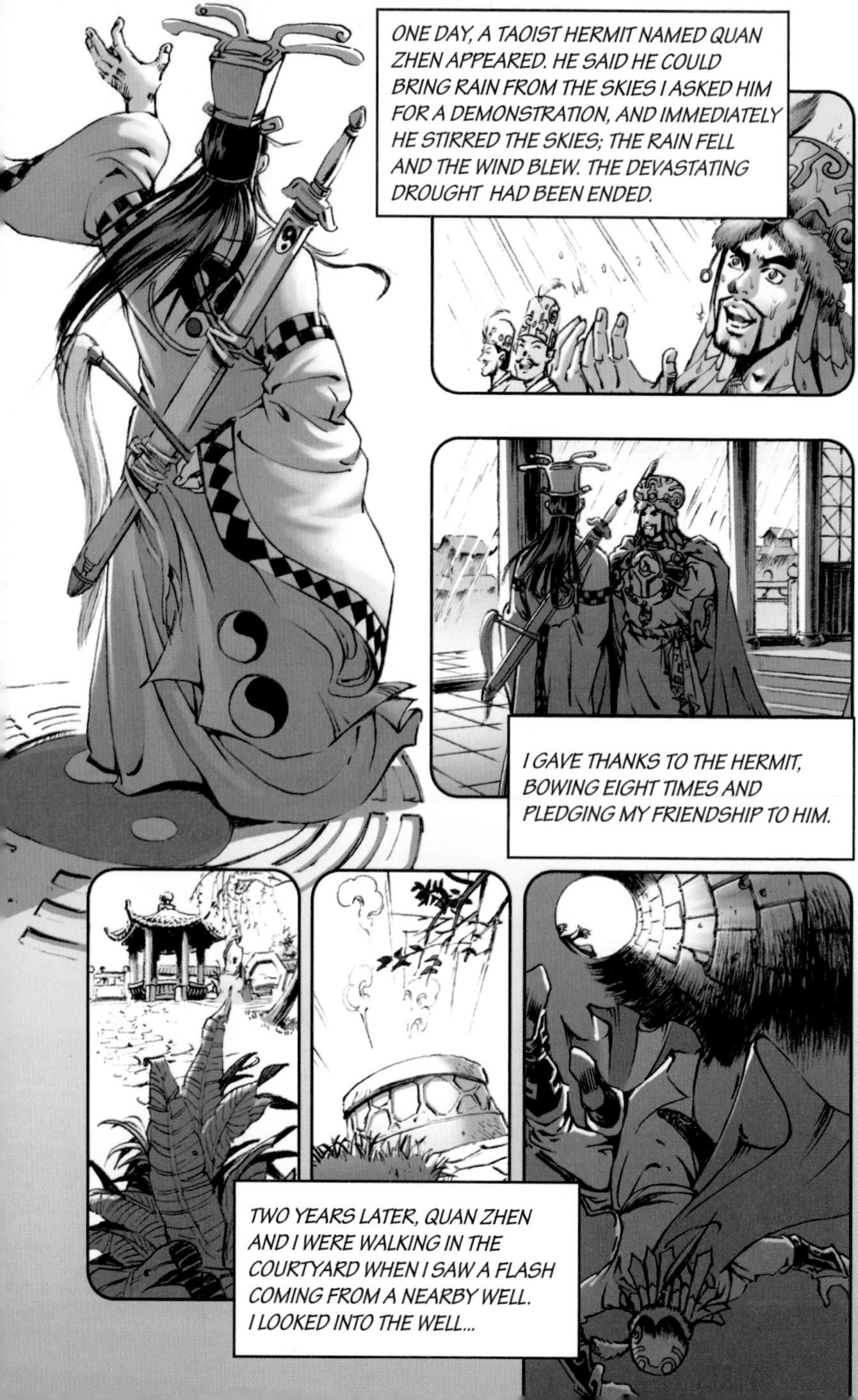
ONE DAY, A TAOIST HERMIT NAMED QUAN ZHEN APPEARED. HE SAID HE COULD BRING RAIN FROM THE SKIES I ASKED HIM FOR A DEMONSTRATION, AND IMMEDIATELY HE STIRRED THE SKIES; THE RAIN FELL AND THE WIND BLEW. THE DEVASTATING DROUGHT HAD BEEN ENDED.
I GAVE THANKS TO THE HERMIT, BOWING EIGHT TIMES AND PLEDGING MY FRIENDSHIP TO HIM.
TWO YEARS LATER, QUAN ZHEN AND I WERE WALKING IN THE COURTYARD WHEN I SAW A FLASH COMING FROM A NEARBY WELL. I LOOKED INTO THE WELL...

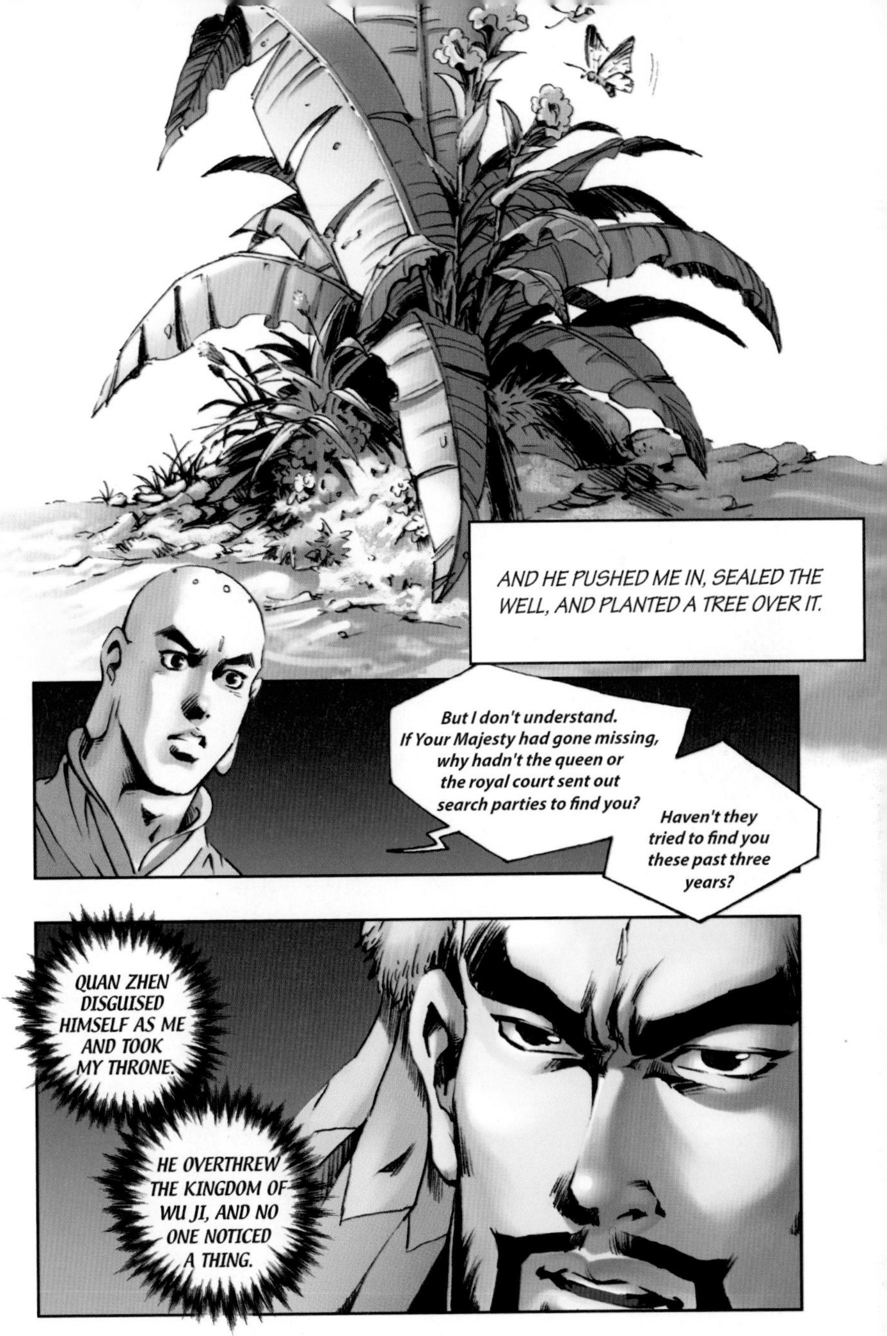
AND HE PUSHED ME IN, SEALED THE WELL, AND PLANTED A TREE OVER IT.
But I don't understand. If Your Majesty had gone missing, why hadn't the queen or the royal court sent out search parties to find you?
Haven't they tried to find you these past three years?
QUAN ZHEN DISGUISED HIMSELF AS ME AND TOOK MY THRONE.
HE OVERTHREW THE KINGDOM OF WU JI, AND NO ONE NOTICED A THING.

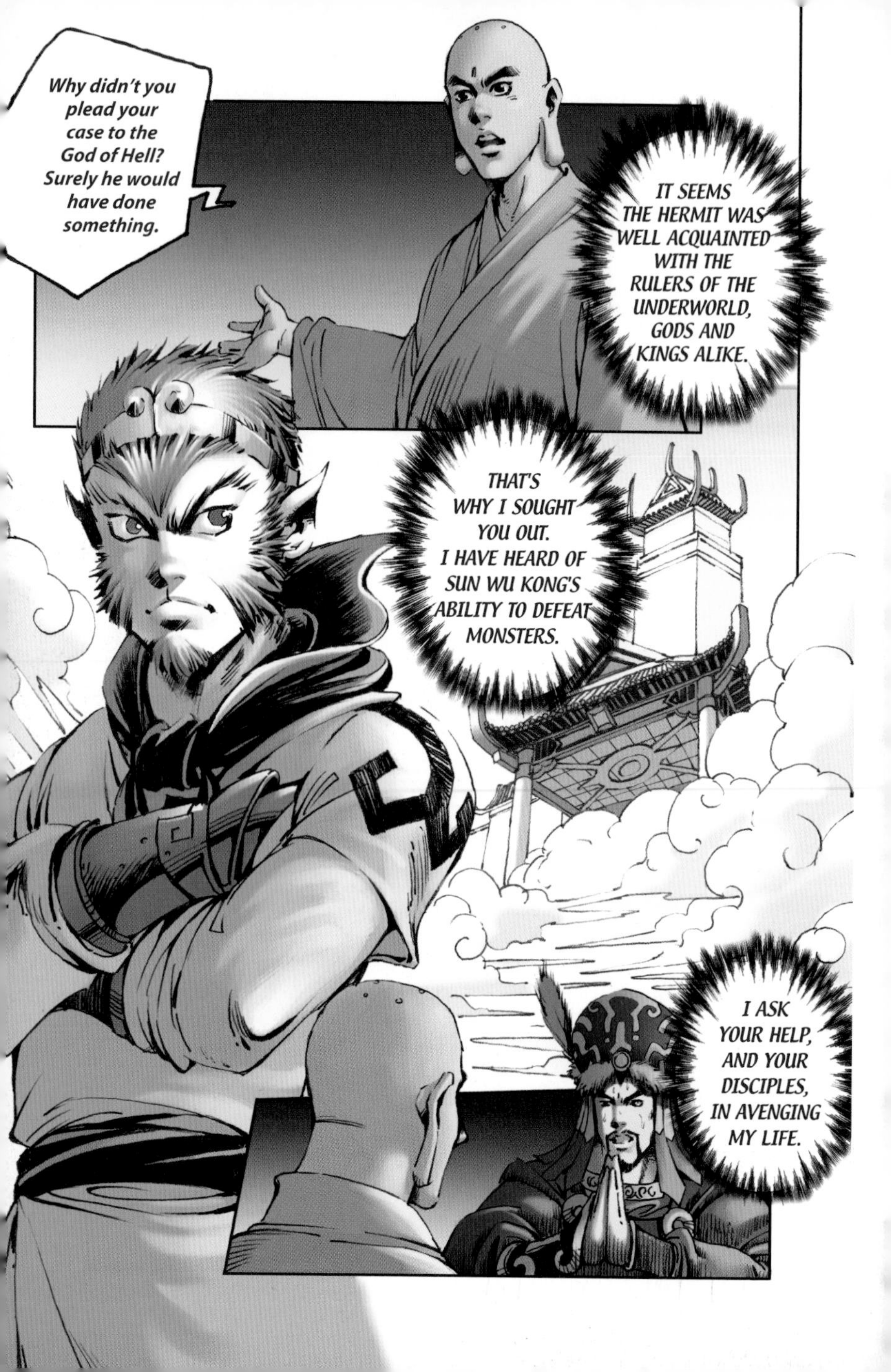
Why didn't you plead your case to the God of Hell? Surely he would have done something.
IT SEEMS THE HERMIT WAS WELL ACQUAINTED WITH THE RULERS OF THE UNDERWORLD, GODS AND KINGS ALIKE.
THAT'S WHY I SOUGHT YOU OUT. I HAVE HEARD OF SUN WU KONG'S ABILITY TO DEFEAT MONSTERS.
I ASK YOUR HELP, AND YOUR DISCIPLES, IN AVENGING MY LIFE.

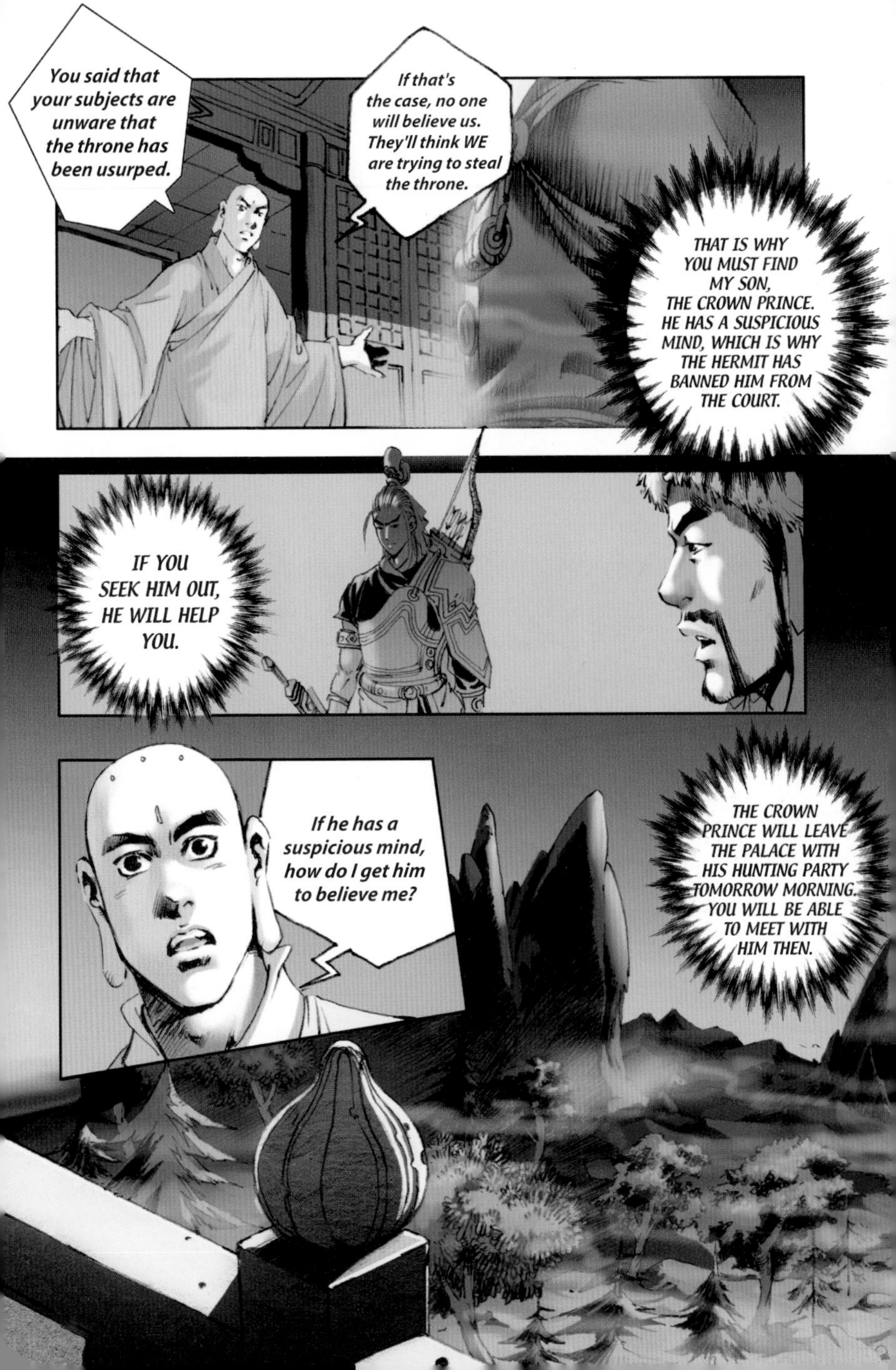
You said that your subjects are unware that the throne has been usurped.
If that's the case, no one will believe us. They'll think WE are trying to steal the throne.
THAT IS WHY YOU MUST FIND MY SON, THE CROWN PRINCE. HE HAS A SUSPICIOUS MIND, WHICH IS WHY THE HERMIT HAS BANNED HIM FROM THE COURT.
IF YOU SEEK HIM OUT, HE WILL HELP YOU.
If he has a suspicious mind, how do I get him to believe me?
THE CROWN PRINCE WILL LEAVE THE PALACE WITH HIS HUNTING PARTY TOMORROW MORNING. YOU WILL BE ABLE TO MEET WITH HIM THEN.

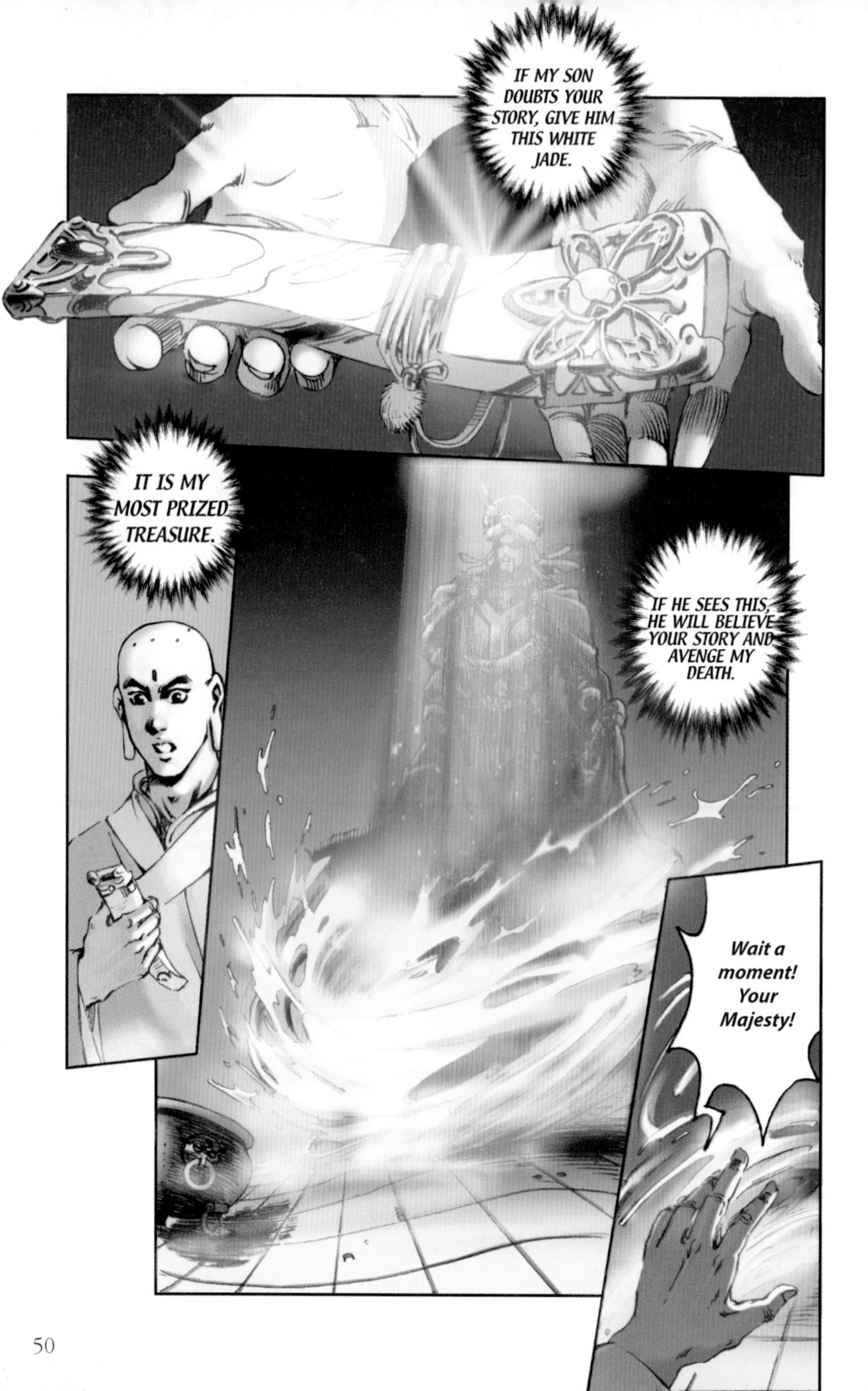
IF MY SON DOUBTS YOUR STORY, GIVE HIM THIS WHITE JADE.
IT IS MY MOST PRIZED TREASURE.
IF HE SEES THIS, HE WILL BELIEVE YOUR STORY AND AVENGE MY DEATH.
Wait a moment! Your Majesty!

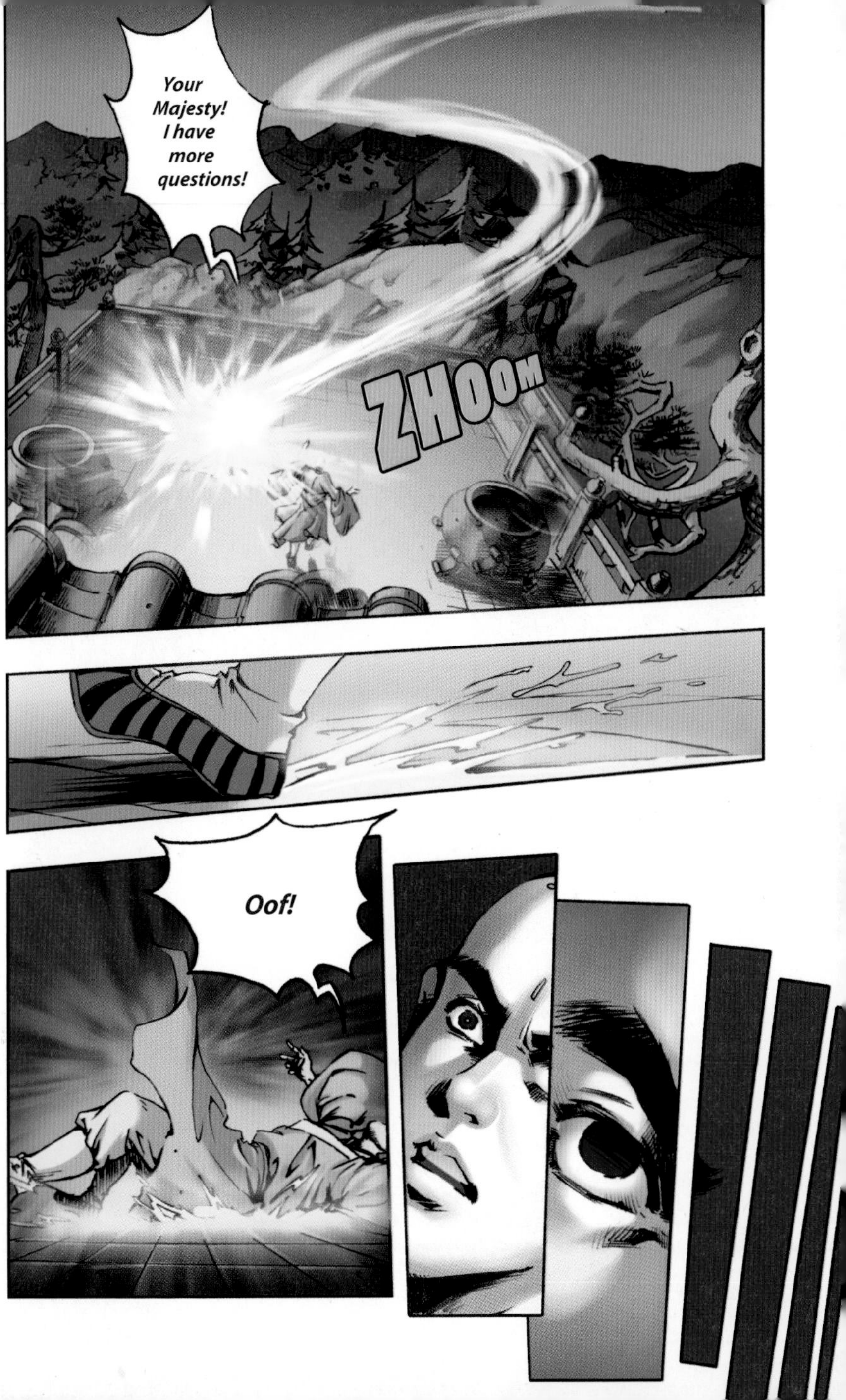
Your Majesty! I have more questions!
ZHOOM
Oof!

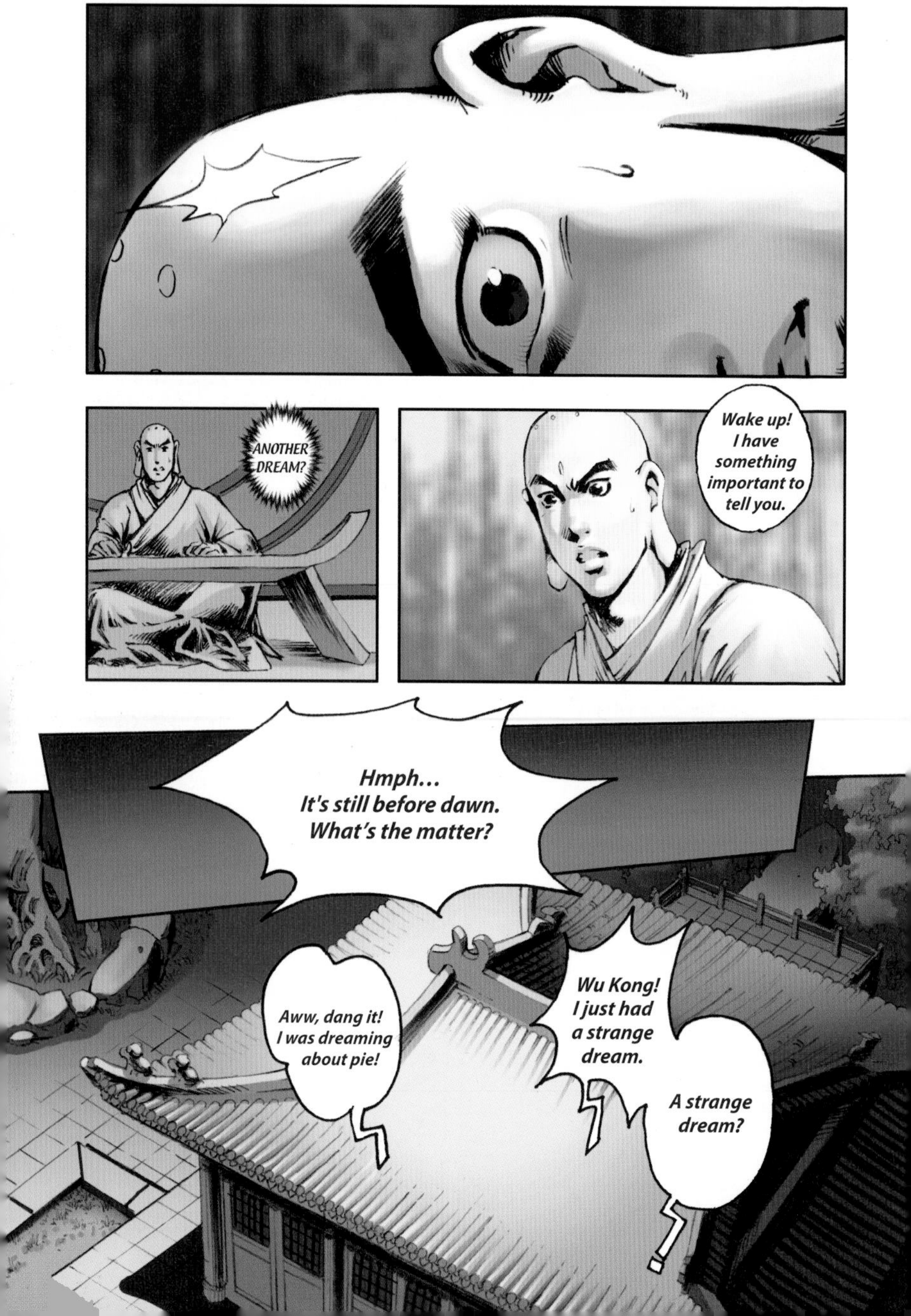
ANOTHER DREAM?
Wake up! I have something important to tell you.
Hmph… It's still before dawn. What's the matter?
Wu Kong! I just had a strange dream.
A strange dream?
Aww, dang it! I was dreaming about pie!

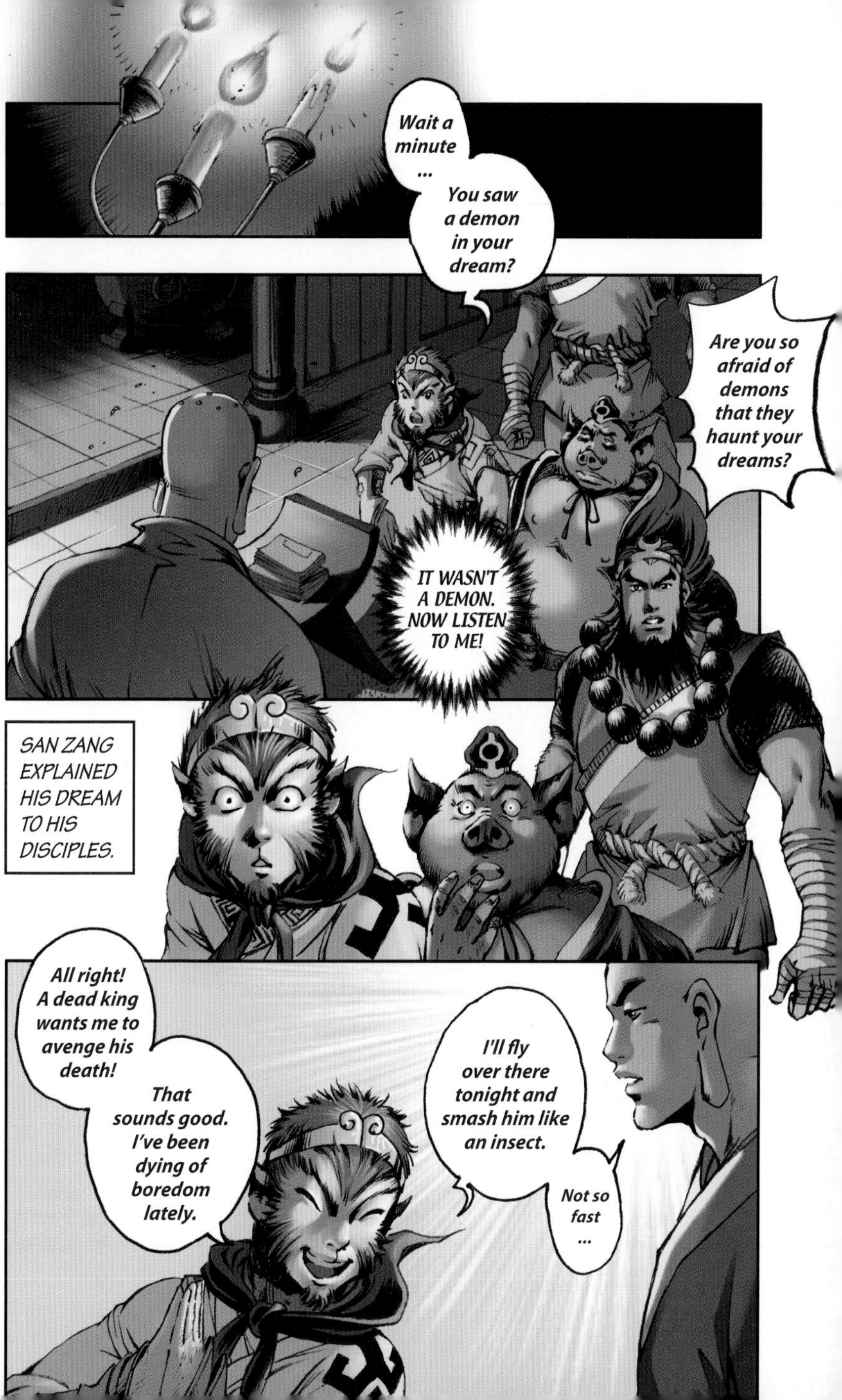

Wait a minute ...
You saw a demon in your dream?
Are you so afraid of demons that they haunt your dreams?
IT WASN'T A DEMON. NOW LISTEN TO ME!
SAN ZANG EXPLAINED HIS DREAM TO HIS DISCIPLES.
All right! A dead king wants me to avenge his death!
That sounds good. I've been dying of boredom lately.
I'll fly over there tonight and smash him like an insect.
Not so fast ...

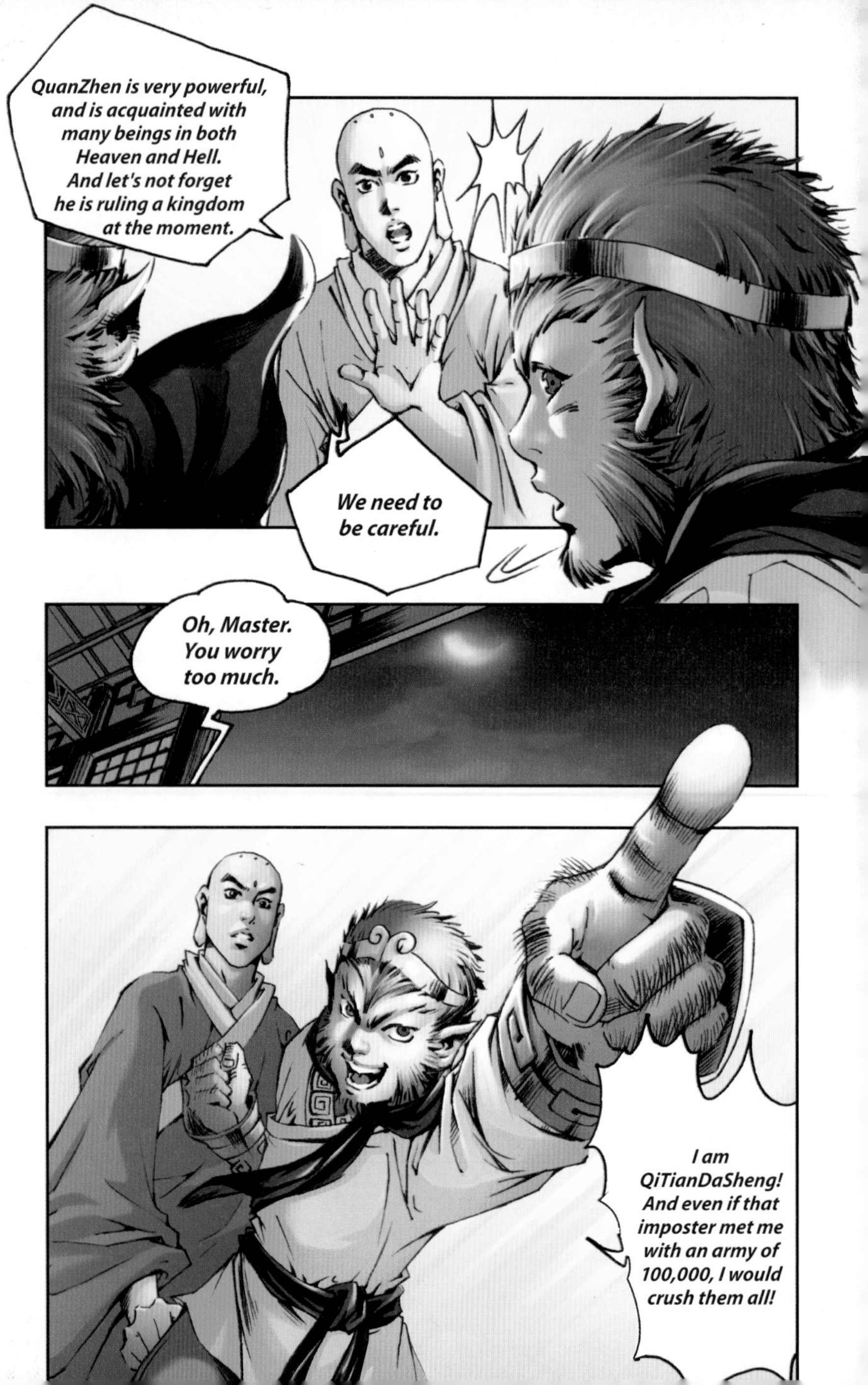
QuanZhen is very powerful, and is acquainted with many beings in both Heaven and Hell. And let's not forget he is ruling a kingdom at the moment.
We need to be careful.
Oh, Master. You worry too much.
I am QiTianDaSheng! And even if that imposter met me with an army of 100,000, I would crush them all!

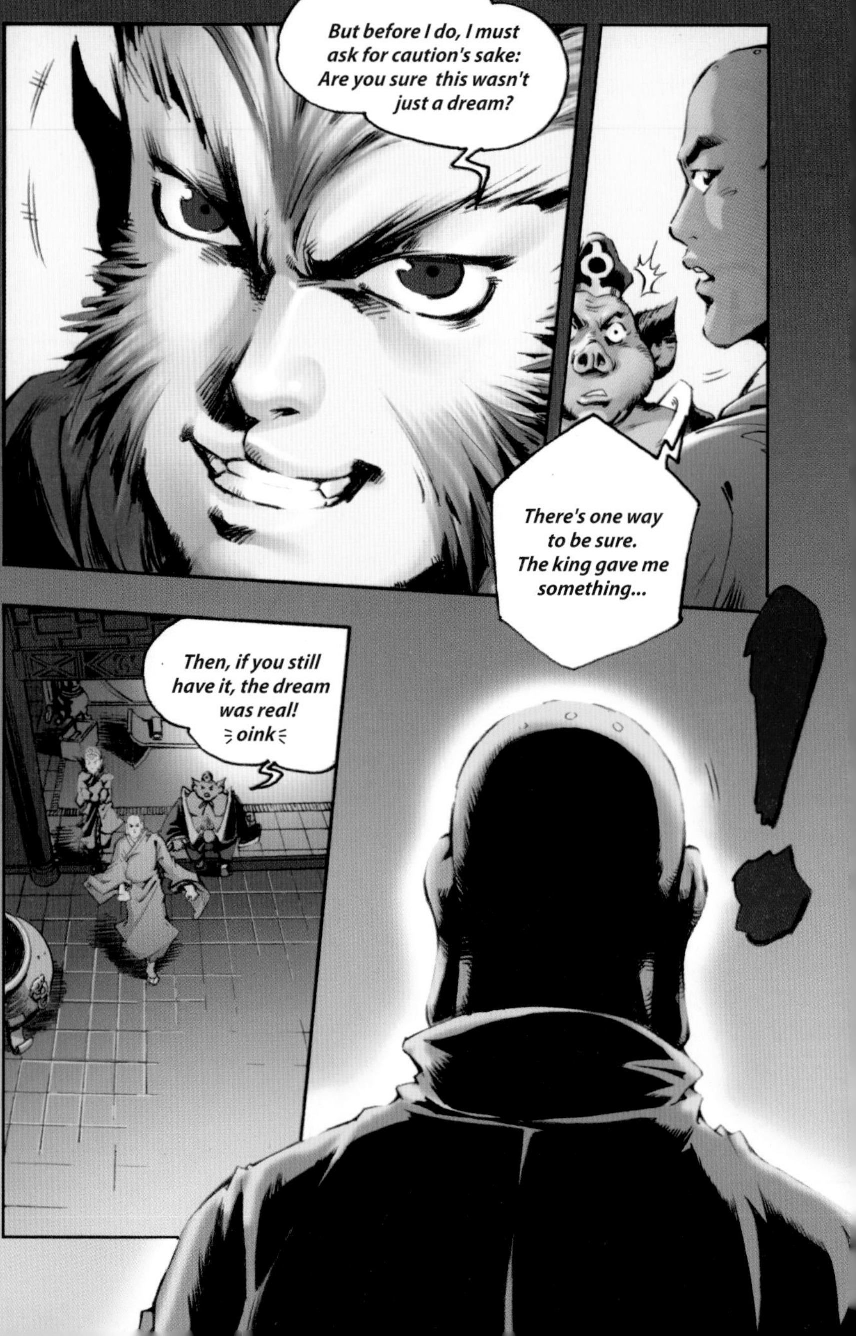
But before I do, I must ask for caution's sake: Are you sure this wasn't just a dream?
There's one way to be sure. The king gave me something...
Then, if you still have it, the dream was real! oink

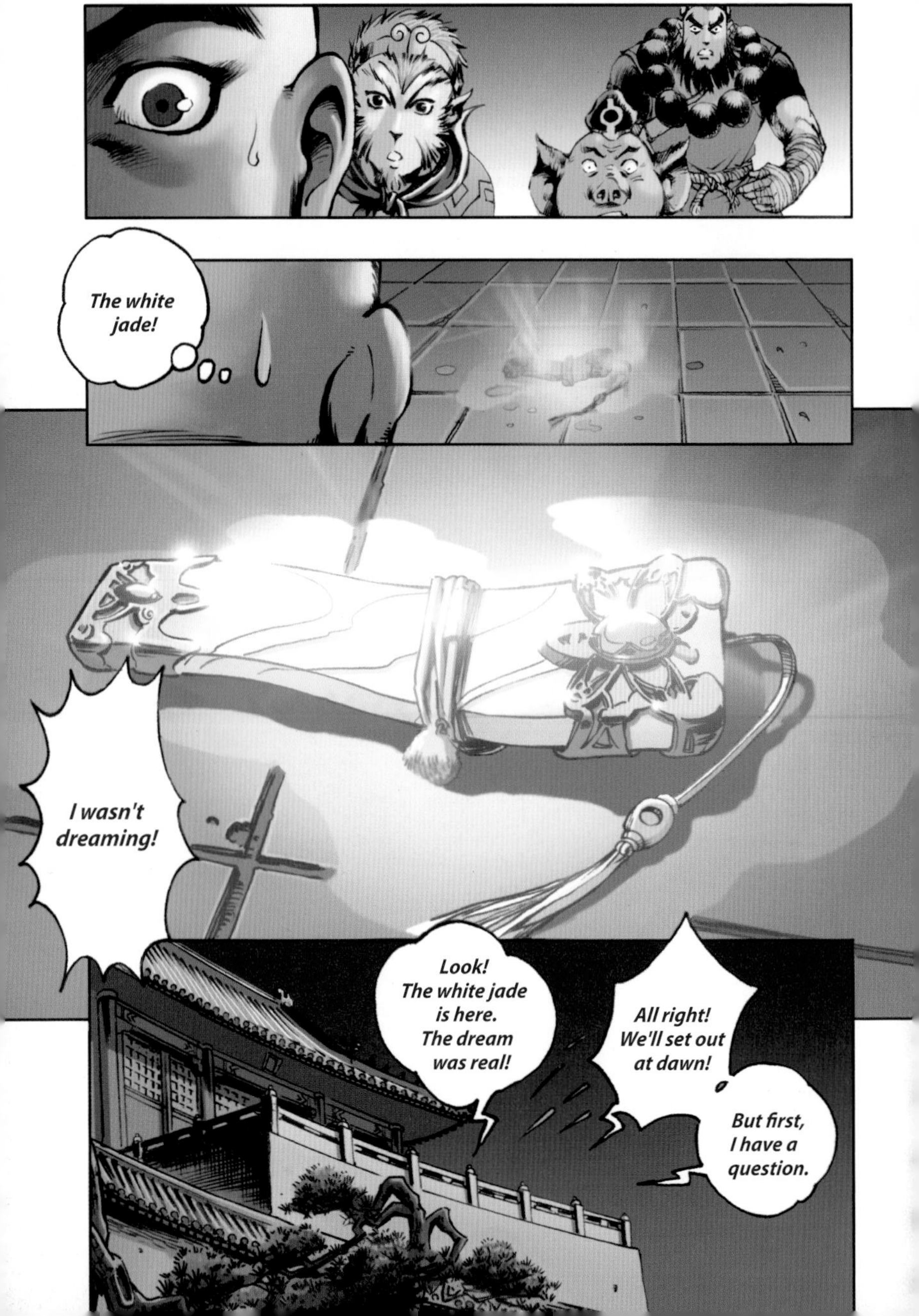
The white jade!
I wasn't dreaming!
Look! The white jade is here. The dream was real!
All right! We'll set out at dawn!
But first, I have a question.

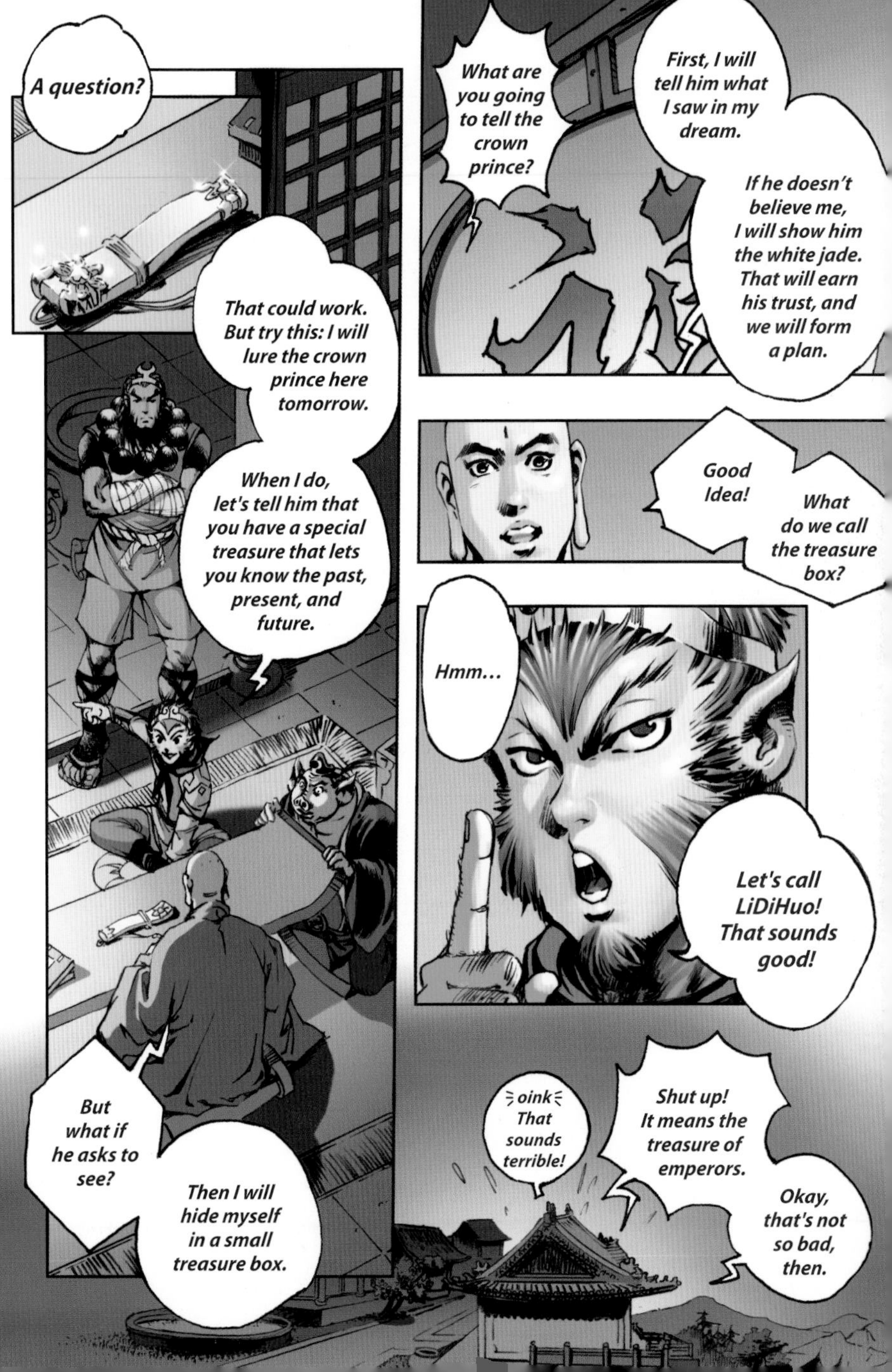
A question?
What are you going to tell the crown prince?
First, I will tell him what I saw in my dream.
If he doesn't believe me, I will show him the white jade. That will earn his trust, and we will form a plan.
That could work. But try this: I will lure the crown prince here tomorrow.
When I do, let's tell him that you have a special treasure that lets you know the past, present, and future.
Good Idea!
What do we call the treasure box?
Hmm…
Let's call LiDiHuo! That sounds good!
But what if he asks to see?
Then I will hide myself in a small treasure box.
oink That sounds terrible!
Shut up! It means the treasure of emperors.
Okay, that's not so bad, then.

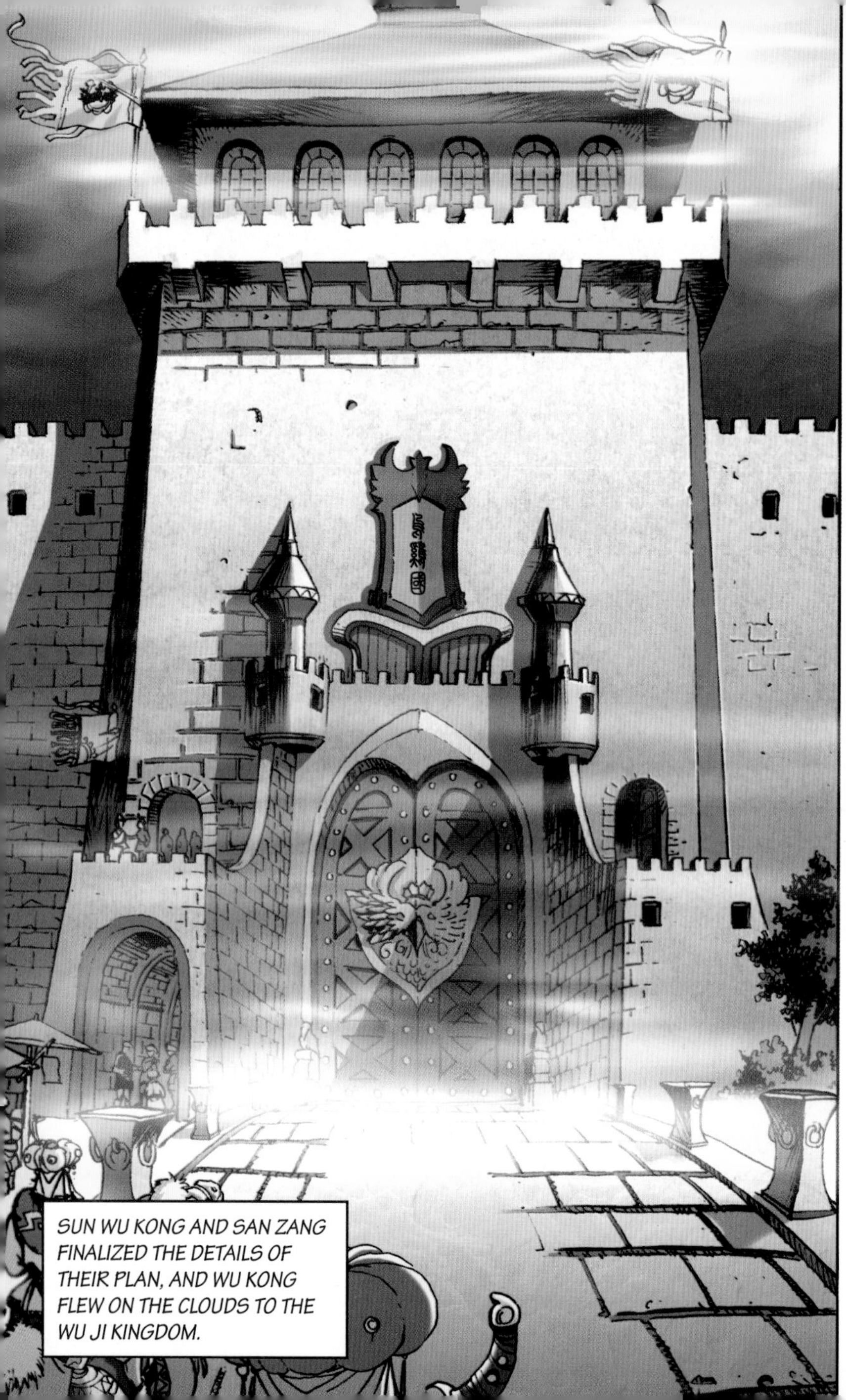
SUN WU KONG AND SAN ZANG FINALIZED THE DETAILS OF THEIR PLAN, AND WU KONG FLEW ON THE CLOUDS TO THE WU JI KINGDOM.

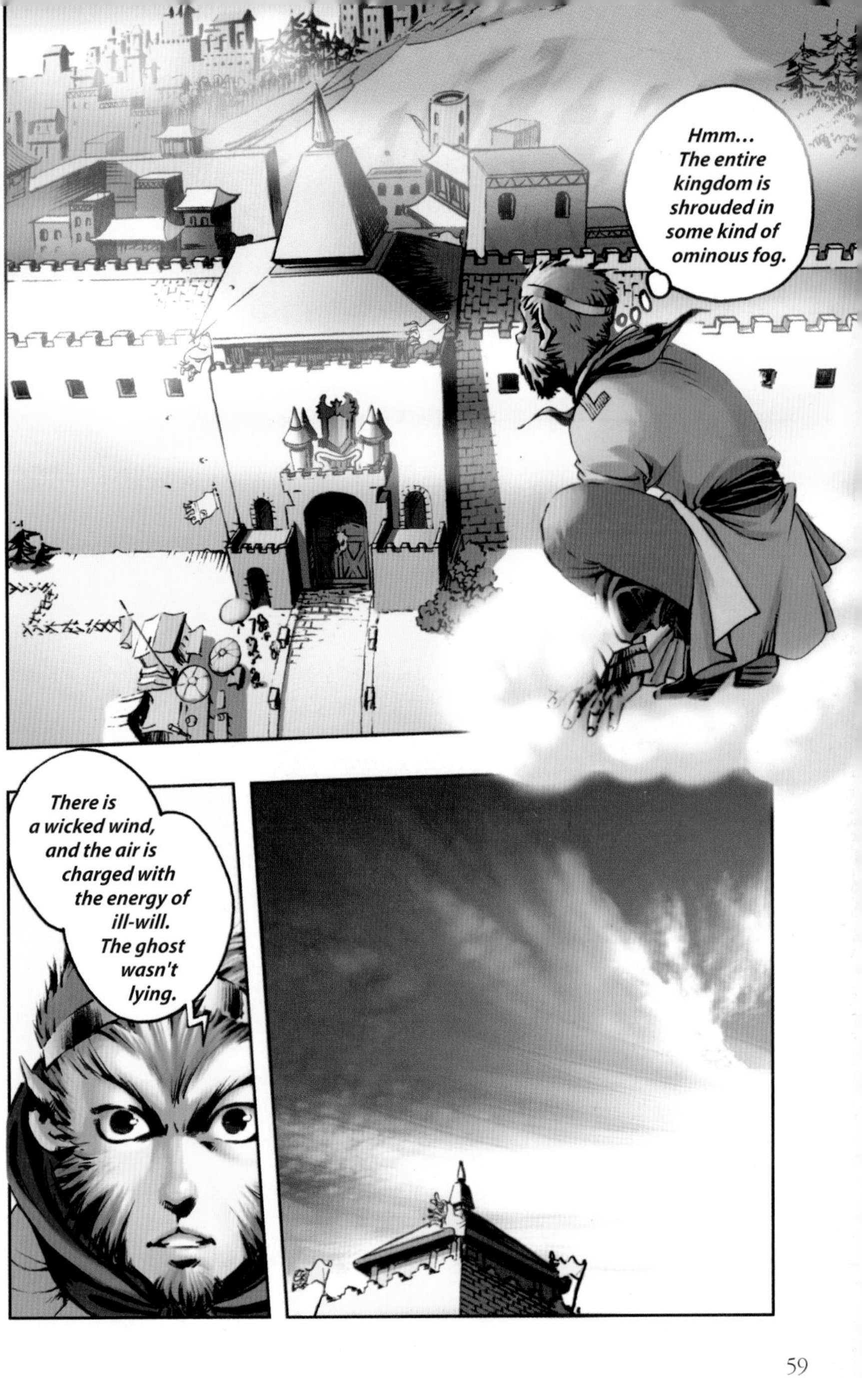
Hmm... The entire kingdom is shrouded in some kind of ominous fog.
There is a wicked wind, and the air is charged with the energy of ill-will. The ghost wasn't lying.

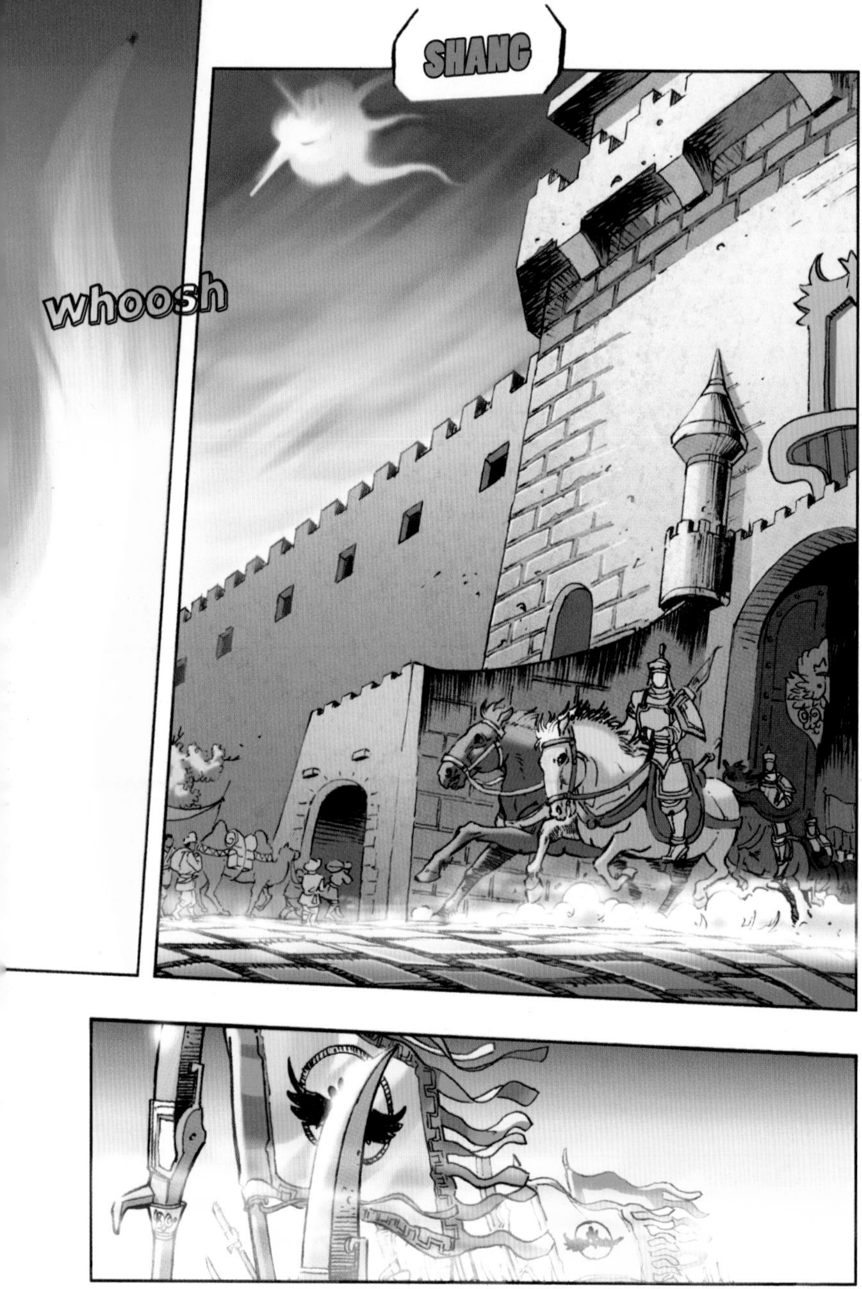
whoosh
SHANG

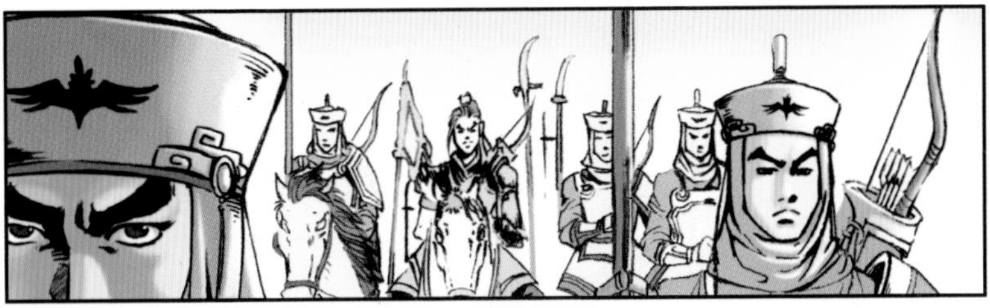

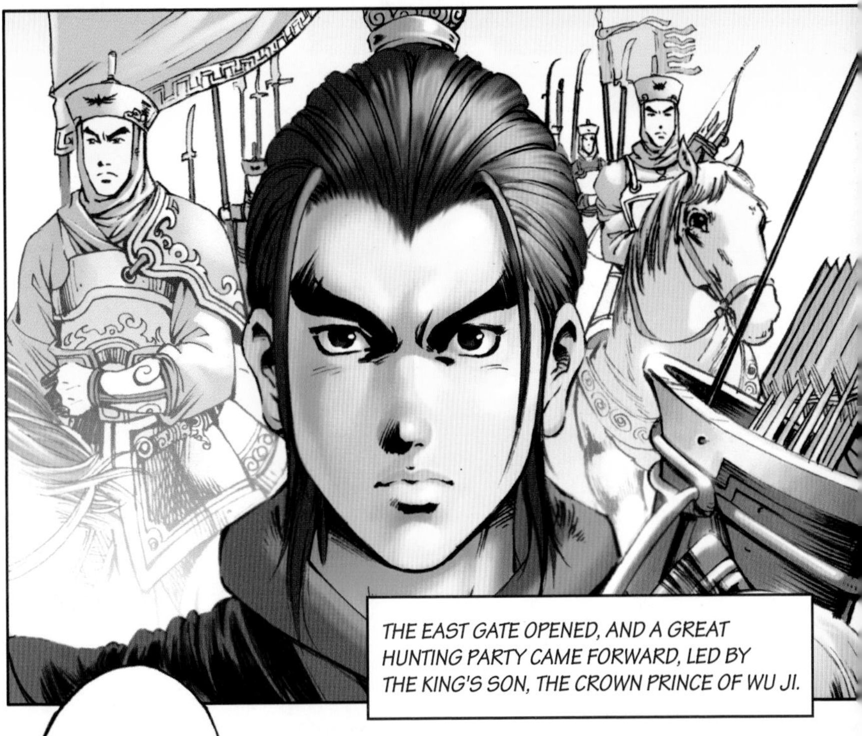
THE EAST GATE OPENED, AND A GREAT HUNTING PARTY CAME FORWARD, LED BY THE KING'S SON, THE CROWN PRINCE OF WU JI.

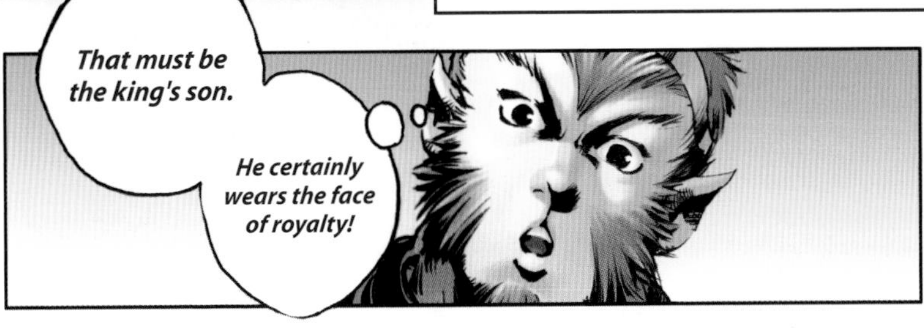
That must be the king's son.
He certainly wears the face of royalty!

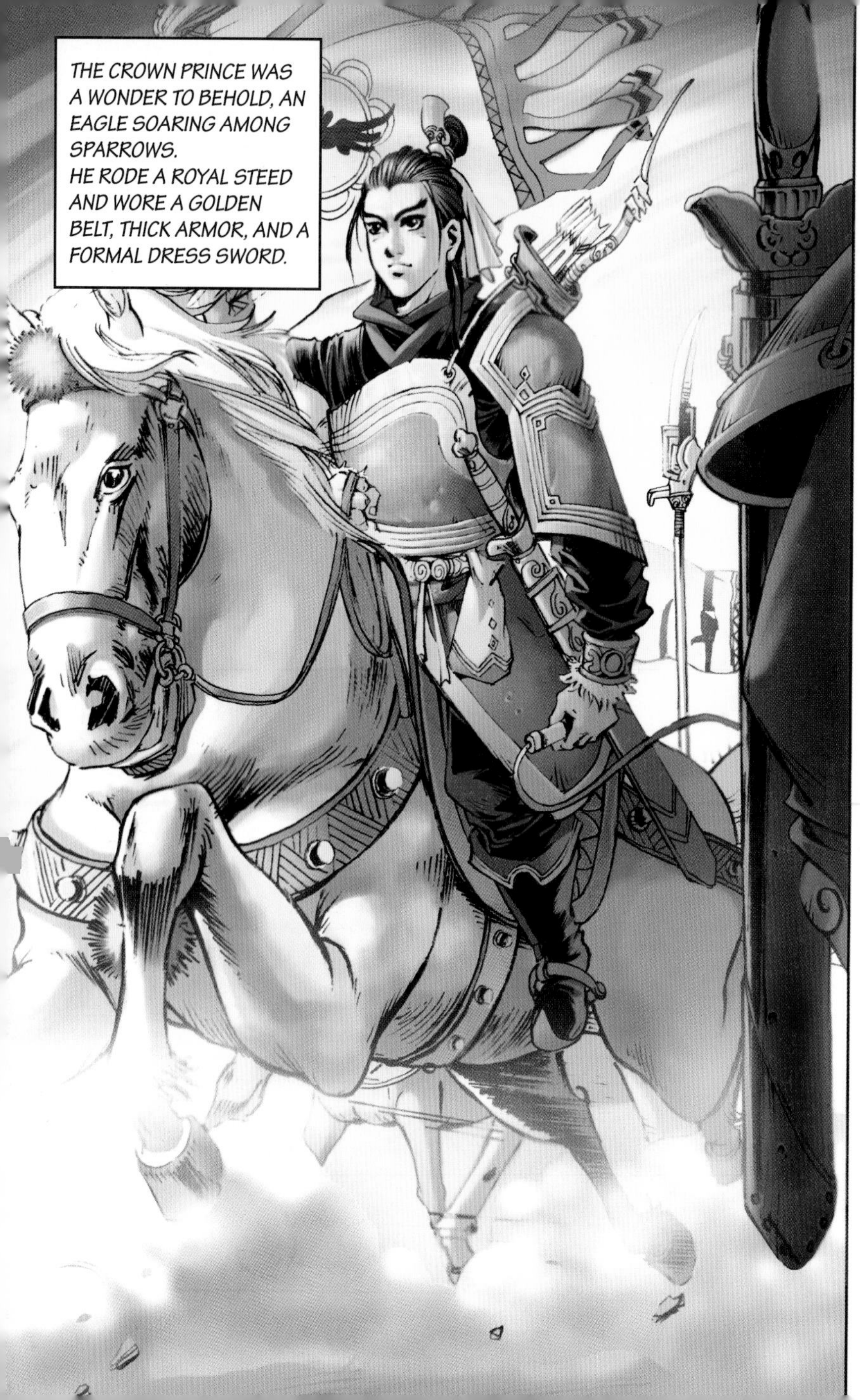
THE CROWN PRINCE WAS A WONDER TO BEHOLD, AN EAGLE SOARING AMONG SPARROWS.
HE RODE A ROYAL STEED AND WORE A GOLDEN BELT, THICK ARMOR, AND A FORMAL DRESS SWORD.

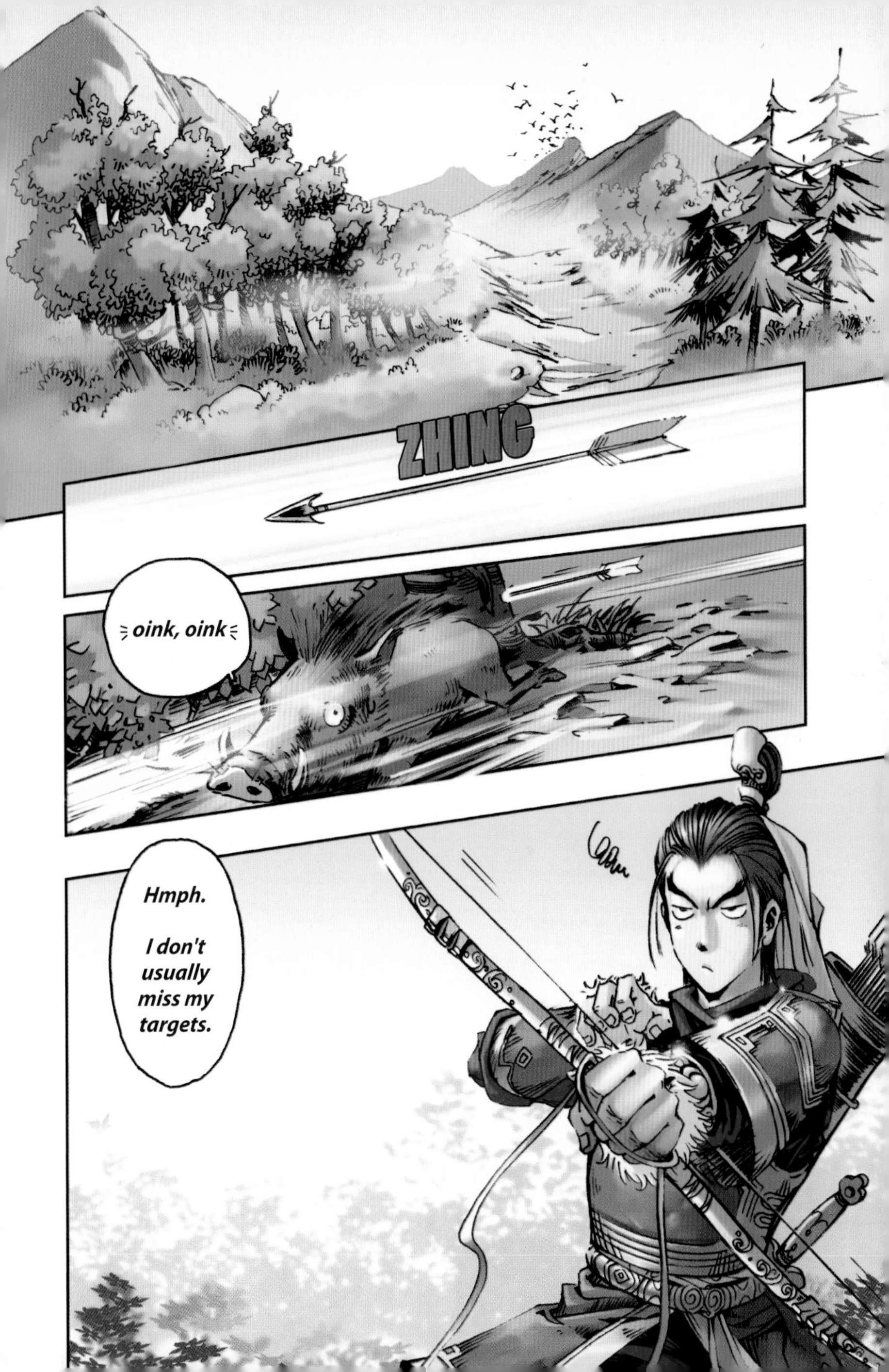
ZHING
oink, oink
Hmph.
I don't usually miss my targets.

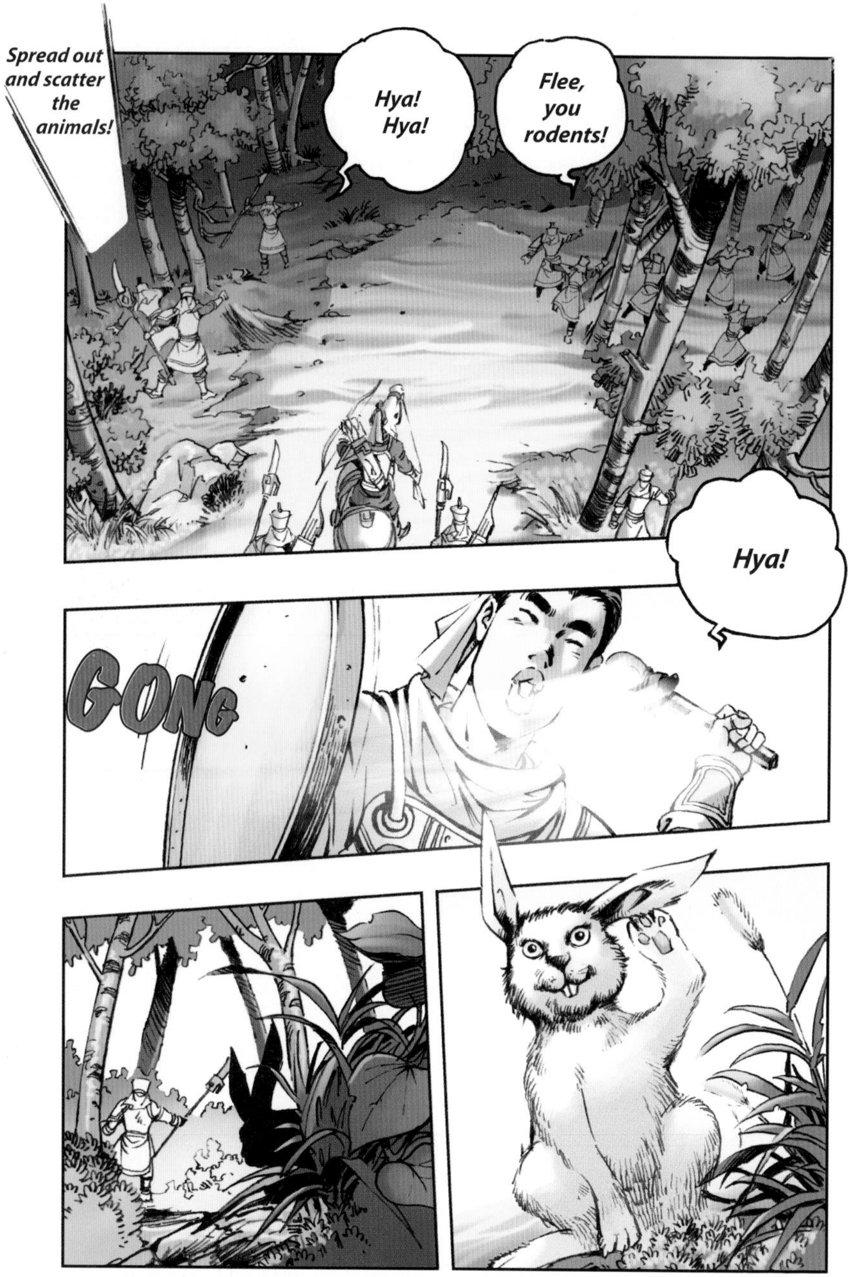
Spread out and scatter the animals!
Hya! Hya!
Flee, you rodents!
Hya!
GONG

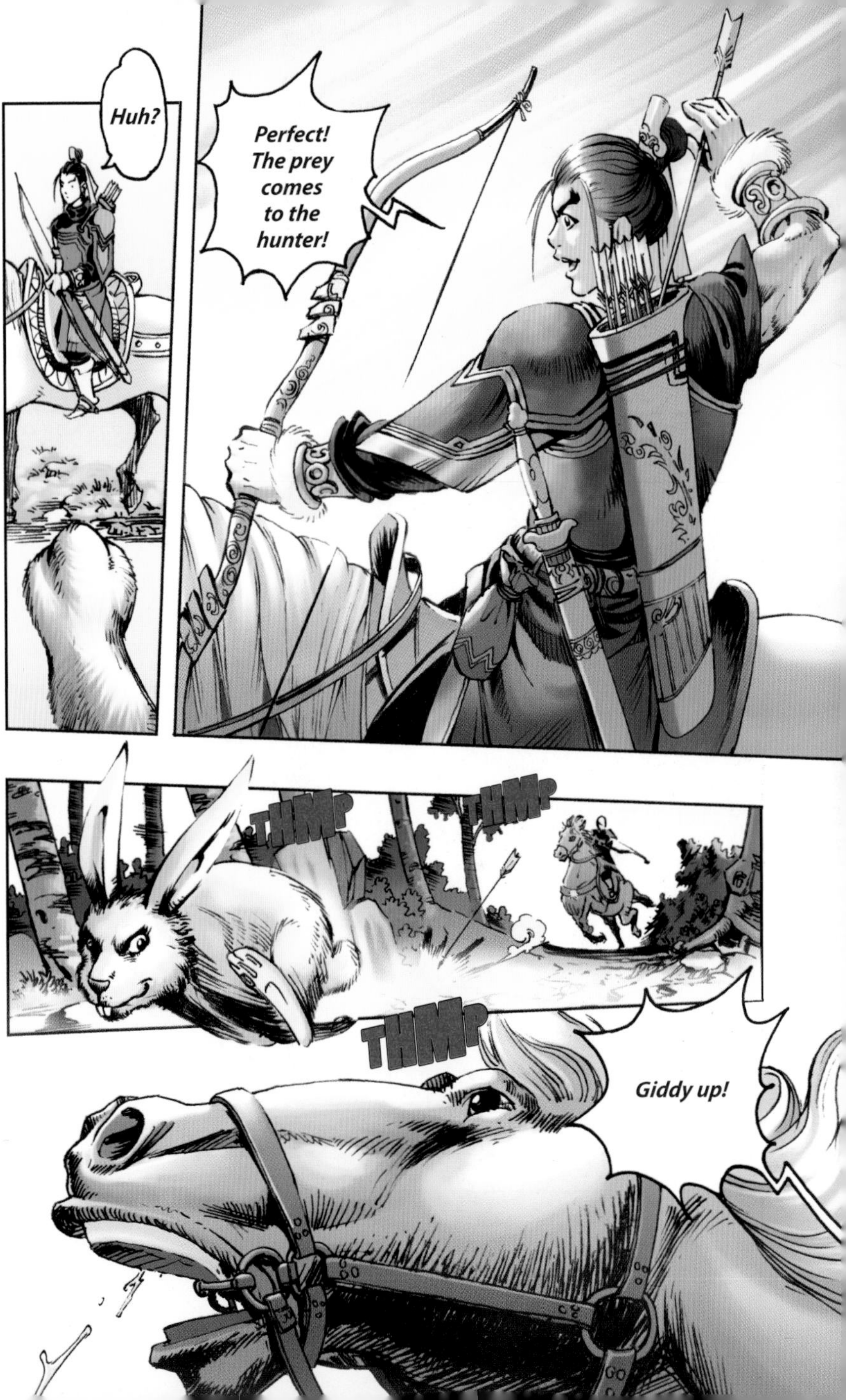
Huh?
Perfect! The prey comes to the hunter!
THMP
THMP
THMP
Giddy up!

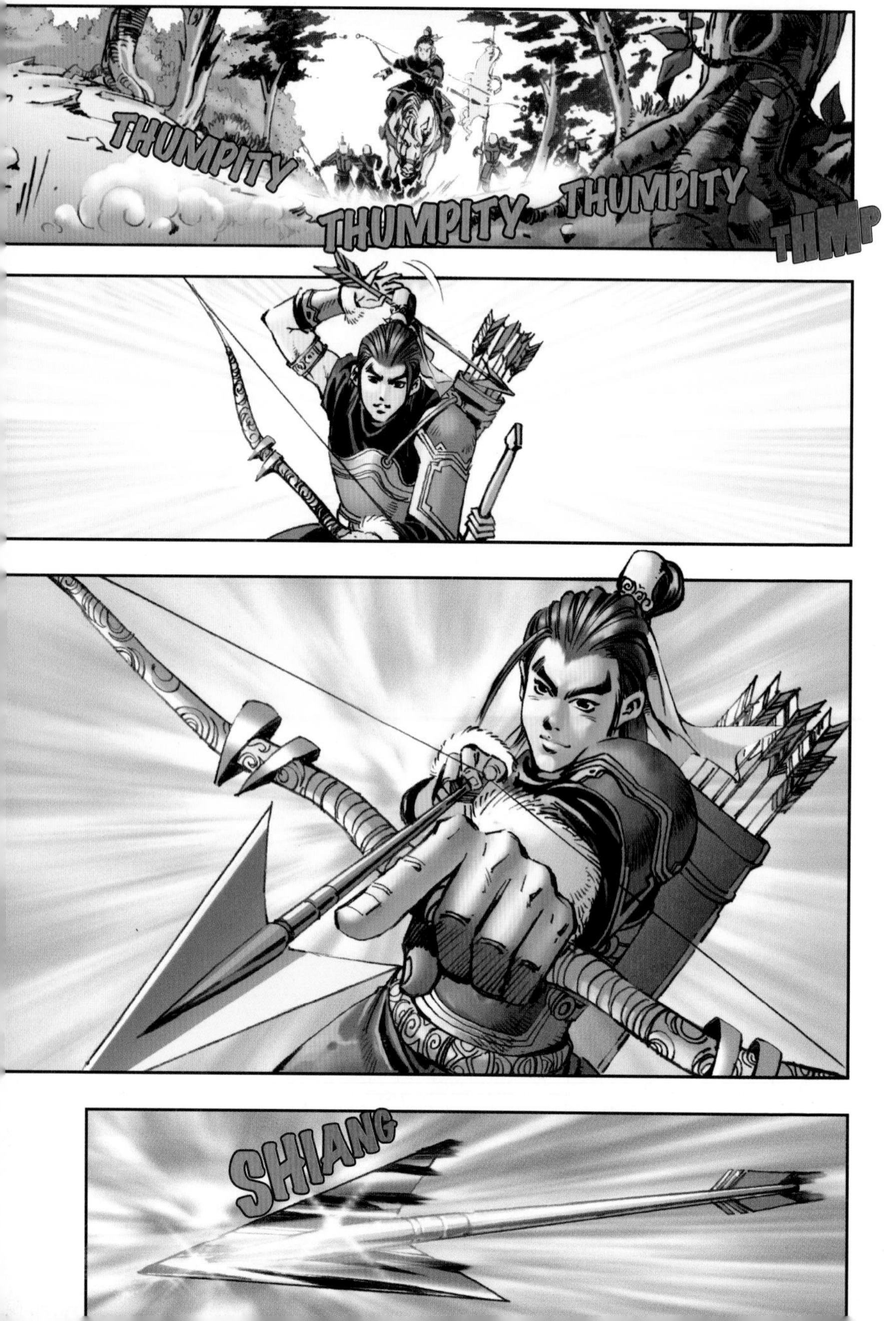
THUMPITY
THUMPITY
THUMPITY
THMP
SHIANG

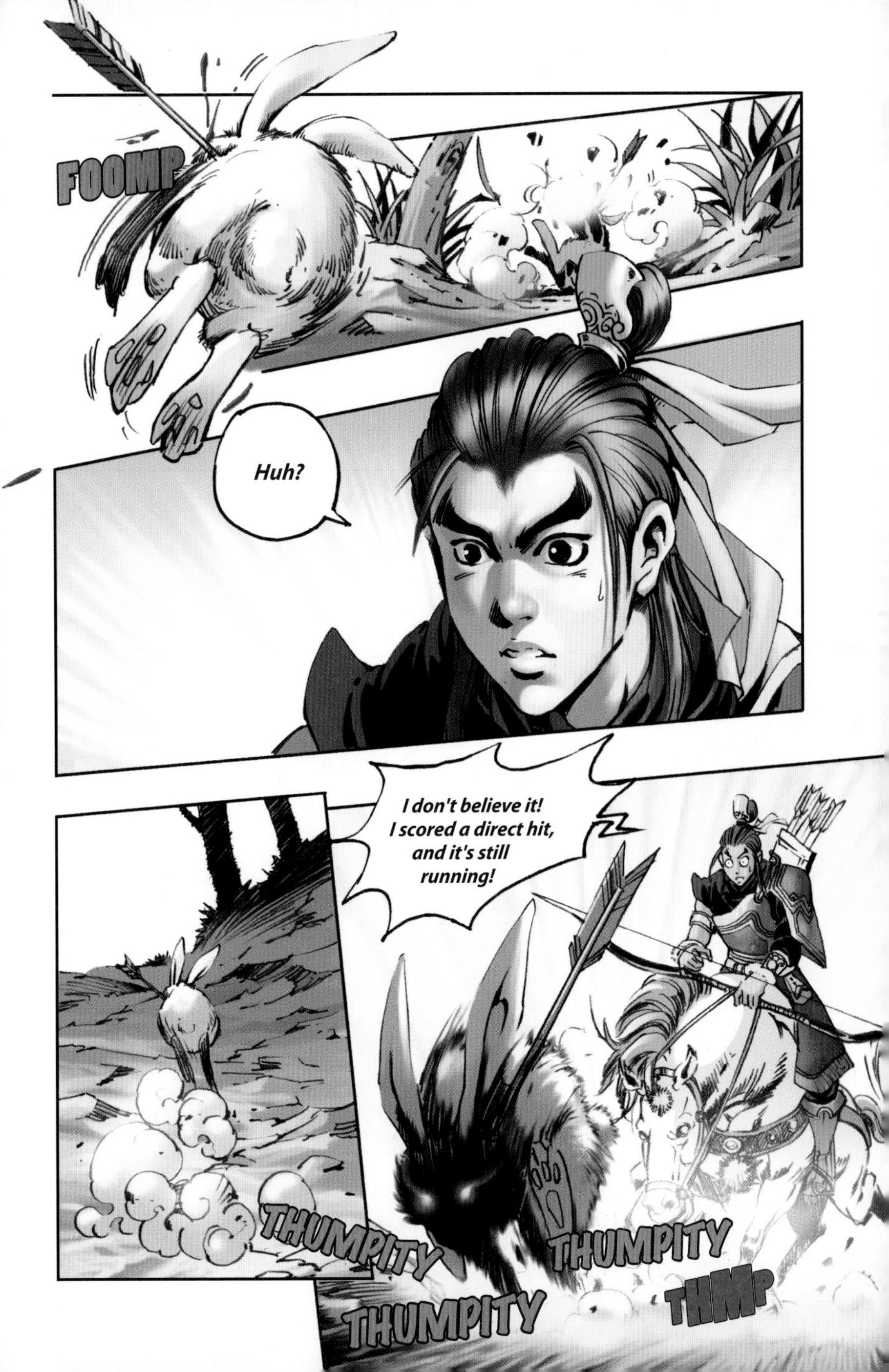
FOOMP
Huh?
I don't believe it! I scored a direct hit, and it's still running!
THUMPITY
THUMPITY
THUMPITY
THMP

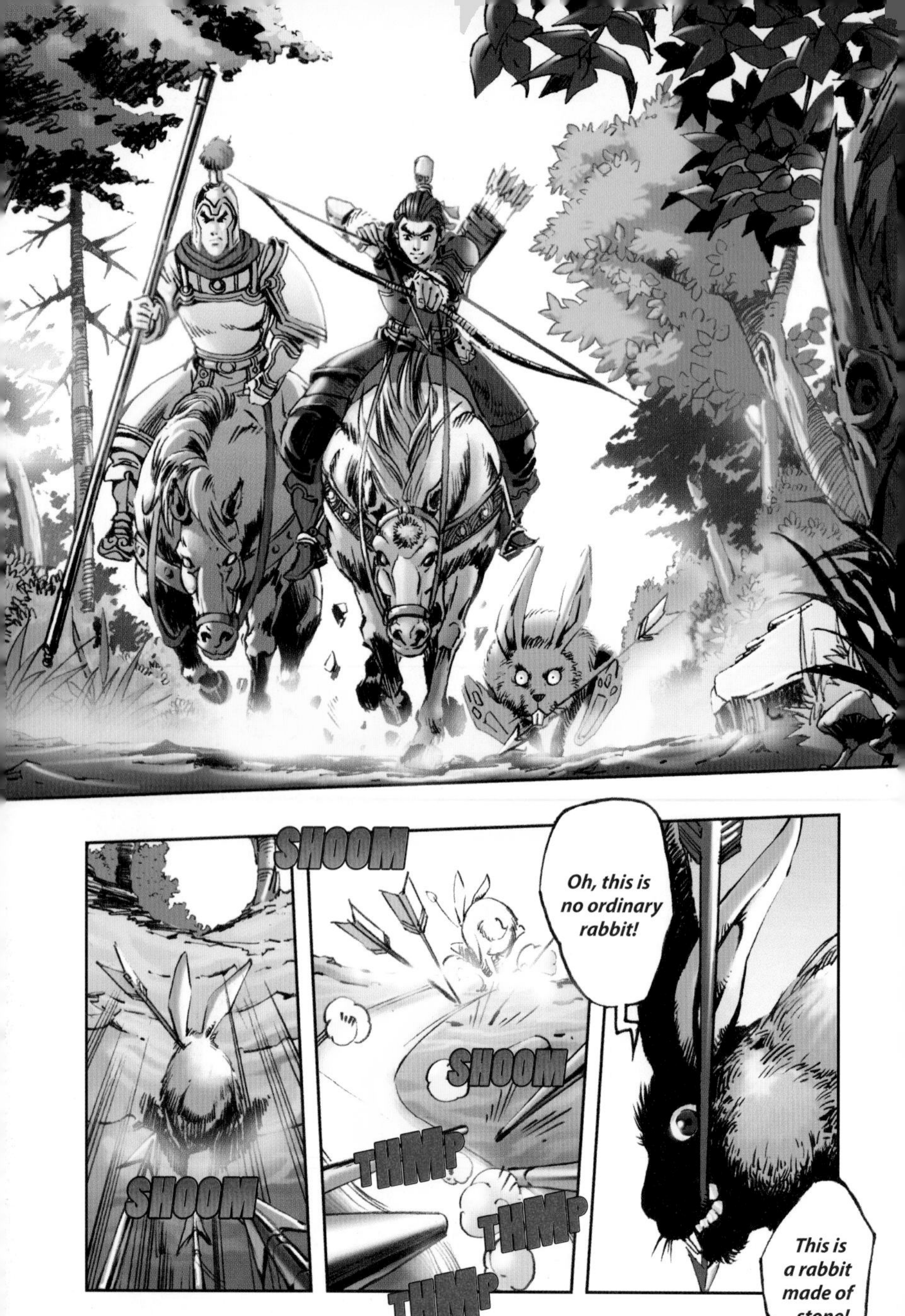
SHOOM
SHOOM
SHOOM
THMP
THMP
THMP
Oh, this is no ordinary rabbit!
This is a rabbit made of stone!

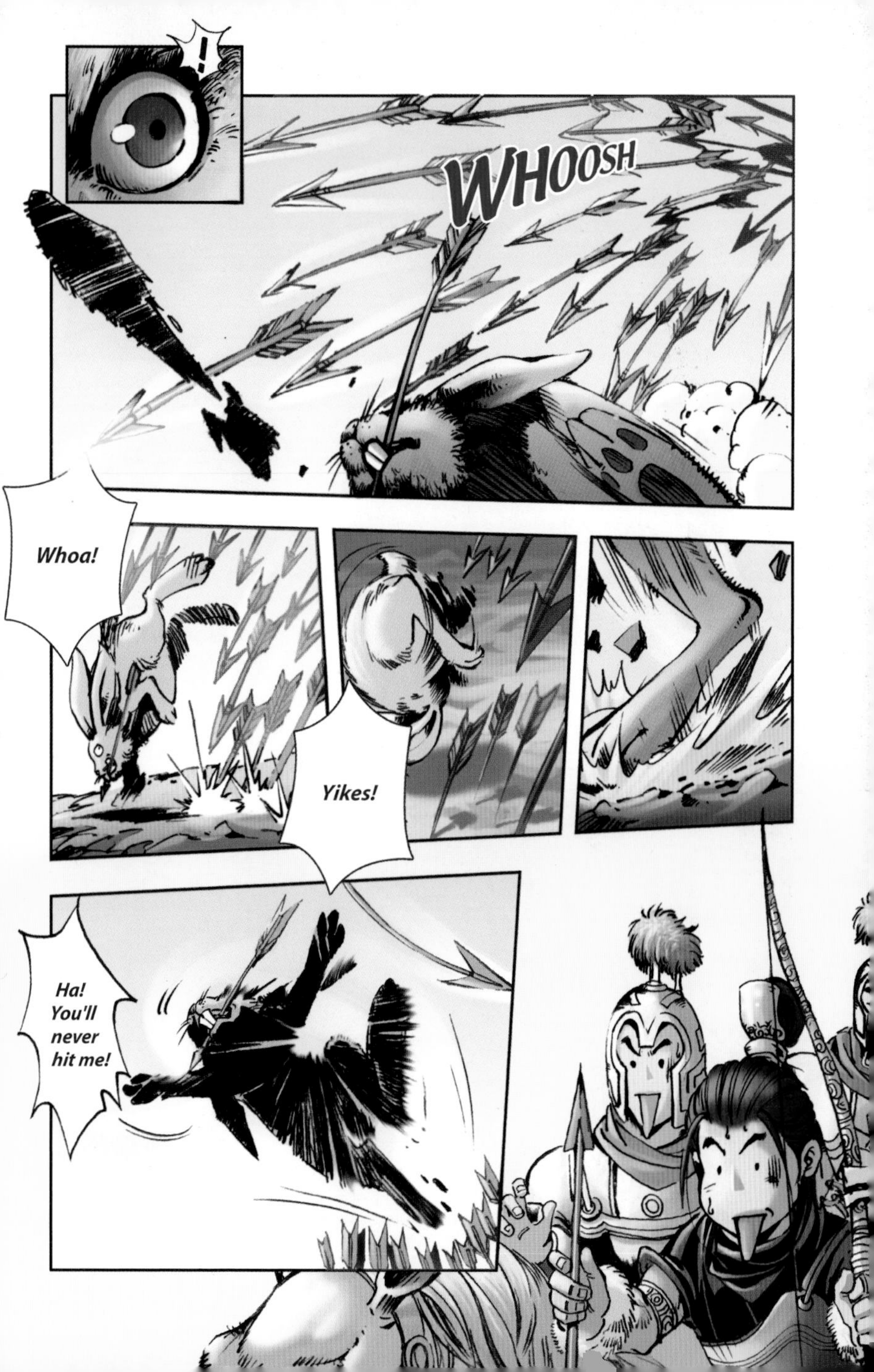
!
WHOOSH
Whoa!
Yikes!
Ha! You'll never hit me!

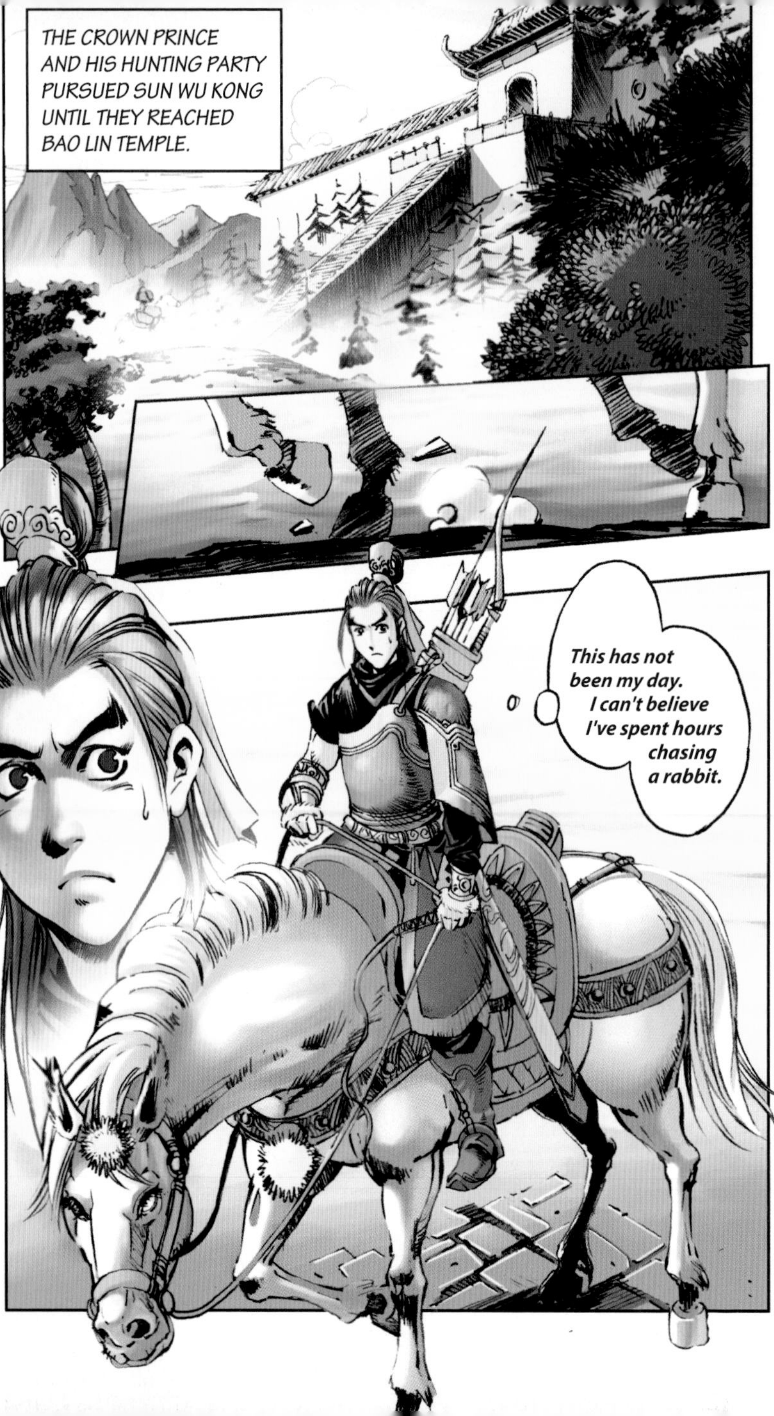
THE CROWN PRINCE AND HIS HUNTING PARTY PURSUED SUN WU KONG UNTIL THEY REACHED BAO LIN TEMPLE.
This has not been my day. I can't believe I've spent hours chasing a rabbit.

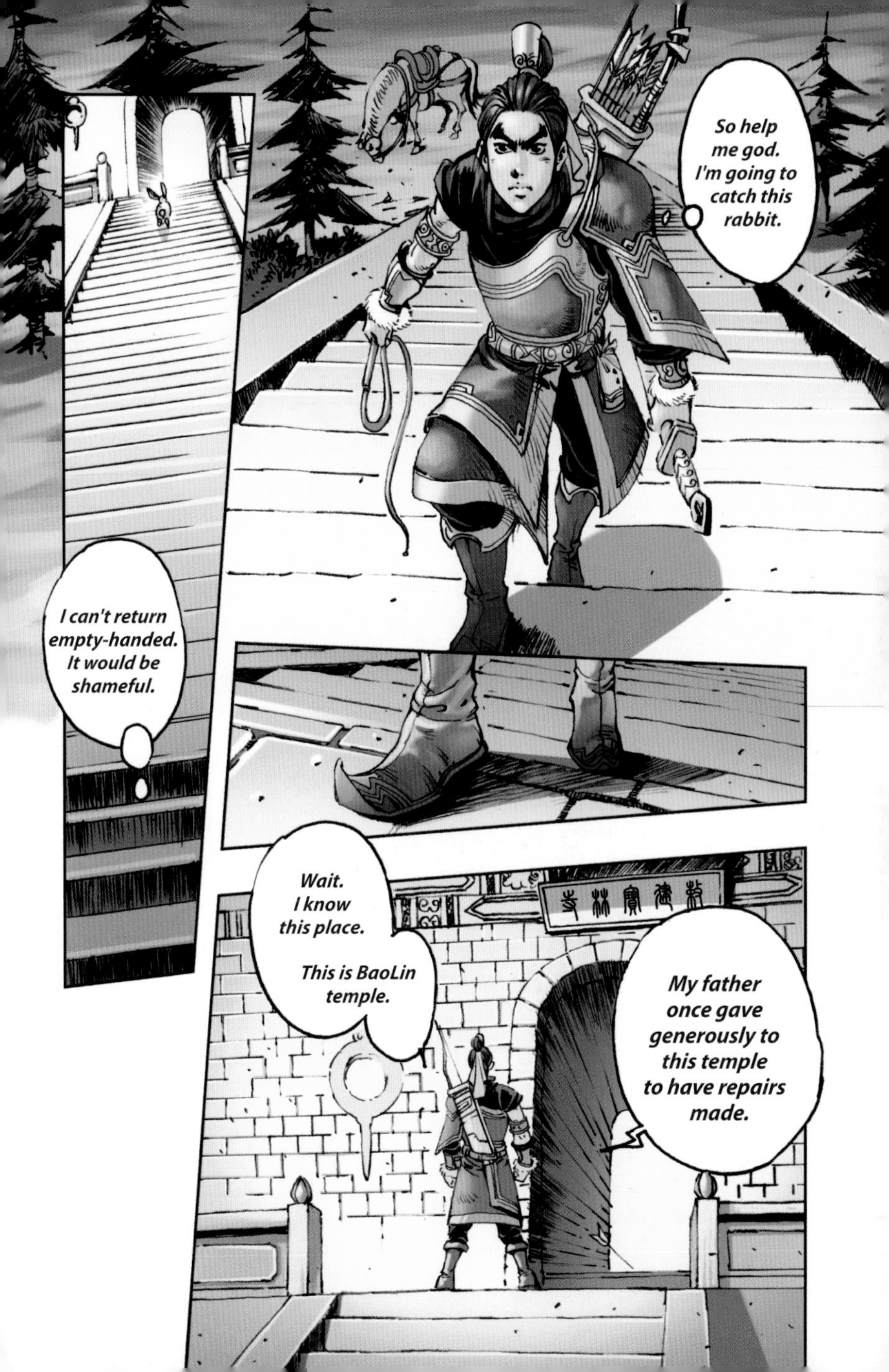
So help me god. I'm going to catch this rabbit.
I can't return empty-handed. It would be shameful.
Wait. I know this place.
This is BaoLin temple.
My father once gave generously to this temple to have repairs made.

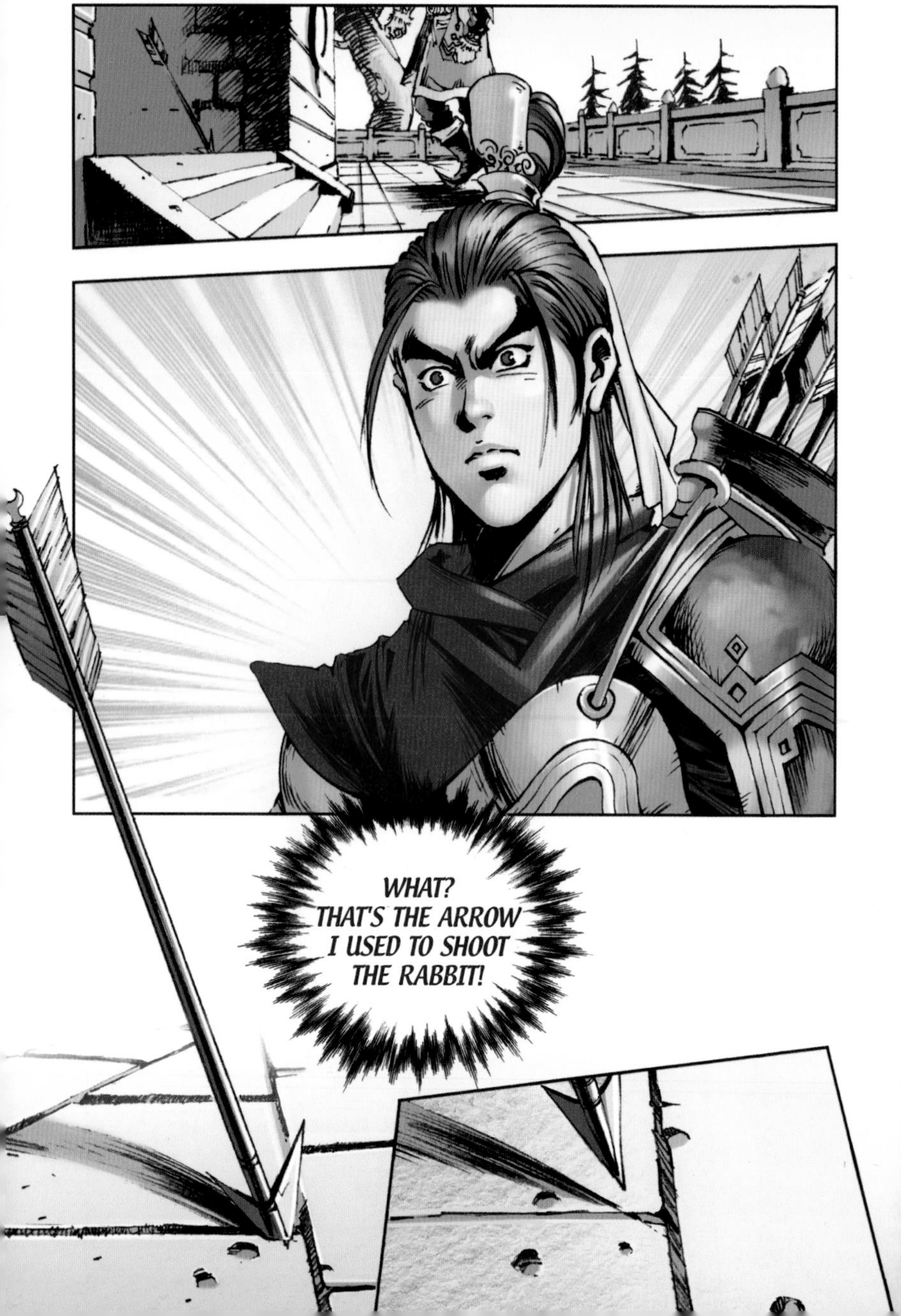
WHAT? THAT'S THE ARROW I USED TO SHOOT THE RABBIT!

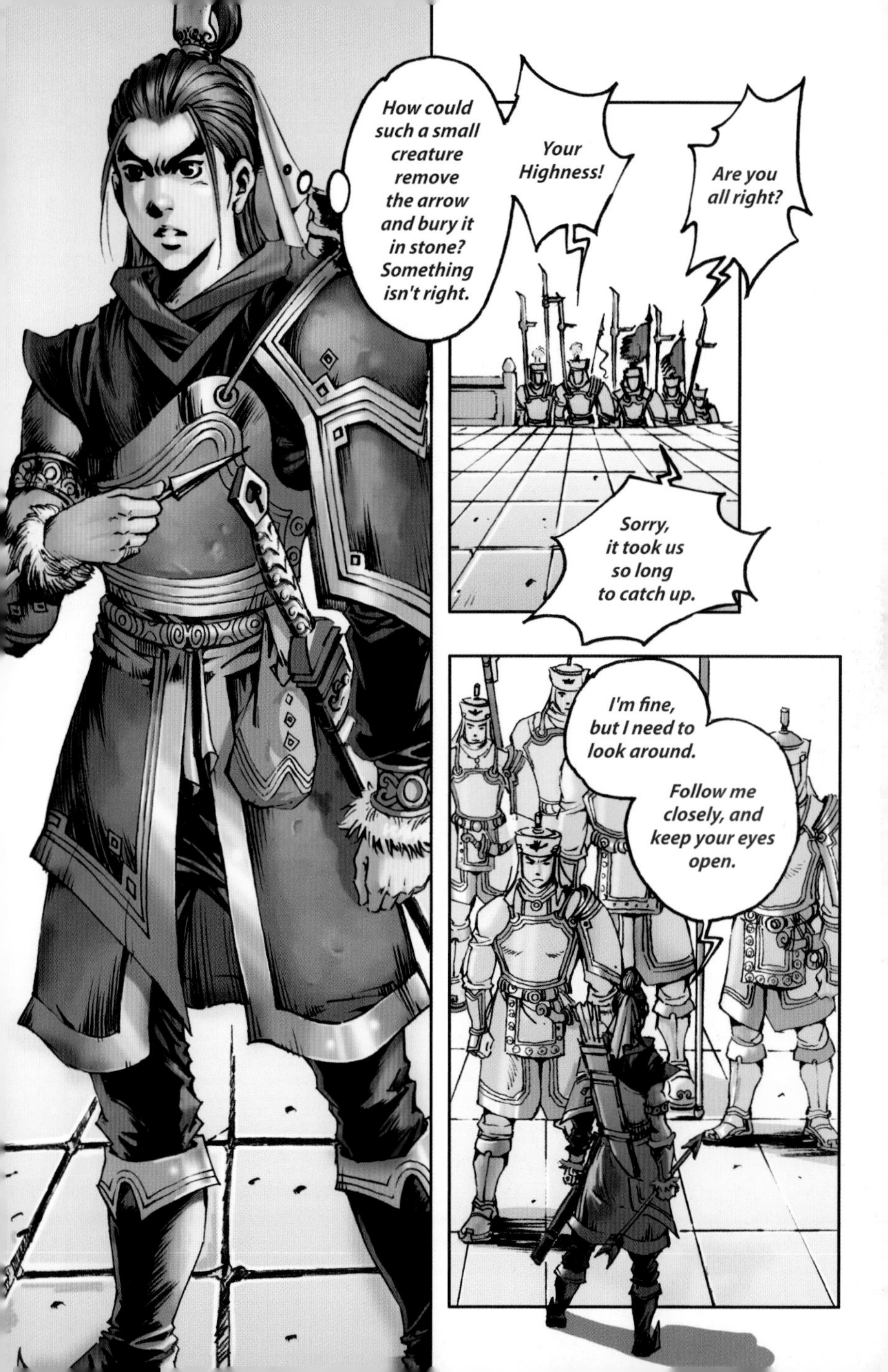
How could such a small creature remove the arrow and bury it in stone? Something isn't right.
Your Highness!
Are you all right?
Sorry, it took us so long to catch up.
I'm fine, but I need to look around.
Follow me closely, and keep your eyes open.

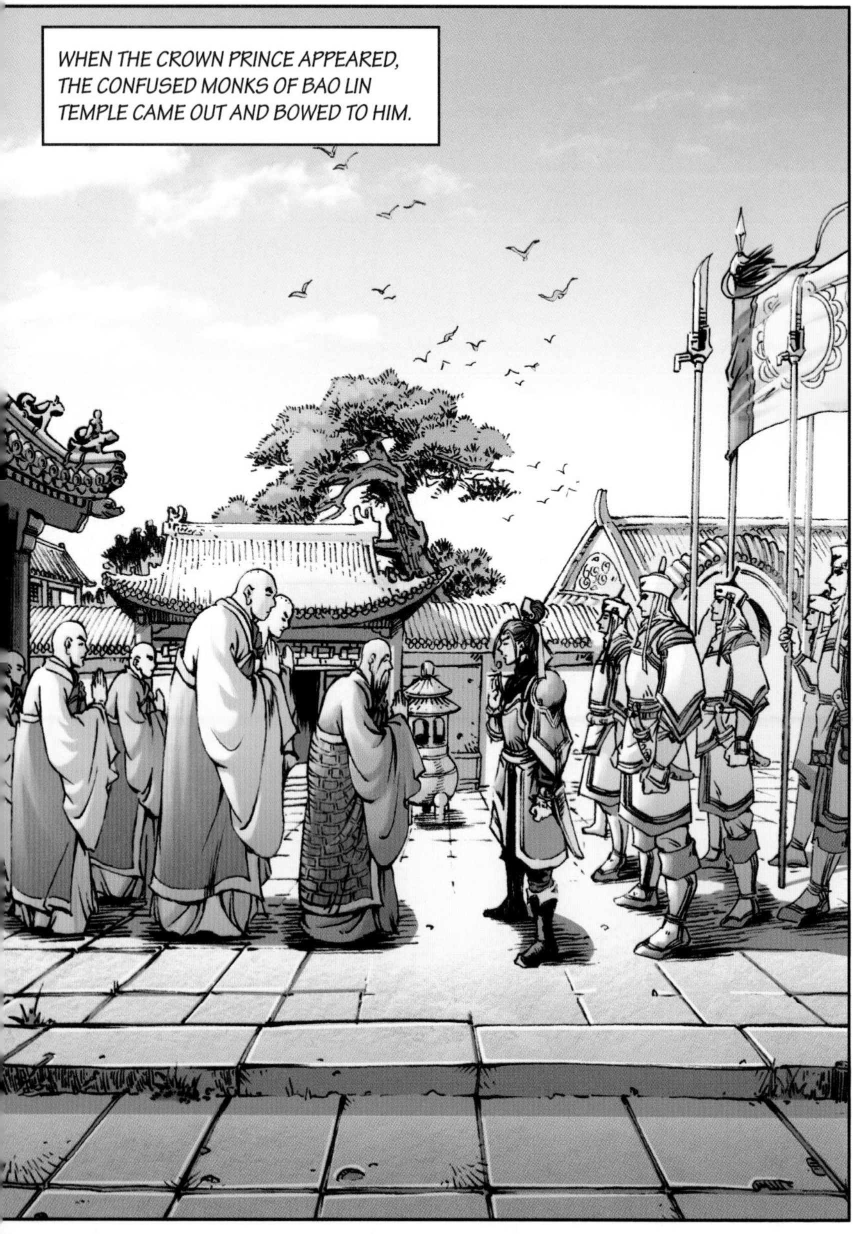
WHEN THE CROWN PRINCE APPEARED, THE CONFUSED MONKS OF BAO LIN TEMPLE CAME OUT AND BOWED TO HIM.

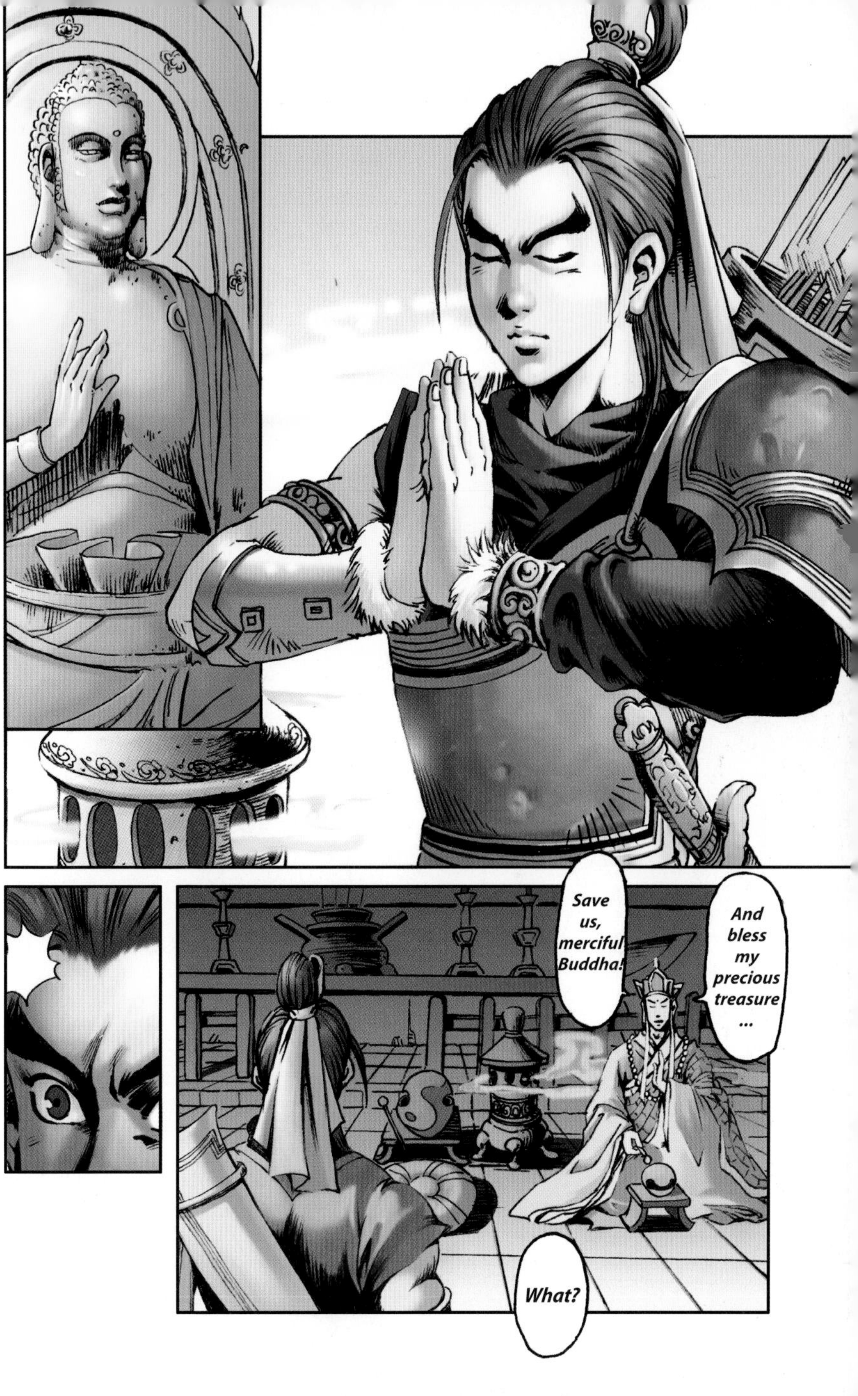
Save us, merciful Buddha!
And bless my precious treasure ...
What?

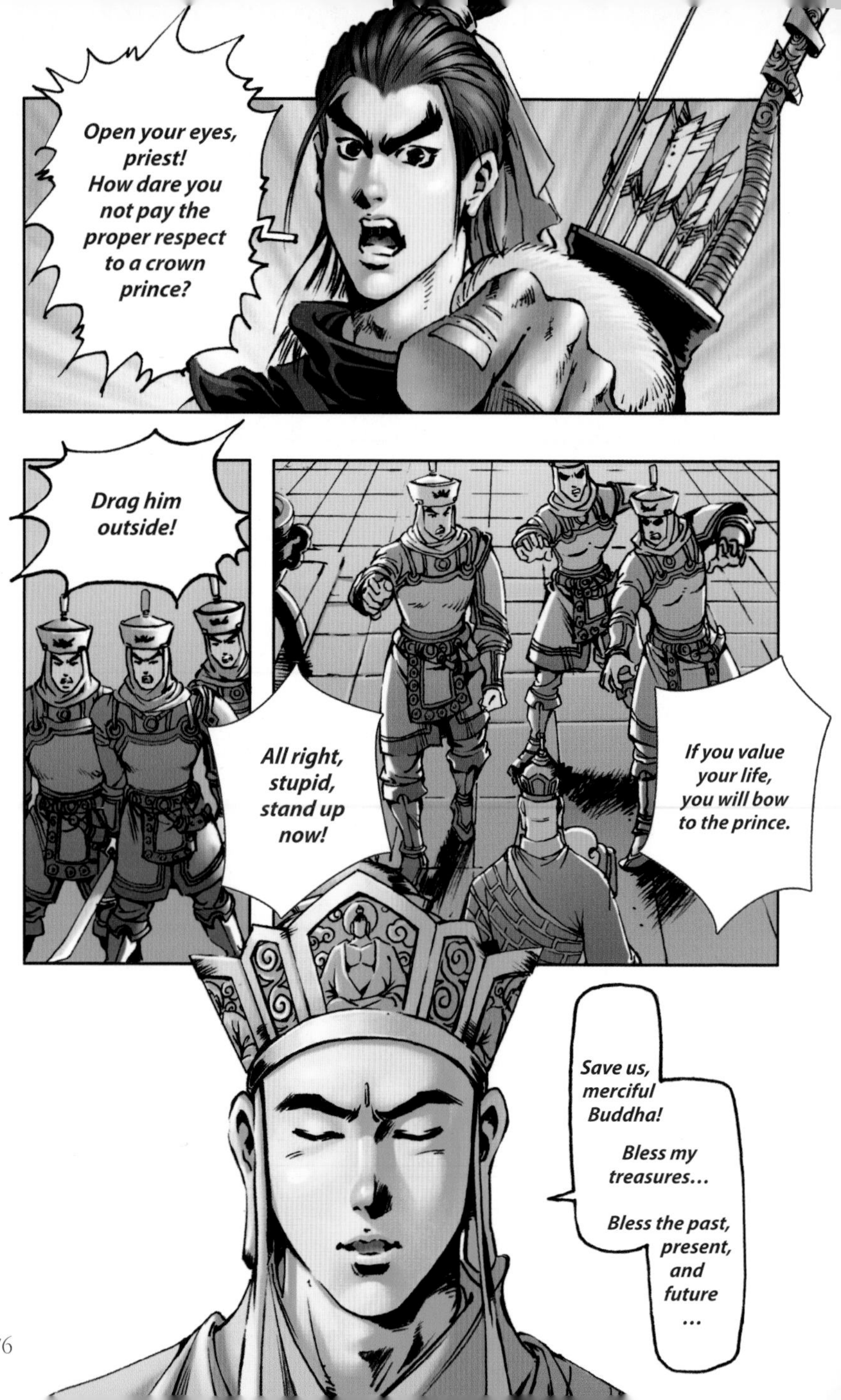
Open your eyes, priest! How dare you not pay the proper respect to a crown prince?
Drag him outside!
All right, stupid, stand up now!
If you value your life, you will bow to the prince.
Save us, merciful Buddha!
Bless my treasures…
Bless the past, present, and future …

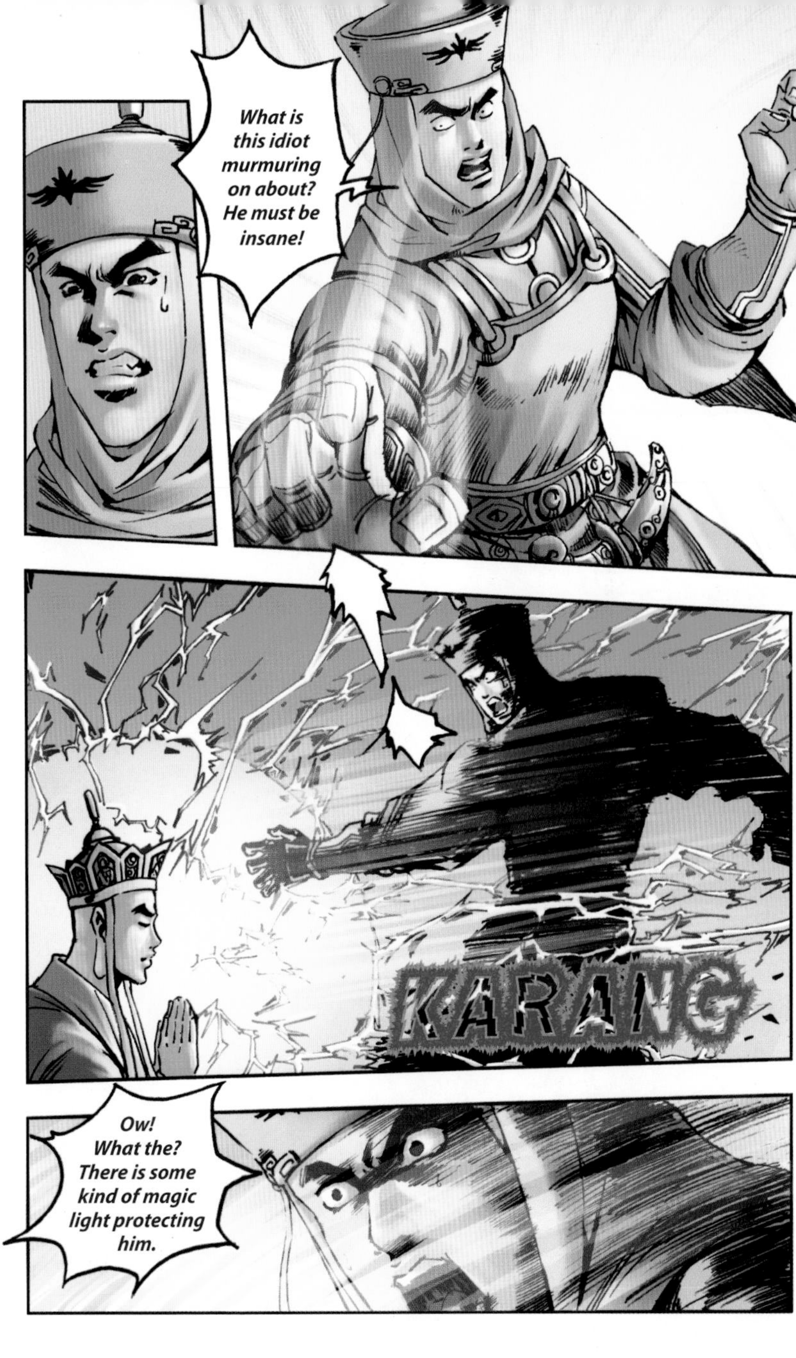
What is this idiot murmuring on about? He must be insane!
KARANG
Ow! What the? There is some kind of magic light protecting him.

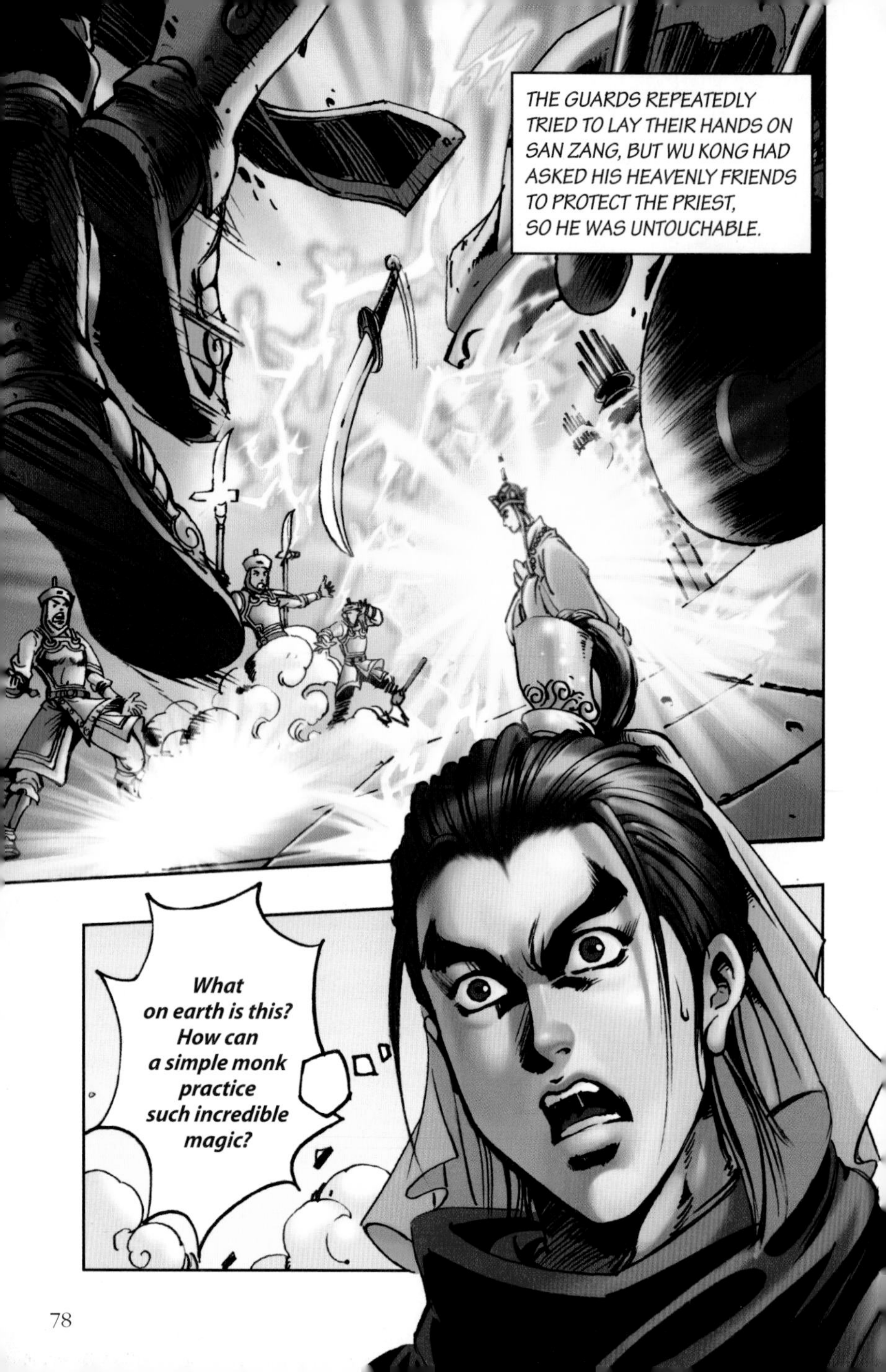
THE GUARDS REPEATEDLY TRIED TO LAY THEIR HANDS ON SAN ZANG, BUT WU KONG HAD ASKED HIS HEAVENLY FRIENDS TO PROTECT THE PRIEST, SO HE WAS UNTOUCHABLE.
What on earth is this? How can a simple monk practice such incredible magic?

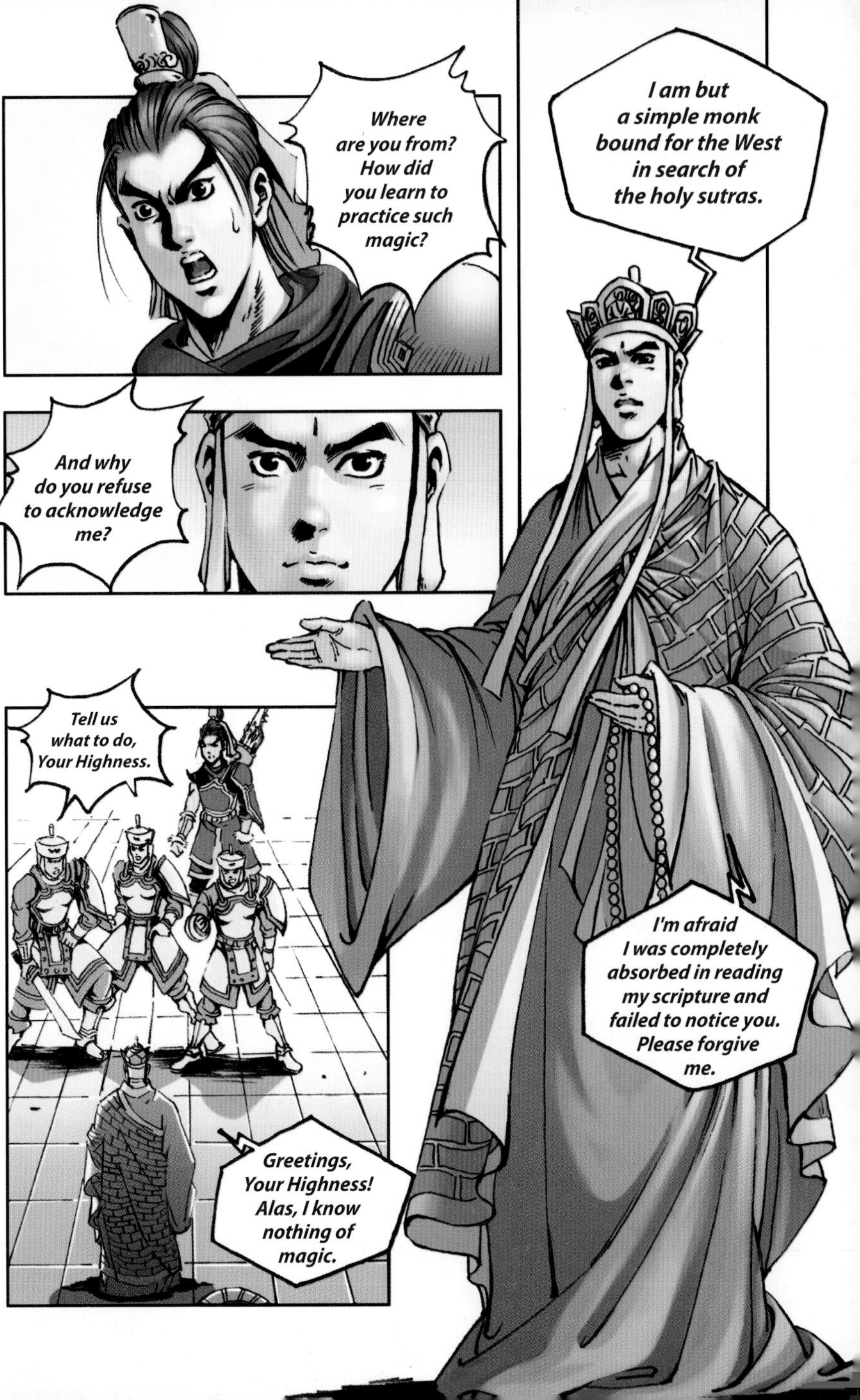
Where are you from? How did you learn to practice such magic?
I am but a simple monk bound for the West in search of the holy sutras.
And why do you refuse to acknowledge me?
Tell us what to do, Your Highness.
Greetings, Your Highness! Alas, I know nothing of magic.
I'm afraid I was completely absorbed in reading my scripture and failed to notice you. Please forgive me.

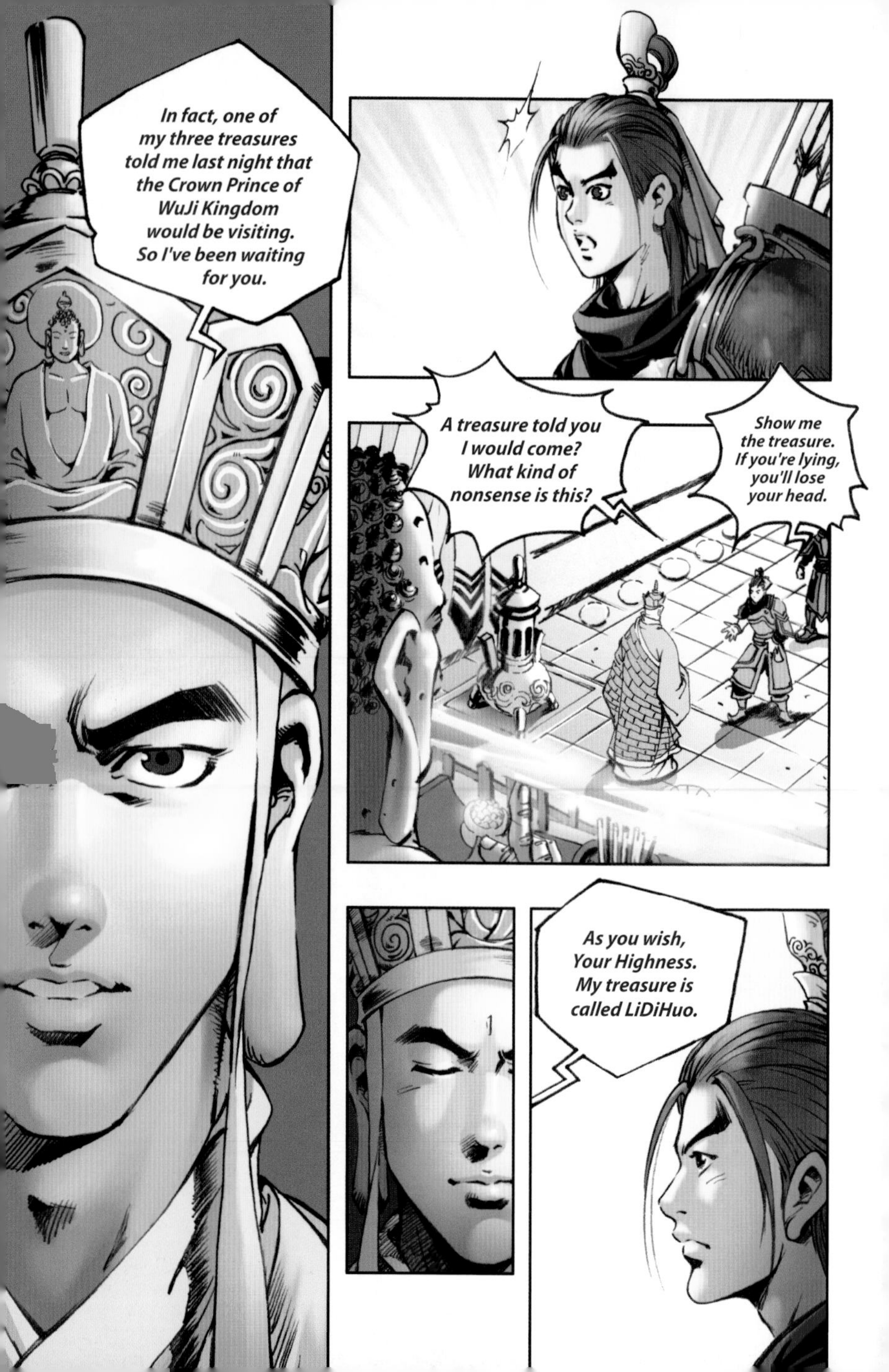
In fact, one of my three treasures told me last night that the Crown Prince of WuJi Kingdom would be visiting. So I've been waiting for you.
A treasure told you I would come? What kind of nonsense is this?
Show me the treasure. If you're lying, you'll lose your head.
As you wish, Your Highness. My treasure is called LiDiHuo.

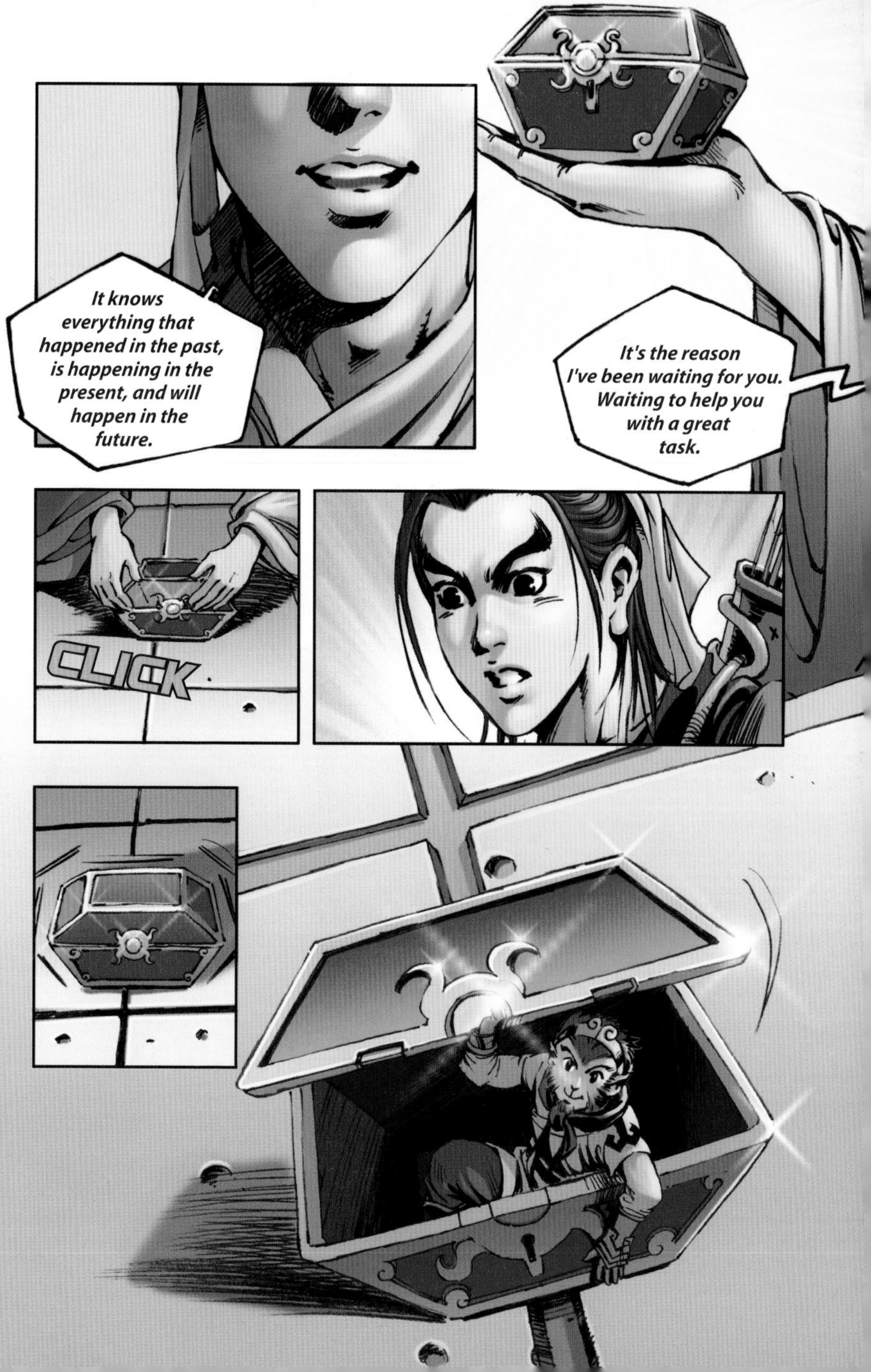
It knows everything that happened in the past, is happening in the present, and will happen in the future.
It's the reason I've been waiting for you. Waiting to help you with a great task.
CLICK

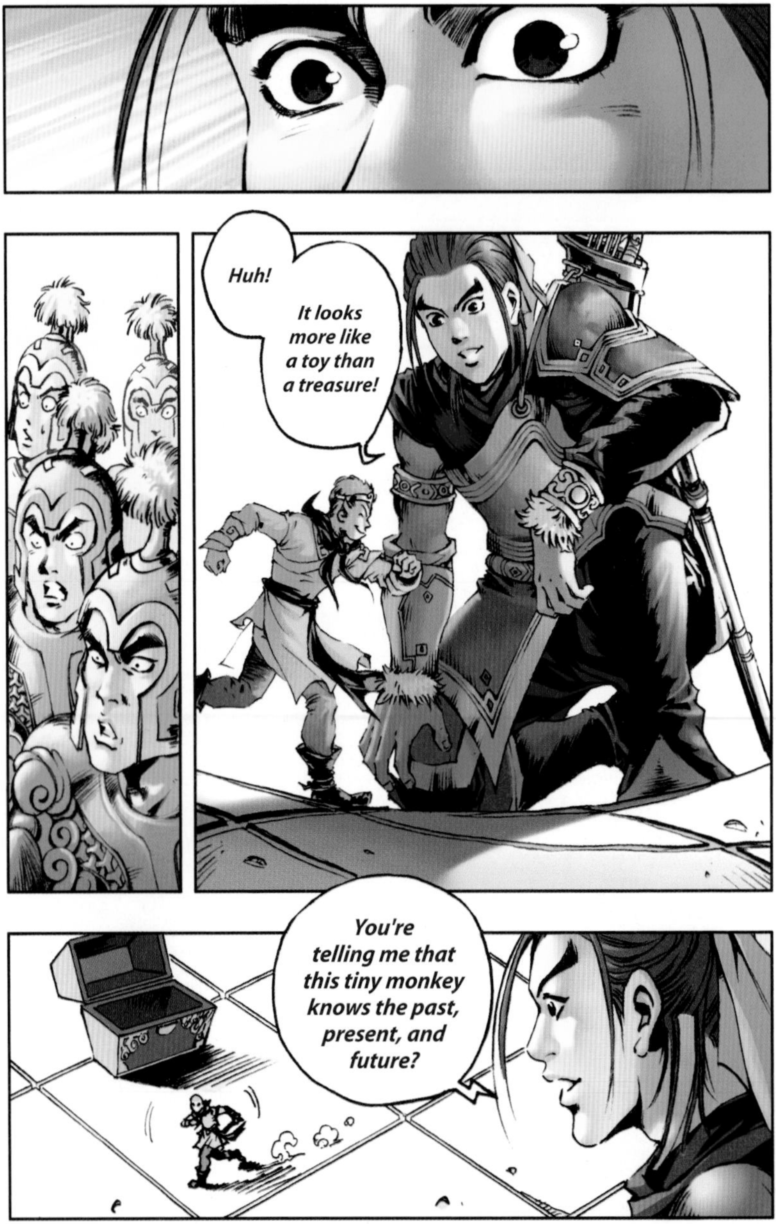
Huh!
It looks more like a toy than a treasure!
You're telling me that this tiny monkey knows the past, present, and future?

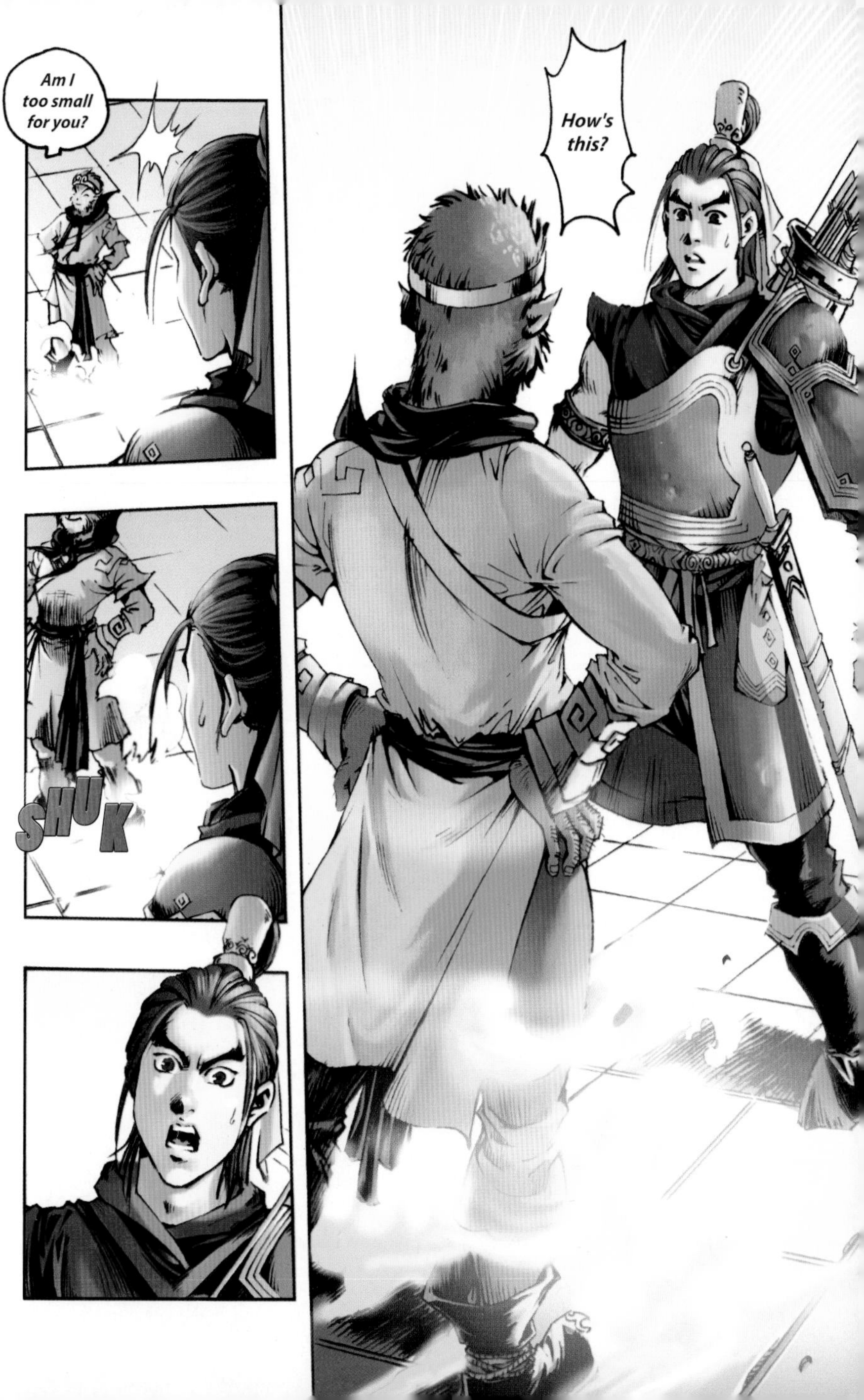
Am I too small for you?
SHUK
How's this?

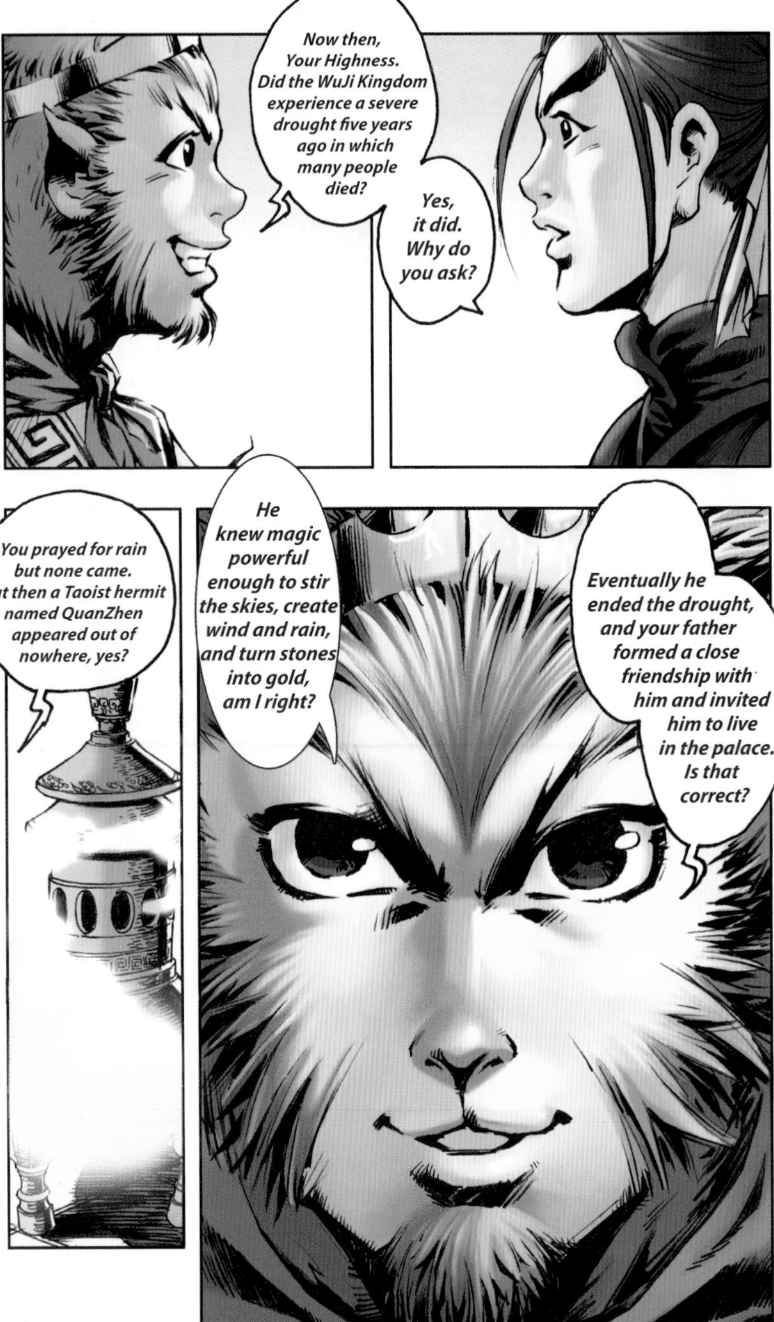
Now then, Your Highness. Did the WuJi Kingdom experience a severe drought five years ago in which many people died?
Yes, it did. Why do you ask?
You prayed for rain but none came. But then a Taoist hermit named QuanZhen appeared out of nowhere, yes?
He knew magic powerful enough to stir the skies, create wind and rain, and turn stones into gold, am I right?
Eventually he ended the drought, and your father formed a close friendship with him and invited him to live in the palace. Is that correct?

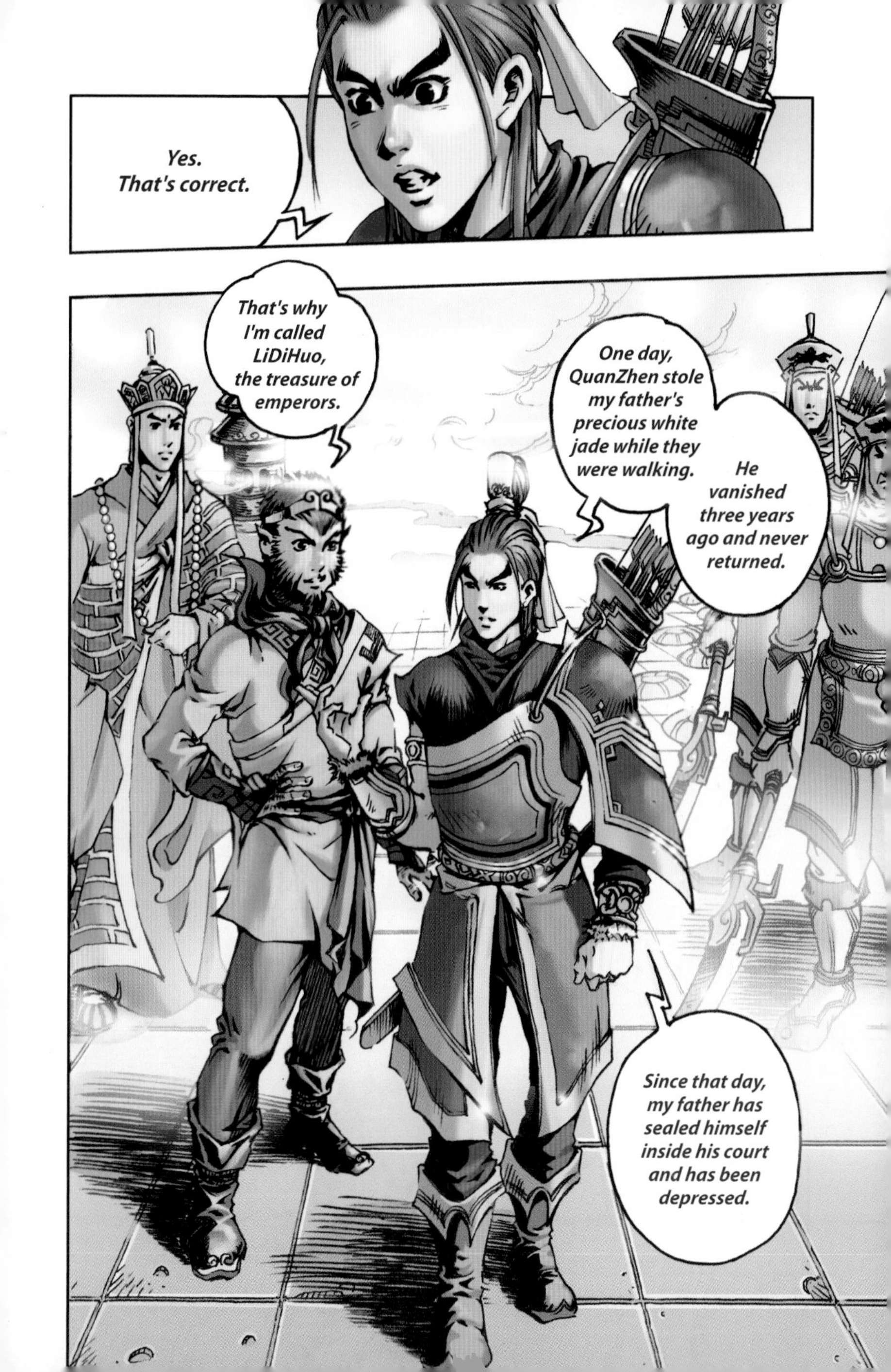
Yes. That's correct.
That's why I'm called LiDiHuo, the treasure of emperors.
One day, QuanZhen stole my father's precious white jade while they were walking.
He vanished three years ago and never returned.
Since that day, my father has sealed himself inside his court and has been depressed.

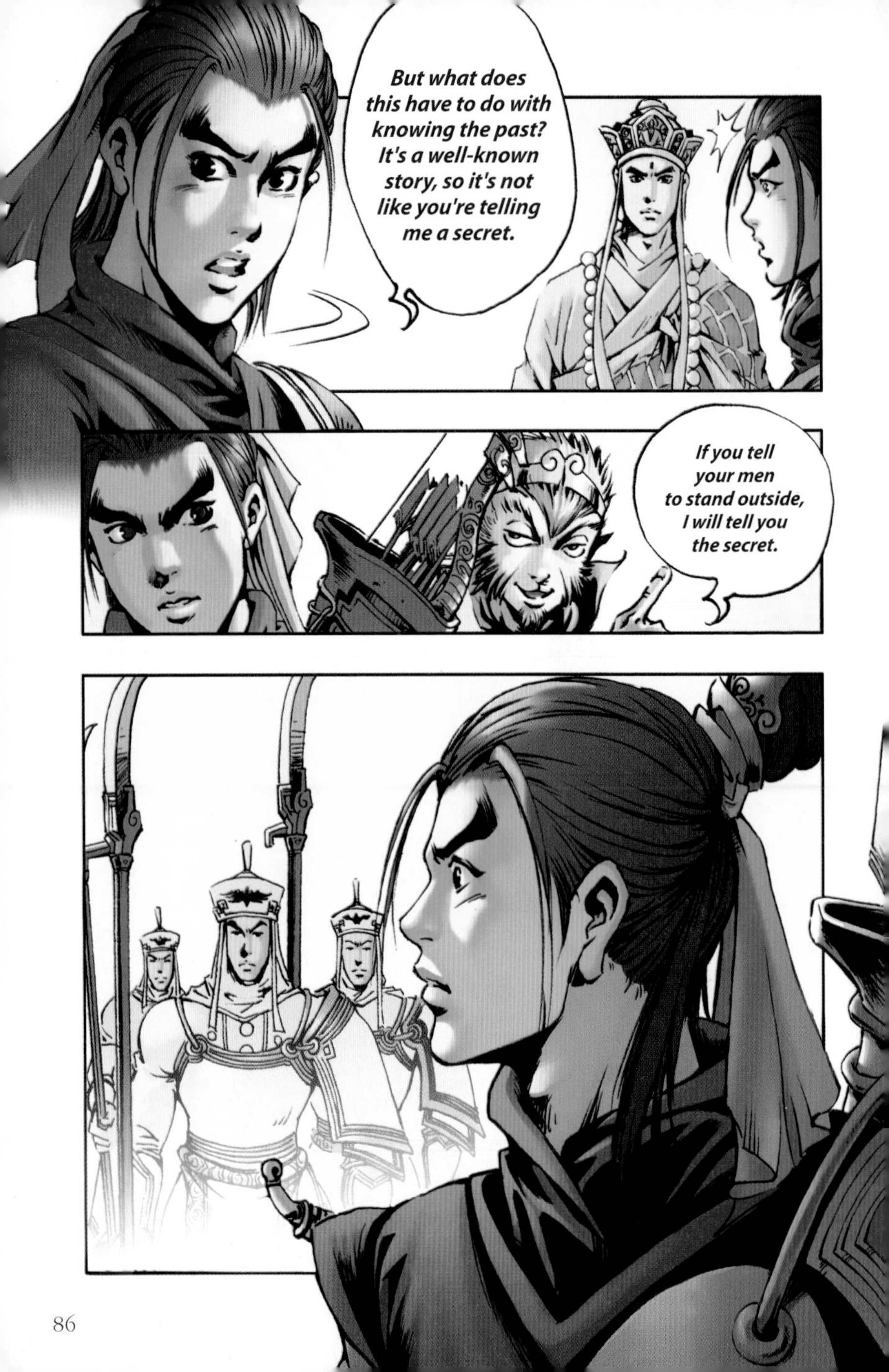
But what does this have to do with knowing the past? It's a well-known story, so it's not like you're telling me a secret.
If you tell your men to stand outside, I will tell you the secret.

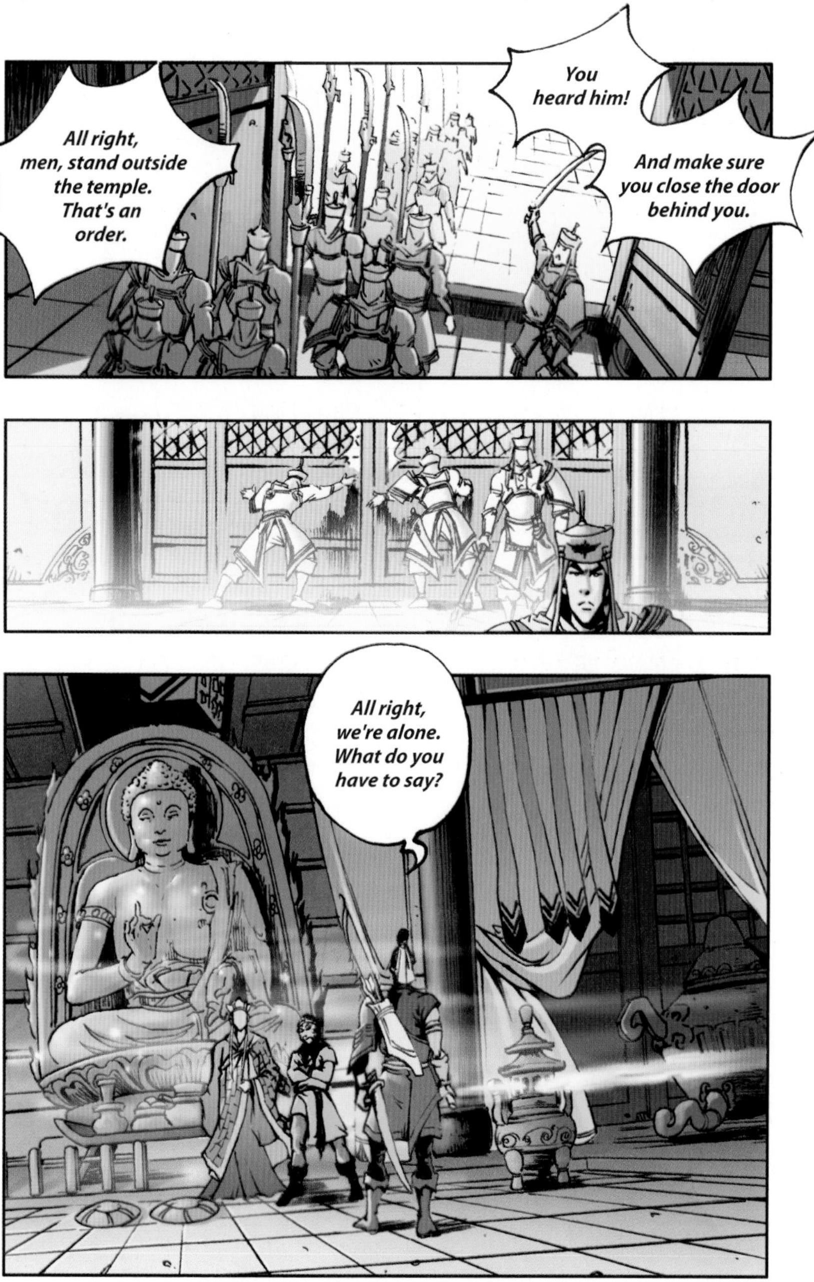
All right, men, stand outside the temple. That's an order.
You heard him!
And make sure you close the door behind you.
All right, we're alone. What do you have to say?

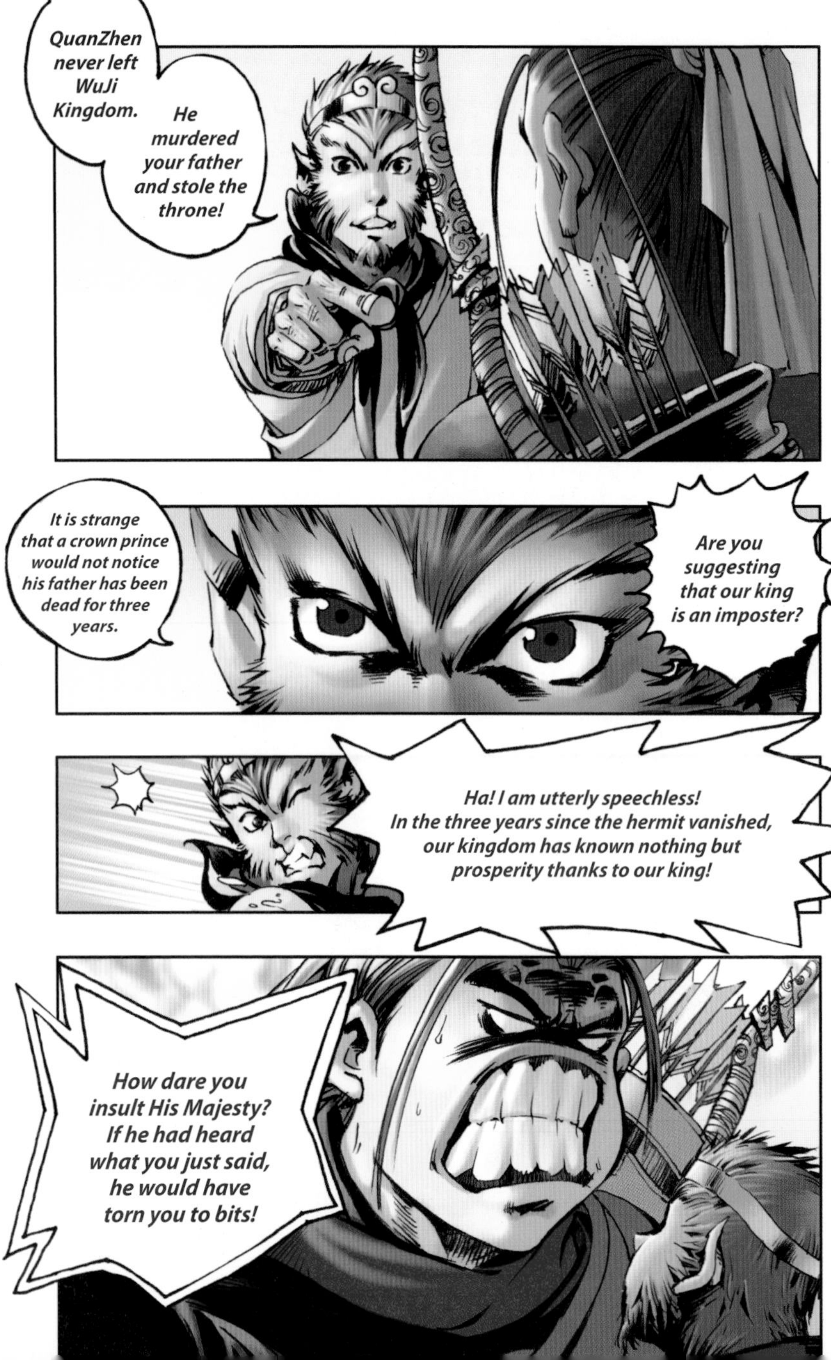
QuanZhen never left WuJi Kingdom.
He murdered your father and stole the throne!
It is strange that a crown prince would not notice his father has been dead for three years.
Are you suggesting that our king is an imposter?
Ha! I am utterly speechless! In the three years since the hermit vanished, our kingdom has known nothing but prosperity thanks to our king!
How dare you insult His Majesty? If he had heard what you just said, he would have torn you to bits!

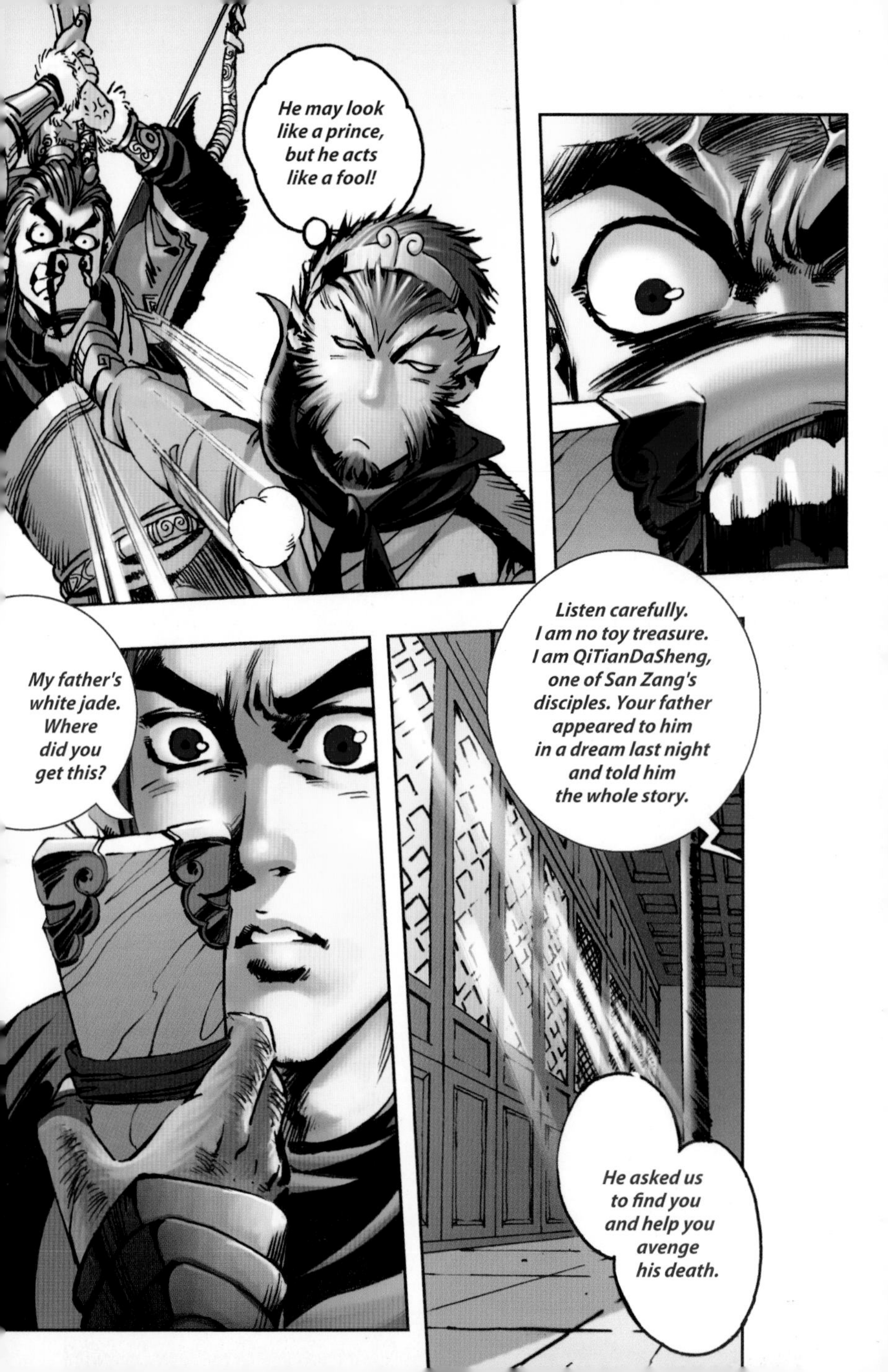
He may look like a prince, but he acts like a fool!
My father's white jade. Where did you get this?
Listen carefully. I am no toy treasure. I am QiTianDaSheng, one of San Zang's disciples. Your father appeared to him in a dream last night and told him the whole story.
He asked us to find you and help you avenge his death.

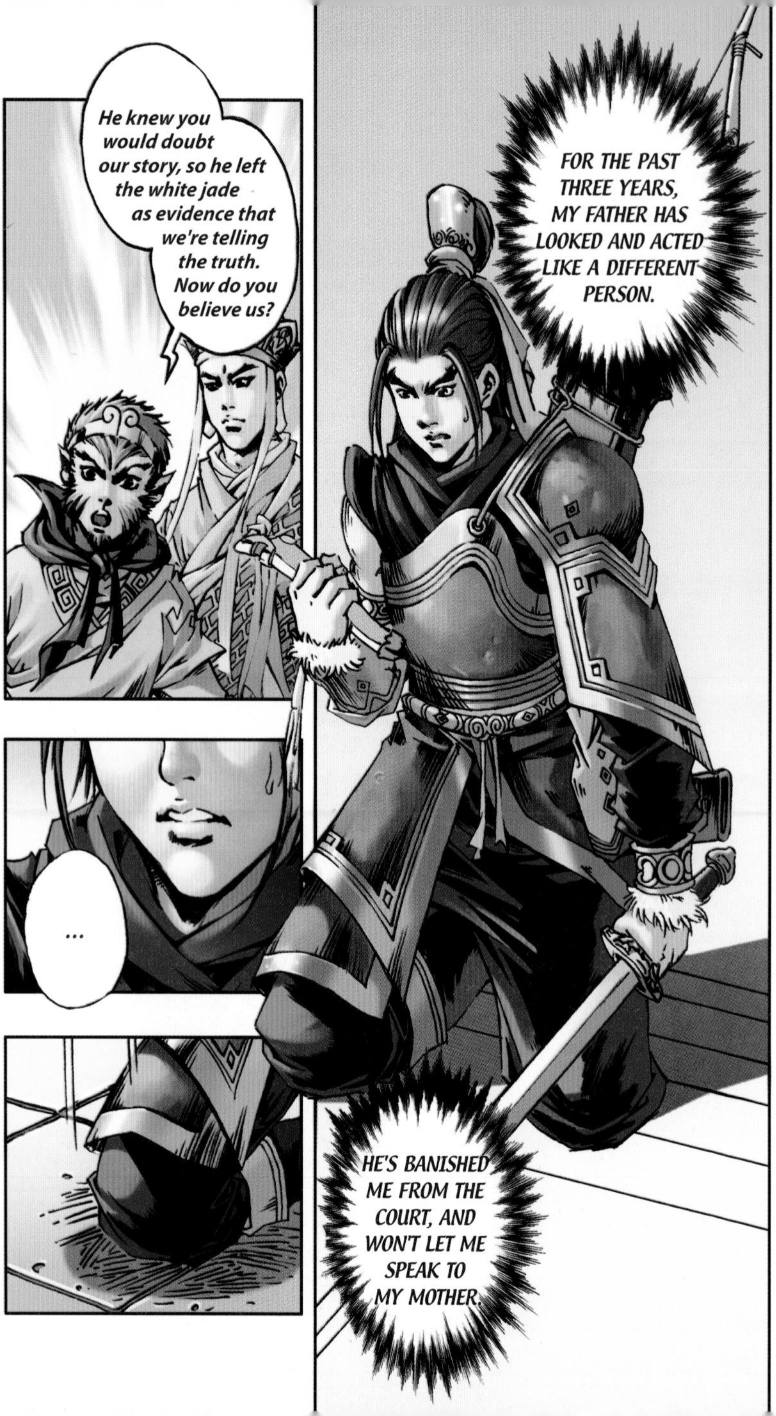
He knew you would doubt our story, so he left the white jade as evidence that we're telling the truth. Now do you believe us?
FOR THE PAST THREE YEARS, MY FATHER HAS LOOKED AND ACTED LIKE A DIFFERENT PERSON.
...
HE'S BANISHED ME FROM THE COURT, AND WON'T LET ME SPEAK TO MY MOTHER.

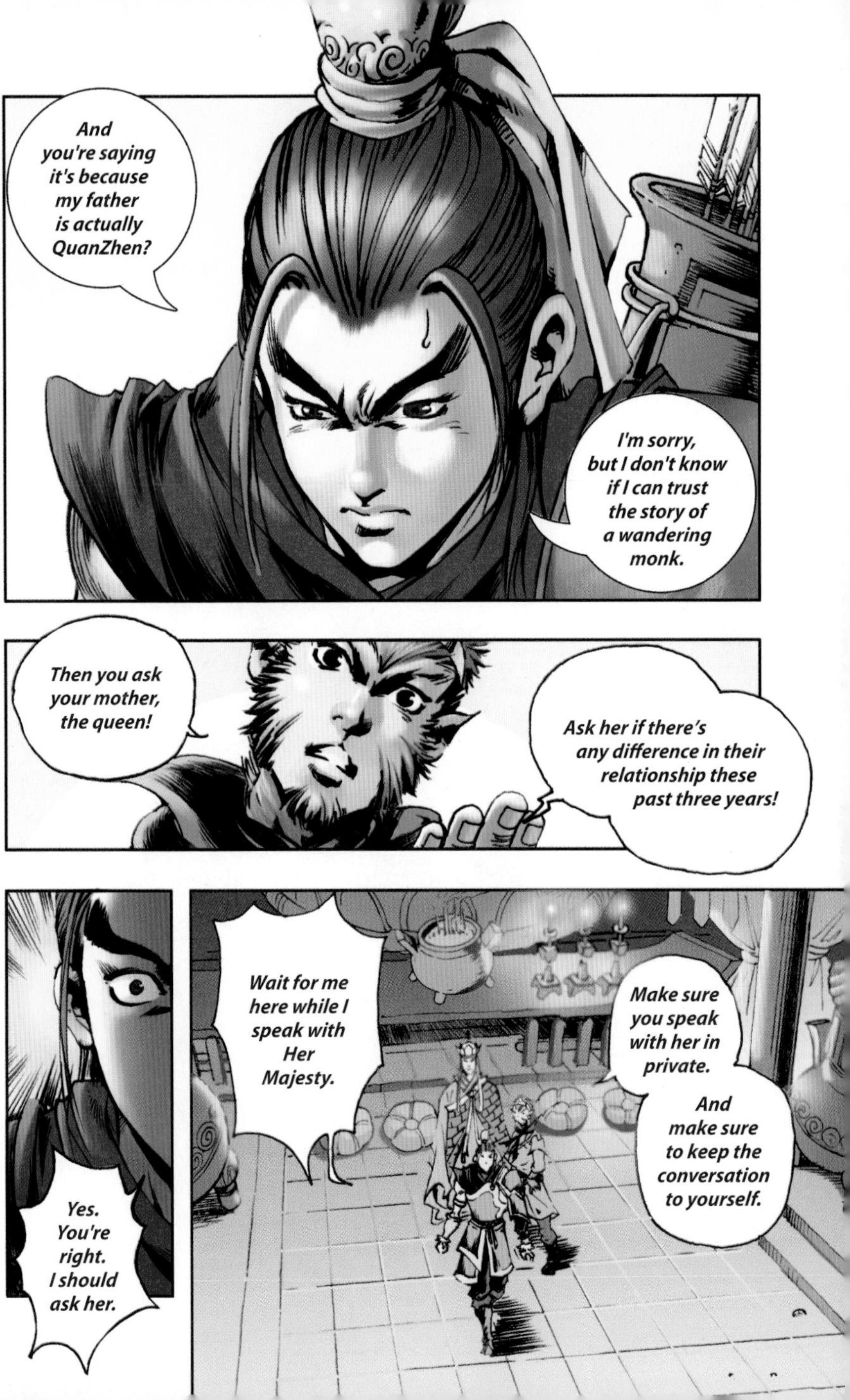
And you're saying it's because my father is actually QuanZhen?
I'm sorry, but I don't know if I can trust the story of a wandering monk.
Then you ask your mother, the queen!
Ask her if there's any difference in their relationship these past three years!
Yes. You're right. I should ask her.
Wait for me here while I speak with Her Majesty.
Make sure you speak with her in private.
And make sure to keep the conversation to yourself.

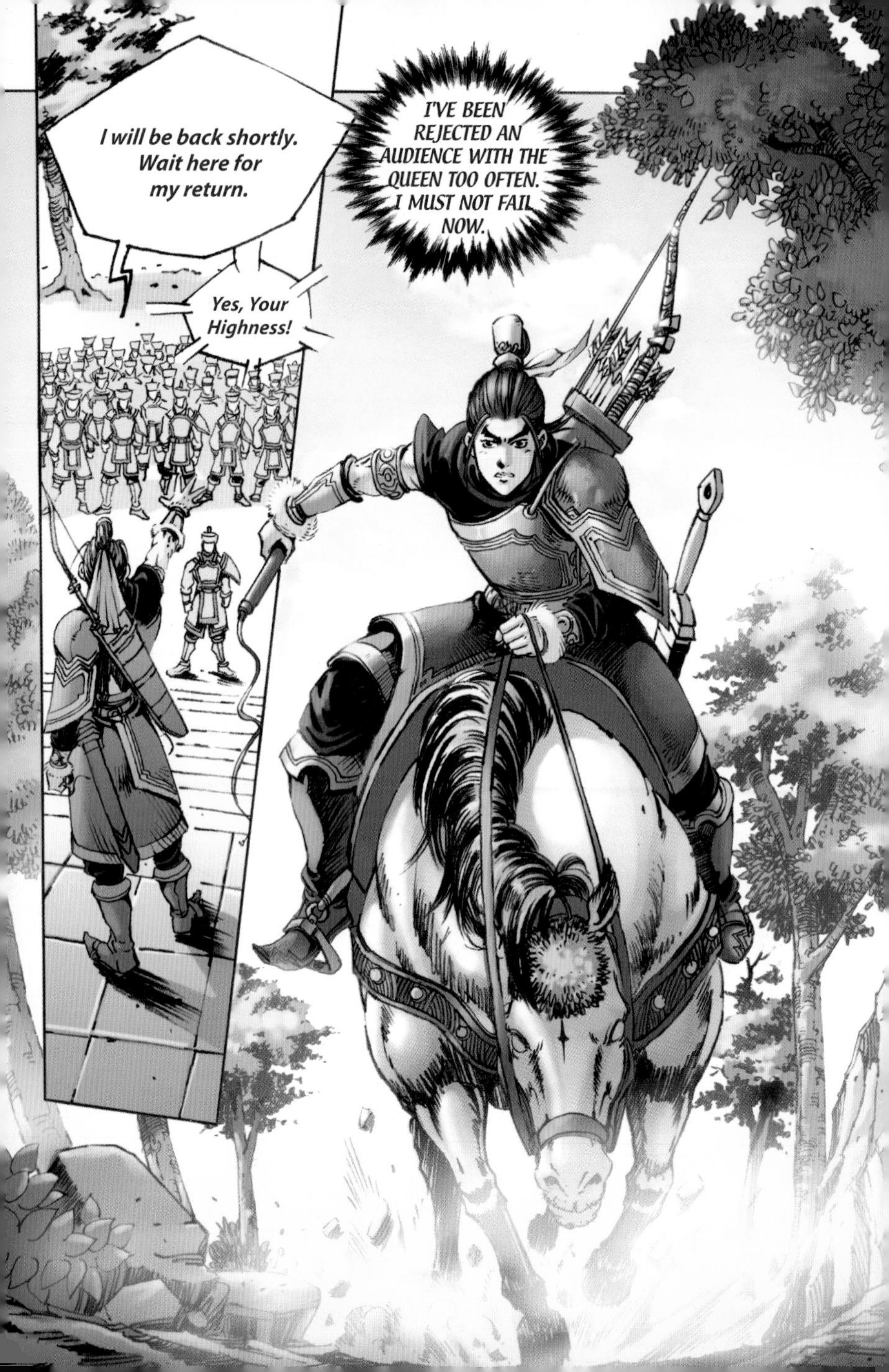
I've been rejected an audience with the queen too often. I must not fail now.
I will be back shortly. Wait here for my return.
Yes, Your Highness!

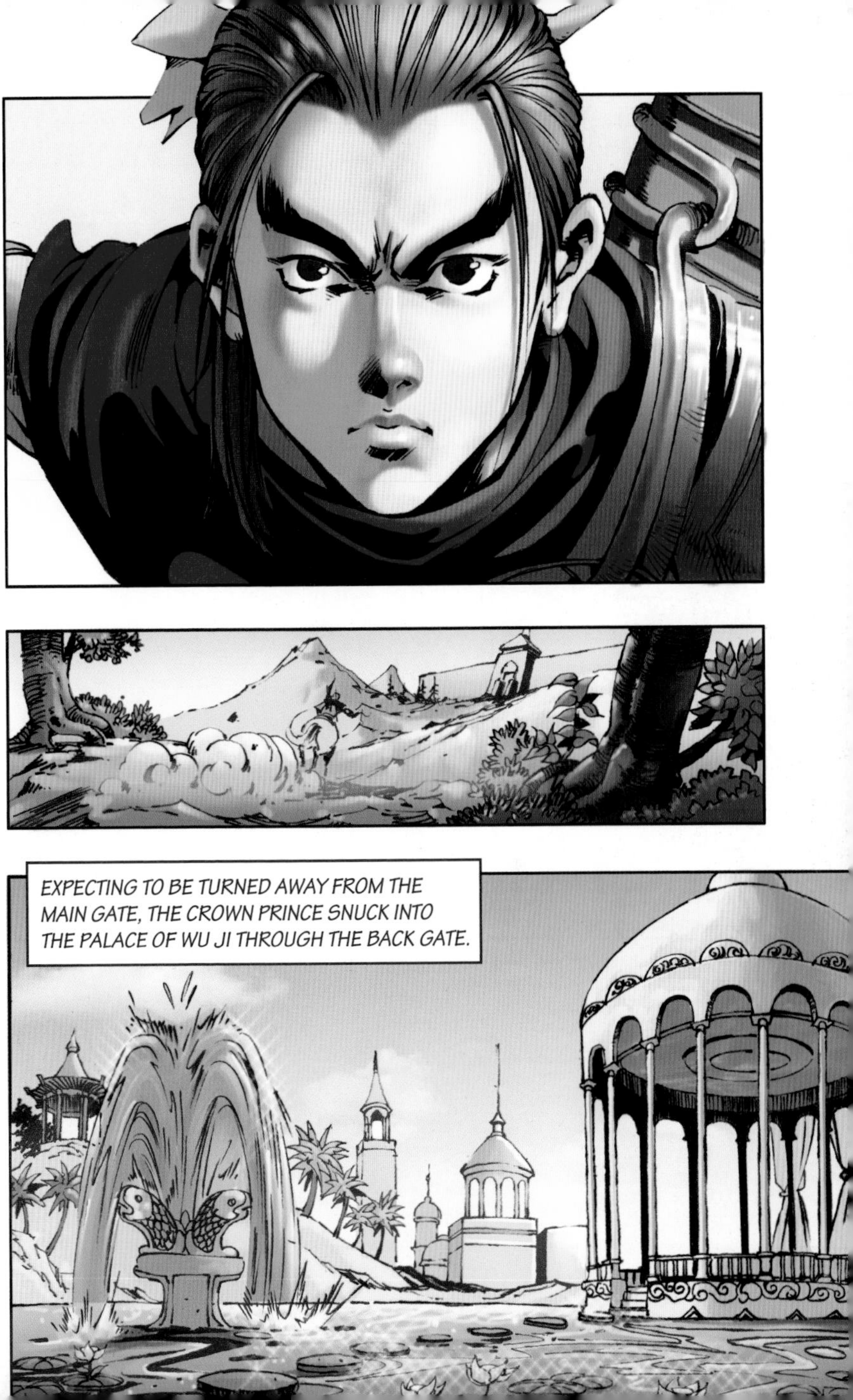
EXPECTING TO BE TURNED AWAY FROM THE MAIN GATE, THE CROWN PRINCE SNUCK INTO THE PALACE OF WU JI THROUGH THE BACK GATE.

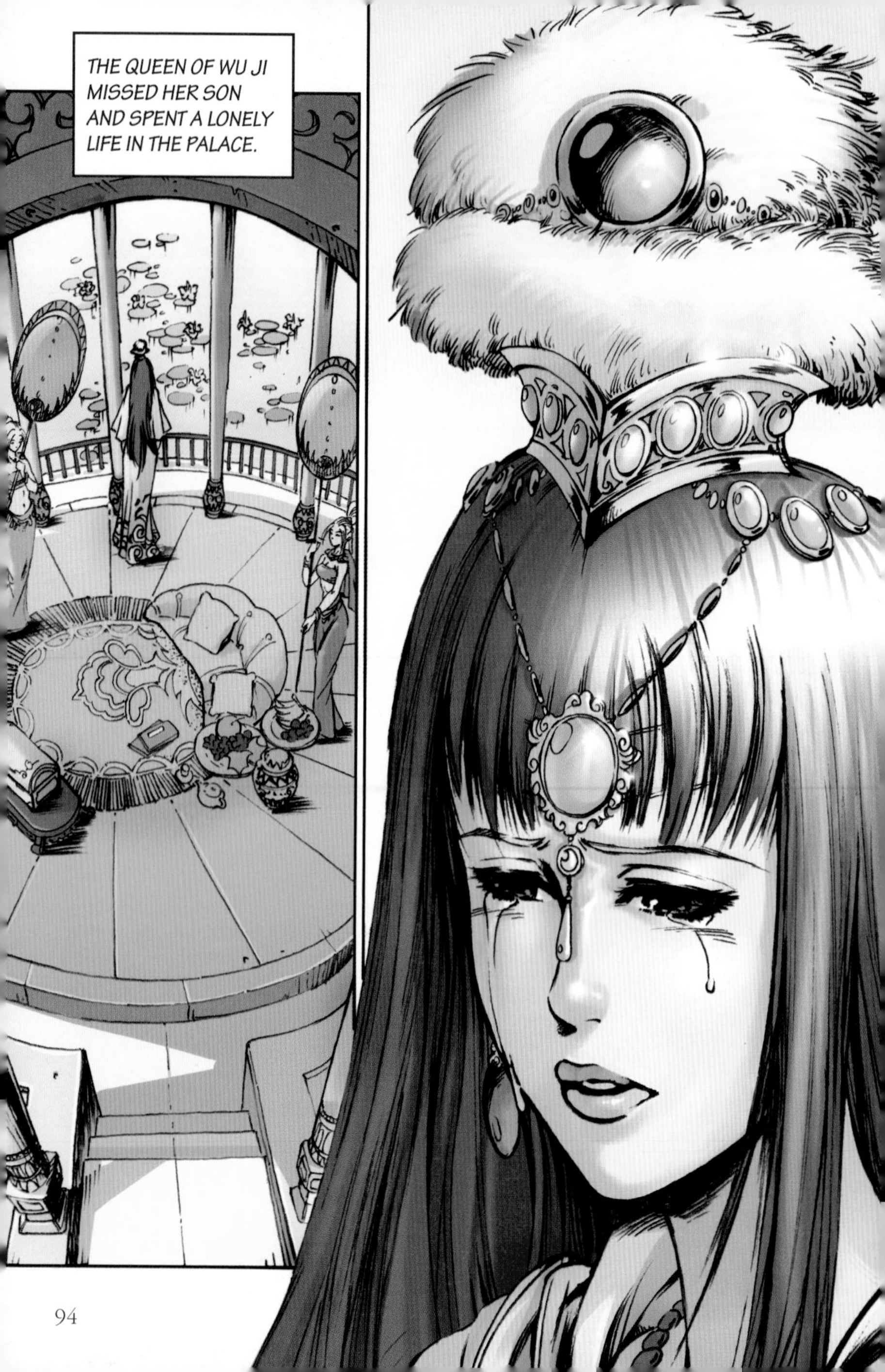
THE QUEEN OF WU JI MISSED HER SON AND SPENT A LONELY LIFE IN THE PALACE.

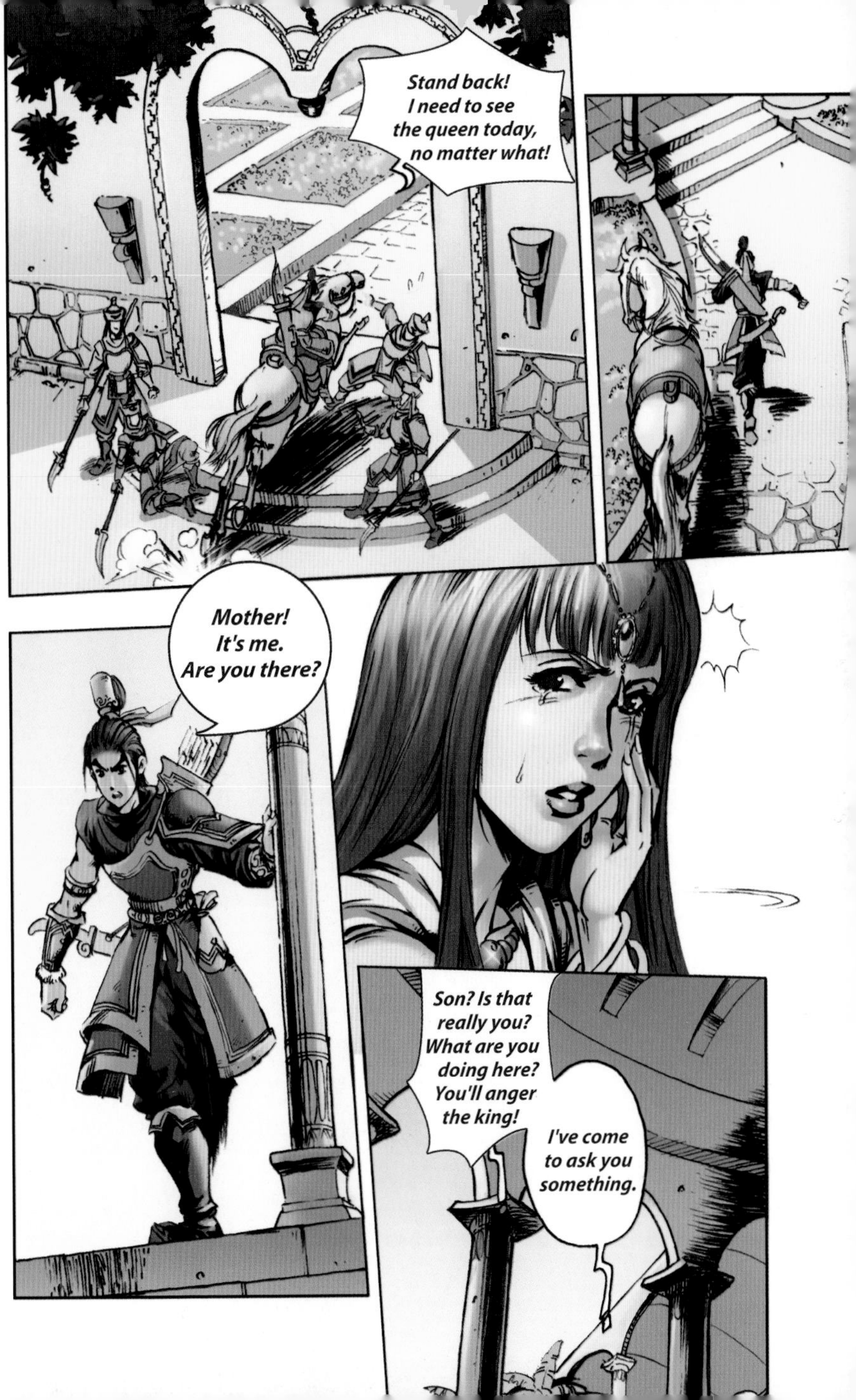
Stand back! I need to see the queen today, no matter what!
Mother! It's me. Are you there?
Son? Is that really you? What are you doing here? You'll anger the king!
I've come to ask you something.

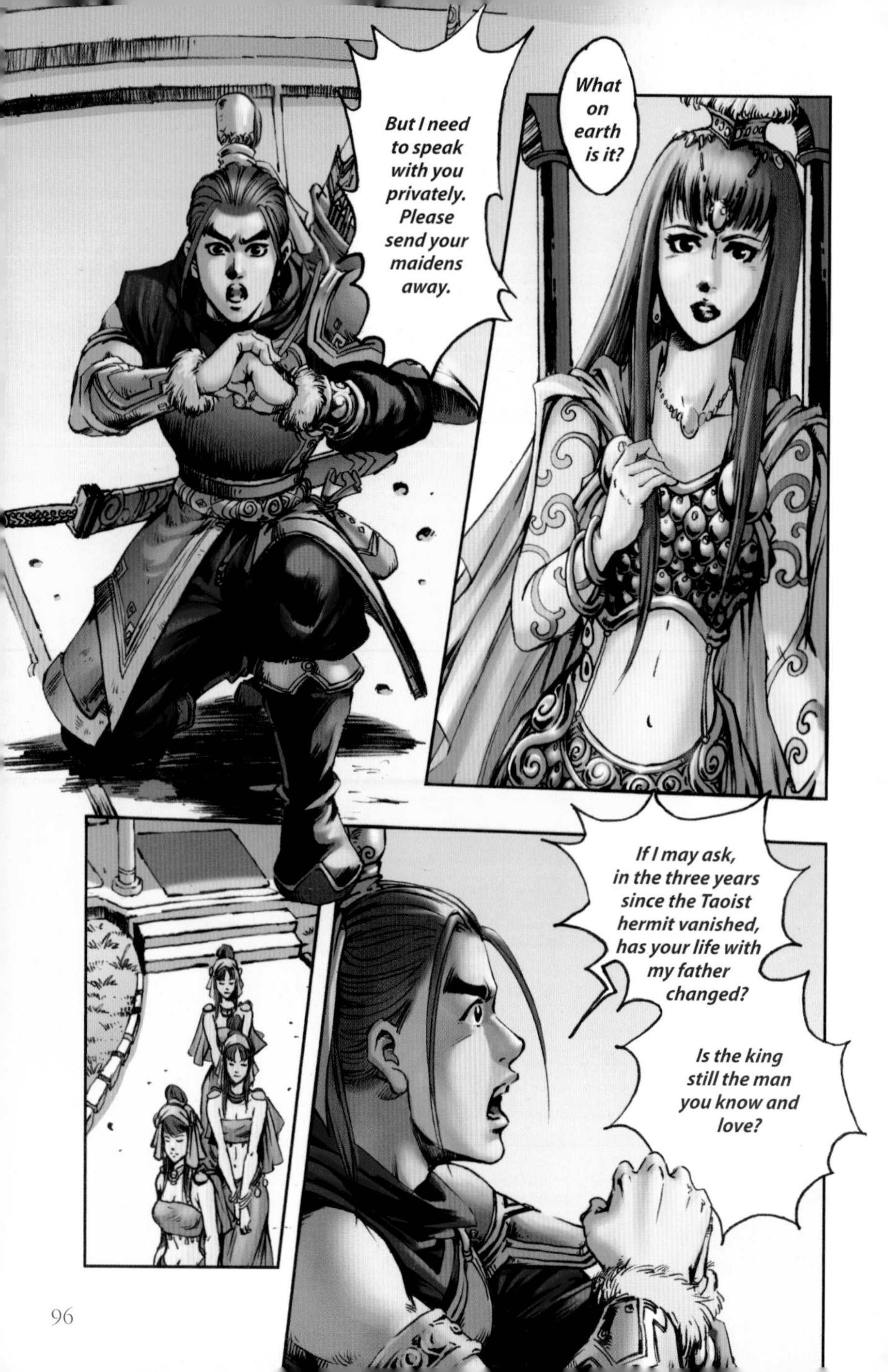
What on earth is it?
But I need to speak with you privately. Please send your maidens away.
If I may ask, in the three years since the Taoist hermit vanished, has your life with my father changed?
Is the king still the man you know and love?

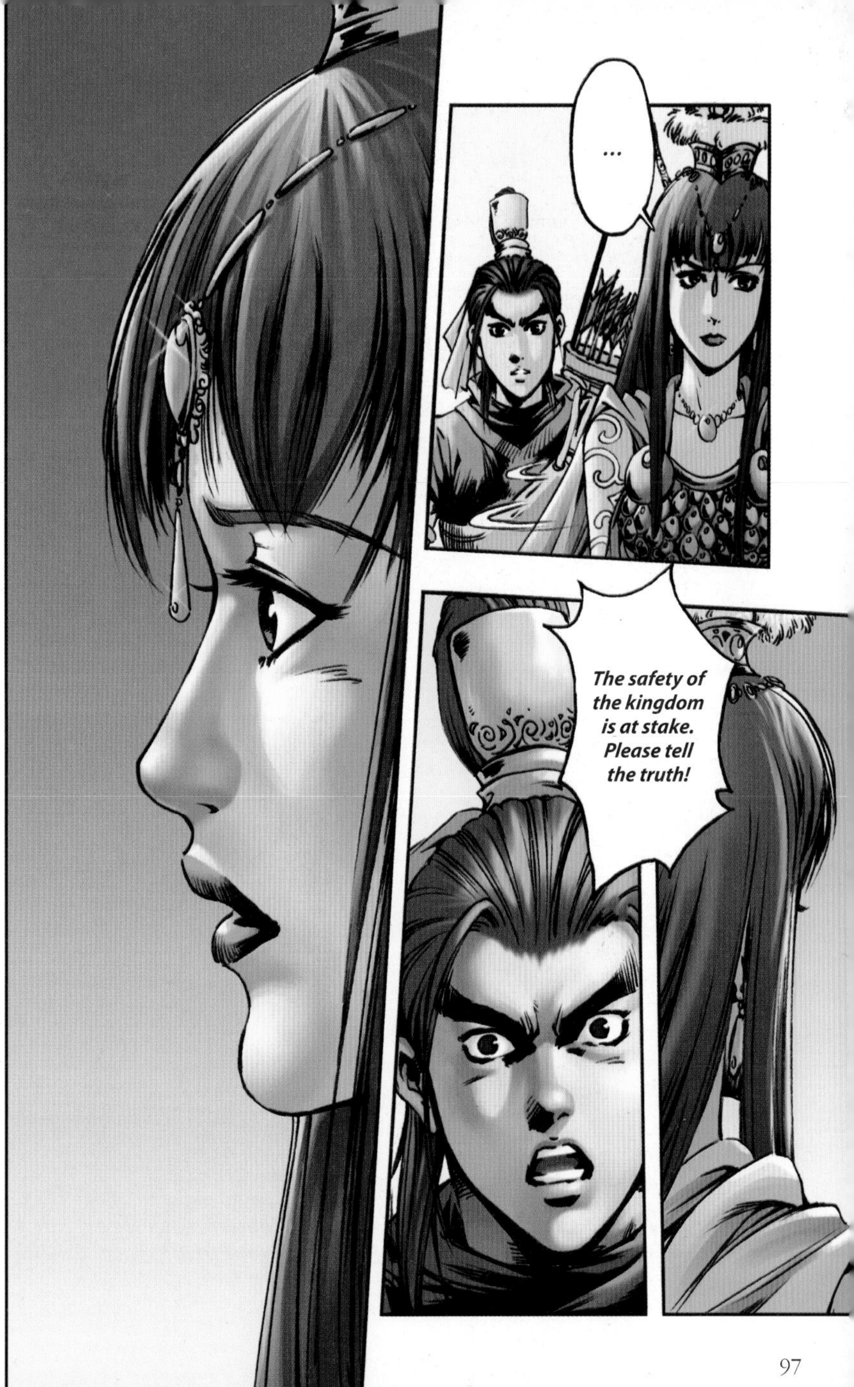
...
The safety of the kingdom is at stake. Please tell the truth!

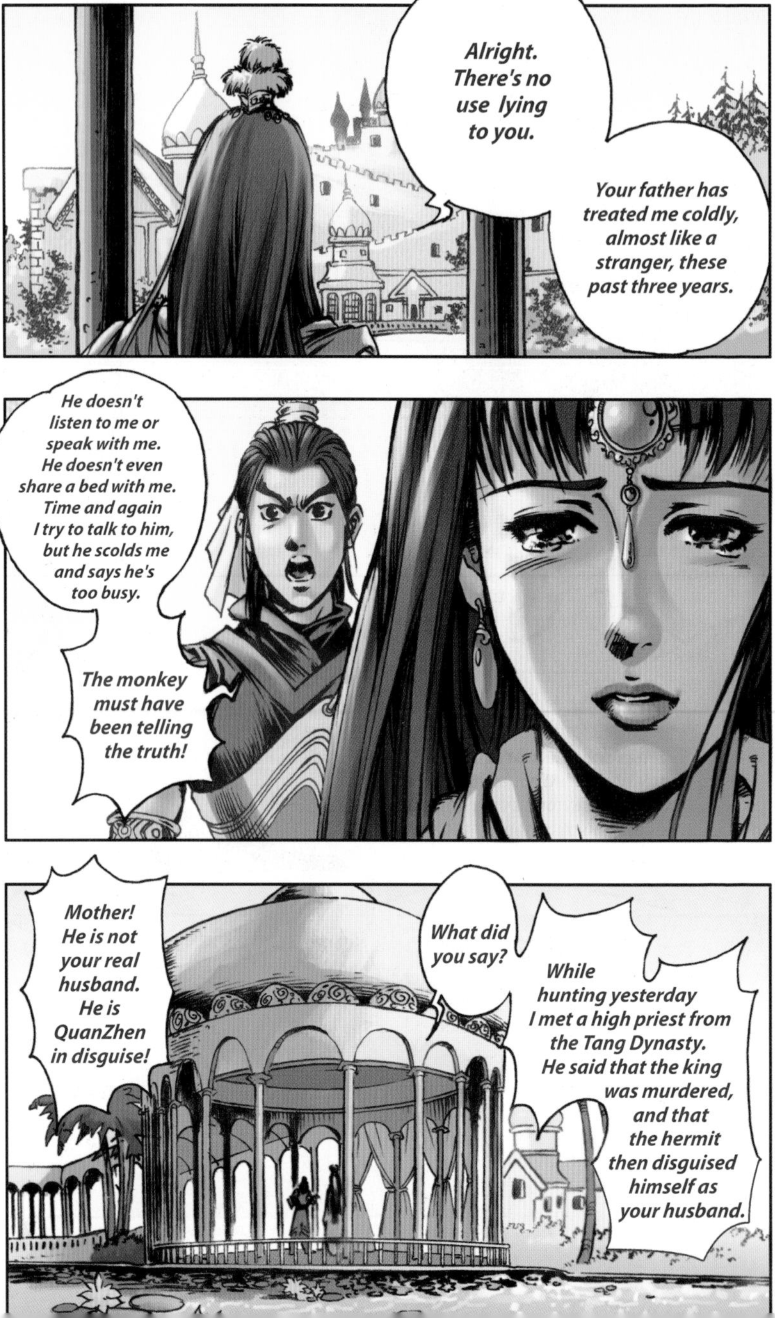
Alright. There's no use lying to you.
Your father has treated me coldly, almost like a stranger, these past three years.
He doesn't listen to me or speak with me. He doesn't even share a bed with me. Time and again I try to talk to him, but he scolds me and says he's too busy.
The monkey must have been telling the truth!
Mother! He is not your real husband. He is QuanZhen in disguise!
What did you say?
While hunting yesterday I met a high priest from the Tang Dynasty. He said that the king was murdered, and that the hermit then disguised himself as your husband.

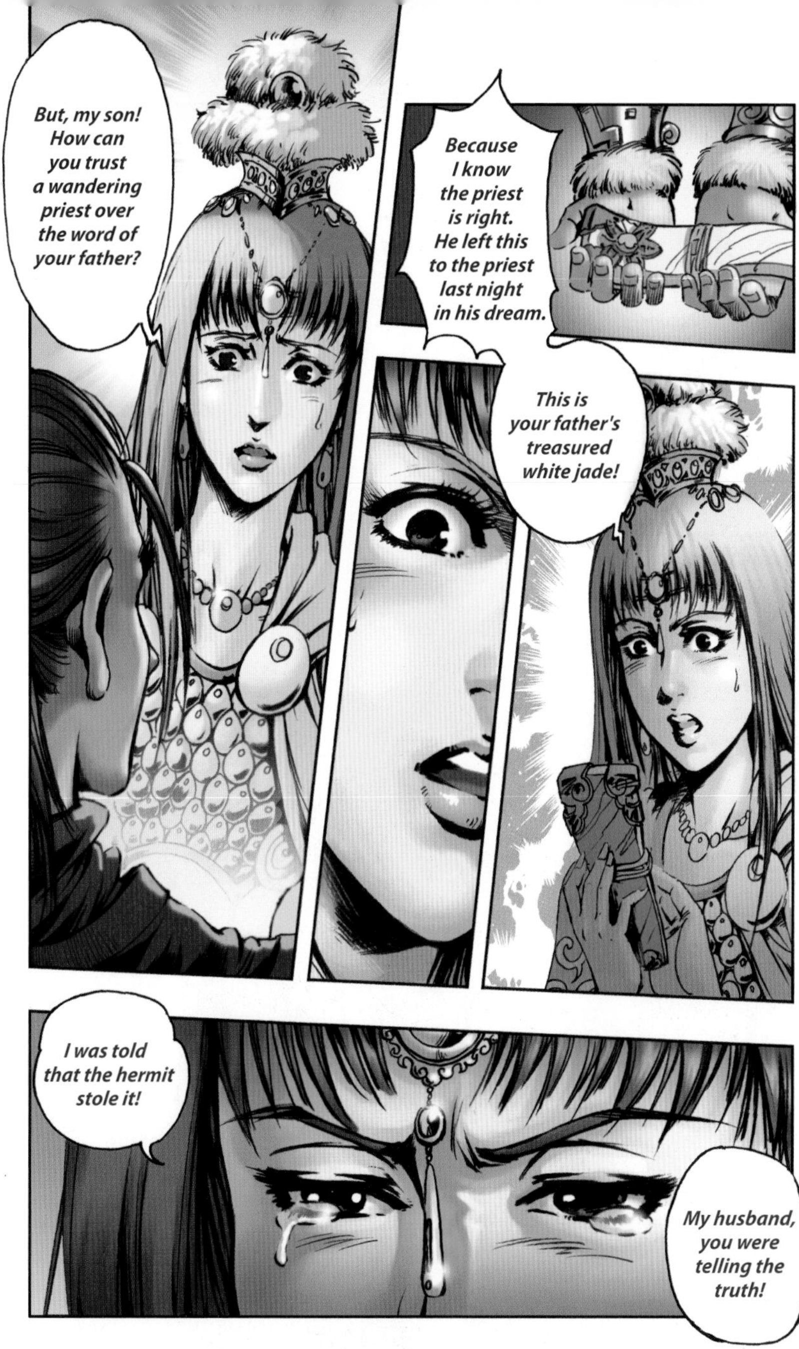
But, my son! How can you trust a wandering priest over the word of your father?
Because I know the priest is right. He left this to the priest last night in his dream.
This is your father's treasured white jade!
I was told that the hermit stole it!
My husband, you were telling the truth!

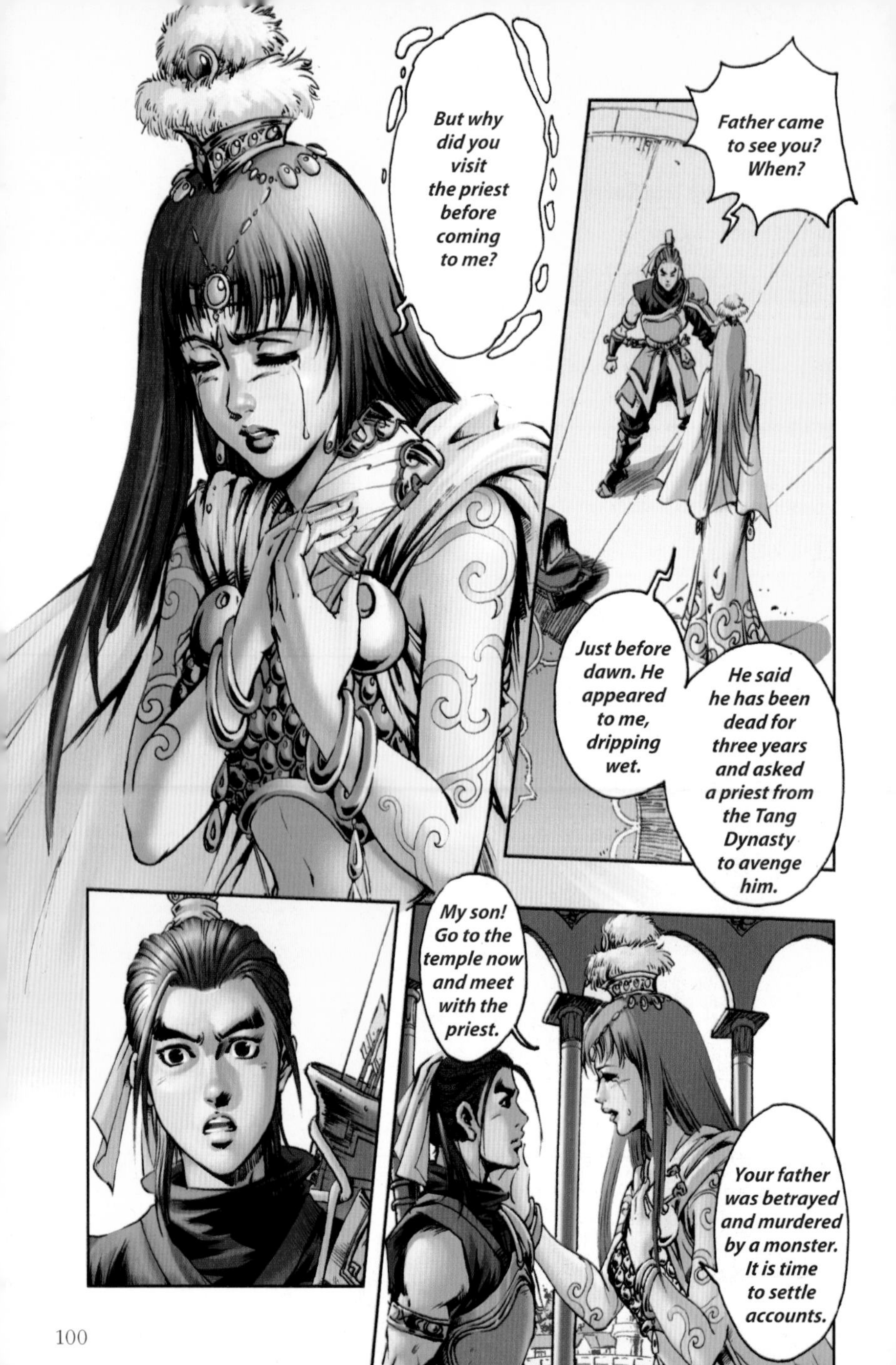
Father came to see you? When?
But why did you visit the priest before coming to me?
Just before dawn. He appeared to me, dripping wet.
He said he has been dead for three years and asked a priest from the Tang Dynasty to avenge him.
My son! Go to the temple now and meet with the priest.
Your father was betrayed and murdered by a monster. It is time to settle accounts.

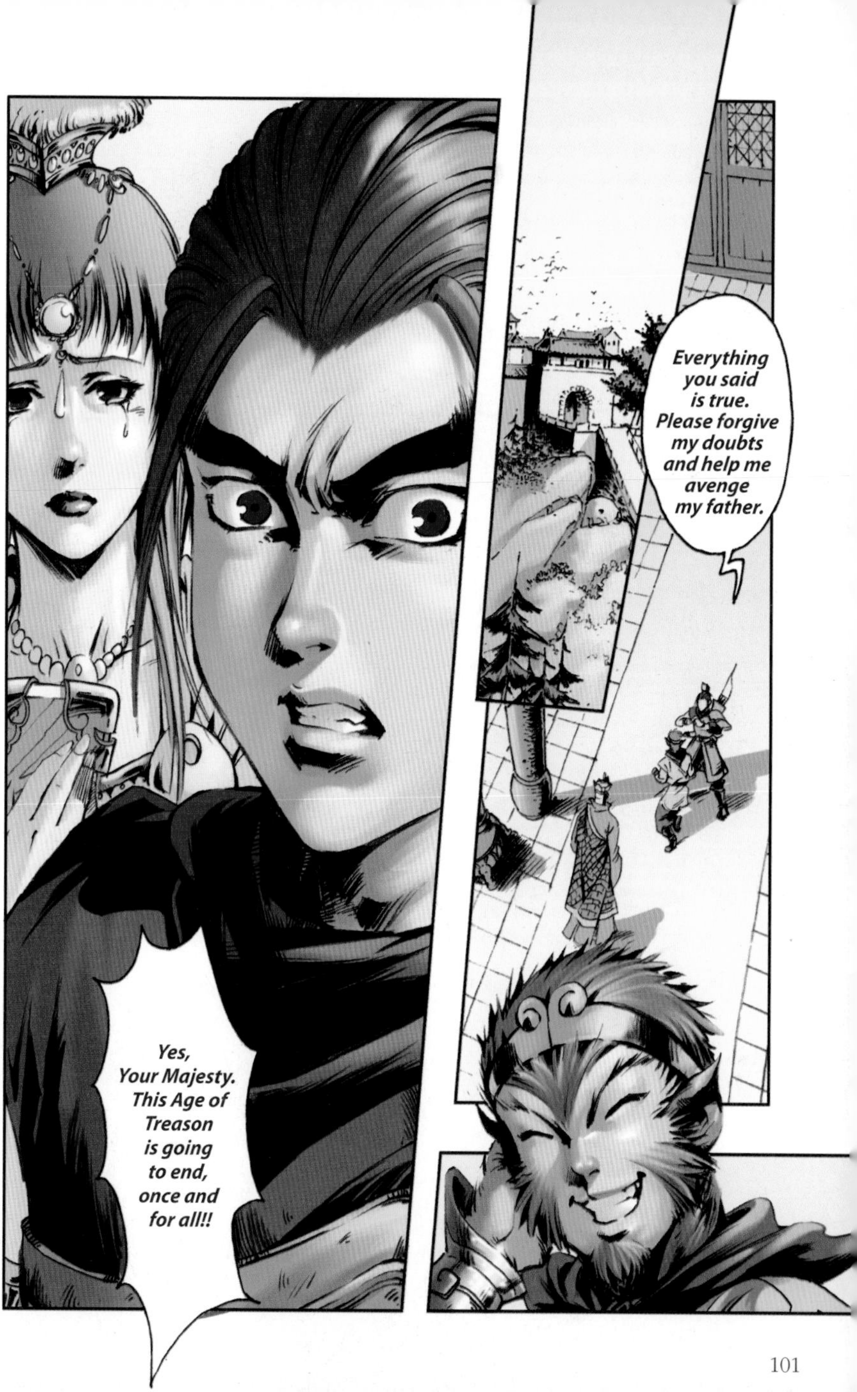
Everything you said is true. Please forgive my doubts and help me avenge my father.
Yes, Your Majesty. This Age of Treason is going to end, once and for all!!

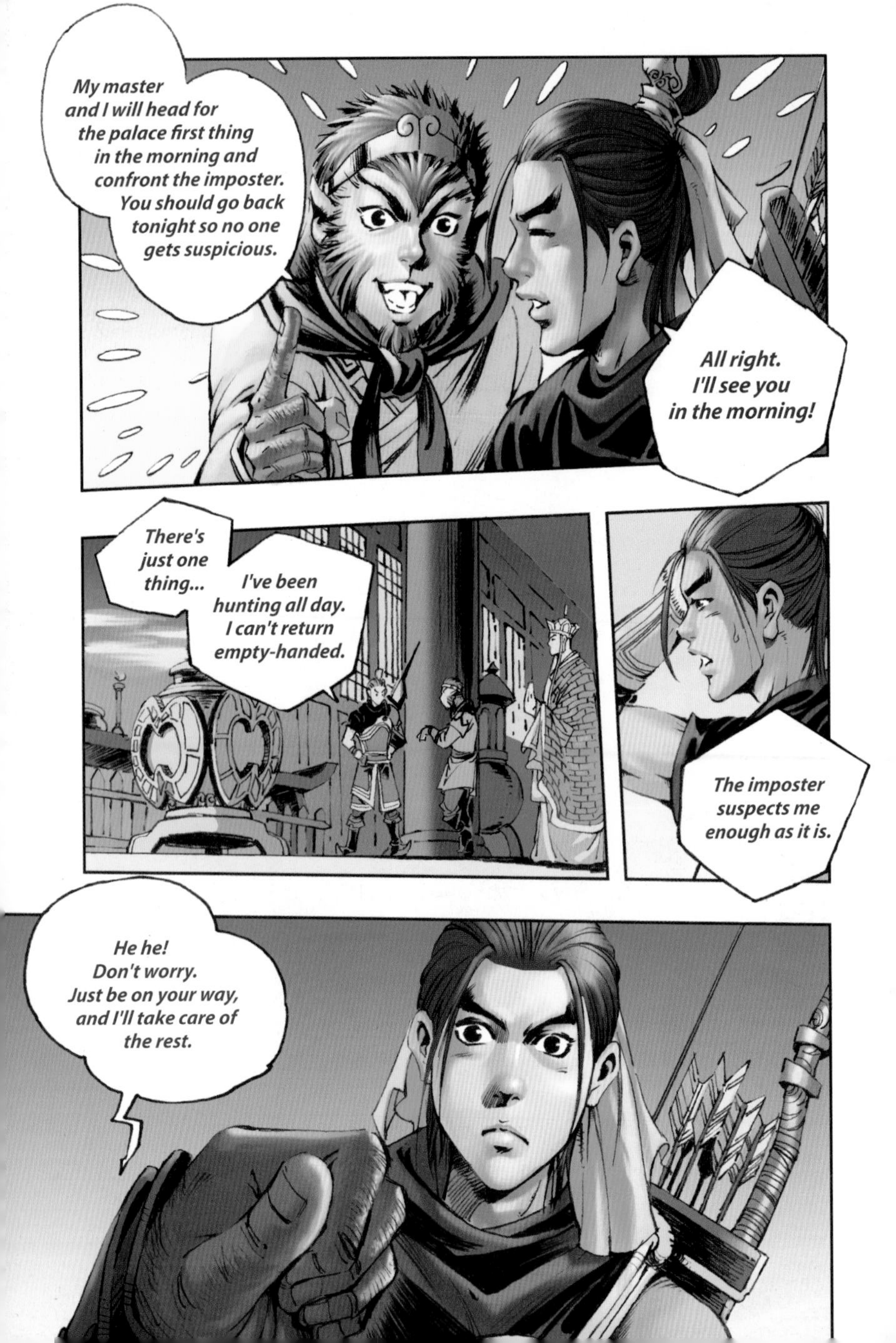
My master and I will head for the palace first thing in the morning and confront the imposter. You should go back tonight so no one gets suspicious.
All right. I'll see you in the morning!
There's just one thing...
I've been hunting all day. I can't return empty-handed.
The imposter suspects me enough as it is.
He he! Don't worry. Just be on your way, and I'll take care of the rest.

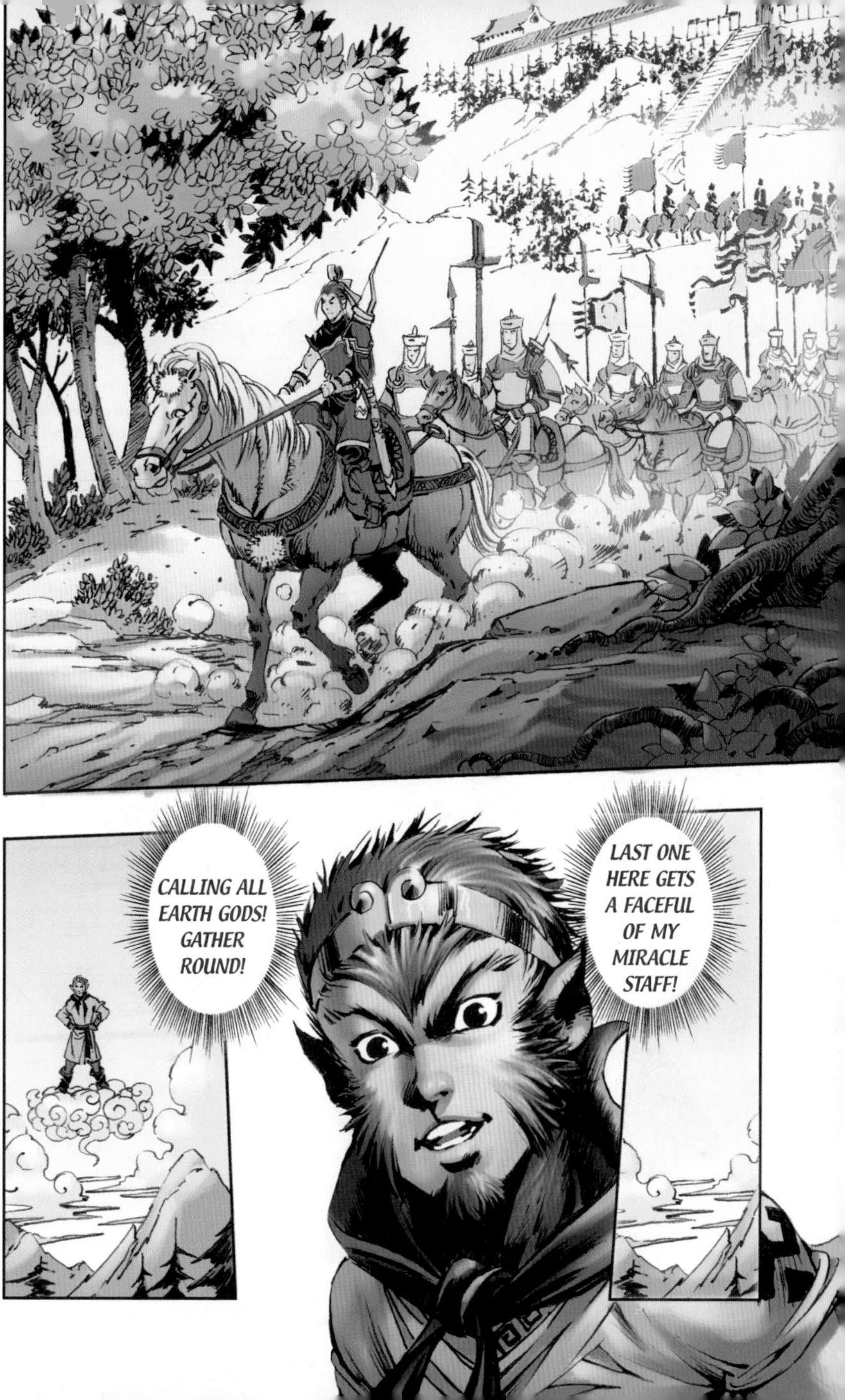
CALLING ALL EARTH GODS! GATHER ROUND!
LAST ONE HERE GETS A FACEFUL OF MY MIRACLE STAFF!

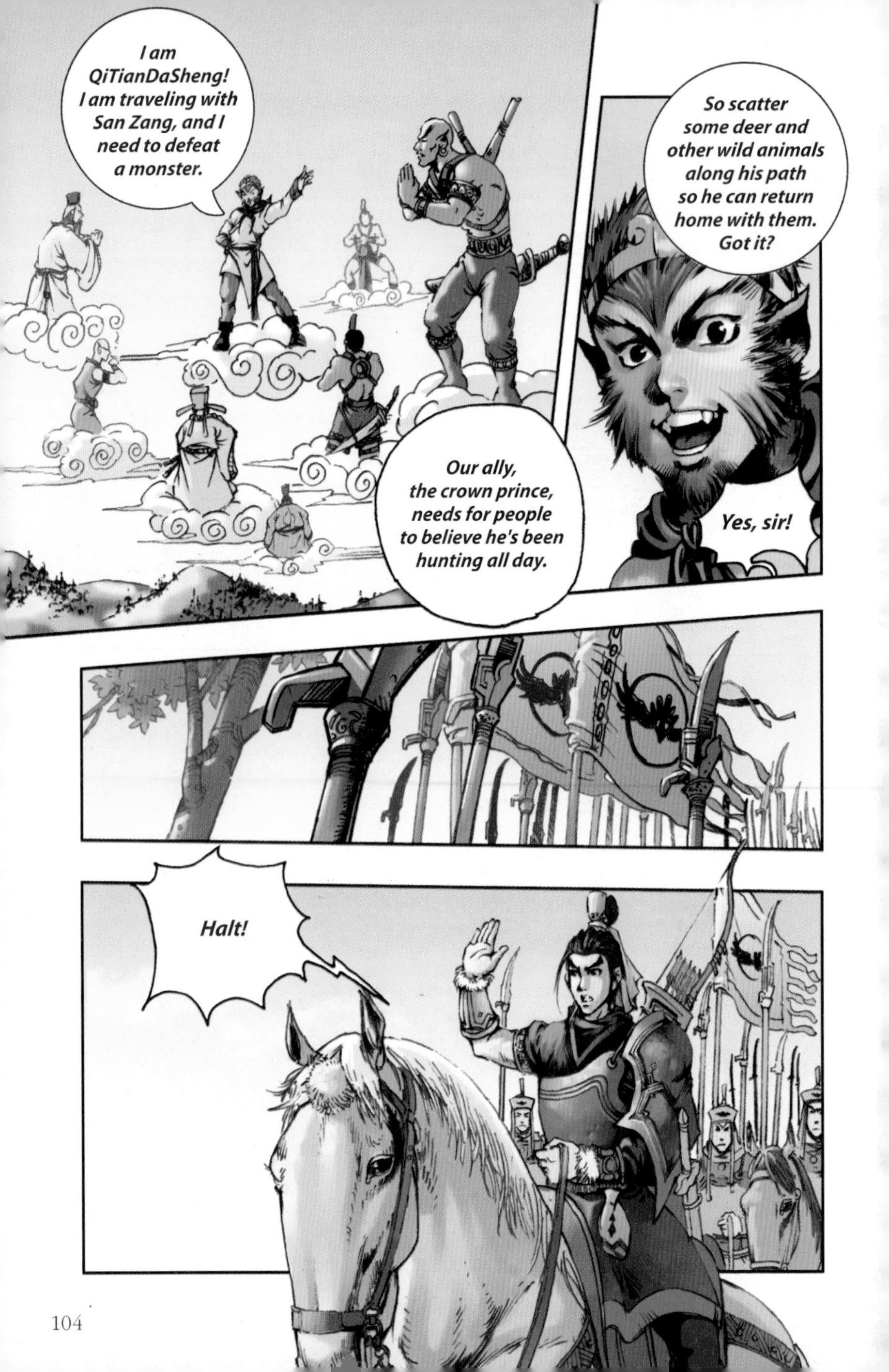
I am QiTianDaSheng! I am traveling with San Zang, and I need to defeat a monster.
So scatter some deer and other wild animals along his path so he can return home with them. Got it?
Our ally, the crown prince, needs for people to believe he's been hunting all day.
Yes, sir!
Halt!

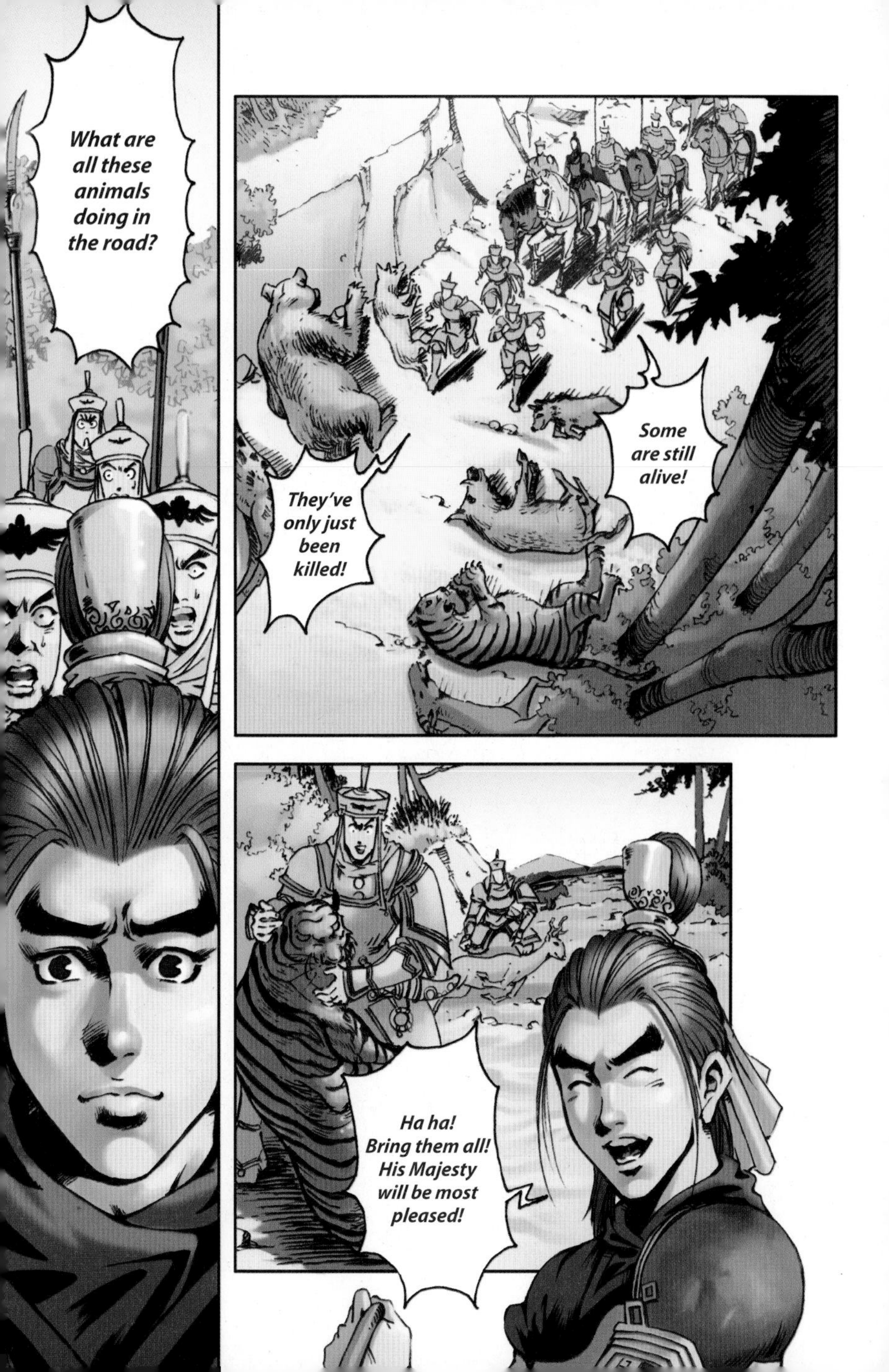
What are all these animals doing in the road?
Some are still alive!
They've only just been killed!
Ha ha! Bring them all! His Majesty will be most pleased!

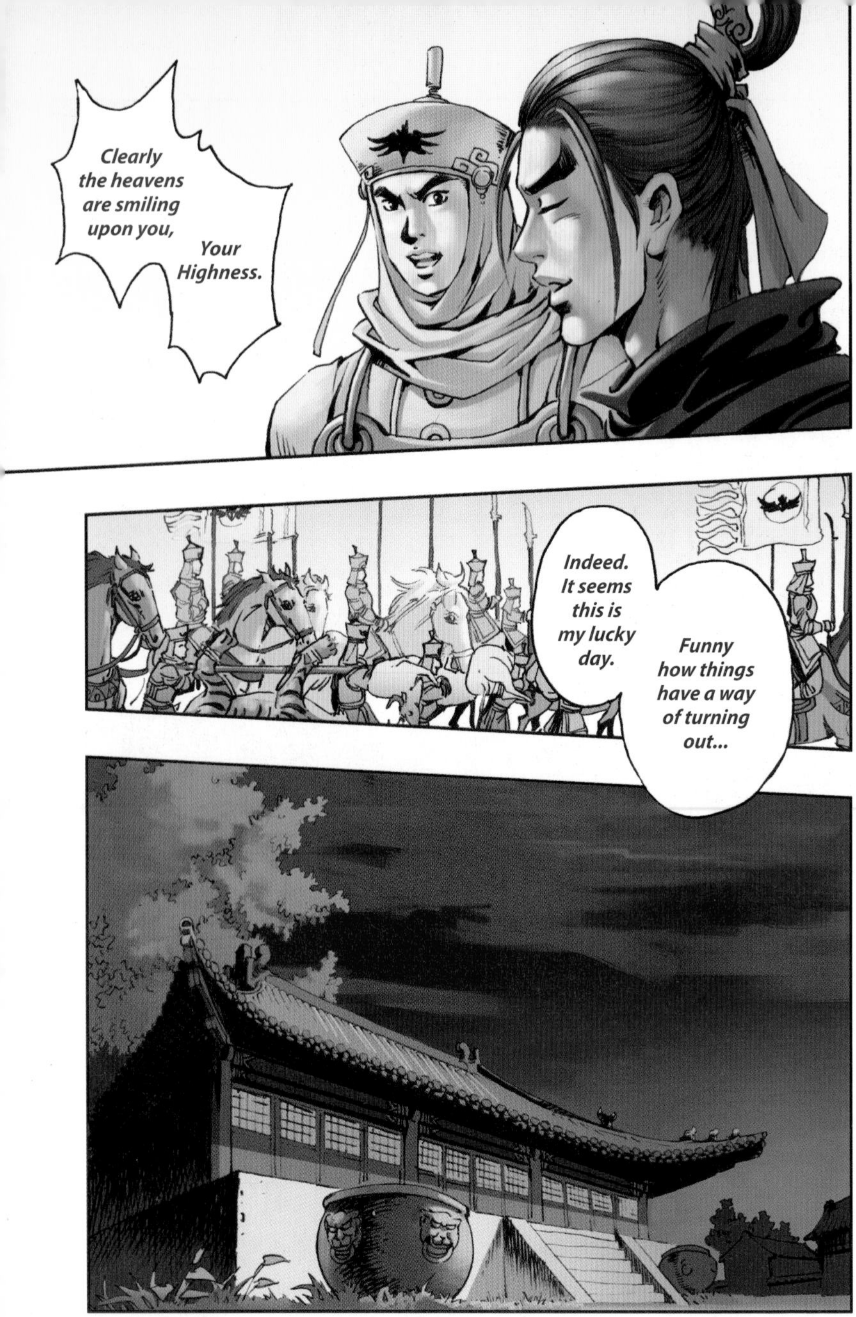
Clearly the heavens are smiling upon you, Your Highness.
Indeed. It seems this is my lucky day.
Funny how things have a way of turning out...

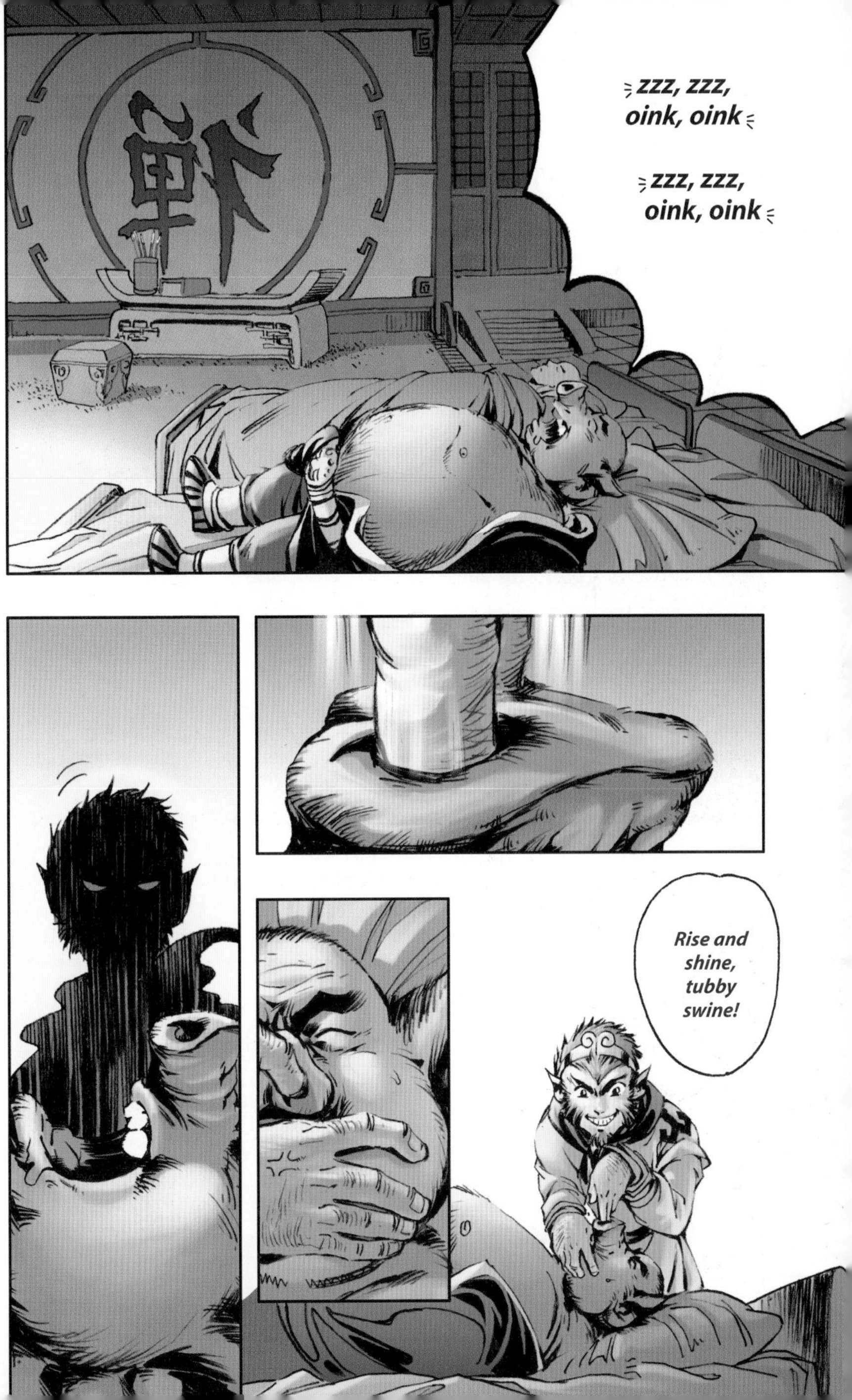
zzz, zzz, oink, oink
zzz, zzz, oink, oink
Rise and shine, tubby swine!

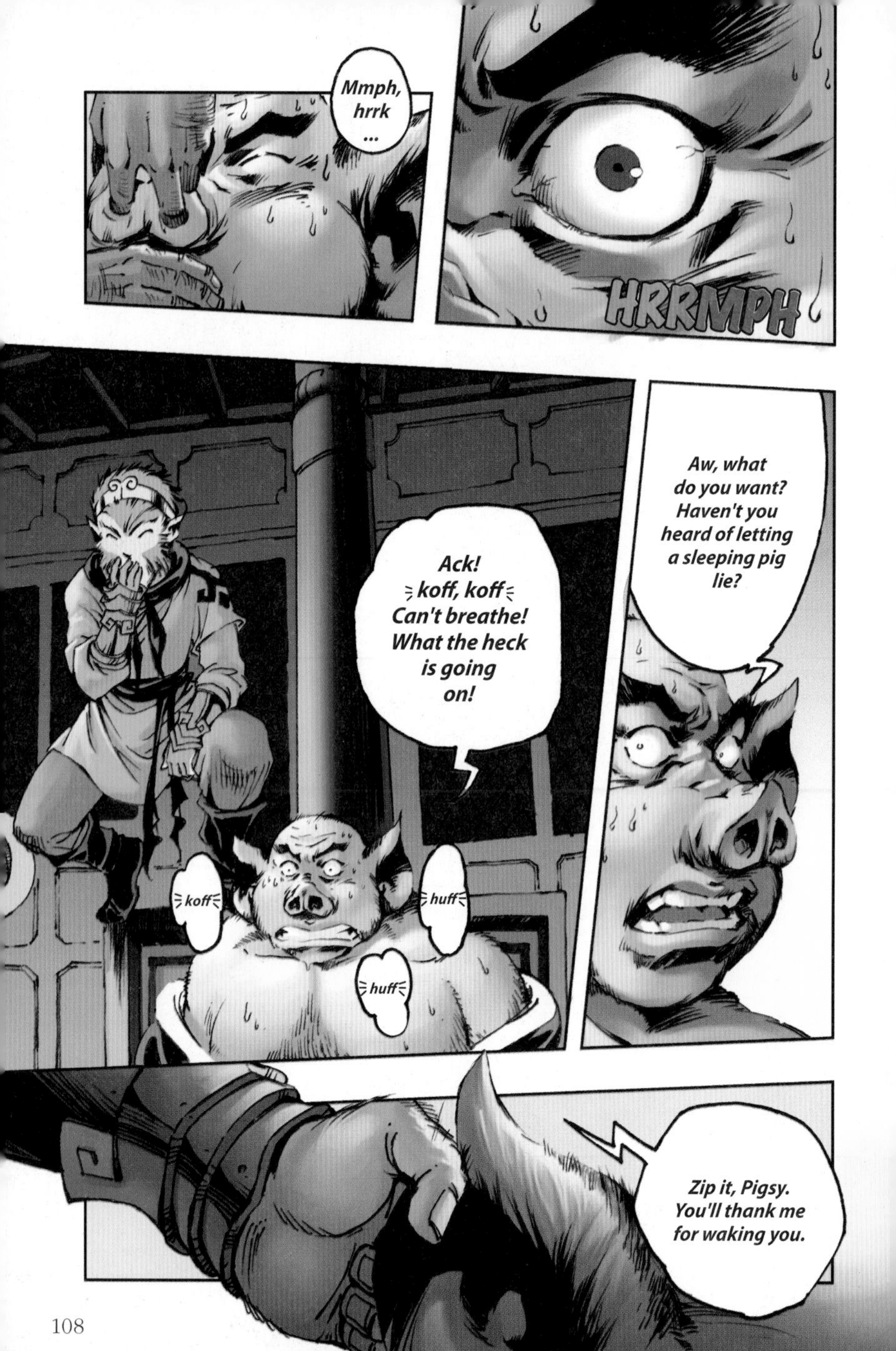
Mmph, hrrk ...
HRRMPH
Ack! koff, koff Can't breathe! What the heck is going on!
Aw, what do you want? Haven't you heard of letting a sleeping pig lie?
koff
huff
huff
Zip it, Pigsy. You'll thank me for waking you.

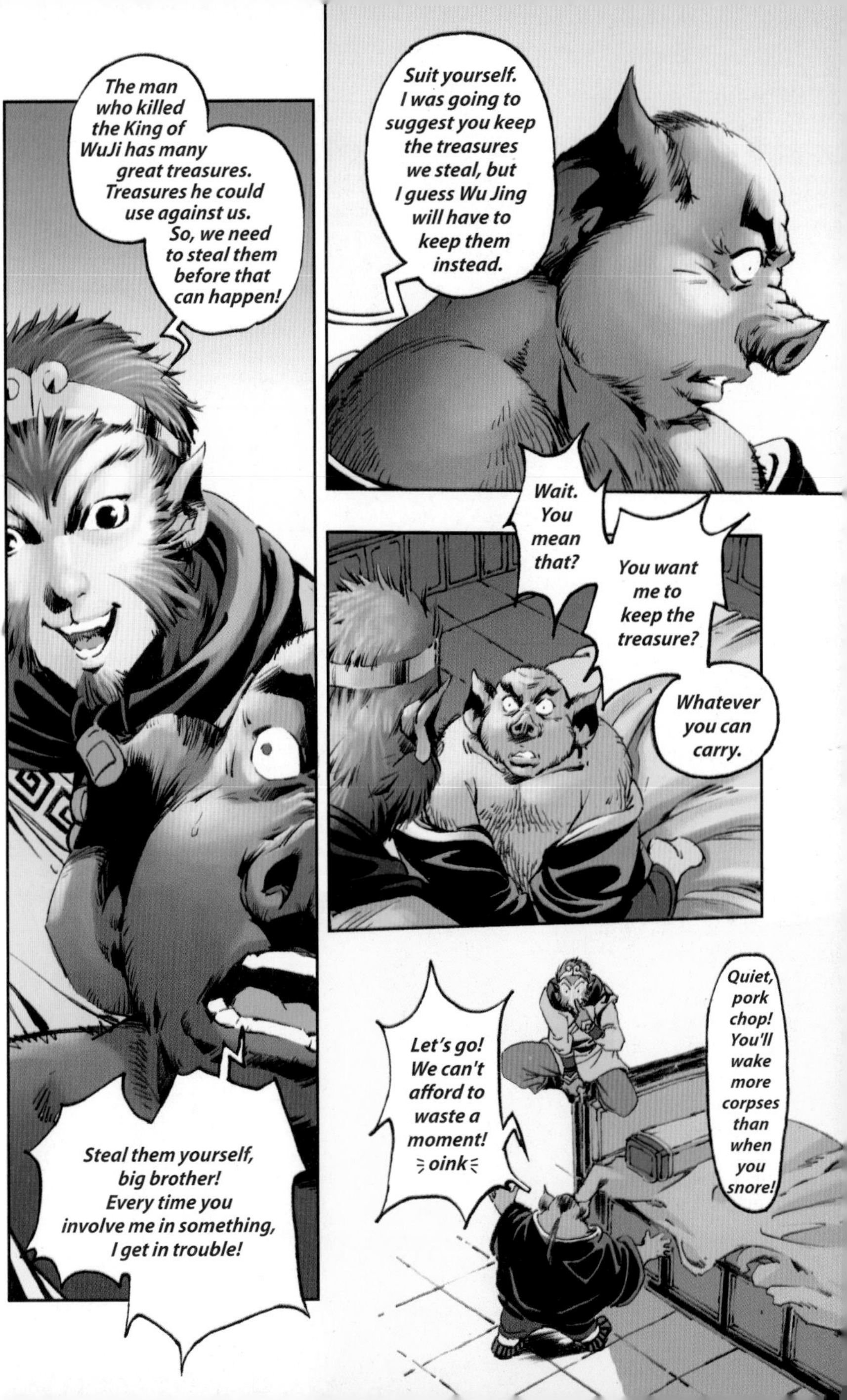
The man who killed the King of WuJi has many great treasures. Treasures he could use against us. So, we need to steal them before that can happen!
Steal them yourself, big brother! Every time you involve me in something, I get in trouble!
Suit yourself. I was going to suggest you keep the treasures we steal, but I guess Wu Jing will have to keep them instead.
Wait. You mean that?
You want me to keep the treasure?
Whatever you can carry.
Quiet, pork chop! You'll wake more corpses than when you snore!
Let's go! We can't afford to waste a moment! ⪢oink⪡

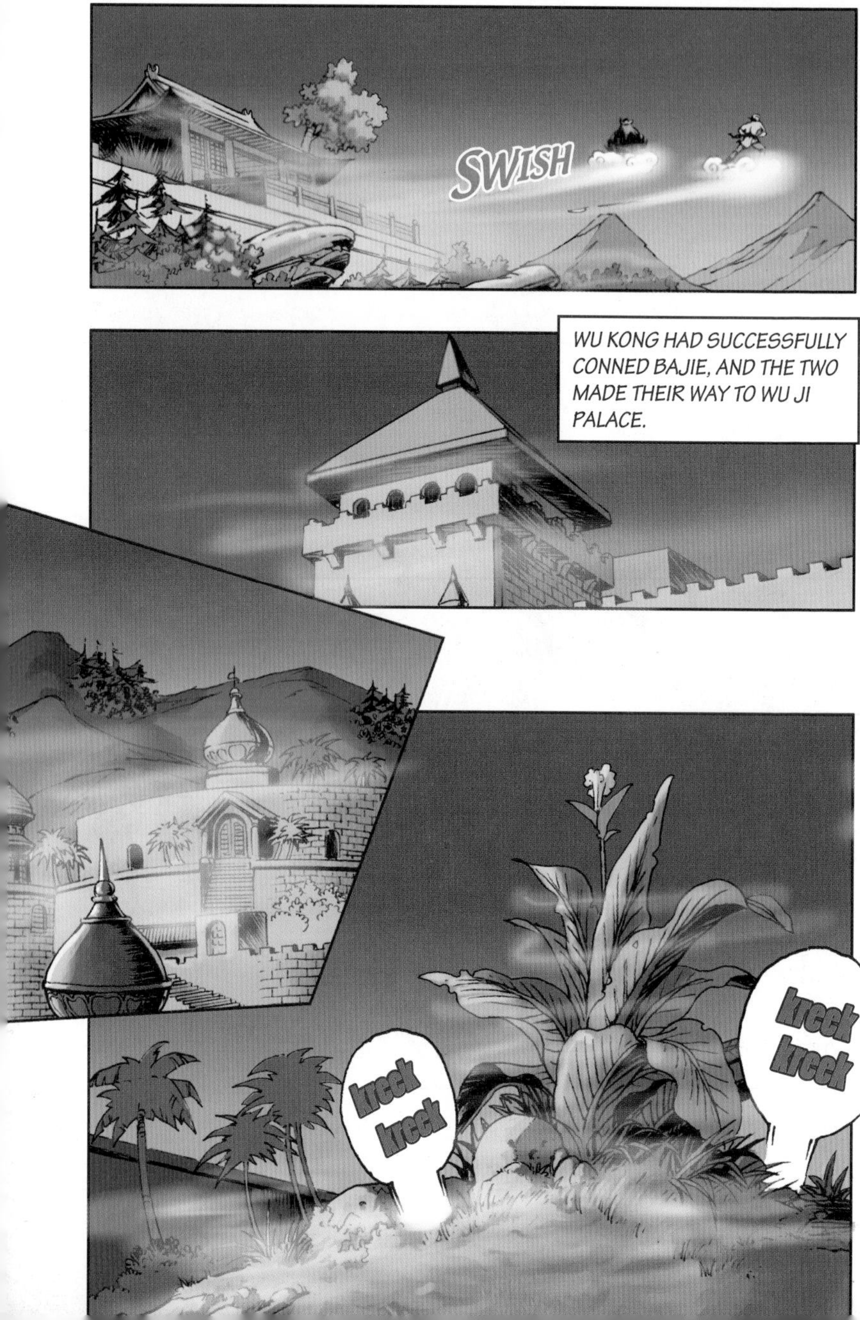
SWISH
WU KONG HAD SUCCESSFULLY CONNED BAJIE, AND THE TWO MADE THEIR WAY TO WU JI PALACE.
kreck kreck
kreck kreck

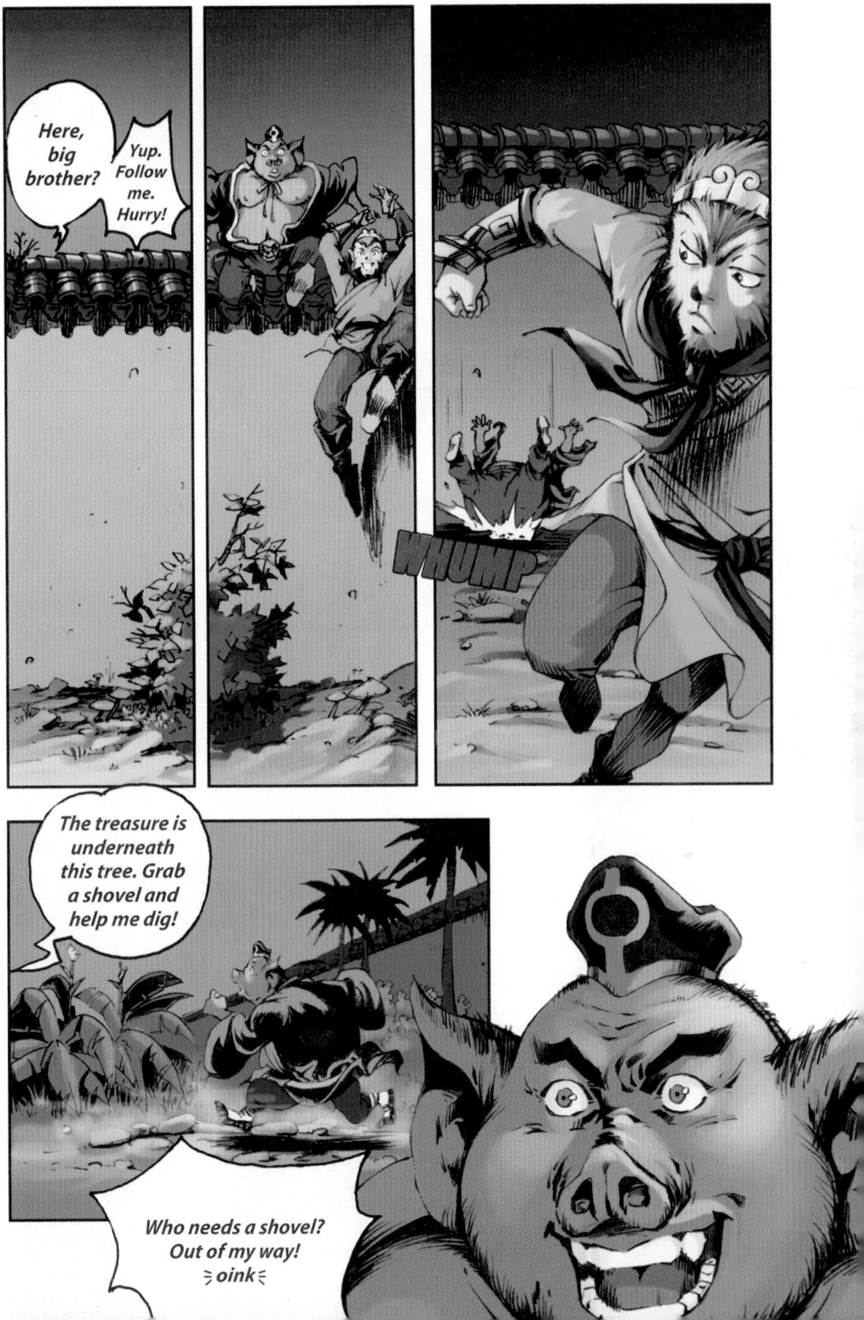

Here, big brother?
Yup. Follow me. Hurry!
WHUMP
The treasure is underneath this tree. Grab a shovel and help me dig!
Who needs a shovel? Out of my way!
oink

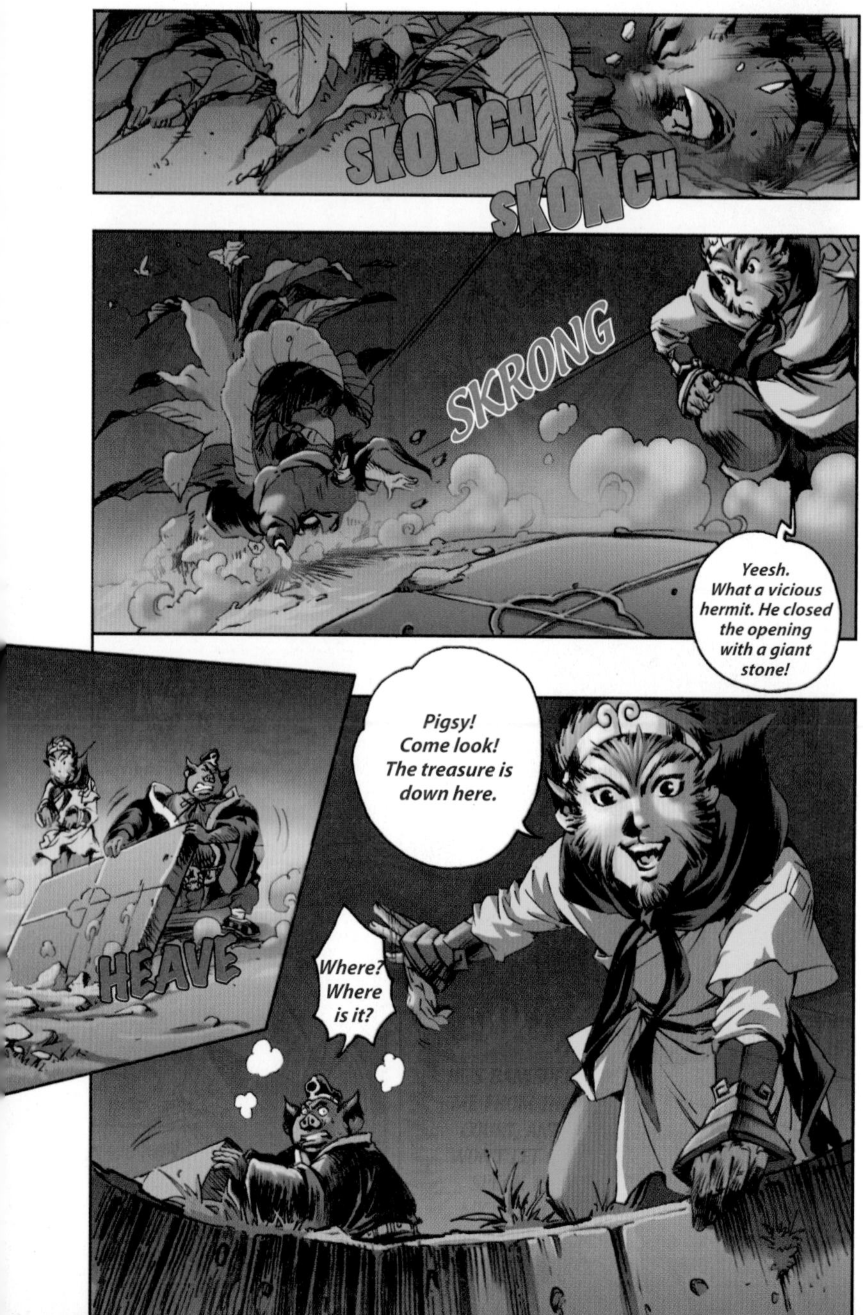
SKONCH
SKONCH
SKRONG
Yeesh. What a vicious hermit. He closed the opening with a giant stone!
HEAVE
Pigsy! Come look! The treasure is down here.
Where? Where is it?

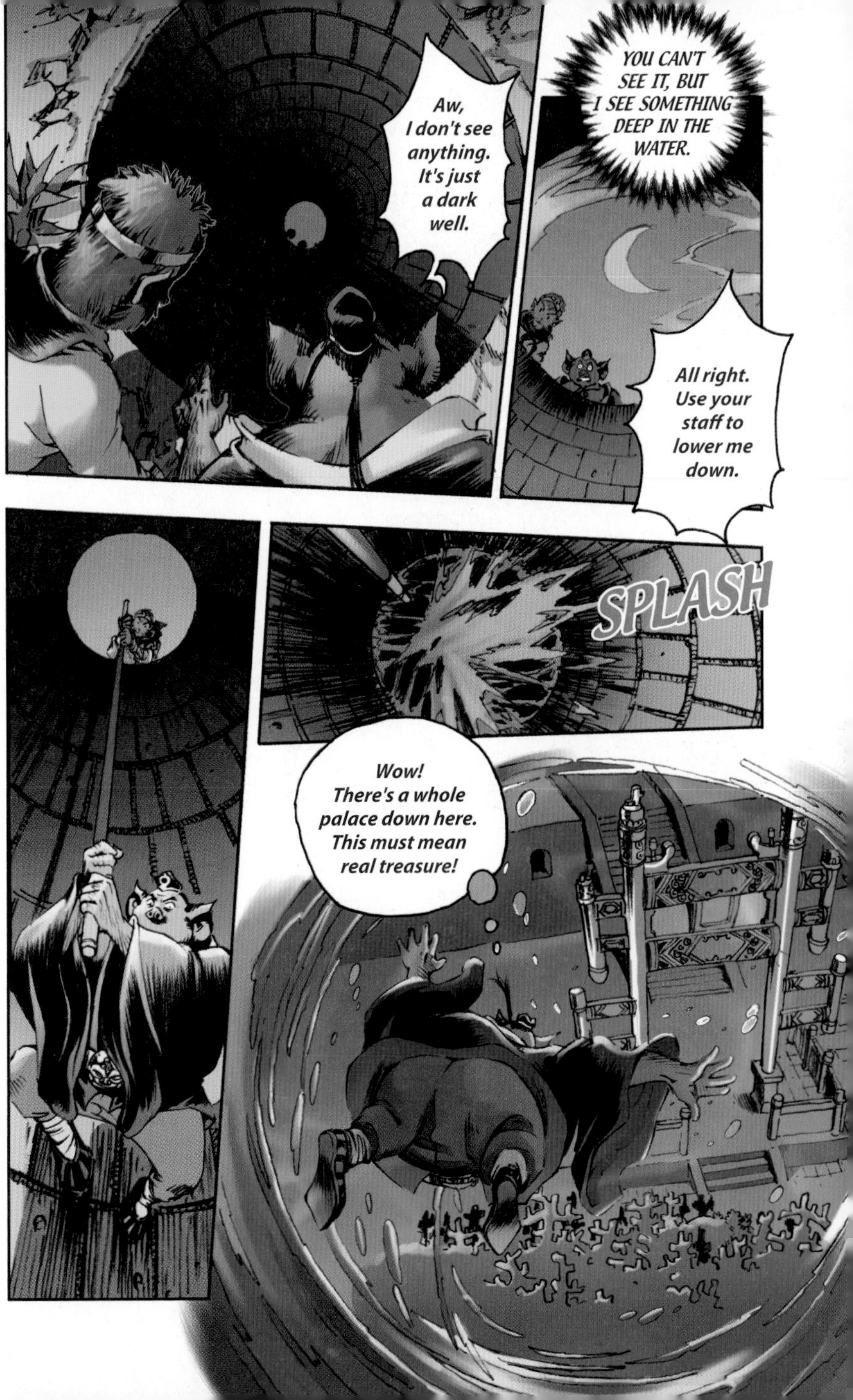
Aw, I don't see anything. It's just a dark well.
YOU CAN'T SEE IT, BUT I SEE SOMETHING DEEP IN THE WATER.
All right. Use your staff to lower me down.
SPLASH
Wow! There's a whole palace down here. This must mean real treasure!

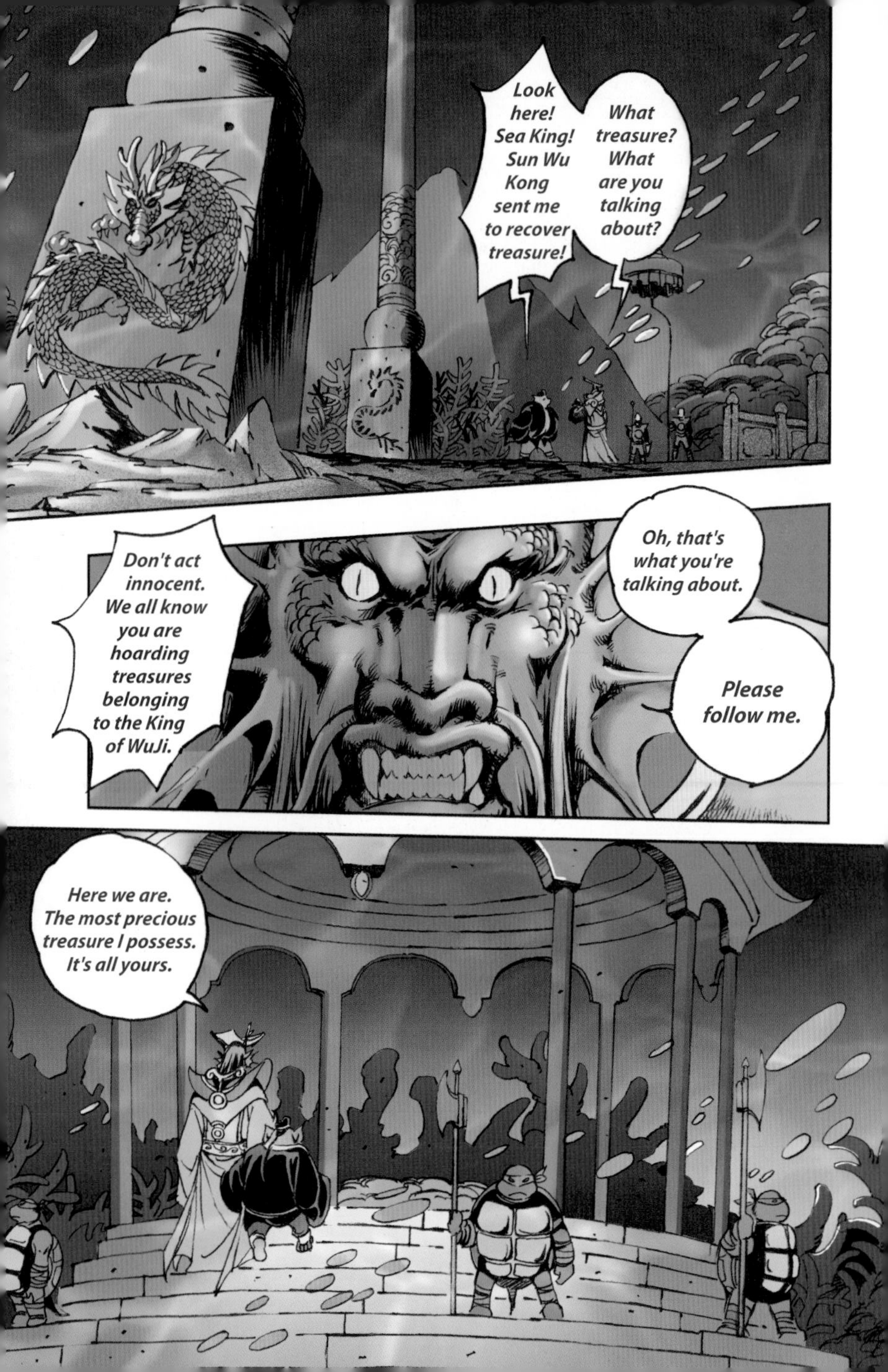

Look here! Sea King! Sun Wu Kong sent me to recover treasure!
What treasure? What are you talking about?
Don't act innocent. We all know you are hoarding treasures belonging to the King of WuJi.
Oh, that's what you're talking about.
Please follow me.
Here we are. The most precious treasure I possess. It's all yours.

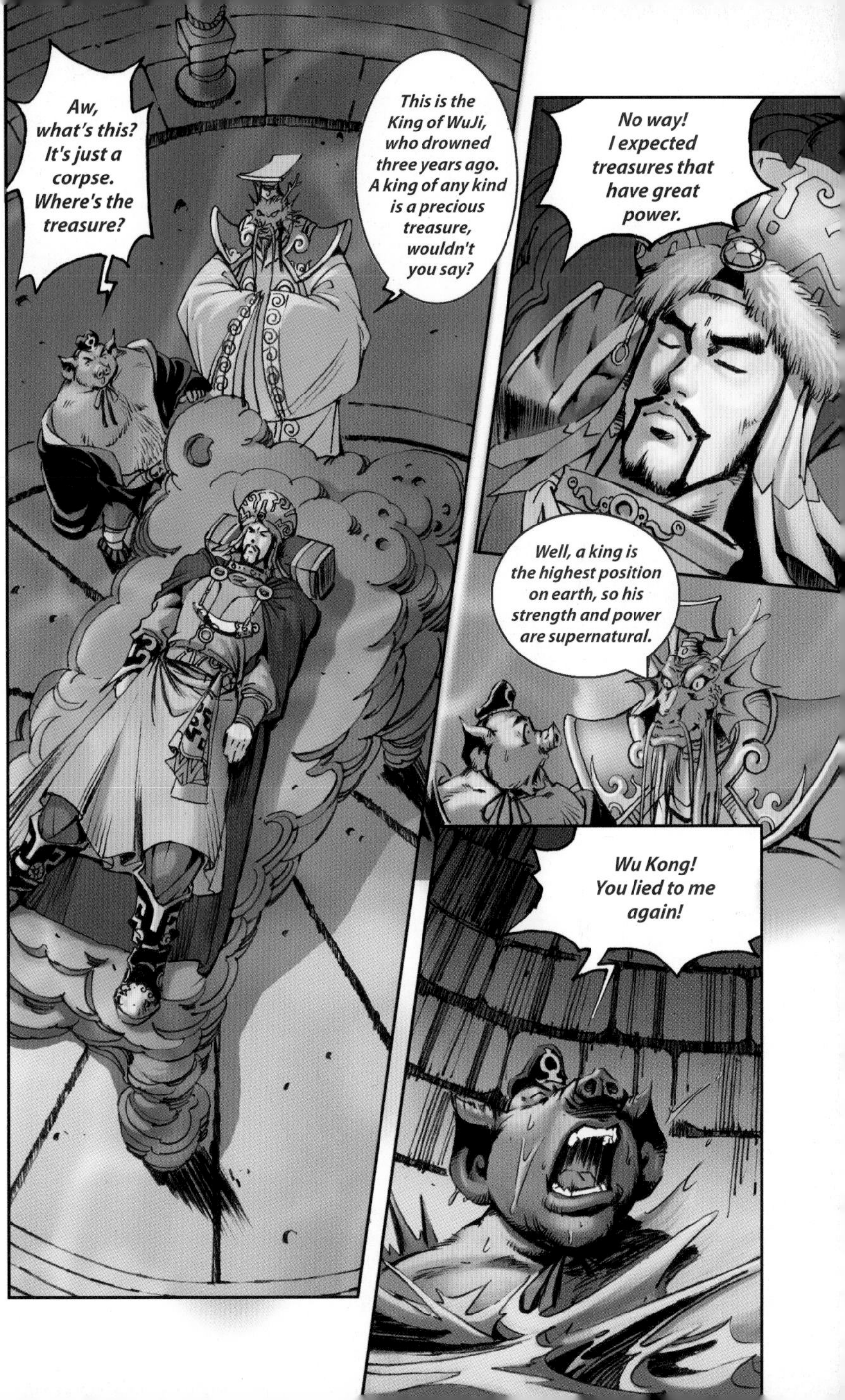
Aw, what's this? It's just a corpse. Where's the treasure?
This is the King of WuJi, who drowned three years ago. A king of any kind is a precious treasure, wouldn't you say?
No way! I expected treasures that have great power.
Well, a king is the highest position on earth, so his strength and power are supernatural.
Wu Kong! You lied to me again!

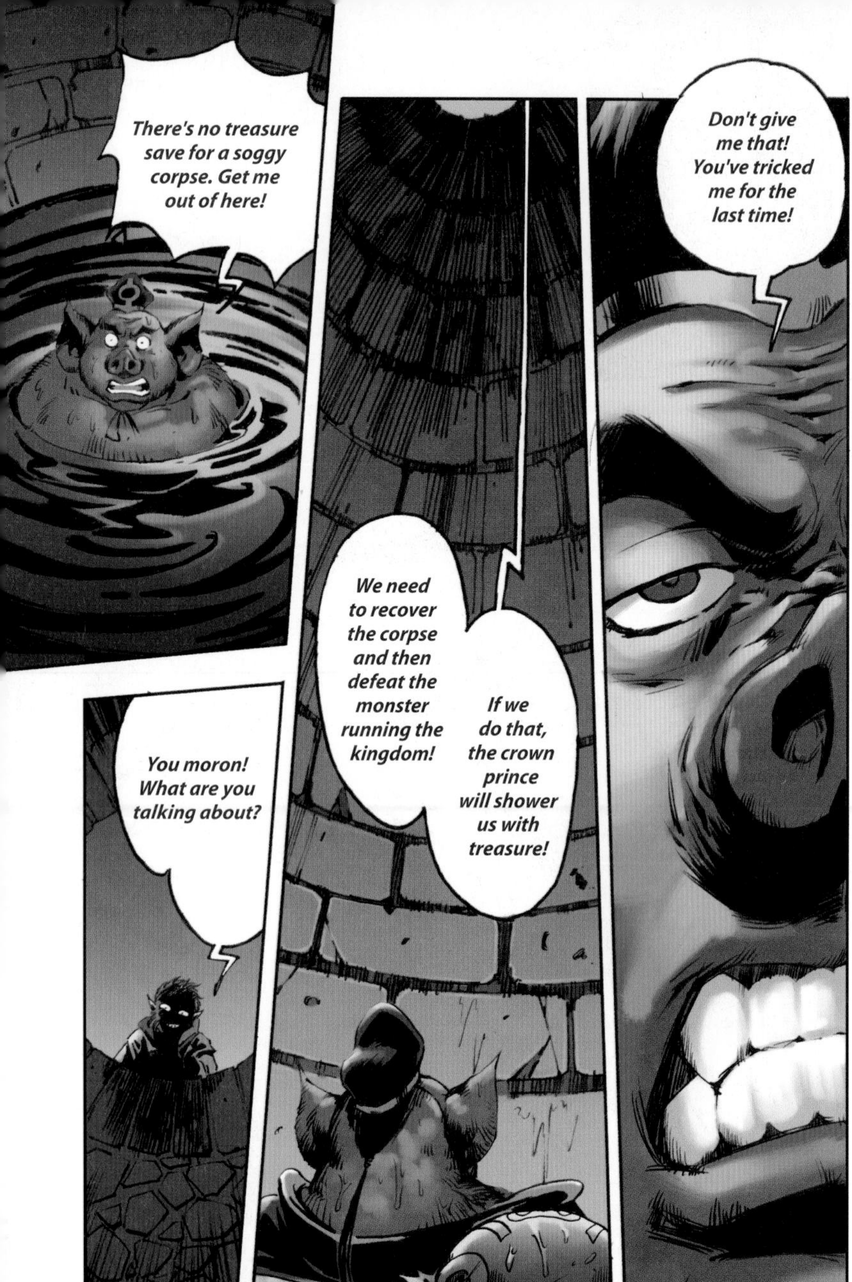
There's no treasure save for a soggy corpse. Get me out of here!
Don't give me that! You've tricked me for the last time!
You moron! What are you talking about?
We need to recover the corpse and then defeat the monster running the kingdom!
If we do that, the crown prince will shower us with treasure!

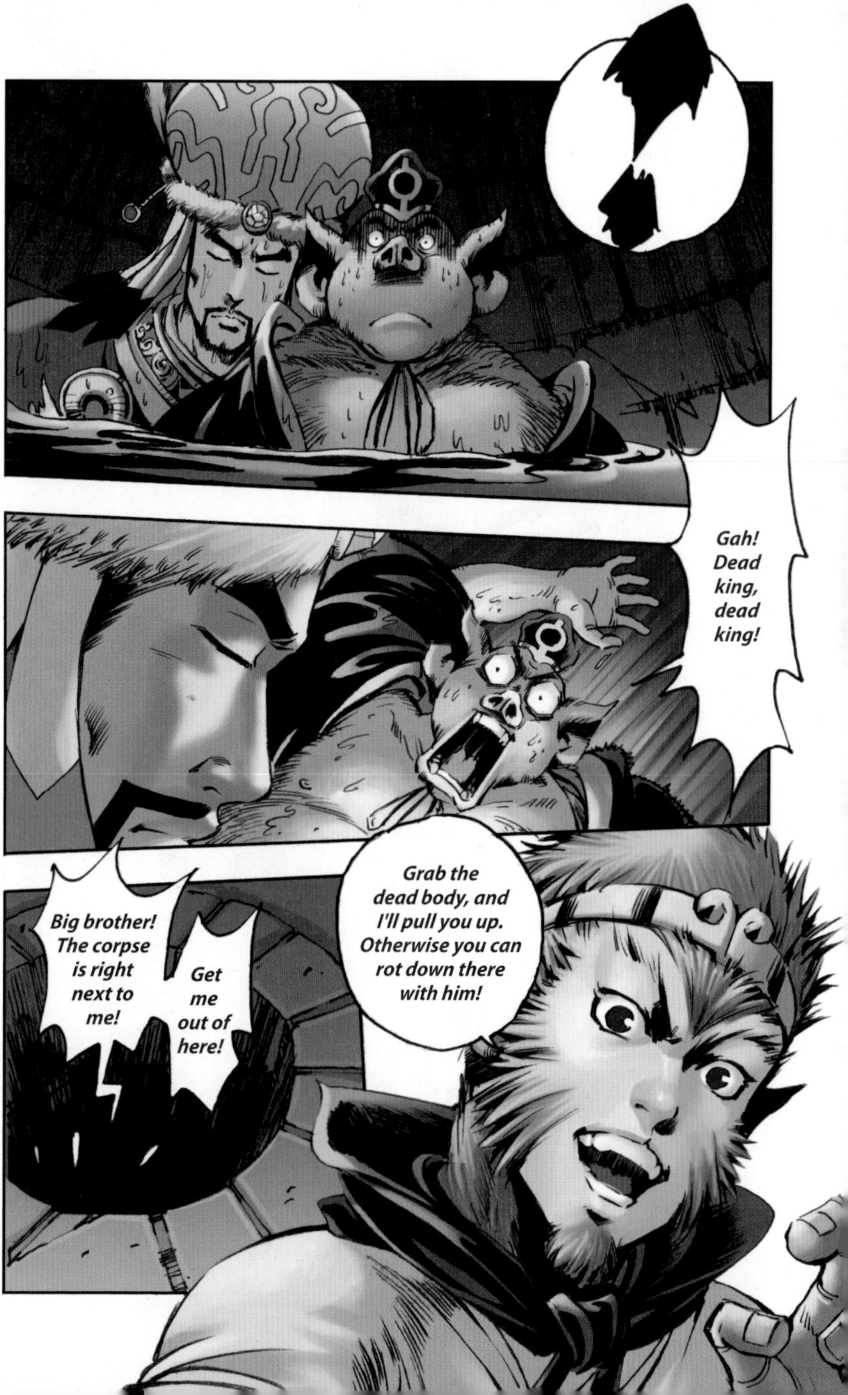
Gah! Dead king, dead king!
Big brother! The corpse is right next to me!
Get me out of here!
Grab the dead body, and I'll pull you up. Otherwise you can rot down there with him!

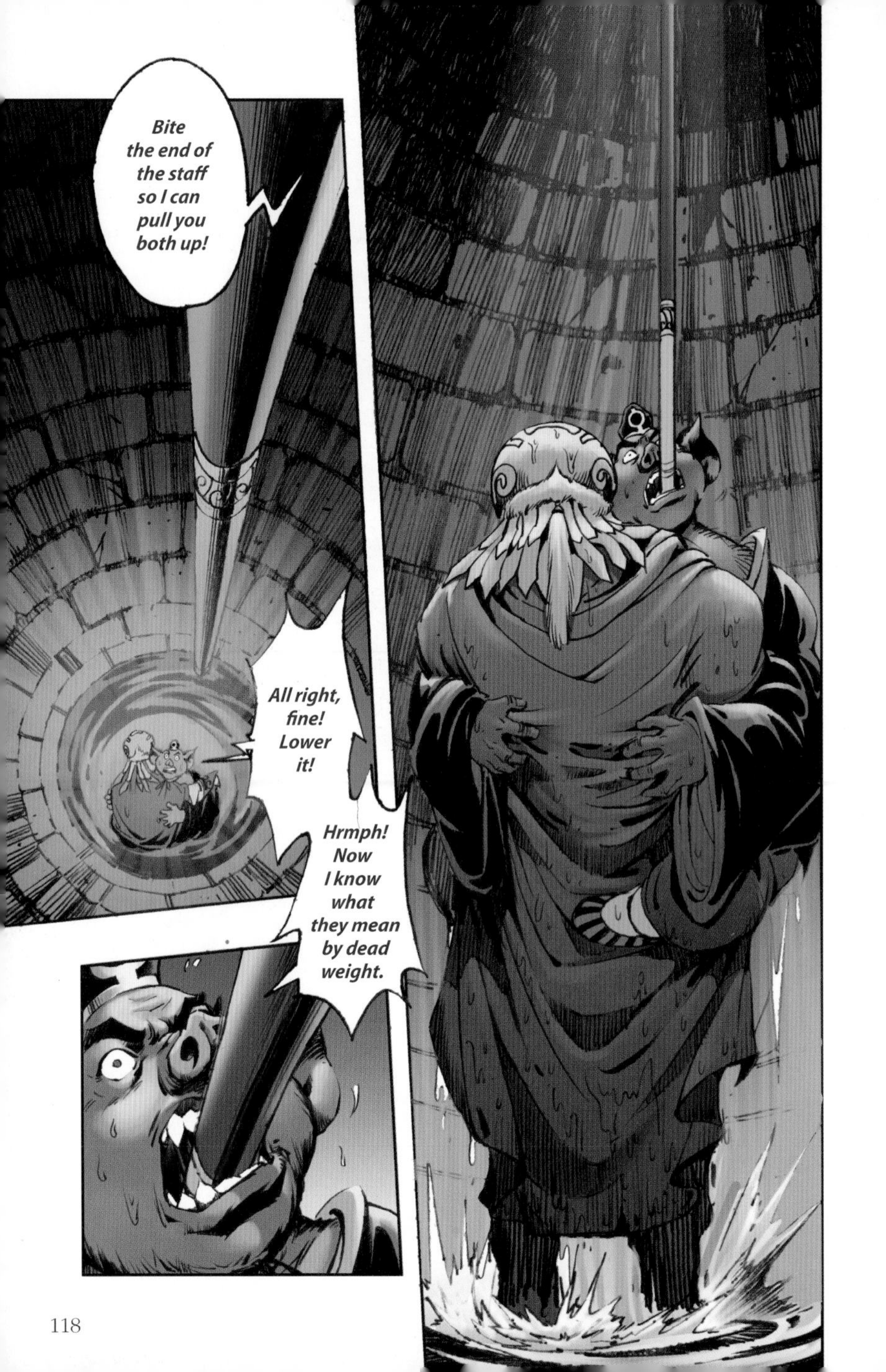
Bite the end of the staff so I can pull you both up!
All right, fine! Lower it!
Hrmph! Now I know what they mean by dead weight.

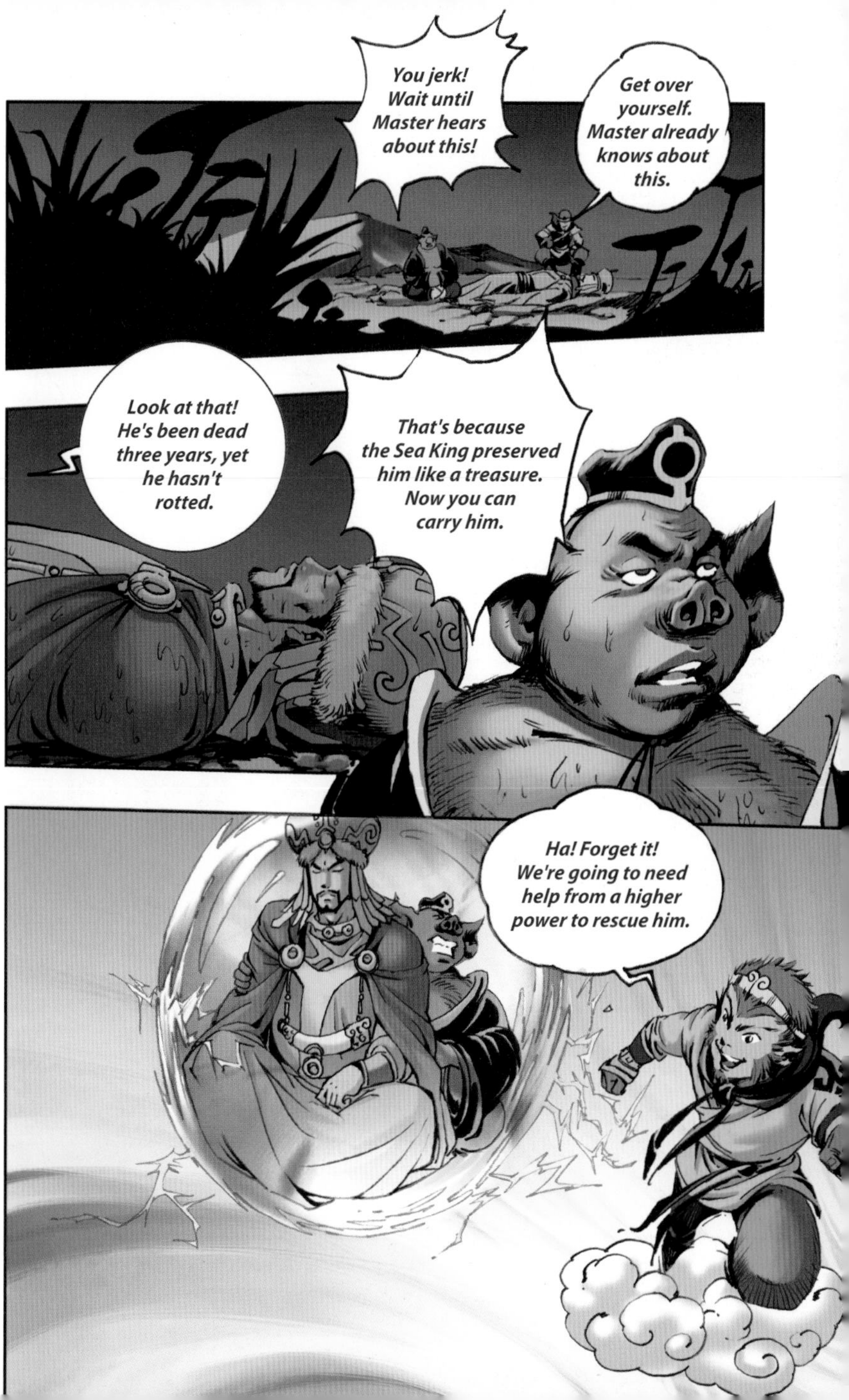
You jerk! Wait until Master hears about this!
Get over yourself. Master already knows about this.
Look at that! He's been dead three years, yet he hasn't rotted.
That's because the Sea King preserved him like a treasure. Now you can carry him.
Ha! Forget it! We're going to need help from a higher power to rescue him.

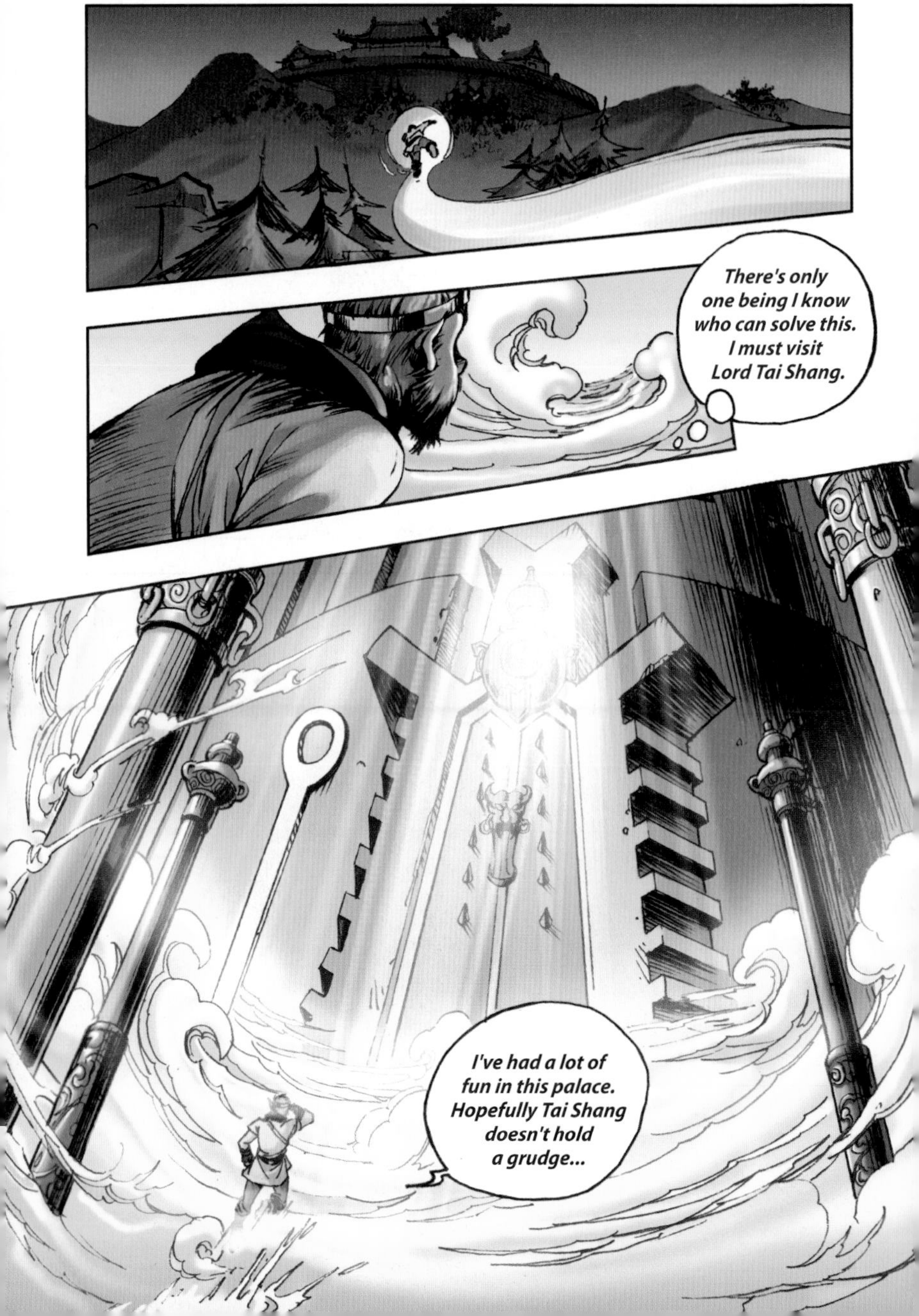
There's only one being I know who can solve this. I must visit Lord Tai Shang.
I've had a lot of fun in this palace. Hopefully Tai Shang doesn't hold a grudge...

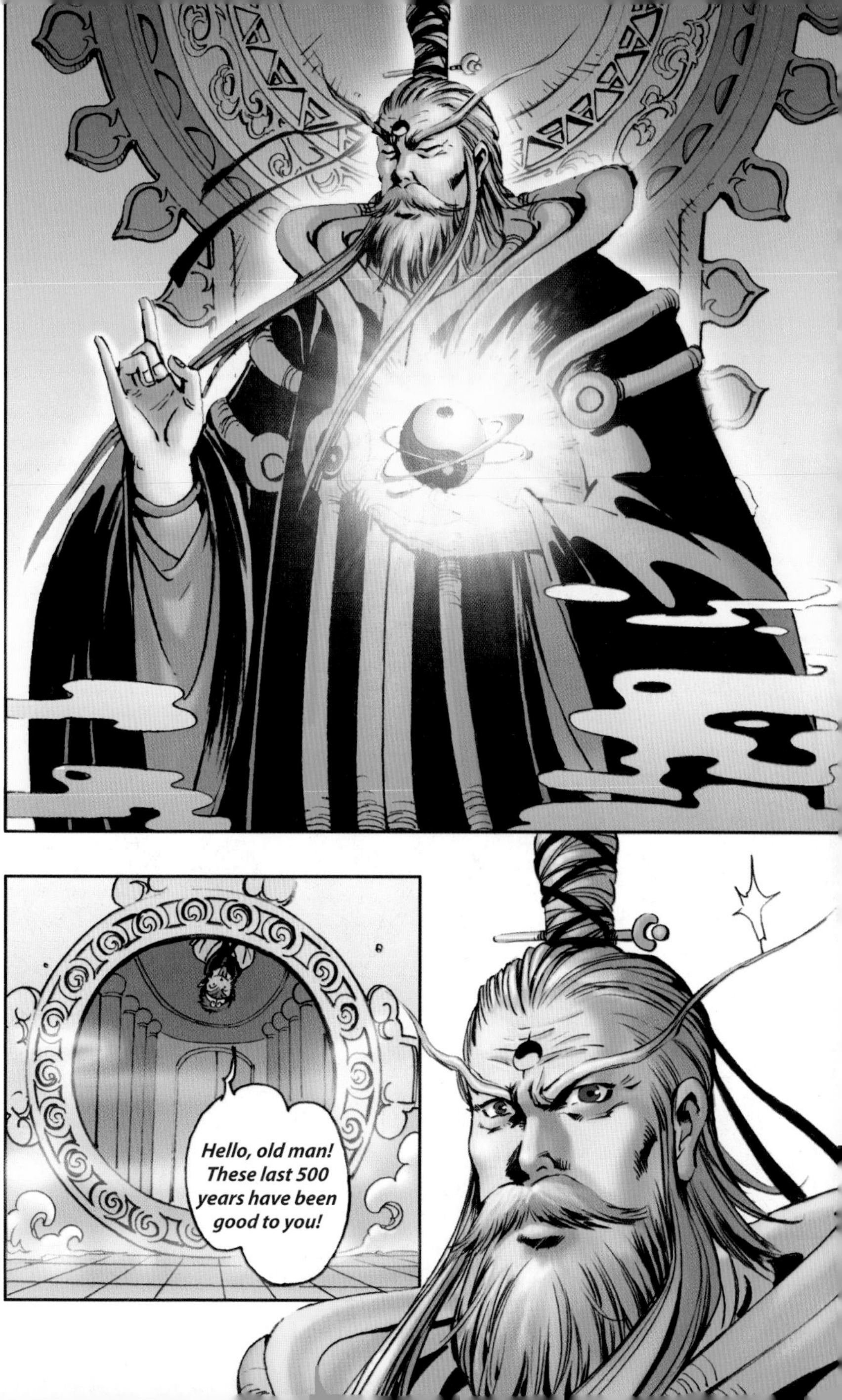
Hello, old man! These last 500 years have been good to you!

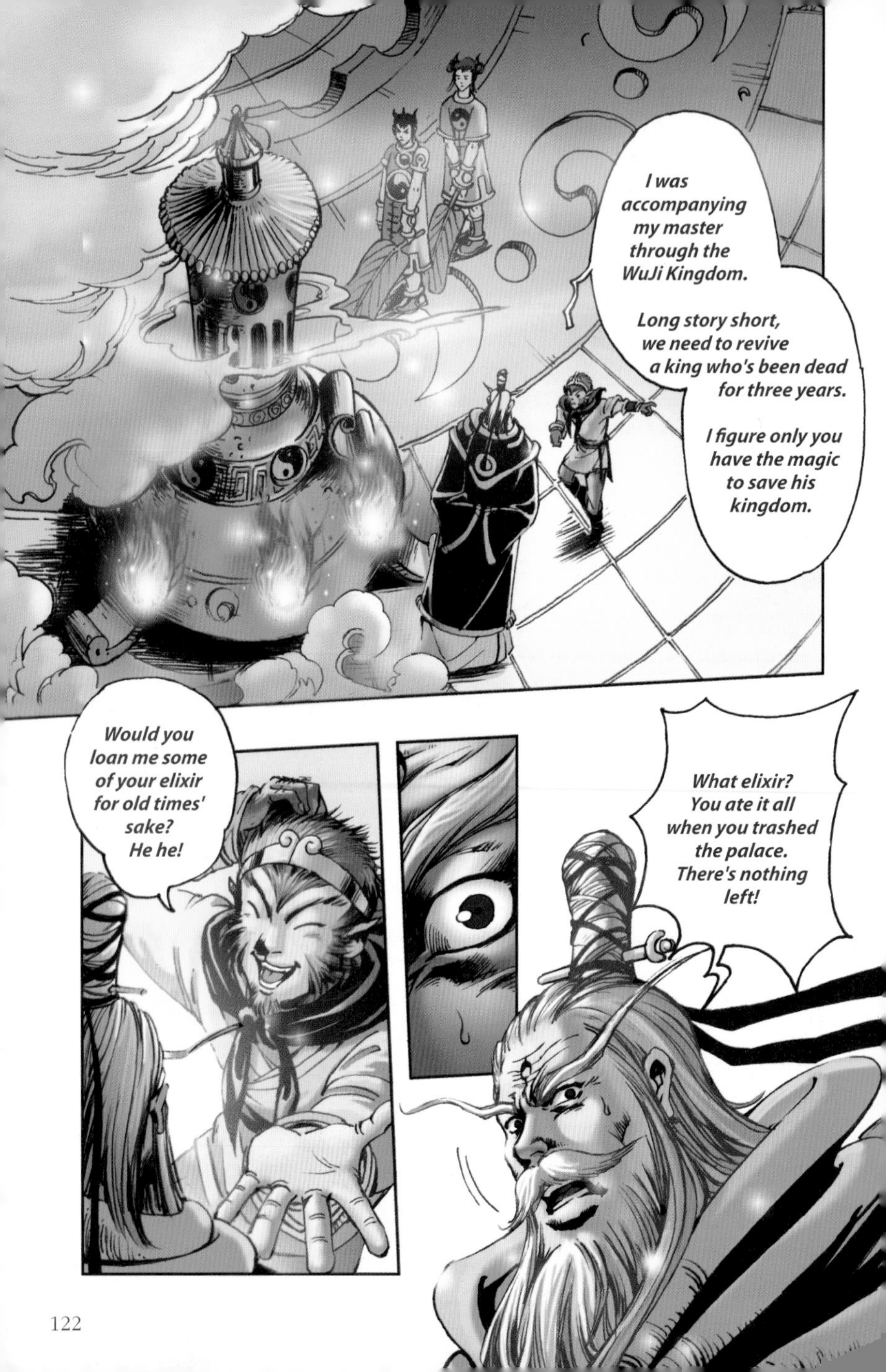
I was accompanying my master through the WuJi Kingdom.
Long story short, we need to revive a king who's been dead for three years.
I figure only you have the magic to save his kingdom.
Would you loan me some of your elixir for old times' sake? He he!
What elixir? You ate it all when you trashed the palace. There's nothing left!

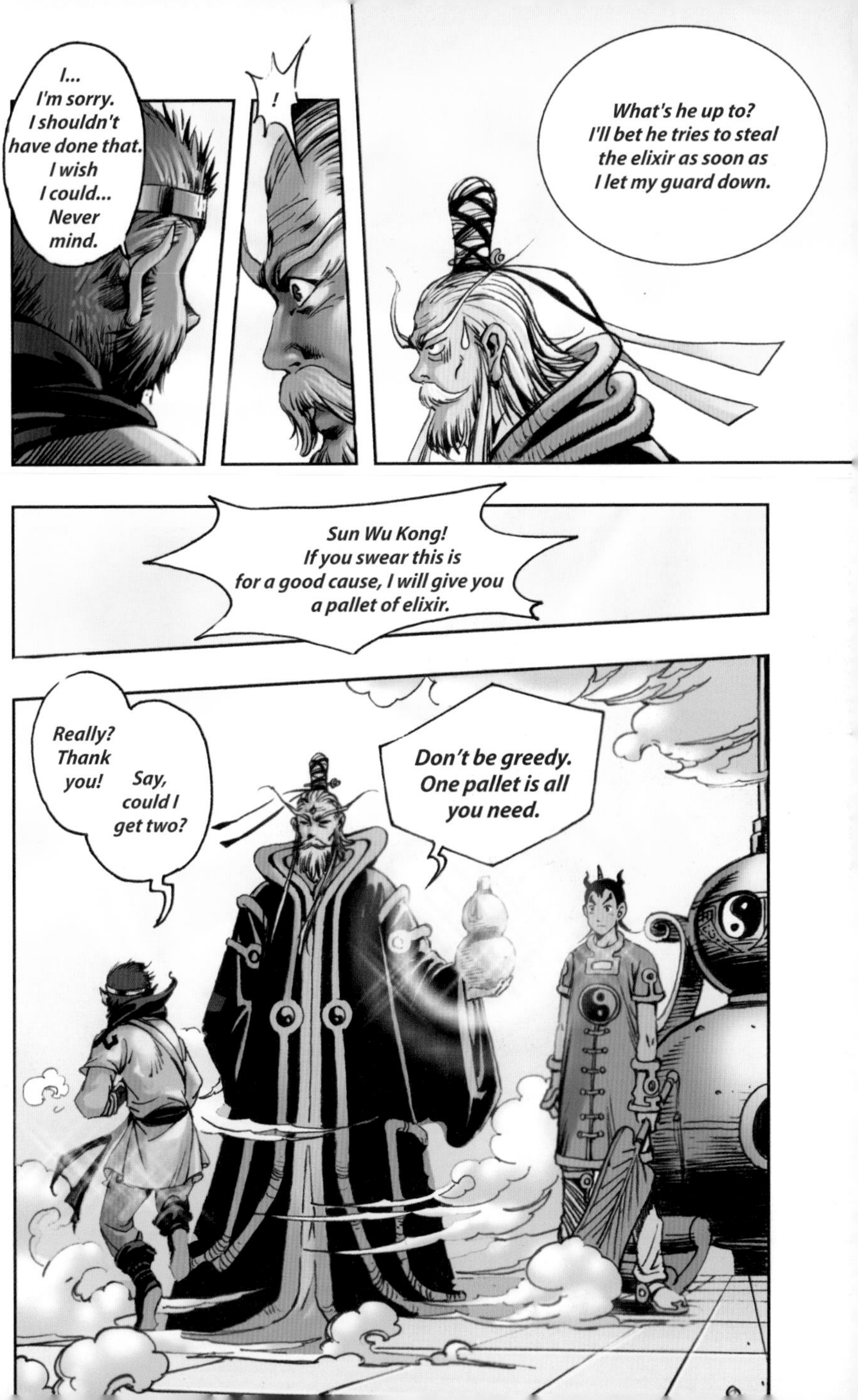

I... I'm sorry. I shouldn't have done that. I wish I could... Never mind.
!
What's he up to? I'll bet he tries to steal the elixir as soon as I let my guard down.
Sun Wu Kong! If you swear this is for a good cause, I will give you a pallet of elixir.
Really? Thank you!
Say, could I get two?
Don't be greedy. One pallet is all you need.

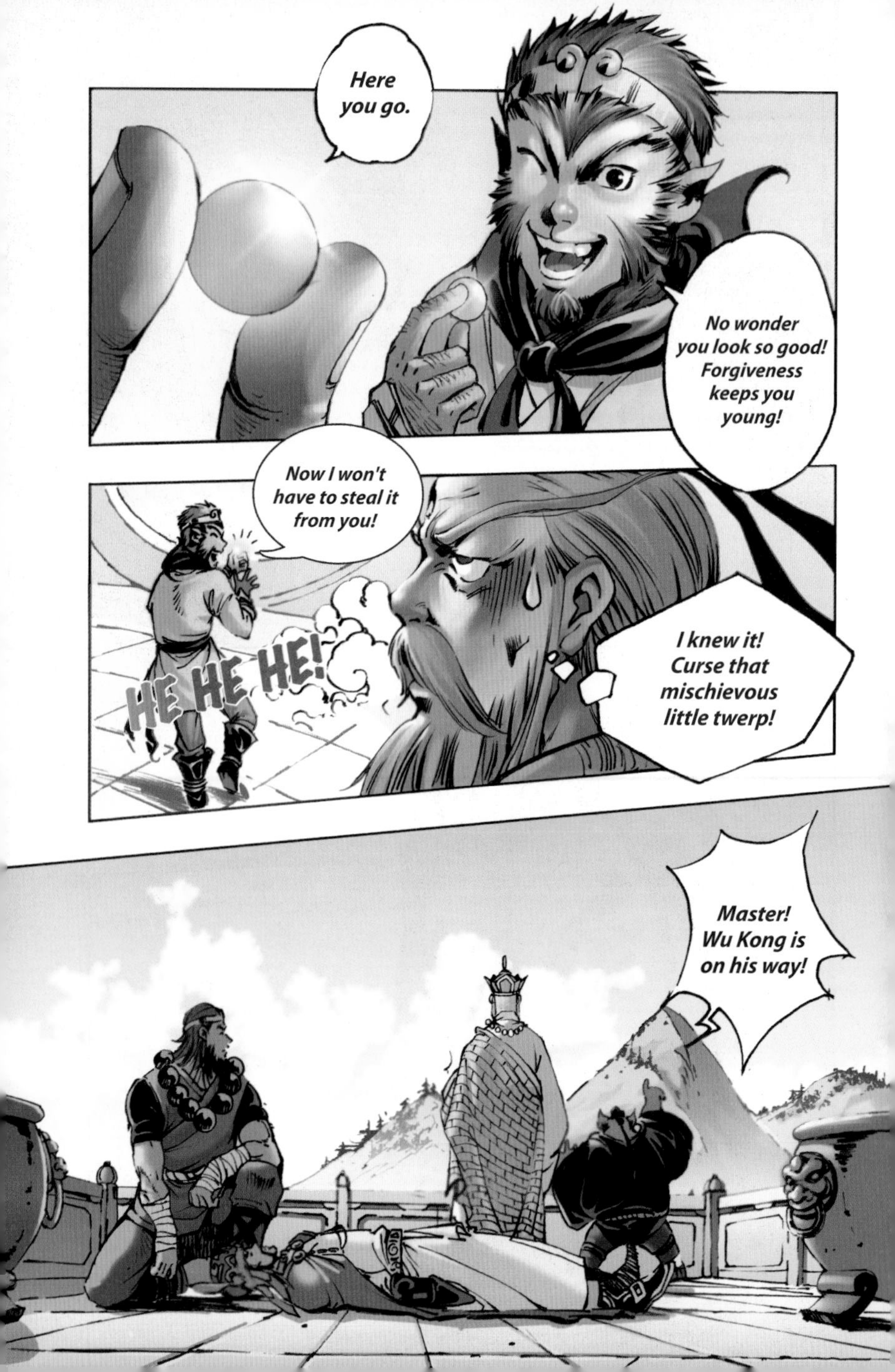
Here you go.
No wonder you look so good! Forgiveness keeps you young!
Now I won't have to steal it from you!
HE HE HE!
I knew it! Curse that mischievous little twerp!
Master! Wu Kong is on his way!

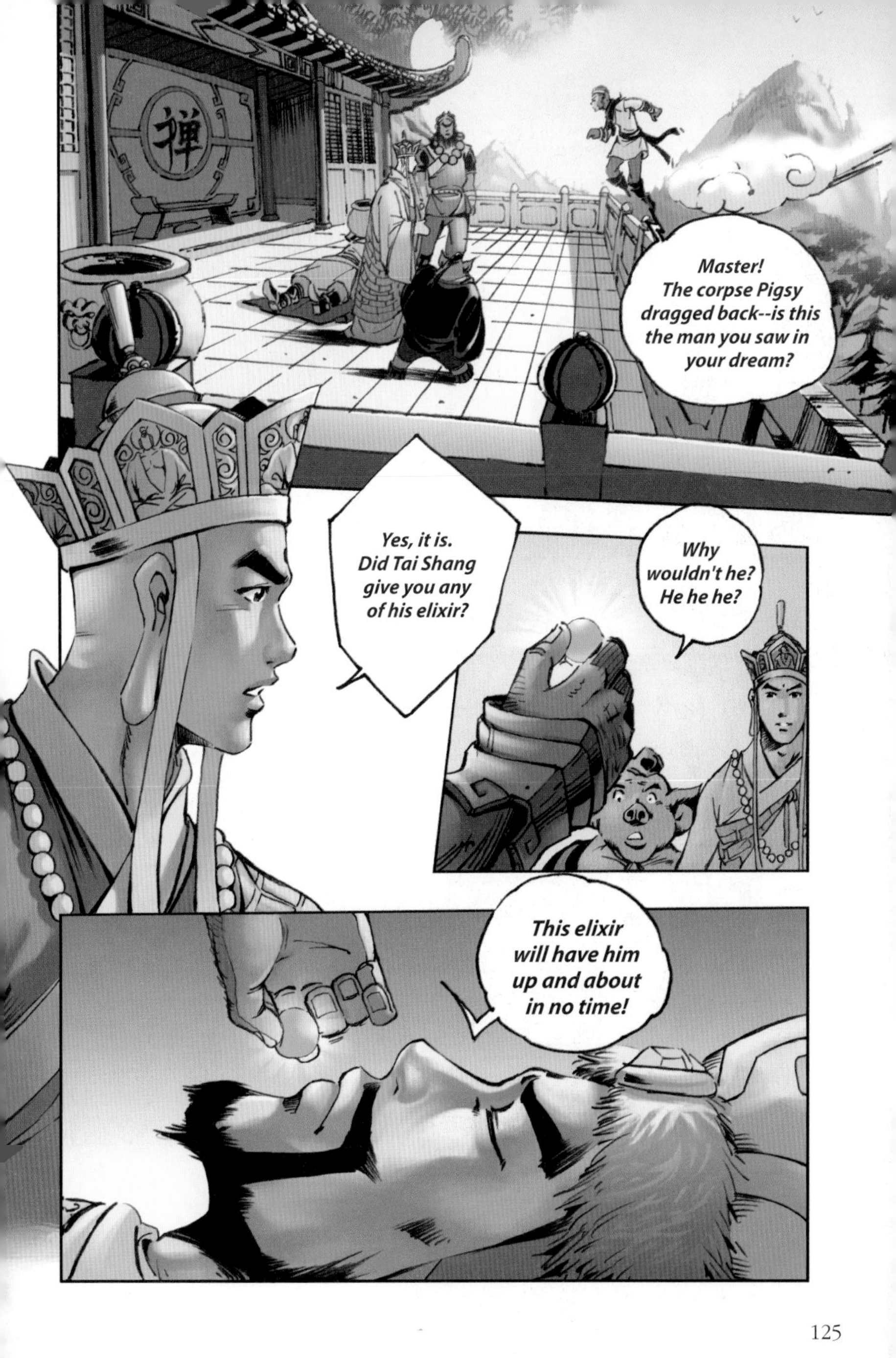
Master! The corpse Pigsy dragged back--is this the man you saw in your dream?
Yes, it is. Did Tai Shang give you any of his elixir?
Why wouldn't he? He he he?
This elixir will have him up and about in no time!

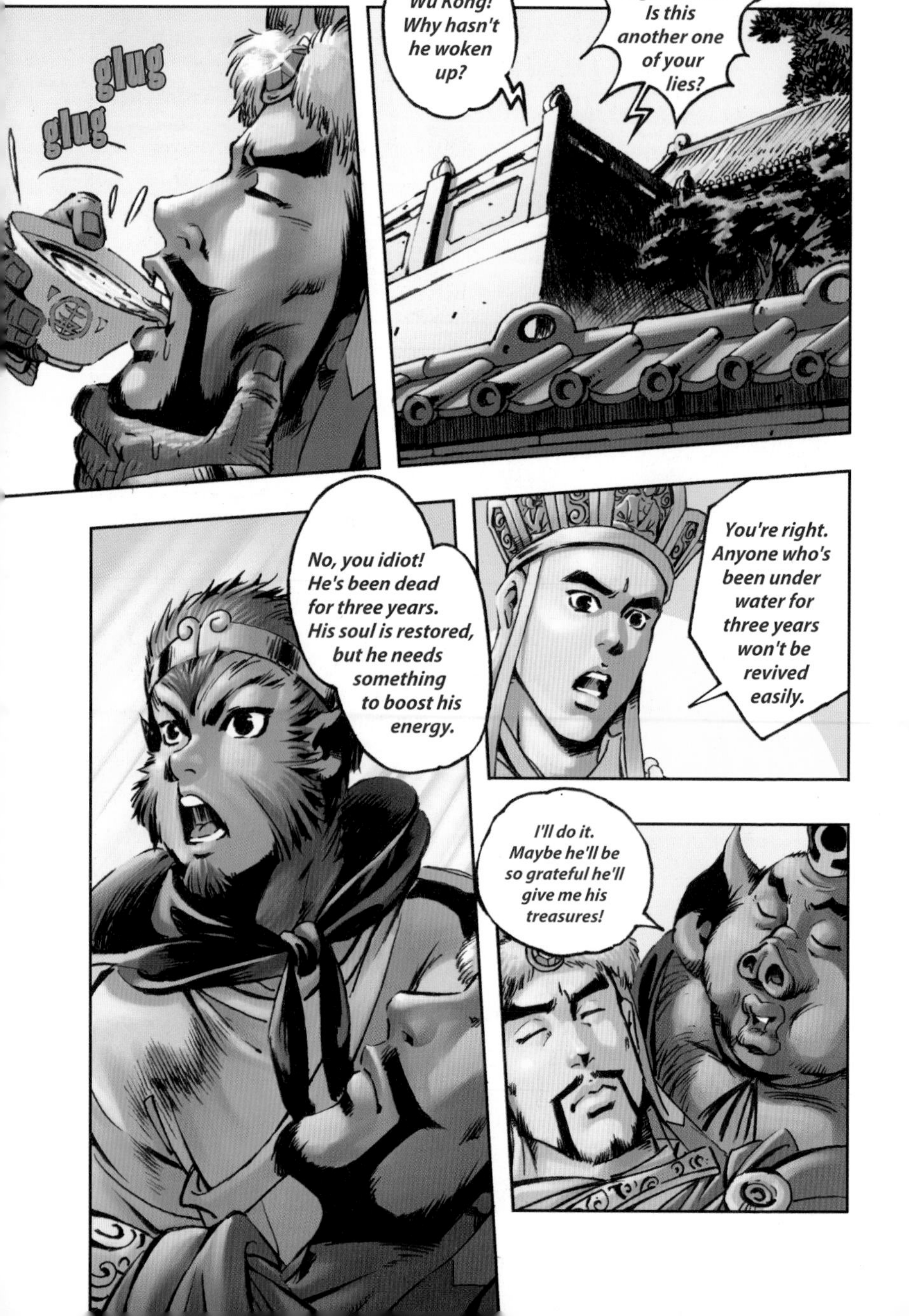
glug
glug
Wu Kong! Why hasn't he woken up?
Aw, big brother! Is this another one of your lies?
No, you idiot! He's been dead for three years. His soul is restored, but he needs something to boost his energy.
You're right. Anyone who's been under water for three years won't be revived easily.
I'll do it. Maybe he'll be so grateful he'll give me his treasures!

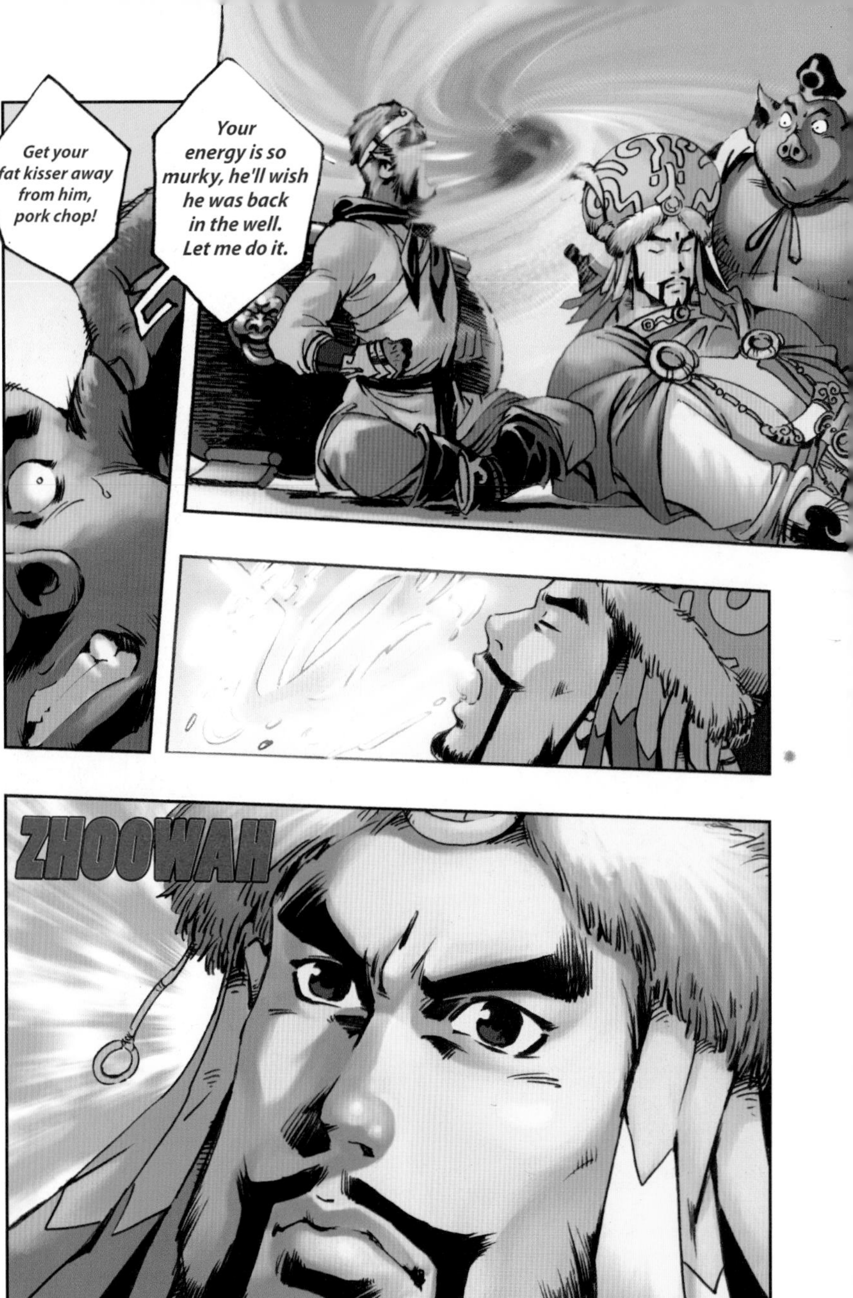
Get your fat kisser away from him, pork chop!
Your energy is so murky, he'll wish he was back in the well. Let me do it.
ZHOOWAH

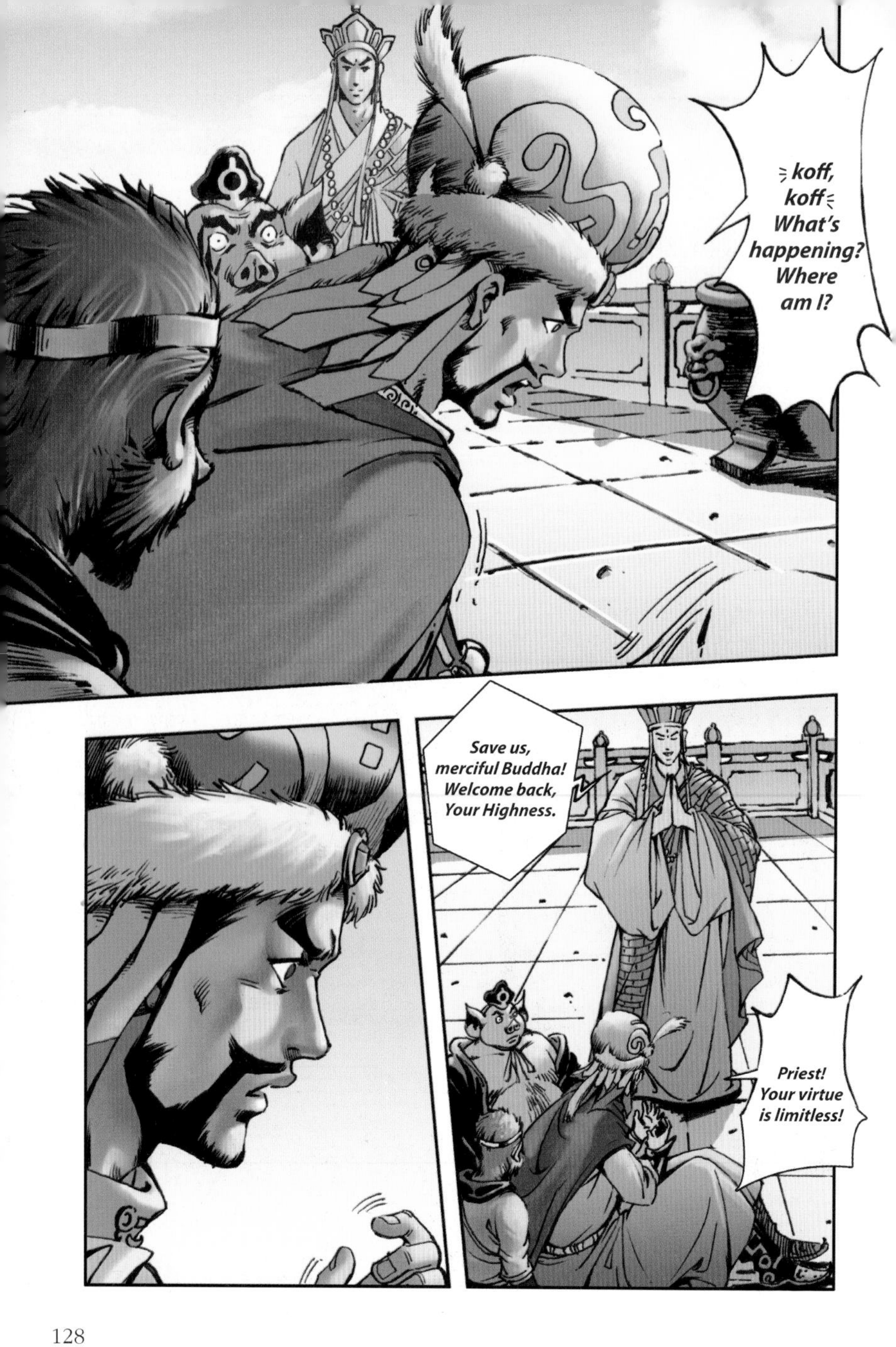
koff, koff What's happening? Where am I?
Save us, merciful Buddha! Welcome back, Your Highness.
Priest! Your virtue is limitless!

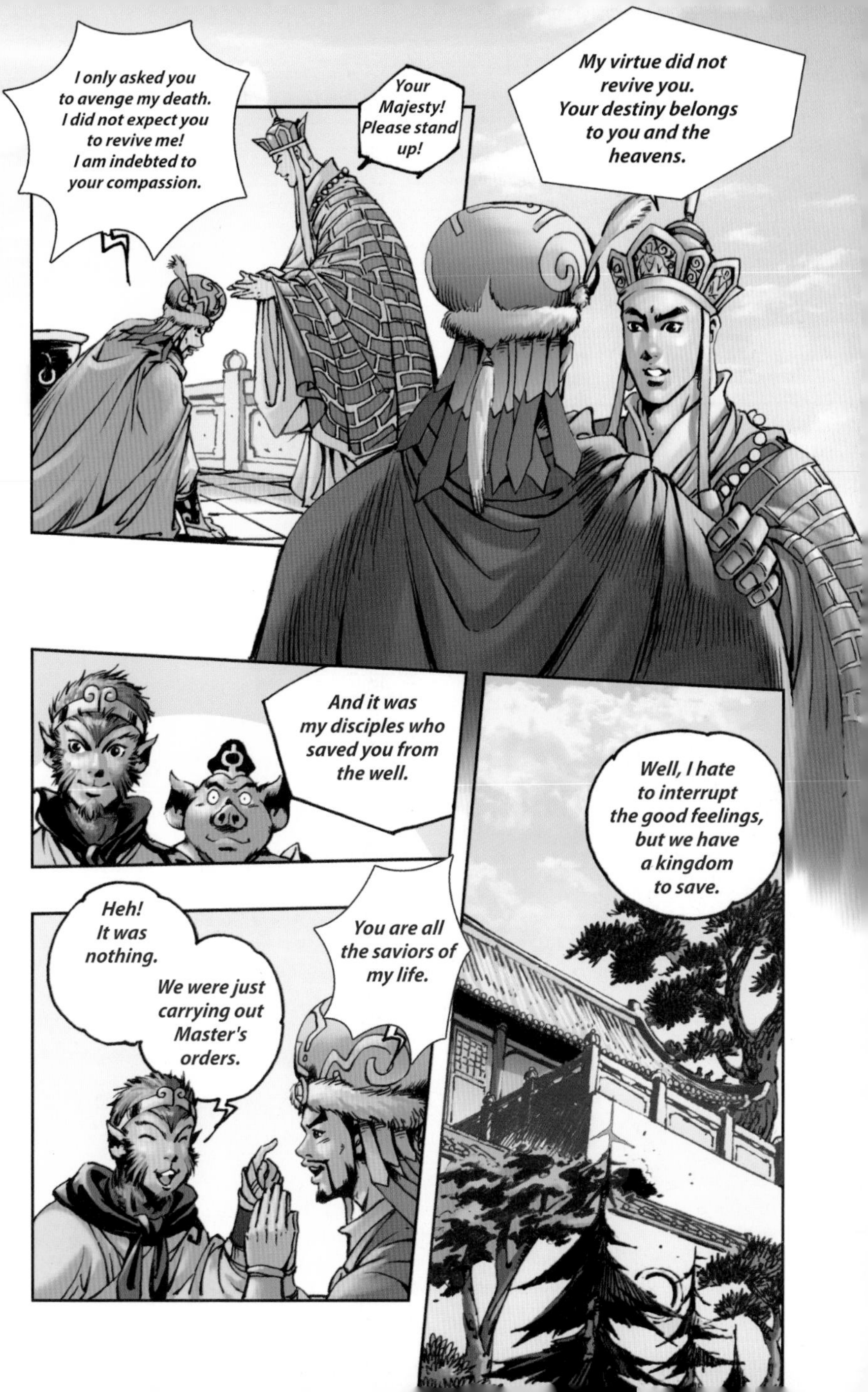
I only asked you to avenge my death. I did not expect you to revive me! I am indebted to your compassion.
Your Majesty! Please stand up!
My virtue did not revive you. Your destiny belongs to you and the heavens.
And it was my disciples who saved you from the well.
Well, I hate to interrupt the good feelings, but we have a kingdom to save.
Heh! It was nothing.
We were just carrying out Master's orders.
You are all the saviors of my life.

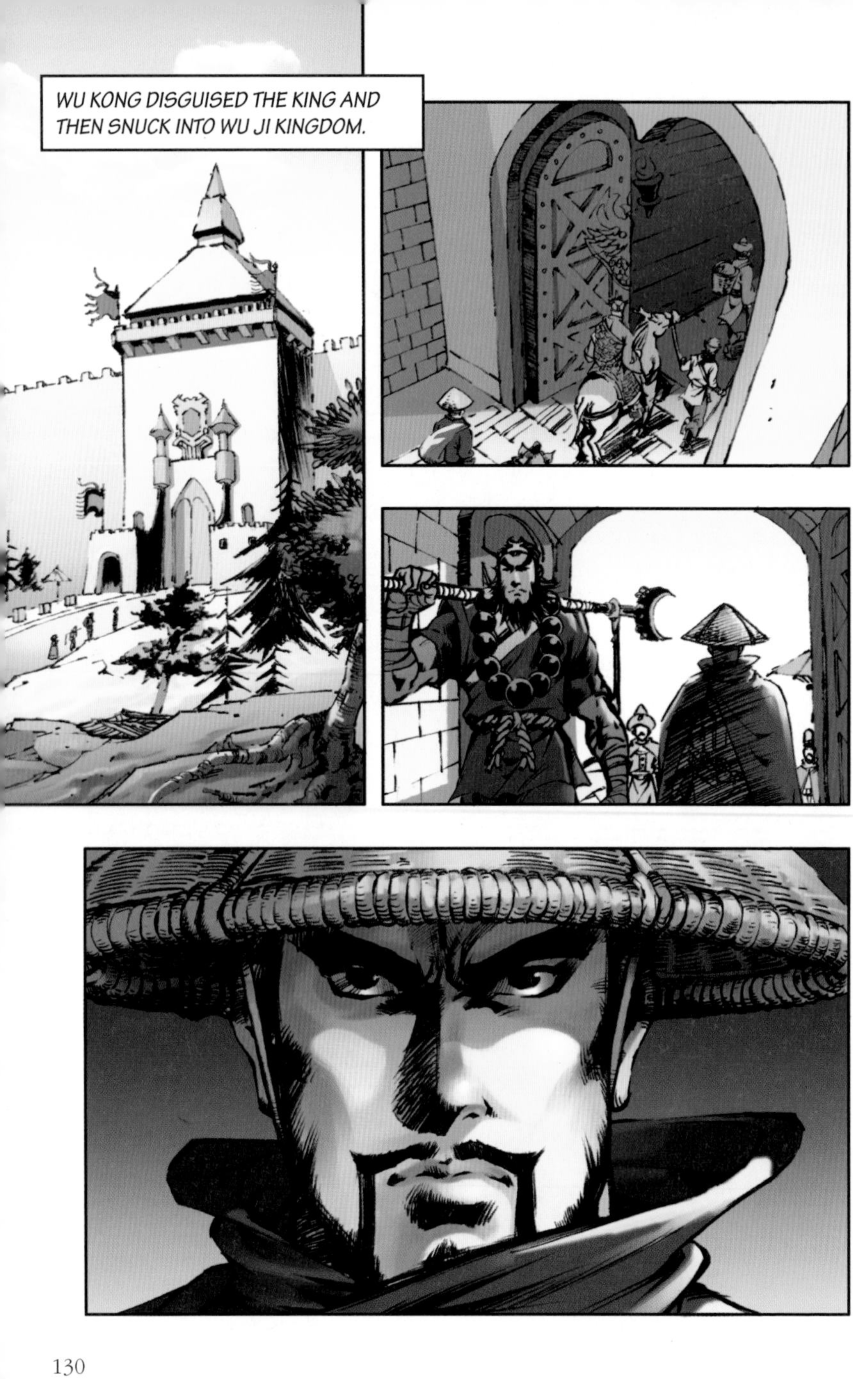
WU KONG DISGUISED THE KING AND
THEN SNUCK INTO WU JI KINGDOM.

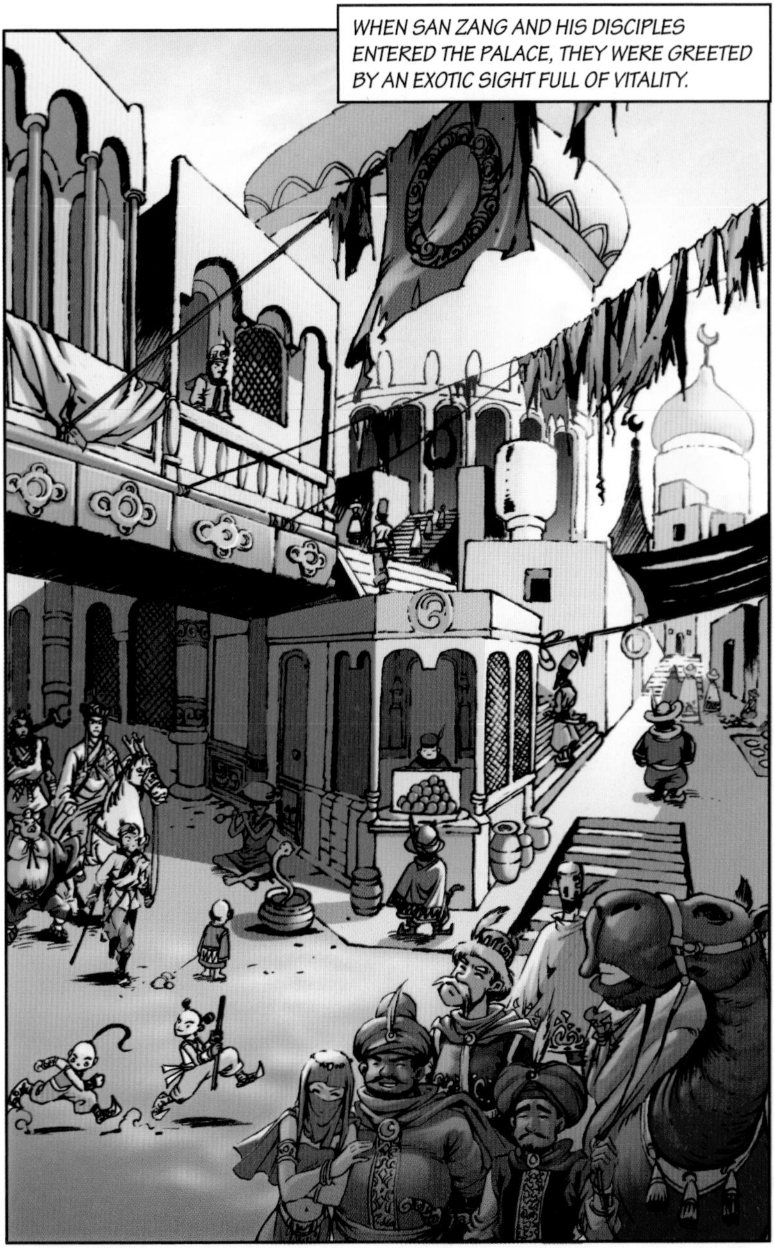
WHEN SAN ZANG AND HIS DISCIPLES ENTERED THE PALACE, THEY WERE GREETED BY AN EXOTIC SIGHT FULL OF VITALITY.

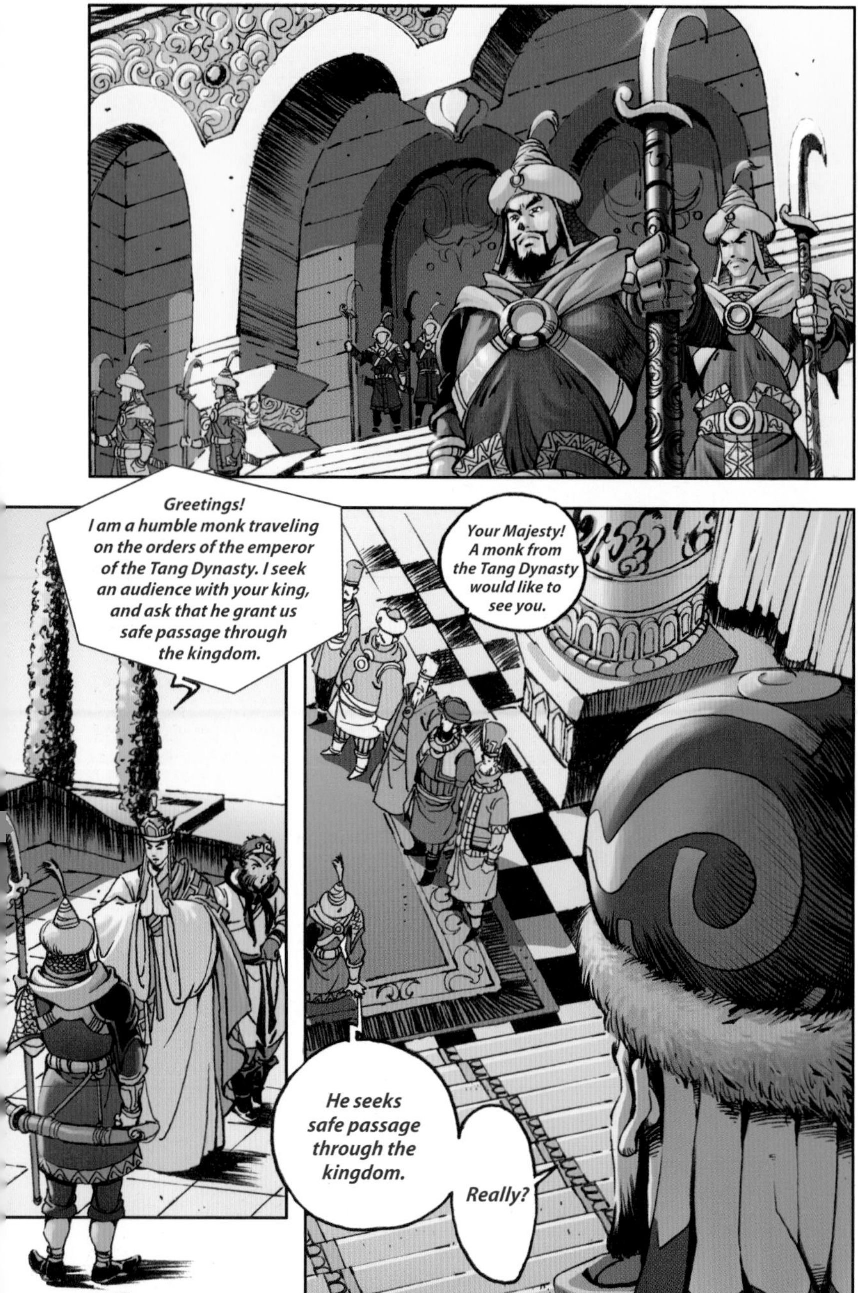
Greetings! I am a humble monk traveling on the orders of the emperor of the Tang Dynasty. I seek an audience with your king, and ask that he grant us safe passage through the kingdom.
Your Majesty! A monk from the Tang Dynasty would like to see you.
He seeks safe passage through the kingdom.
Really?

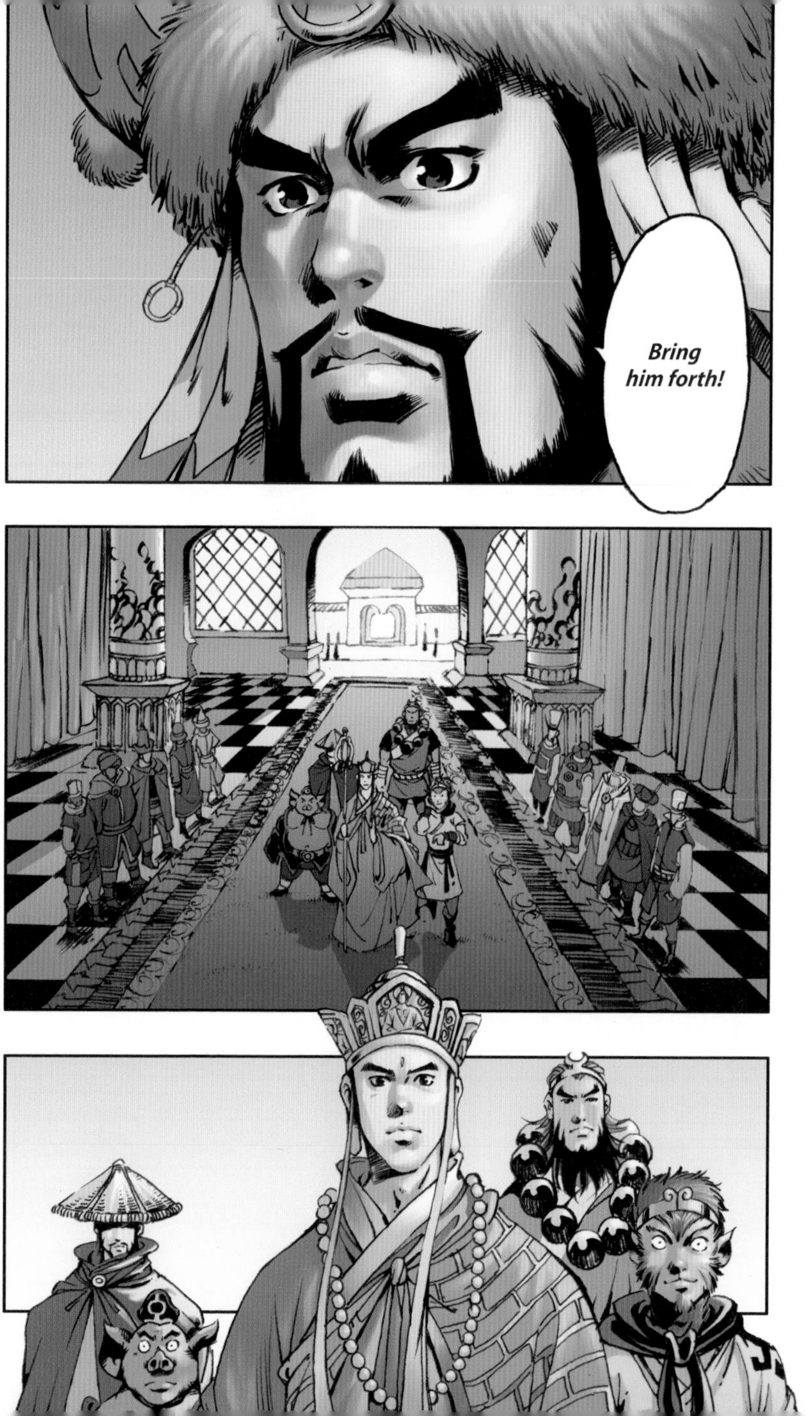
Bring him forth!

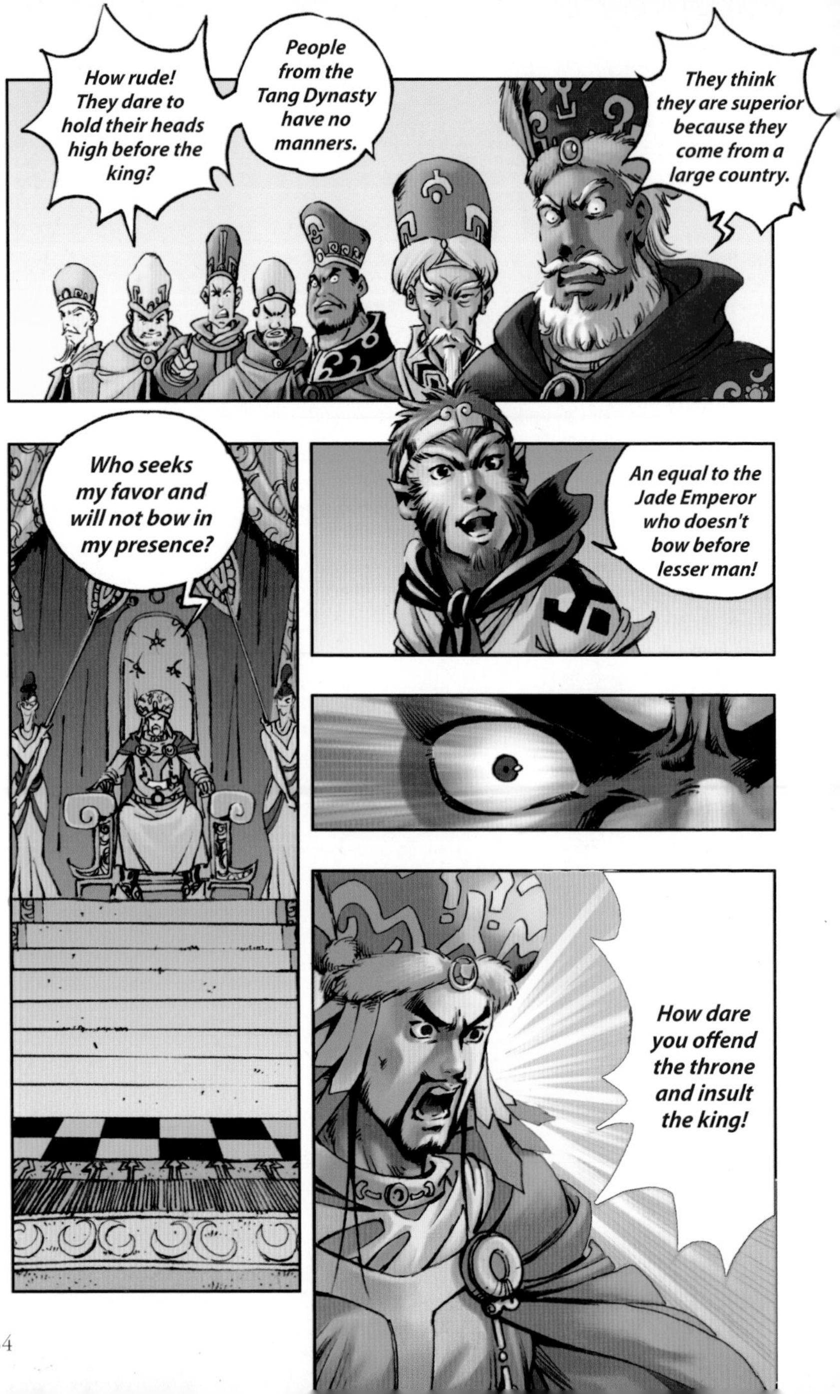
How rude! They dare to hold their heads high before the king?
People from the Tang Dynasty have no manners.
They think they are superior because they come from a large country.
Who seeks my favor and will not bow in my presence?
An equal to the Jade Emperor who doesn't bow before lesser man!
How dare you offend the throne and insult the king!

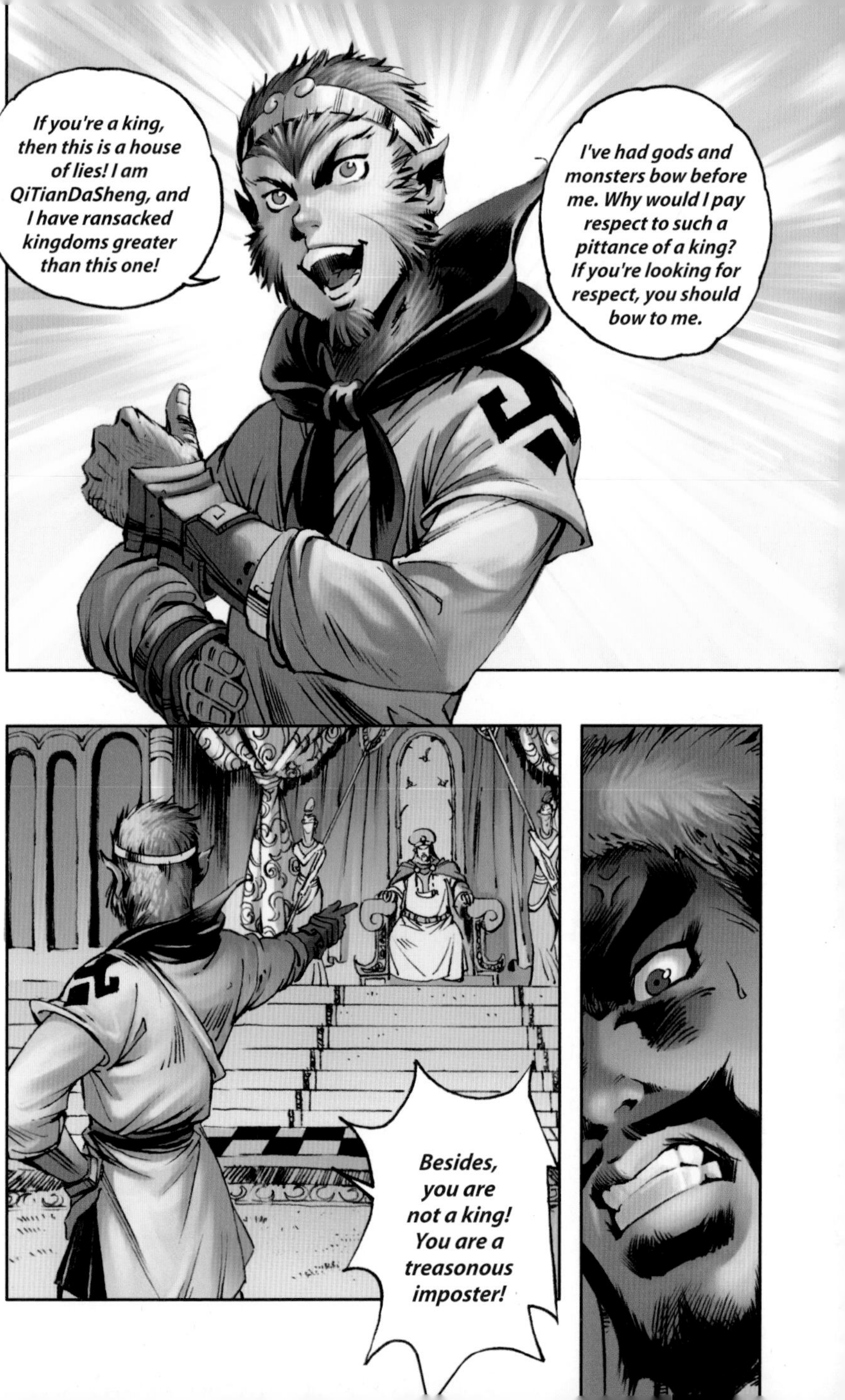
If you're a king, then this is a house of lies! I am QiTianDaSheng, and I have ransacked kingdoms greater than this one!
I've had gods and monsters bow before me. Why would I pay respect to such a pittance of a king? If you're looking for respect, you should bow to me.
Besides, you are not a king! You are a treasonous imposter!

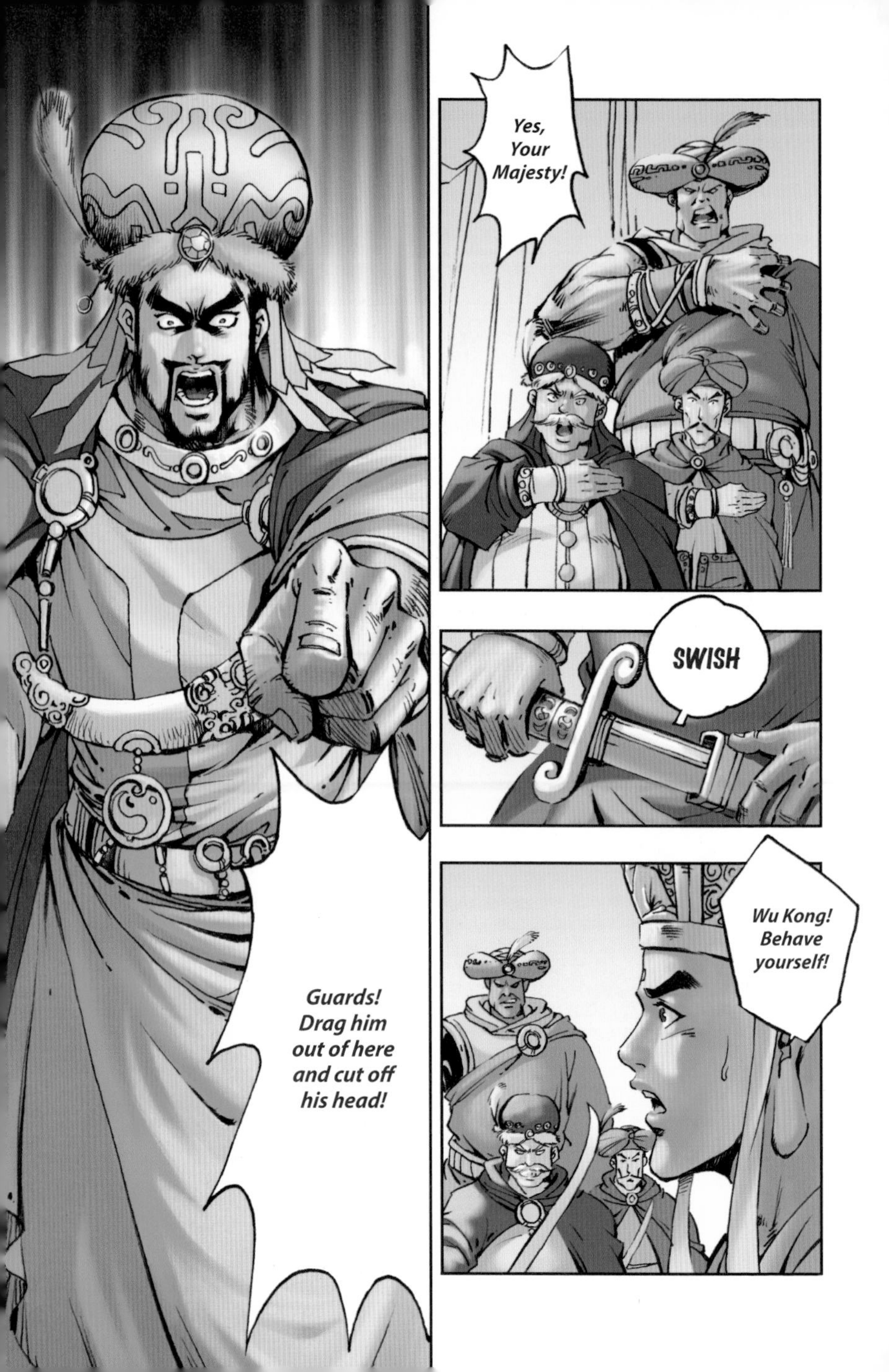
Guards! Drag him out of here and cut off his head!
Yes, Your Majesty!
SWISH
Wu Kong! Behave yourself!

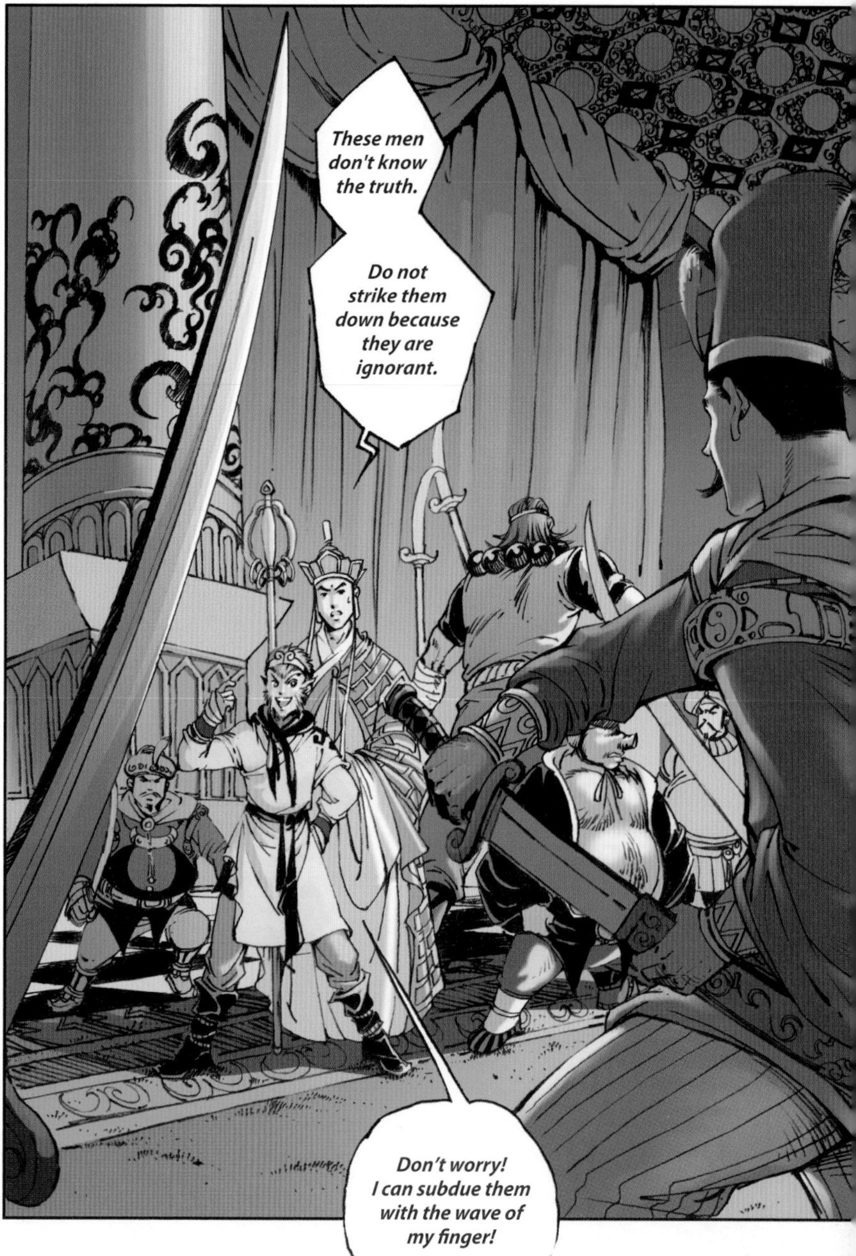
These men don't know the truth.
Do not strike them down because they are ignorant.
Don't worry! I can subdue them with the wave of my finger!

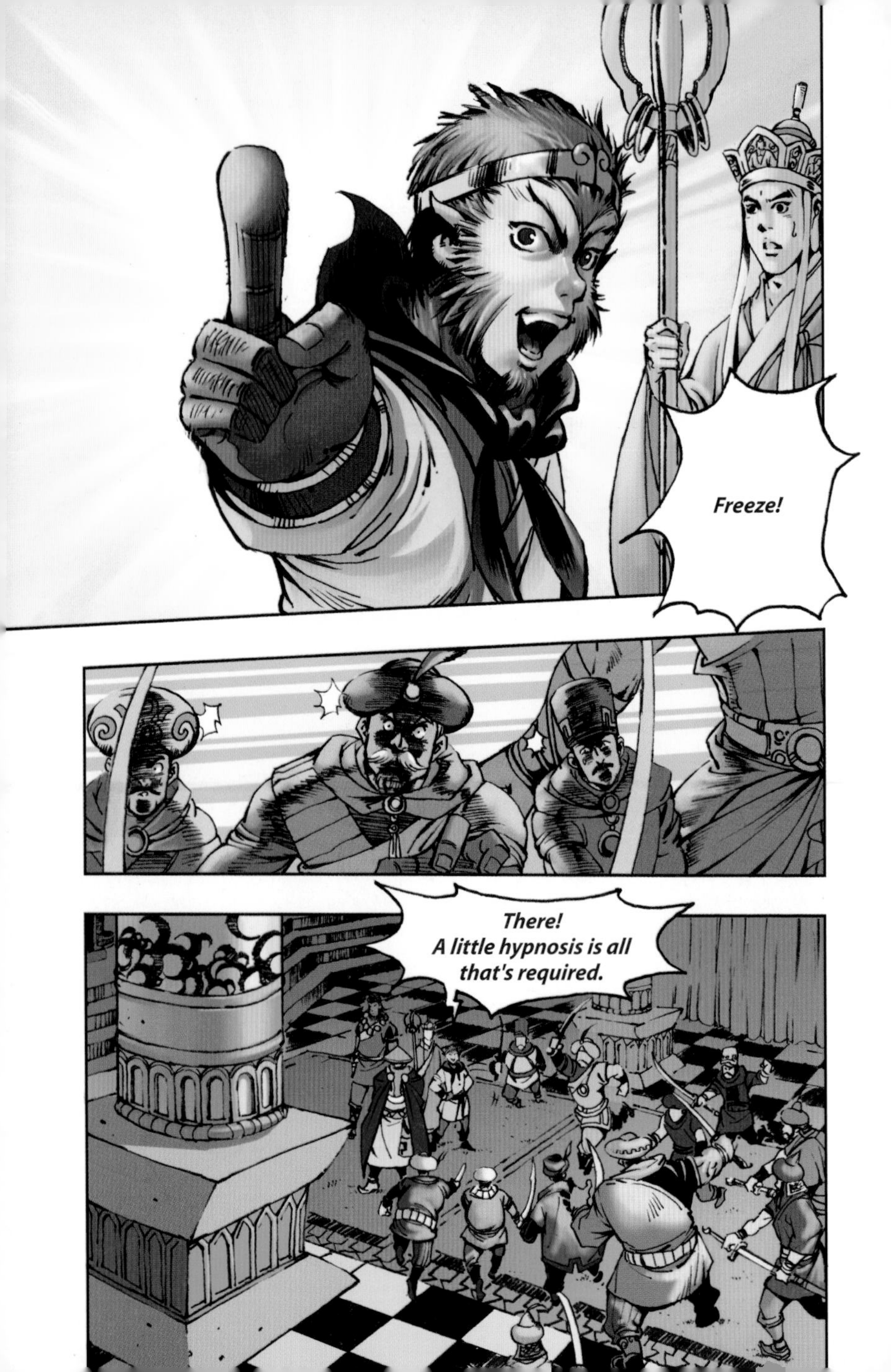
Freeze!
There!
A little hypnosis is all
that's required.

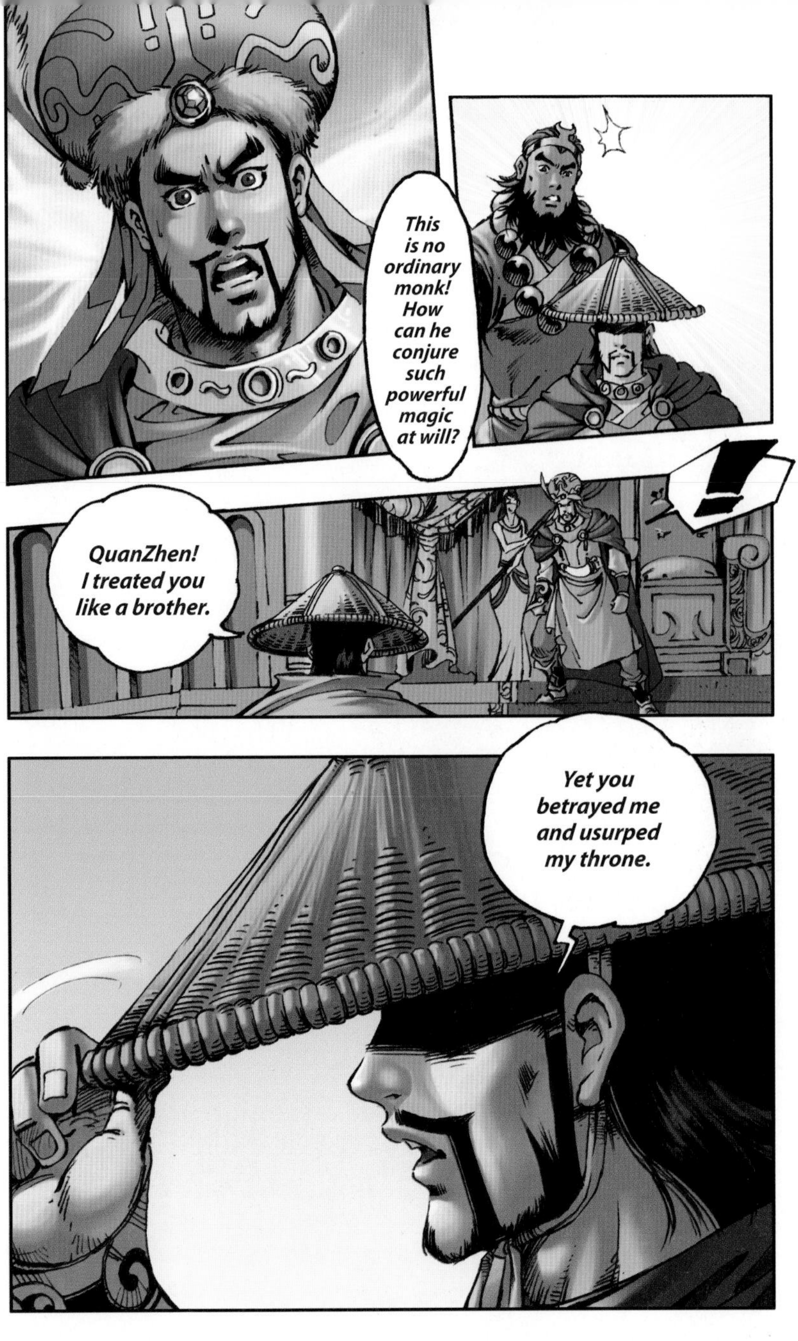
This is no ordinary monk! How can he conjure such powerful magic at will?
QuanZhen! I treated you like a brother.
Yet you betrayed me and usurped my throne.

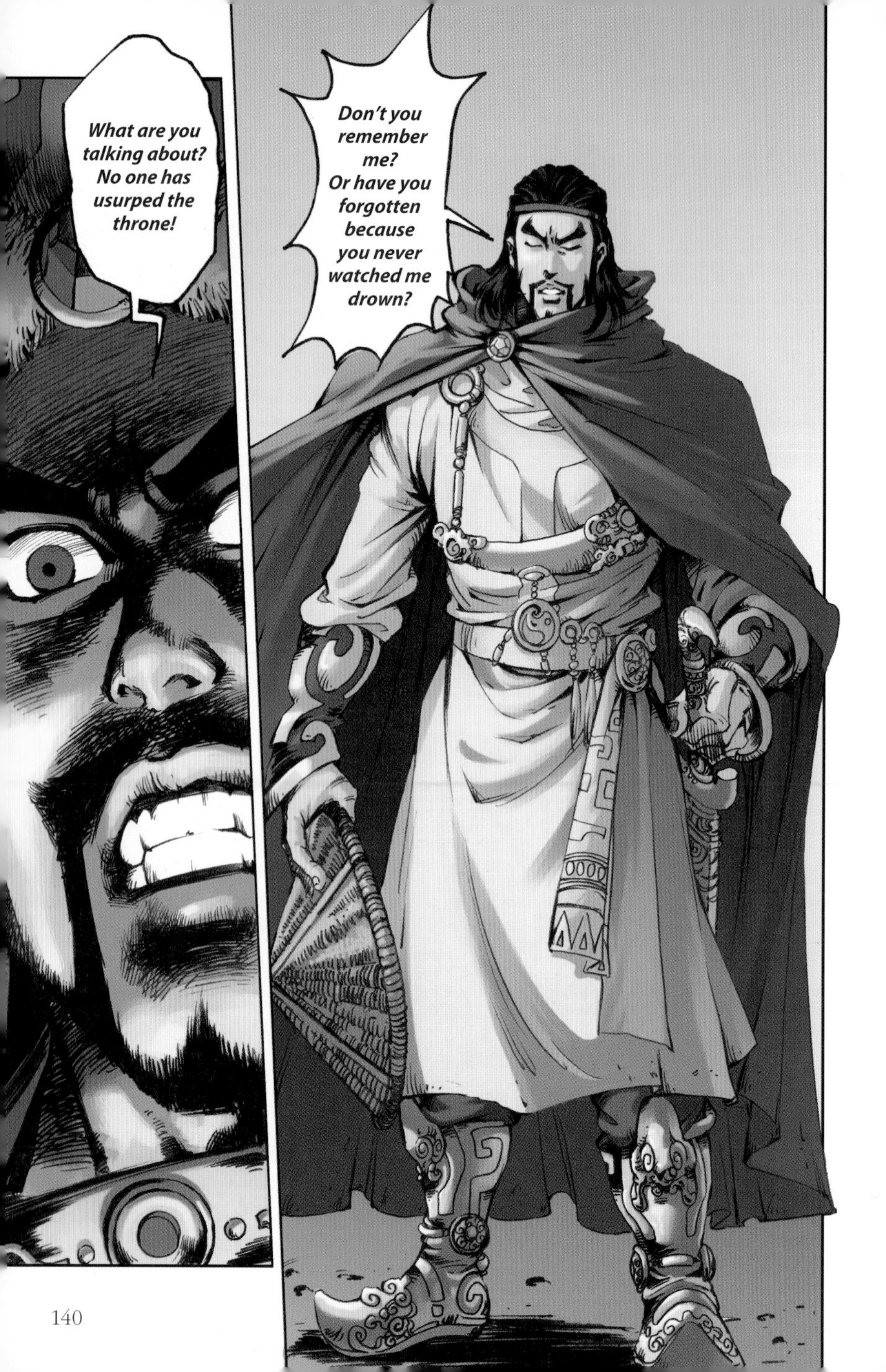
What are you talking about? No one has usurped the throne!
Don't you remember me? Or have you forgotten because you never watched me drown?

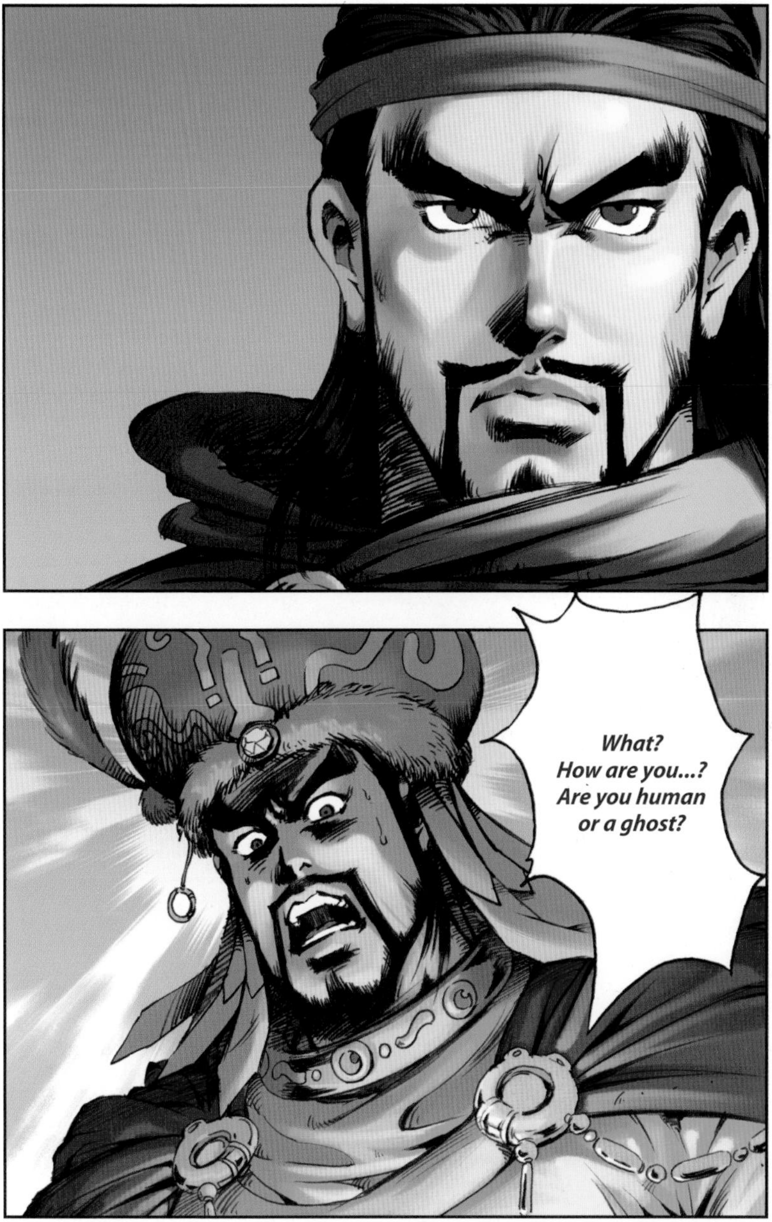
What?
How are you...?
Are you human
or a ghost?

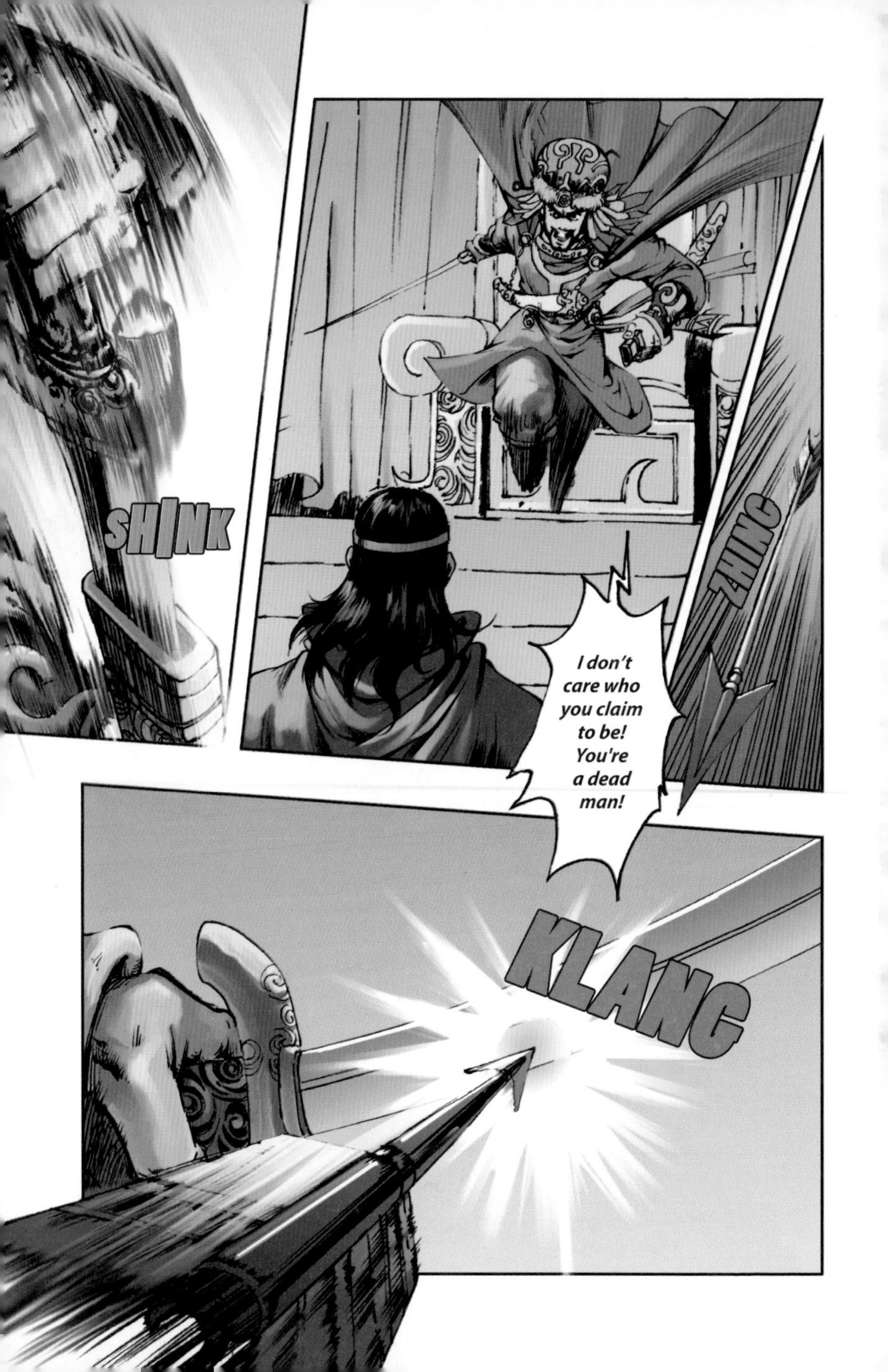
SHIINK
I don't care who you claim to be! You're a dead man!
ZHING
KLANG

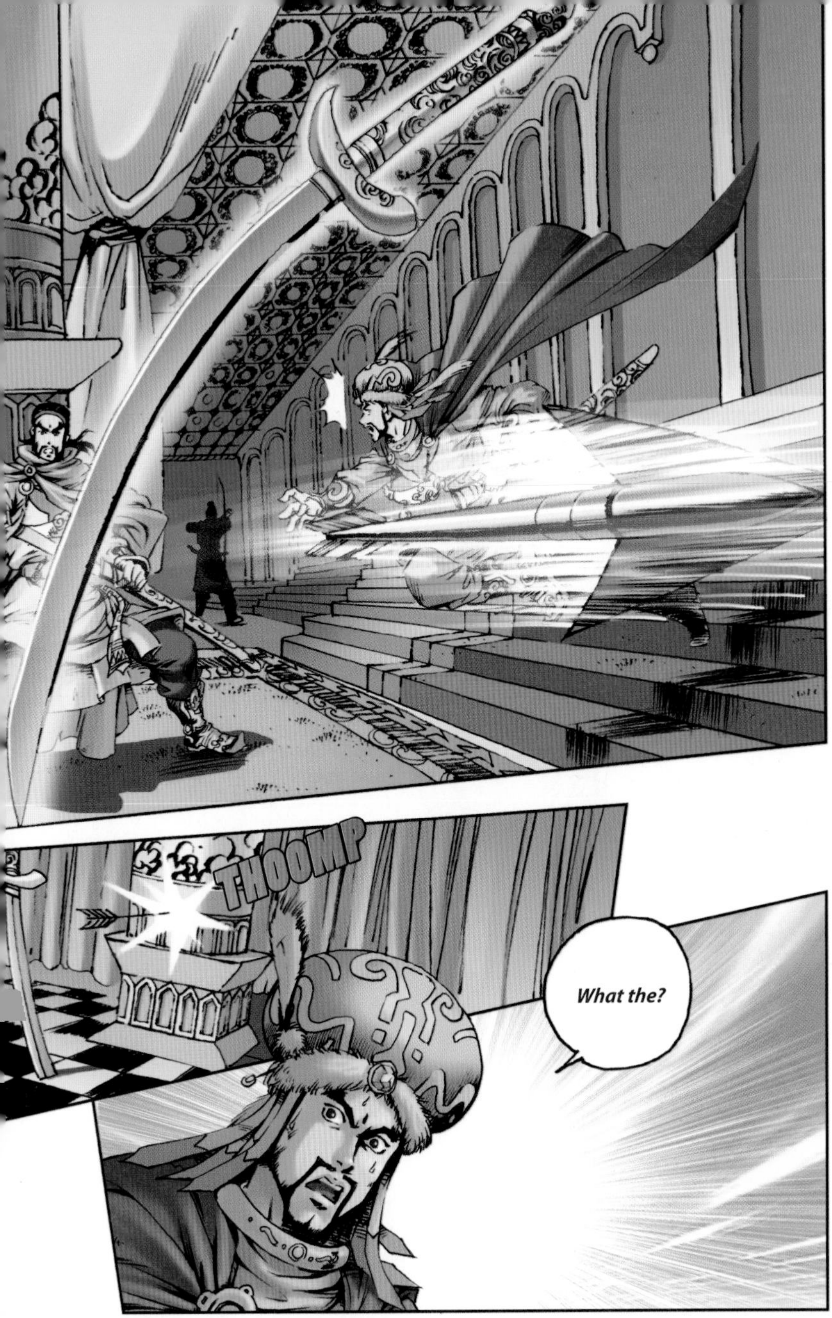
THOOMP
What the?

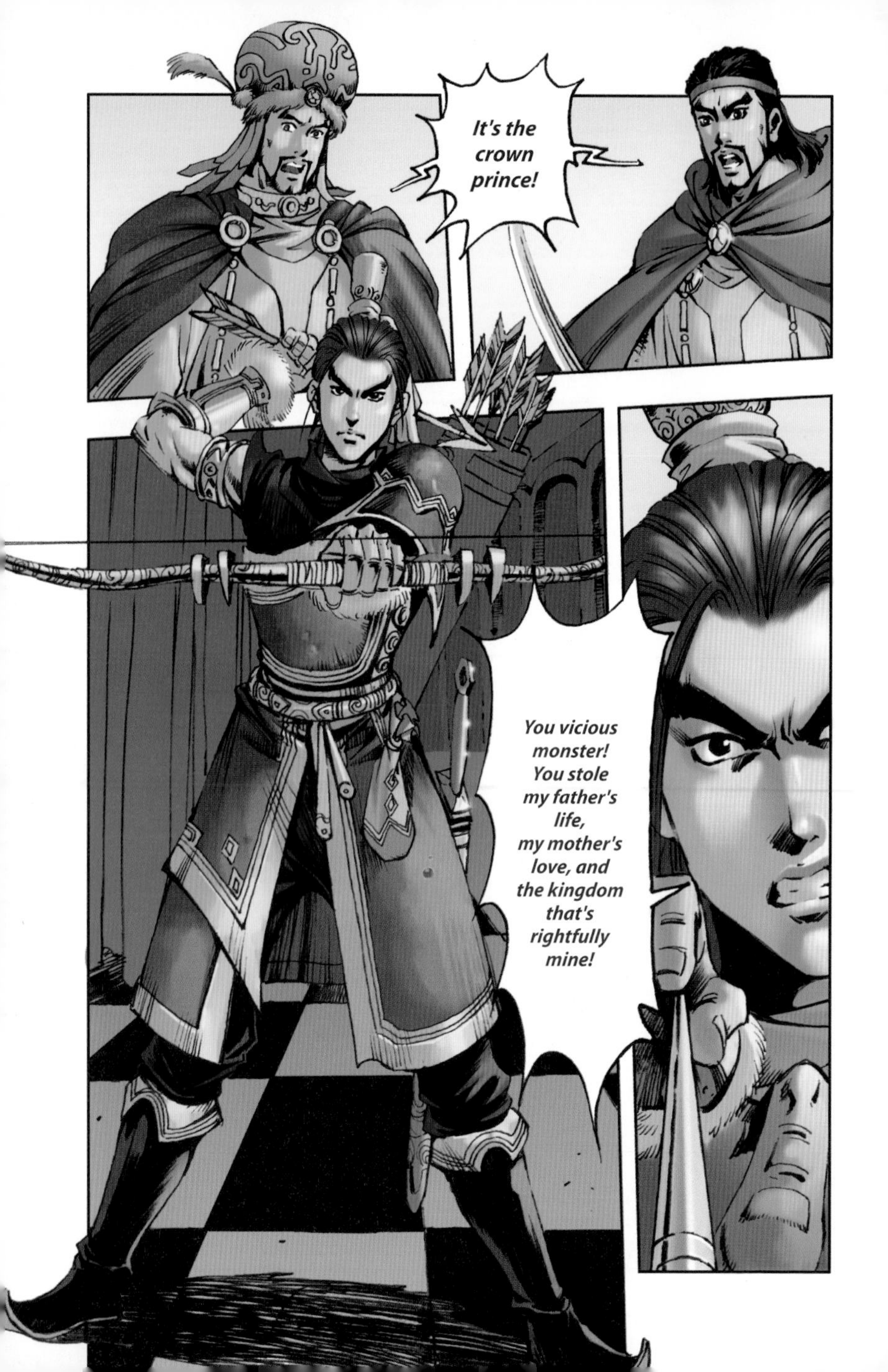
It's the crown prince!
You vicious monster! You stole my father's life, my mother's love, and the kingdom that's rightfully mine!

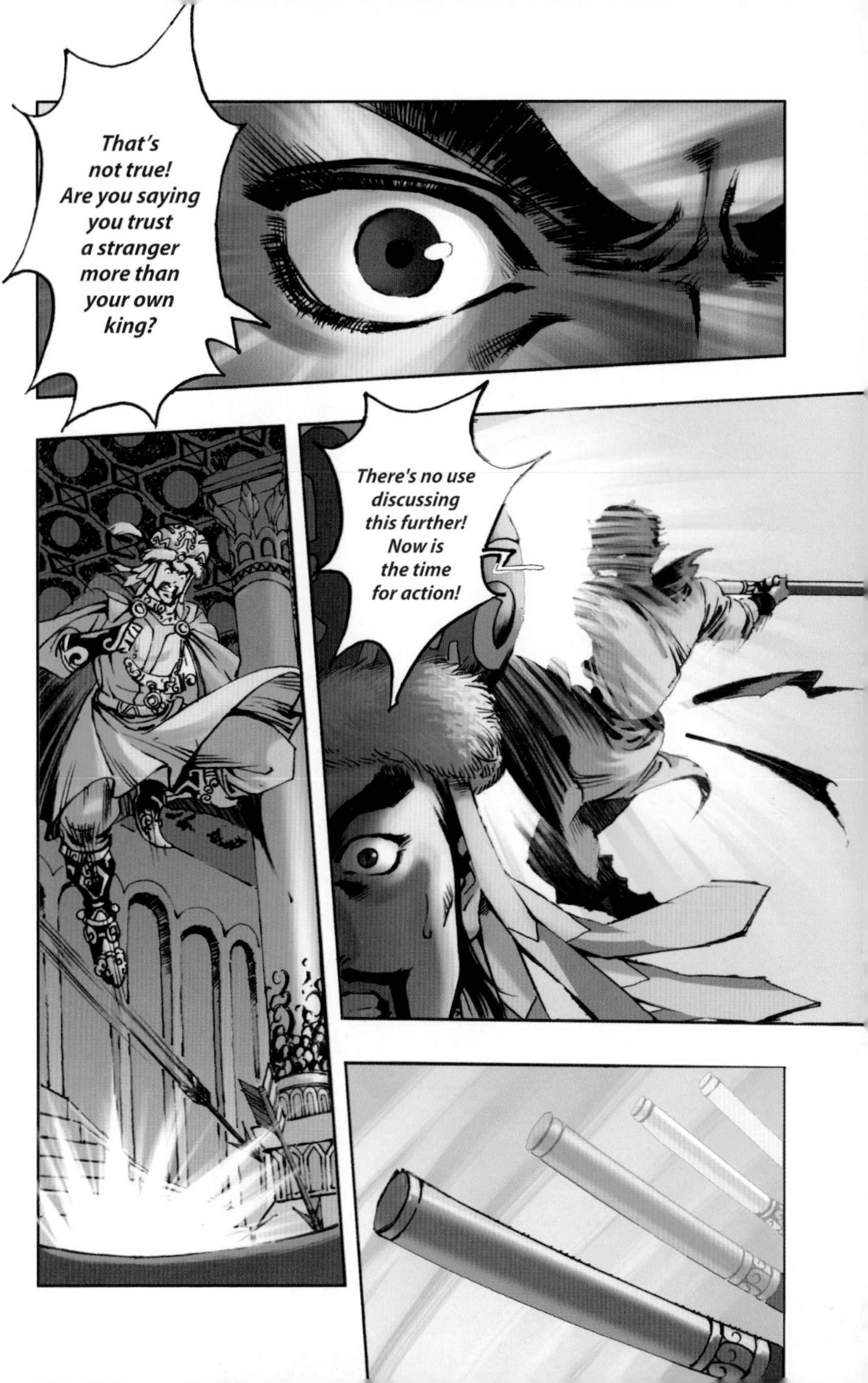
That's not true! Are you saying you trust a stranger more than your own king?
There's no use discussing this further! Now is the time for action!

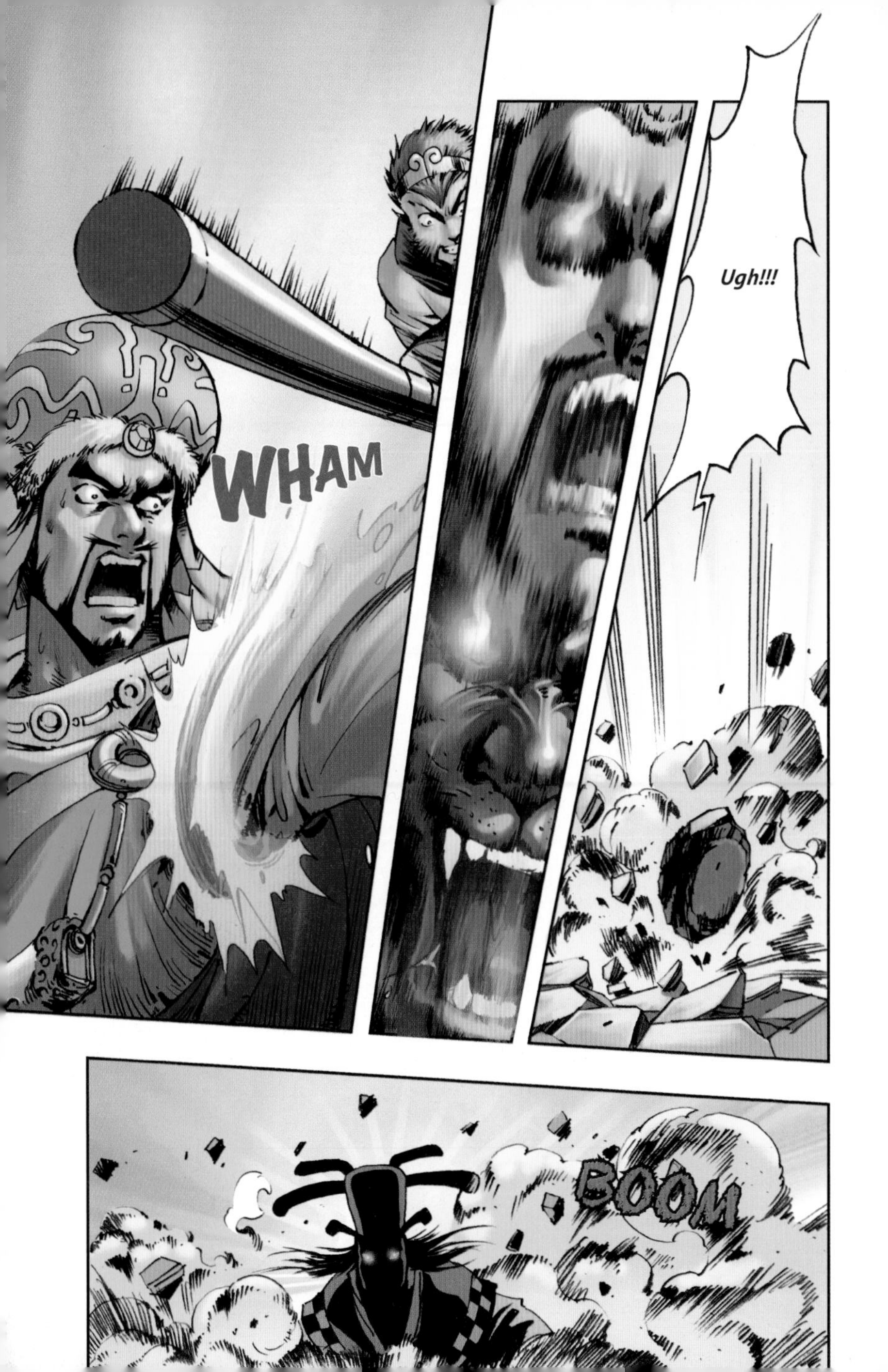
WHAM
Ugh!!!
BOOM

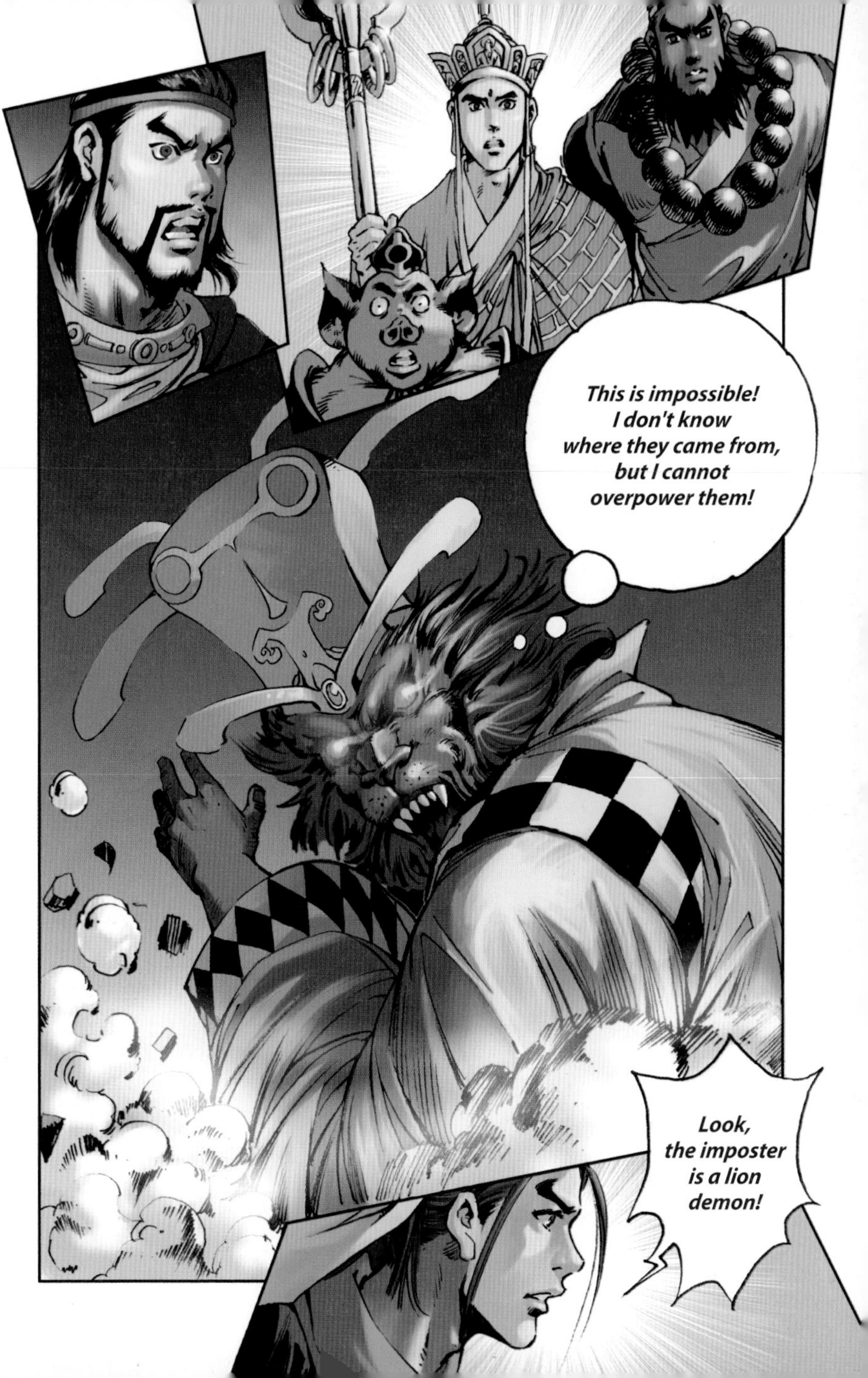
This is impossible! I don't know where they came from, but I cannot overpower them!
Look, the imposter is a lion demon!

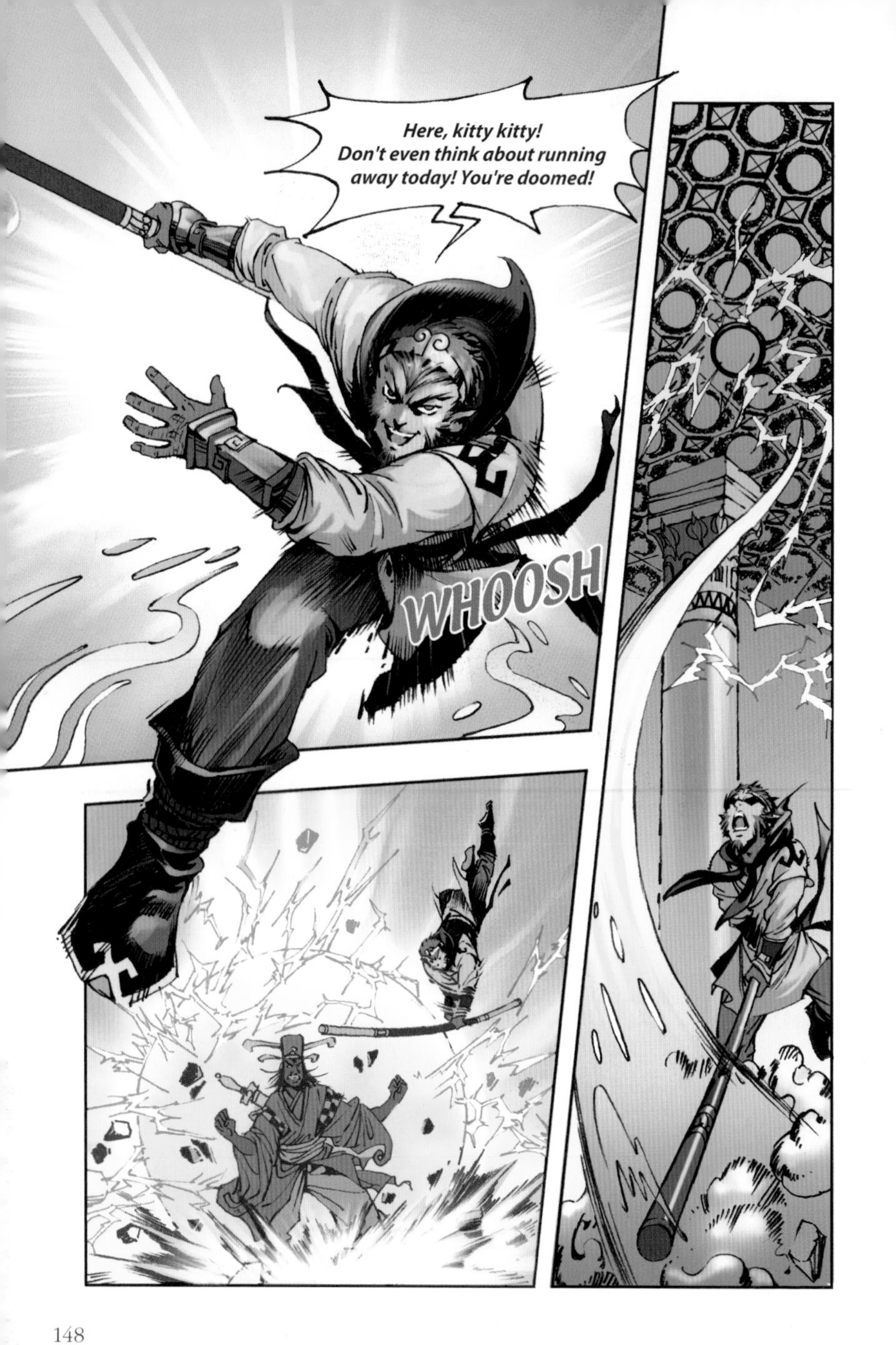
Here, kitty kitty!
Don't even think about running away today! You're doomed!
WHOOSH

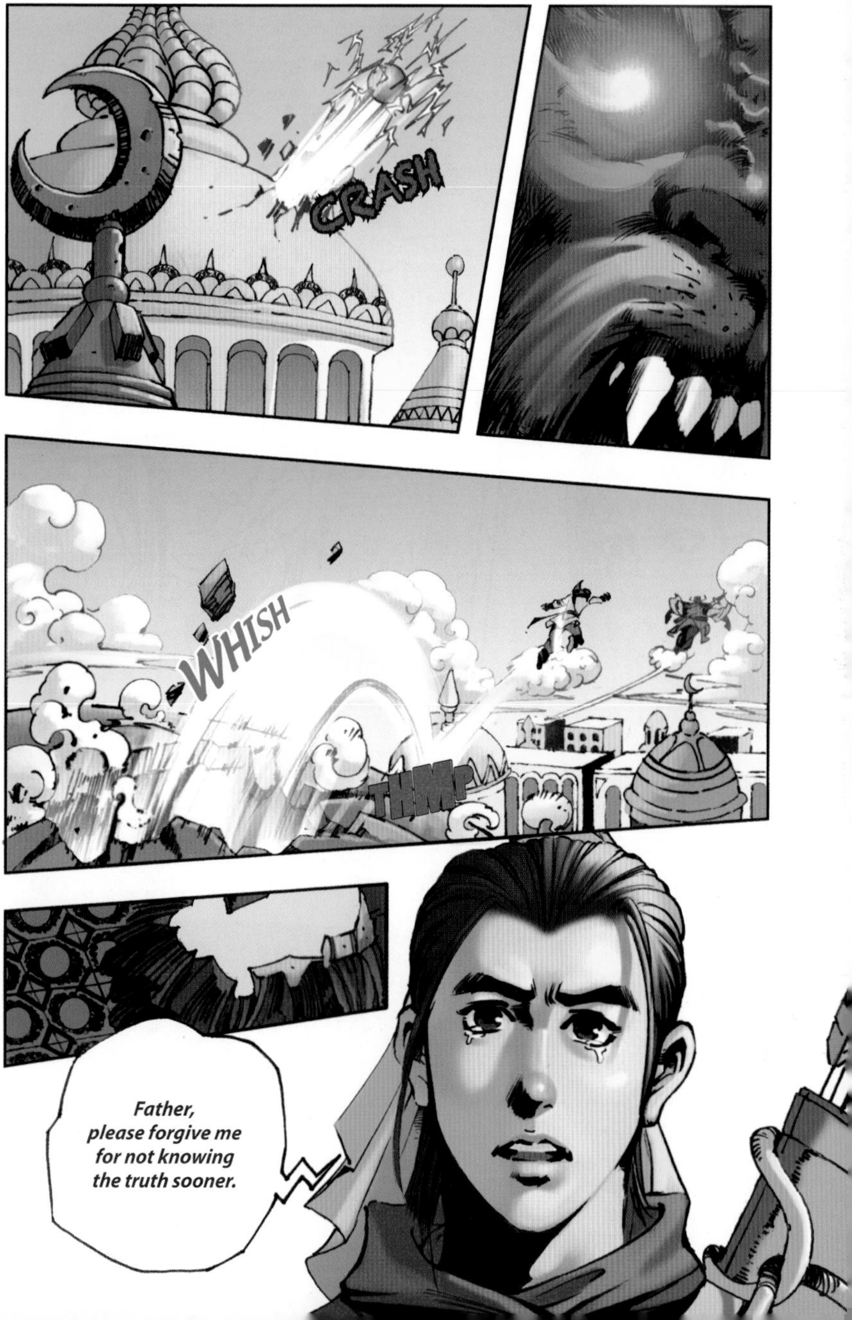
CRASH
WHISH
THMP
Father,
please forgive me
for not knowing
the truth sooner.

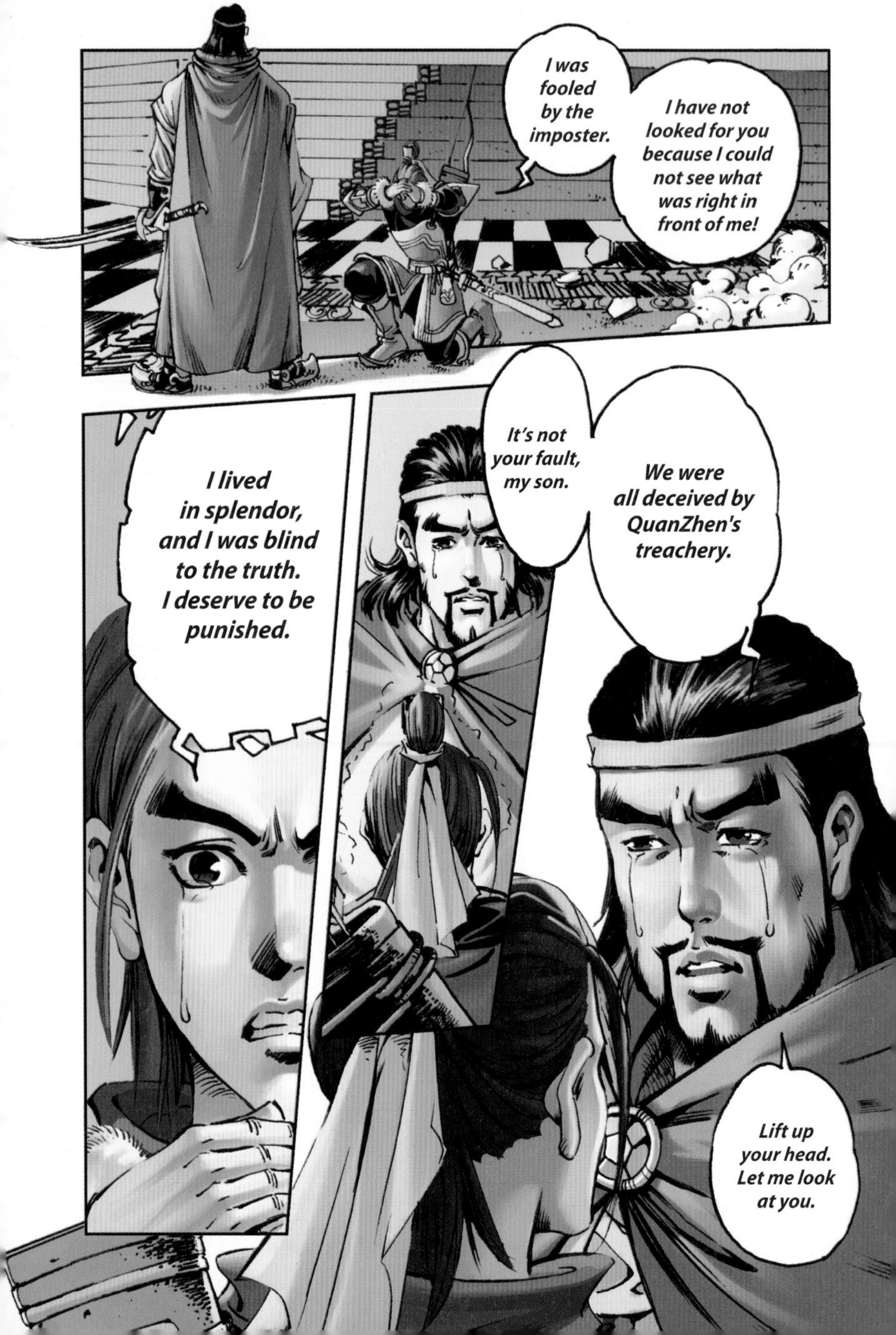
I was fooled by the imposter.
I have not looked for you because I could not see what was right in front of me!
I lived in splendor, and I was blind to the truth. I deserve to be punished.
It's not your fault, my son.
We were all deceived by QuanZhen's treachery.
Lift up your head. Let me look at you.

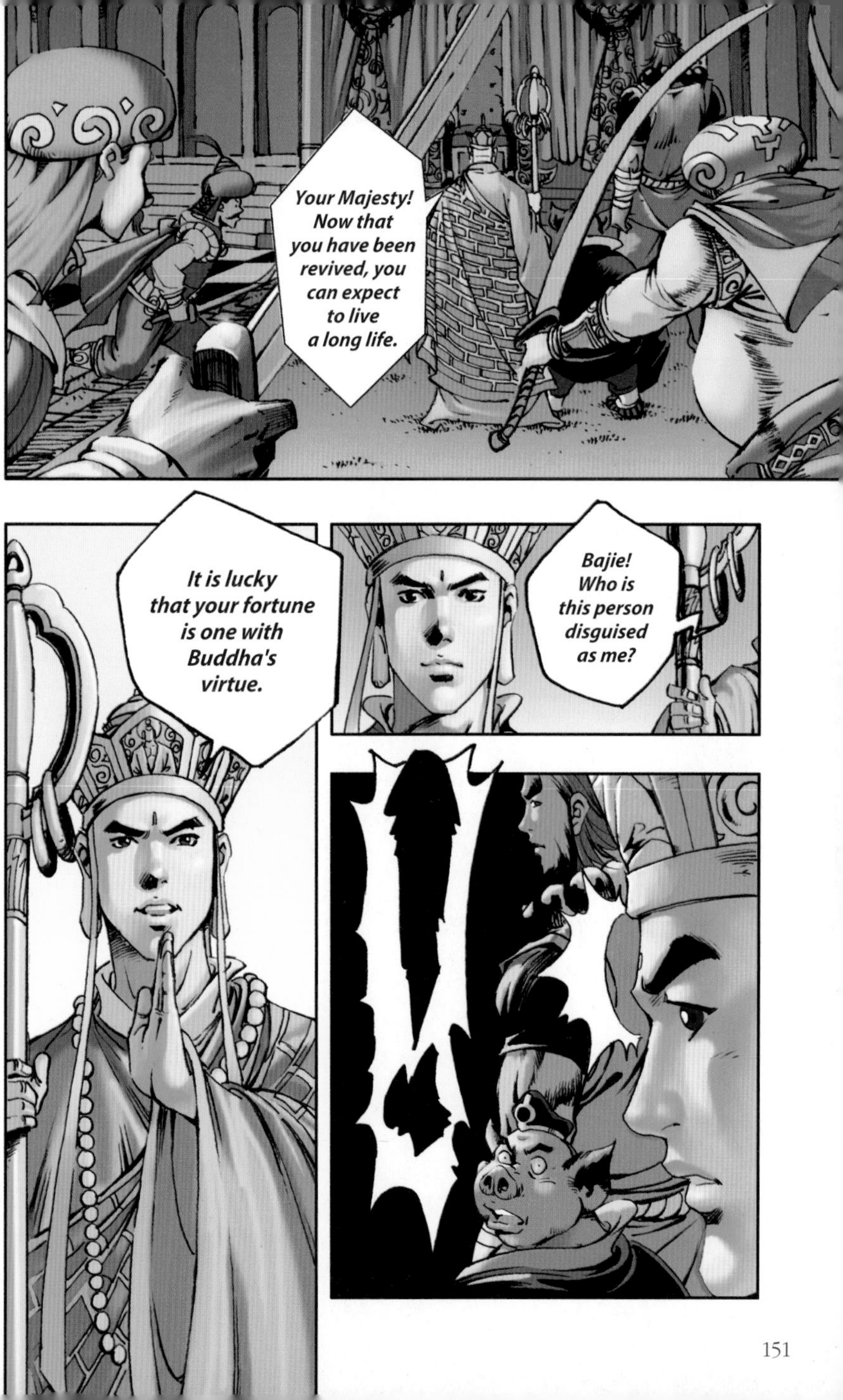
Your Majesty! Now that you have been revived, you can expect to live a long life.
It is lucky that your fortune is one with Buddha's virtue.
Bajie! Who is this person disguised as me?

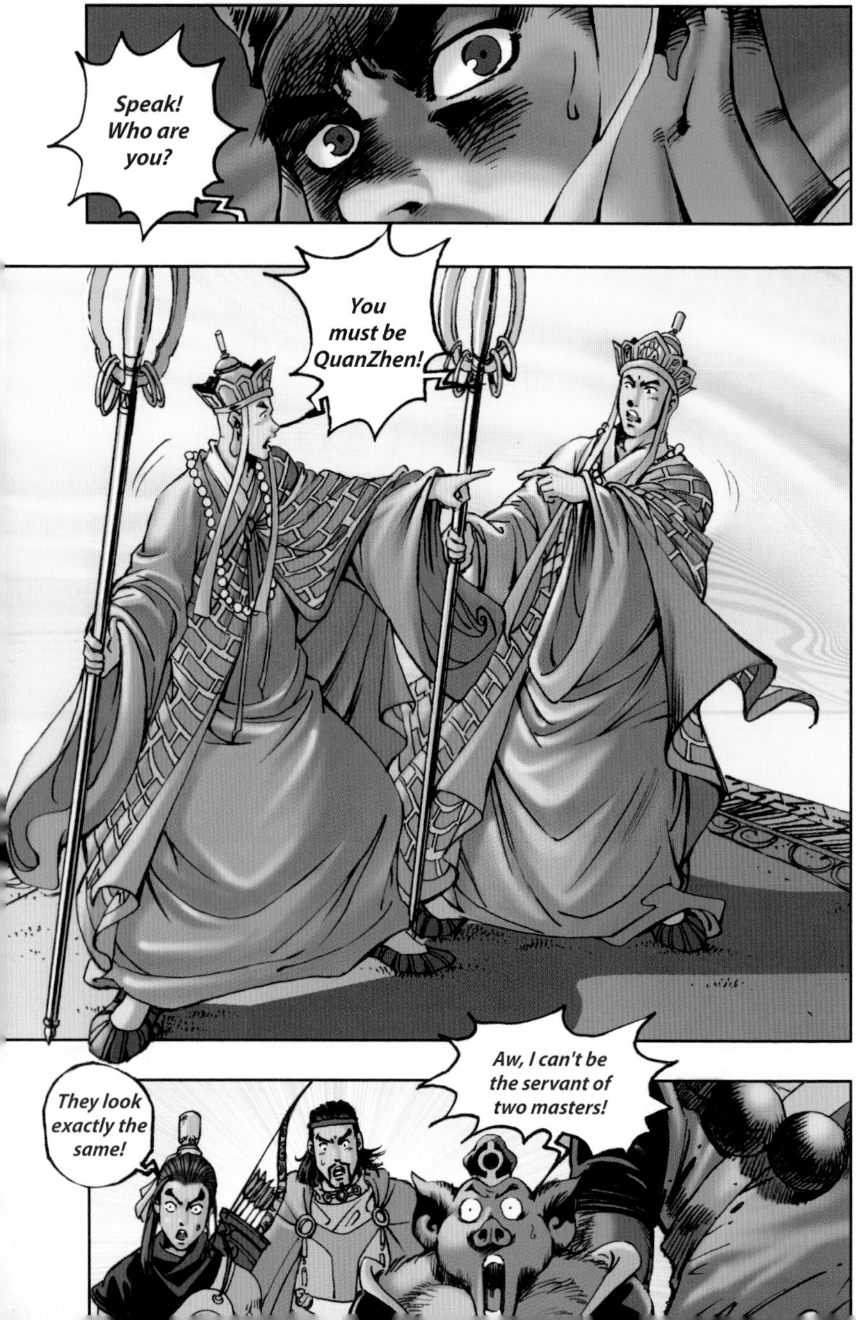
Speak! Who are you?
You must be QuanZhen!
Aw, I can't be the servant of two masters!
They look exactly the same!

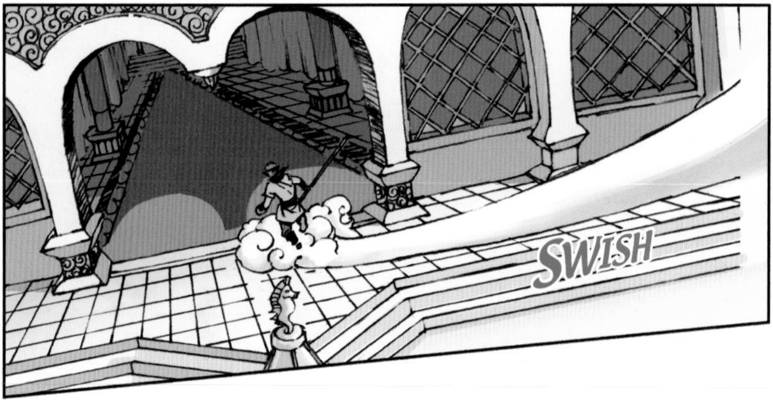
SWISH

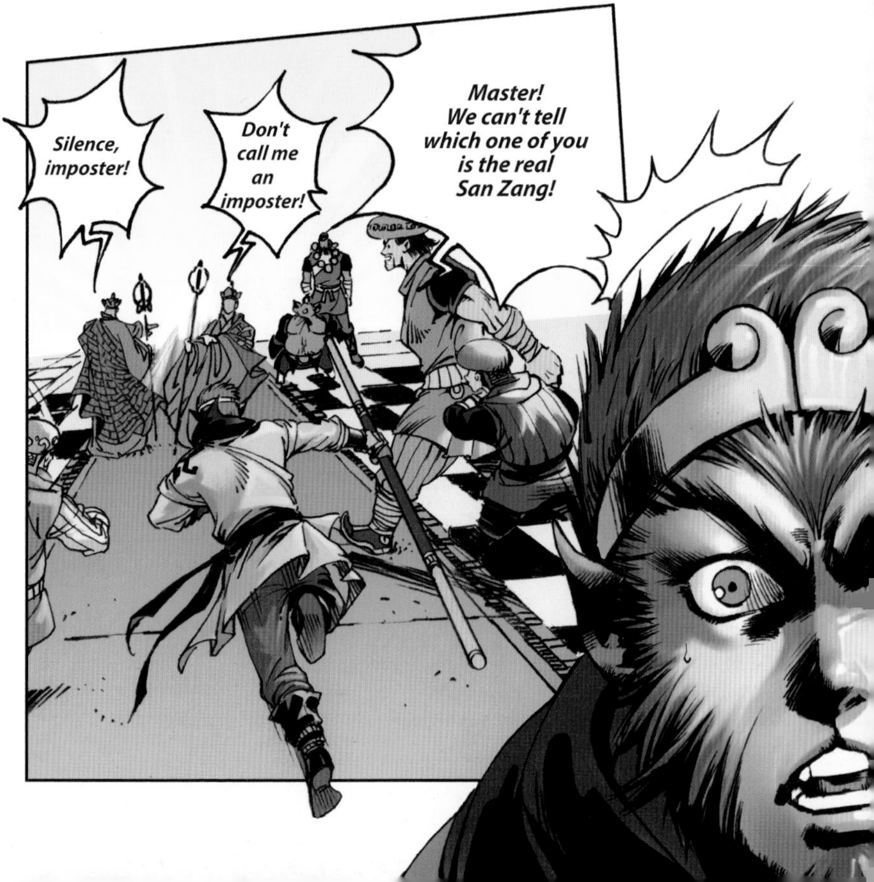
Master! We can't tell which one of you is the real San Zang!
Don't call me an imposter!
Silence, imposter!

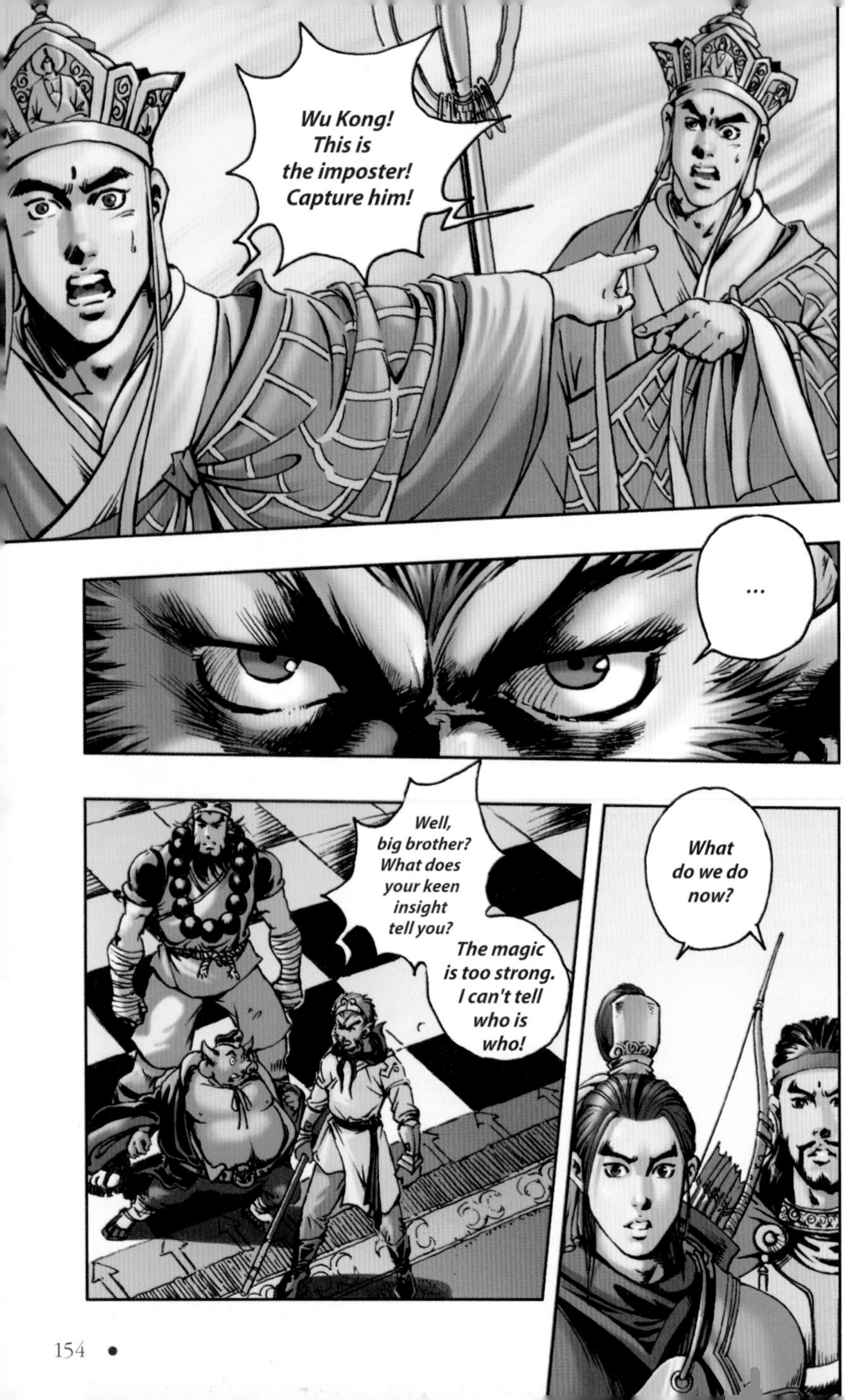
Wu Kong! This is the imposter! Capture him!
...
Well, big brother? What does your keen insight tell you?
The magic is too strong. I can't tell who is who!
What do we do now?

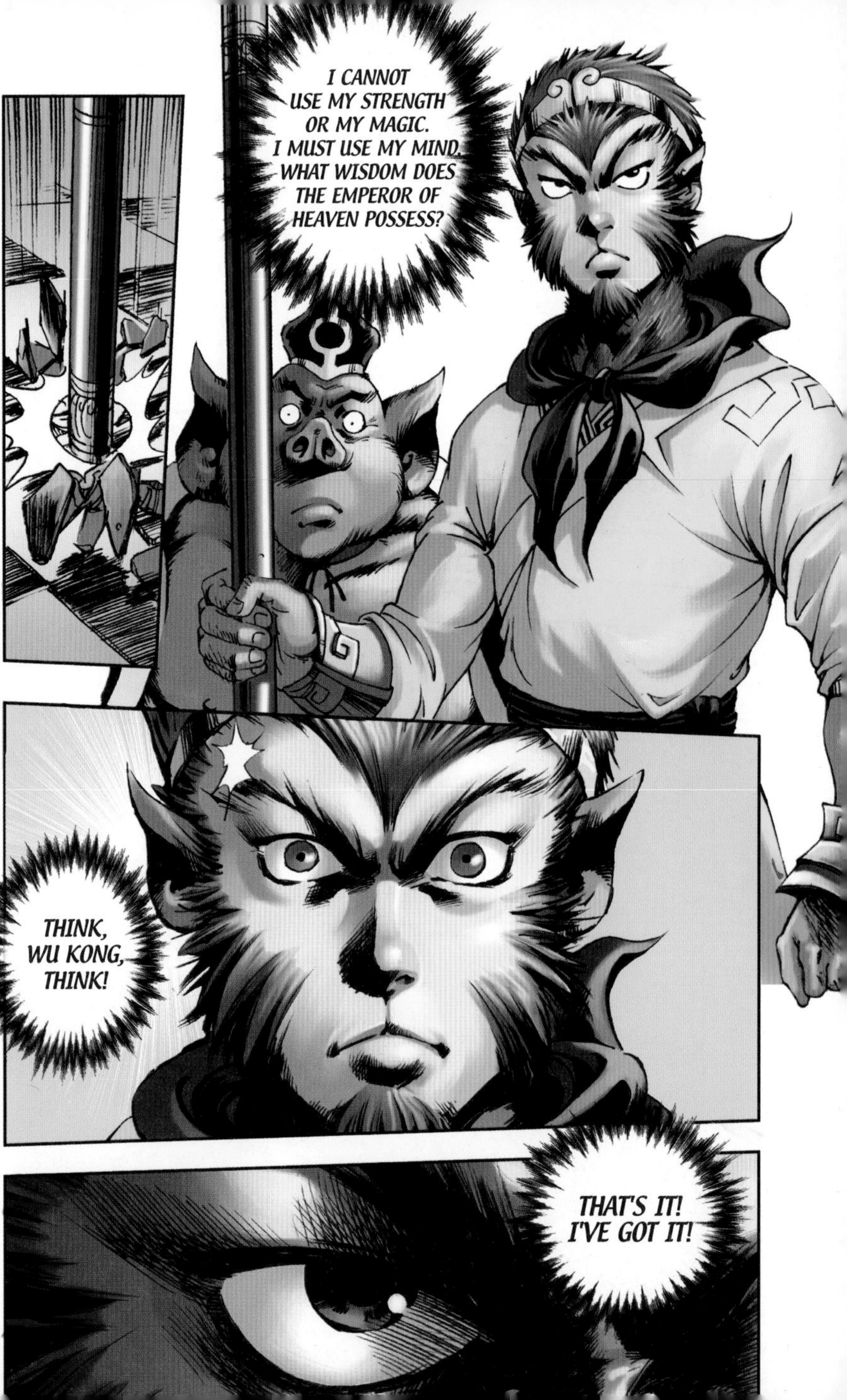
I CANNOT USE MY STRENGTH OR MY MAGIC. I MUST USE MY MIND. WHAT WISDOM DOES THE EMPEROR OF HEAVEN POSSESS?
THINK, WU KONG, THINK!
THAT'S IT! I'VE GOT IT!

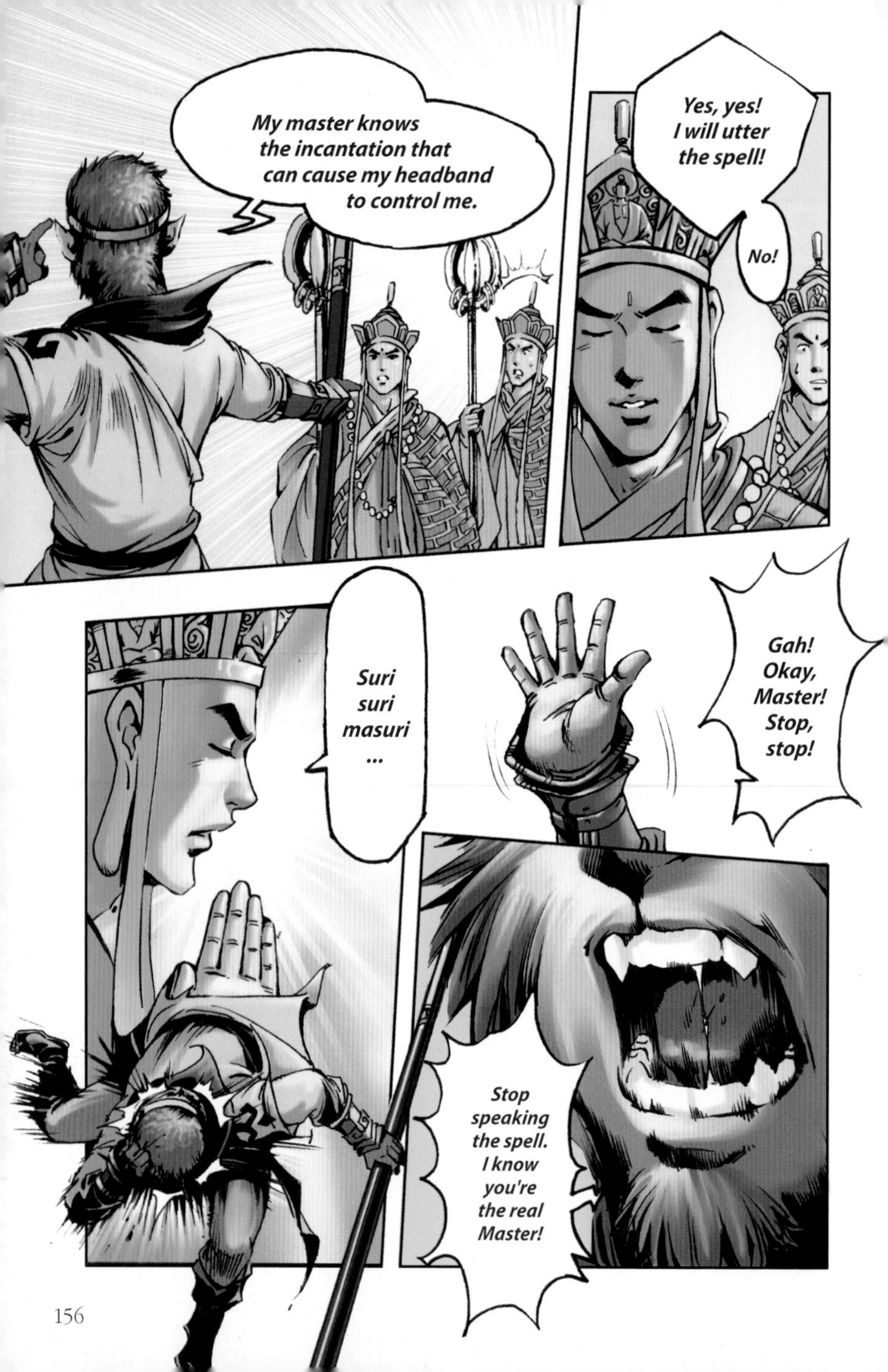
My master knows the incantation that can cause my headband to control me.
Yes, yes! I will utter the spell!
No!
Suri suri masuri ...
Gah! Okay, Master! Stop, stop!
Stop speaking the spell. I know you're the real Master!

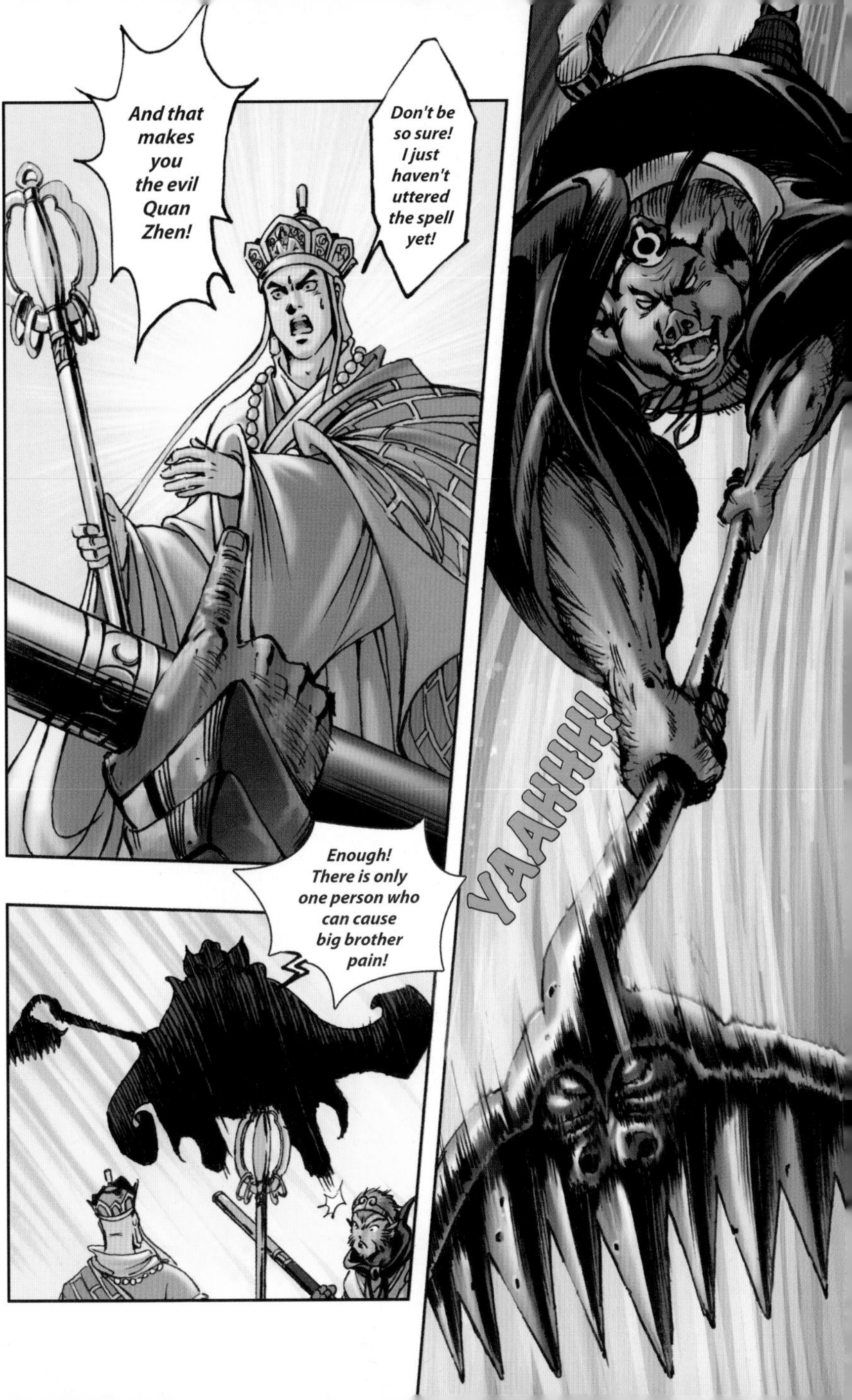
And that makes you the evil Quan Zhen!
Don't be so sure! I just haven't uttered the spell yet!
Enough! There is only one person who can cause big brother pain!
YAAHHH!

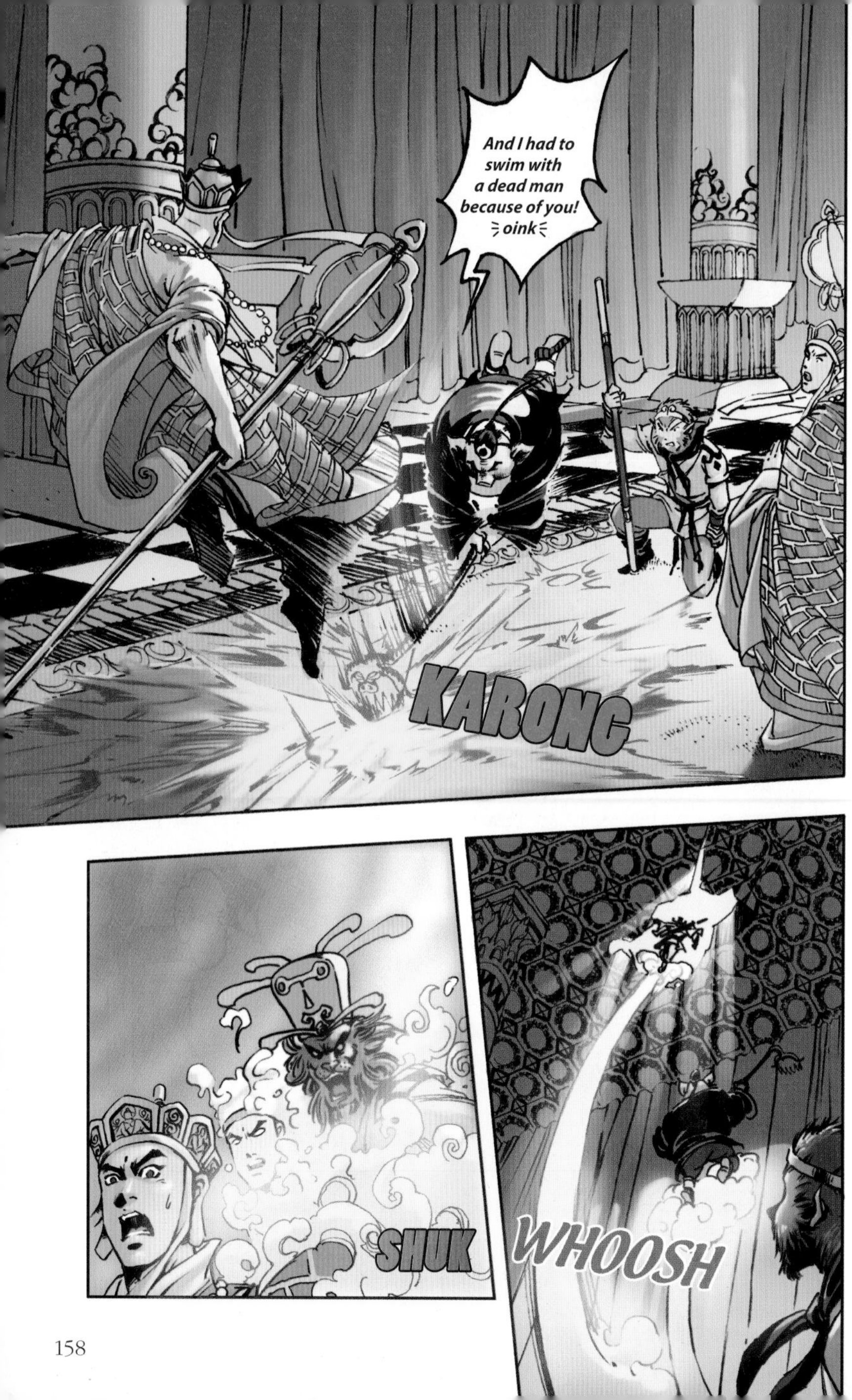
And I had to swim with a dead man because of you! oink
KARONG
SHUK
WHOOSH

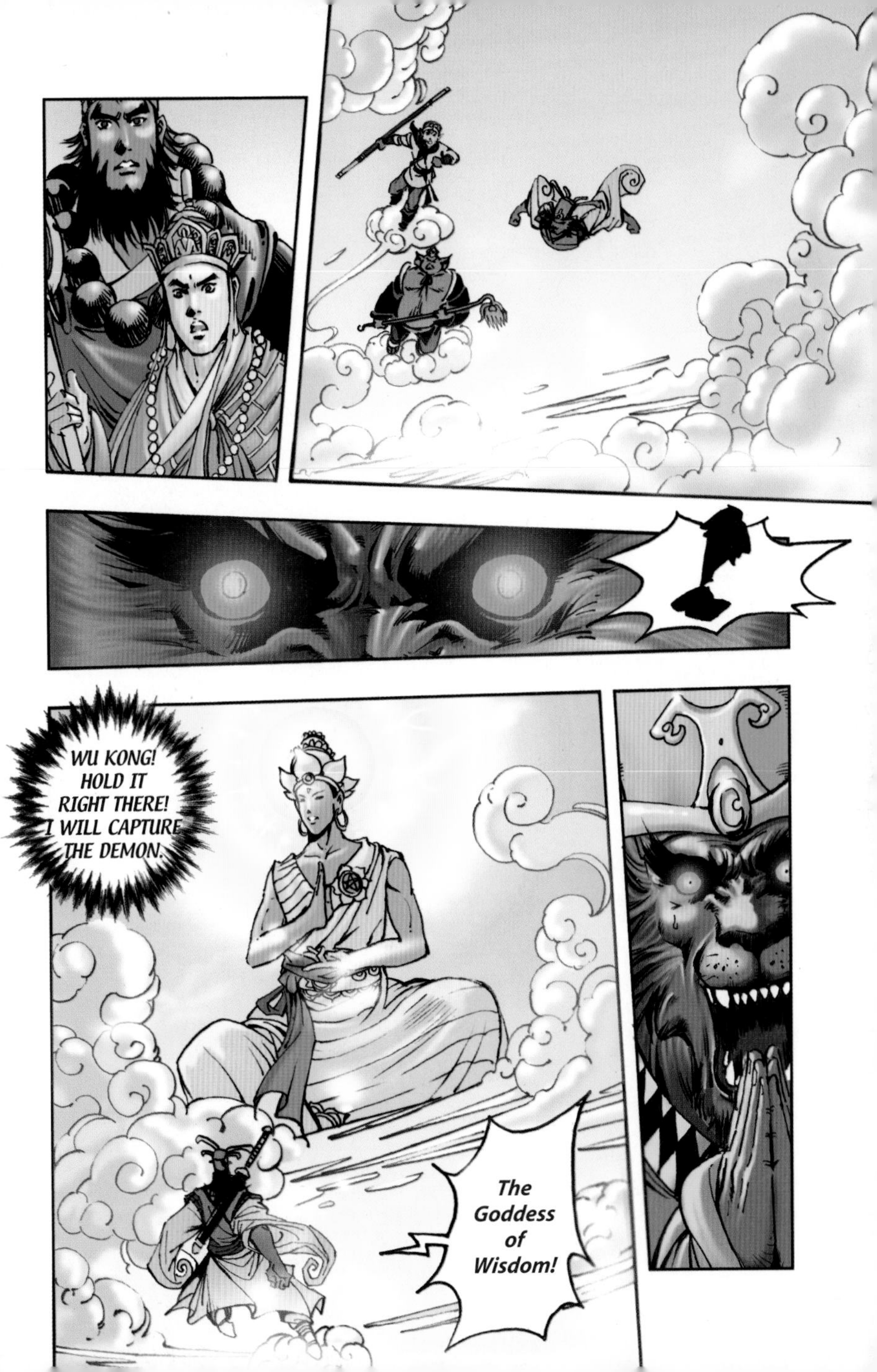

WU KONG! HOLD IT RIGHT THERE! I WILL CAPTURE THE DEMON.
The Goddess of Wisdom!

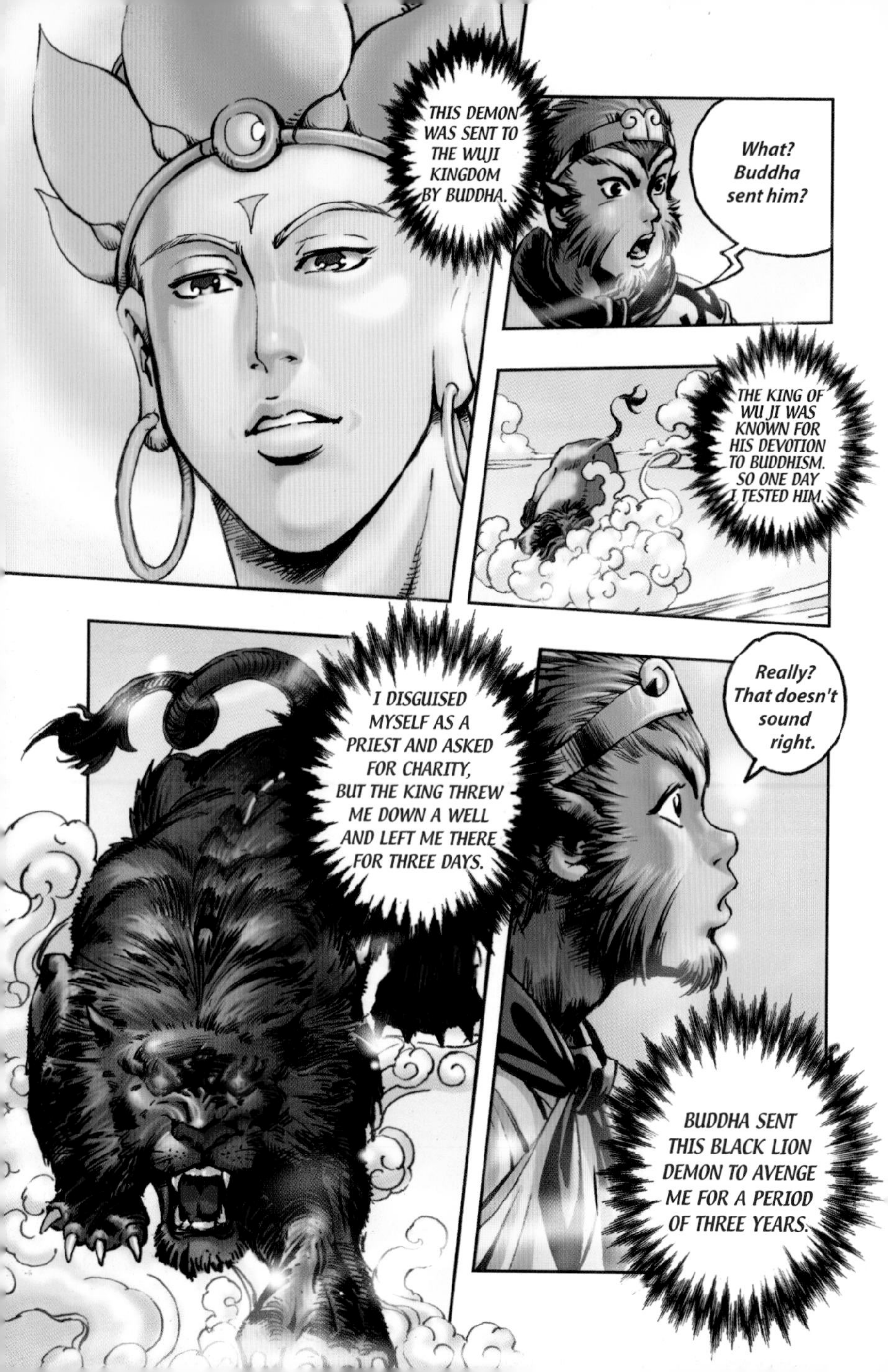
THIS DEMON WAS SENT TO THE WUJI KINGDOM BY BUDDHA.
What? Buddha sent him?
THE KING OF WU JI WAS KNOWN FOR HIS DEVOTION TO BUDDHISM. SO ONE DAY I TESTED HIM.
I DISGUISED MYSELF AS A PRIEST AND ASKED FOR CHARITY, BUT THE KING THREW ME DOWN A WELL AND LEFT ME THERE FOR THREE DAYS.
Really? That doesn't sound right.
BUDDHA SENT THIS BLACK LION DEMON TO AVENGE ME FOR A PERIOD OF THREE YEARS.

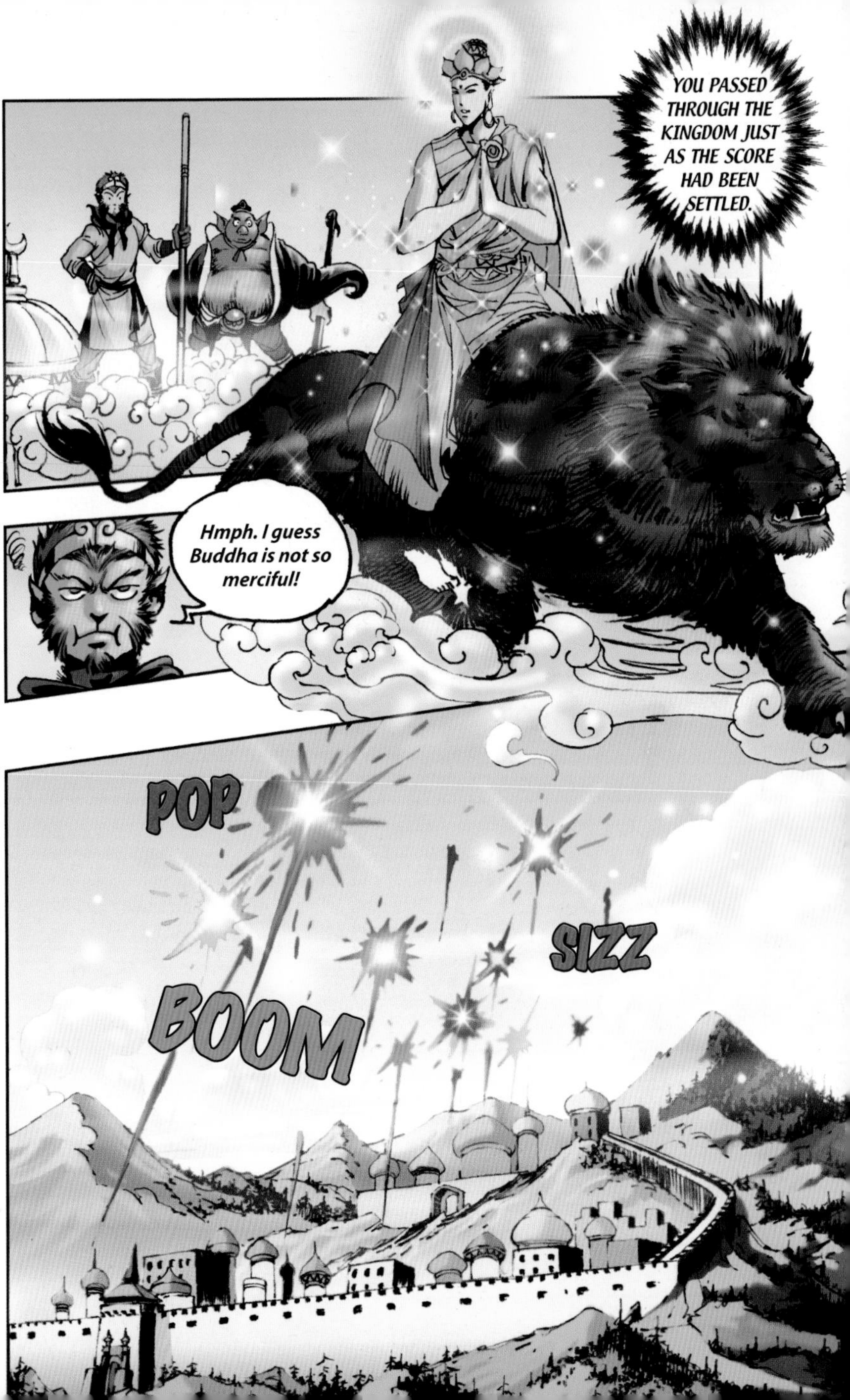
YOU PASSED THROUGH THE KINGDOM JUST AS THE SCORE HAD BEEN SETTLED.
Hmph. I guess Buddha is not so merciful!
POP
SIZZ
BOOM

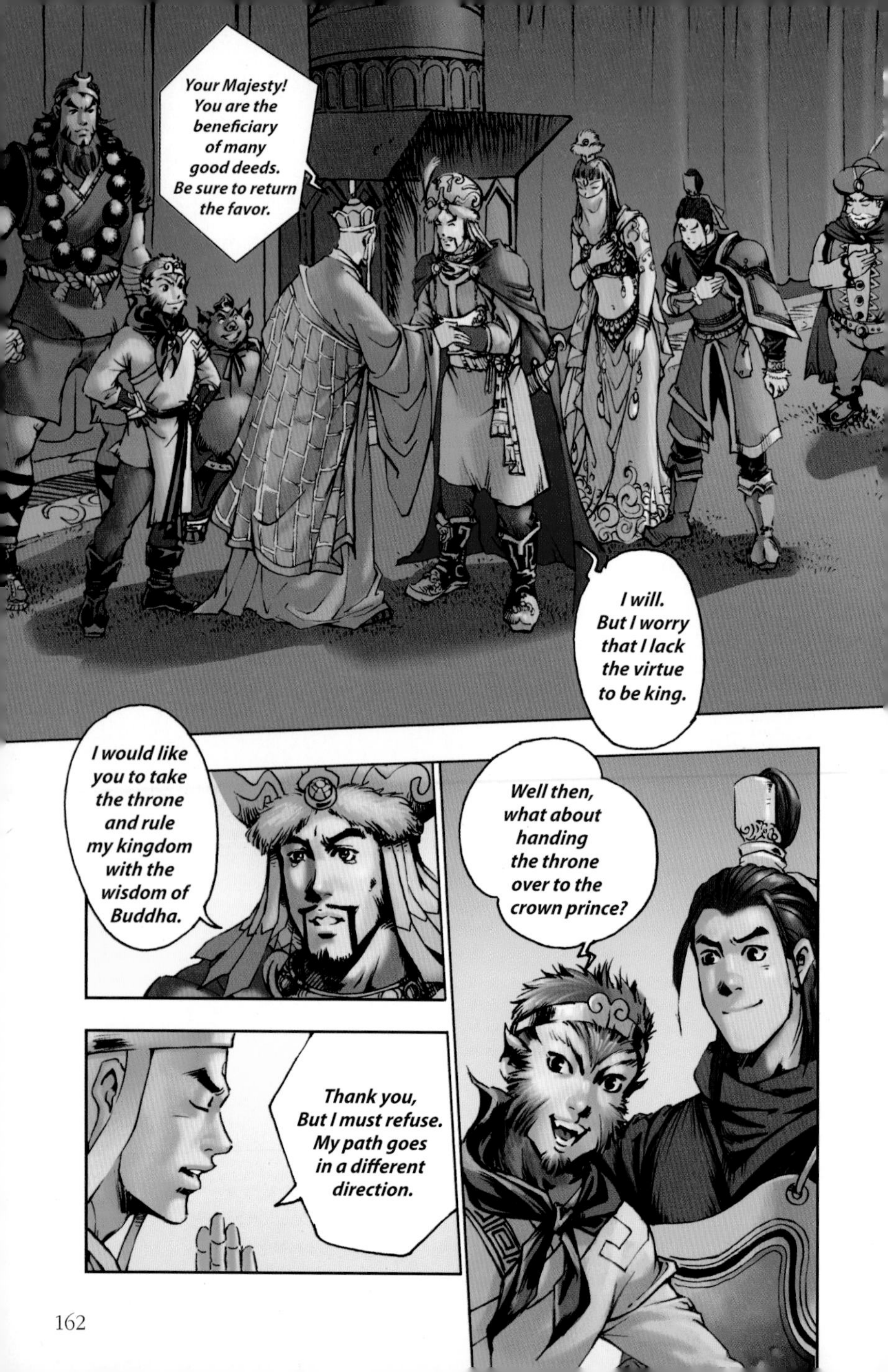
Your Majesty! You are the beneficiary of many good deeds. Be sure to return the favor.
I will. But I worry that I lack the virtue to be king.
I would like you to take the throne and rule my kingdom with the wisdom of Buddha.
Thank you, But I must refuse. My path goes in a different direction.
Well then, what about handing the throne over to the crown prince?

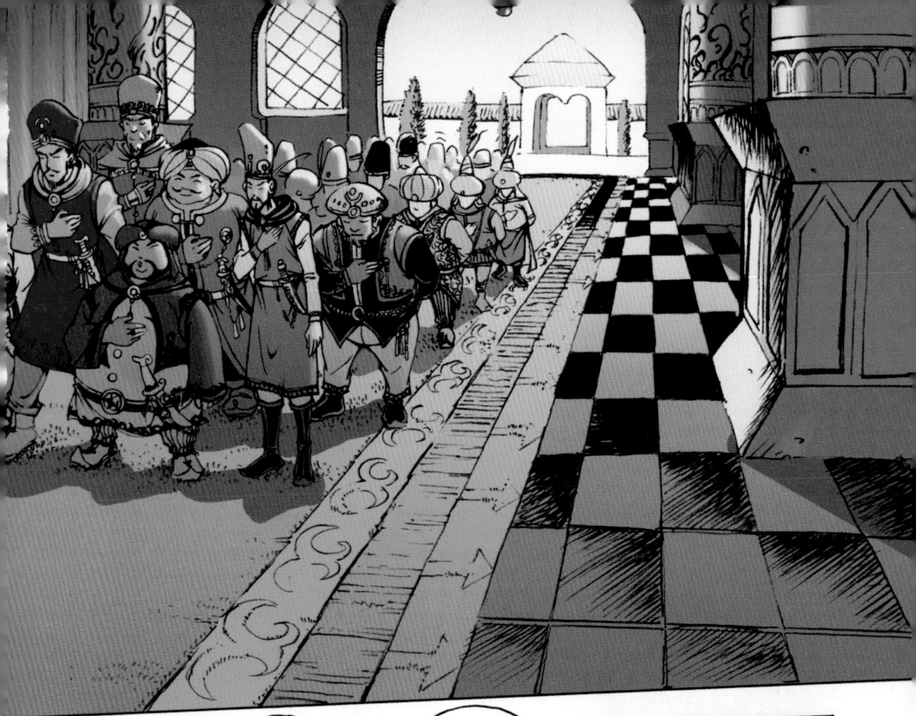

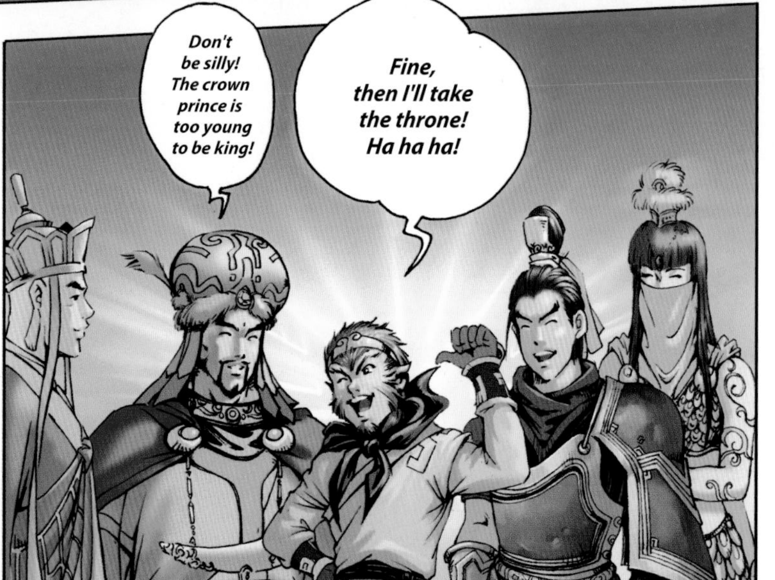
Don't be silly! The crown prince is too young to be king!
Fine, then I'll take the throne! Ha ha ha!

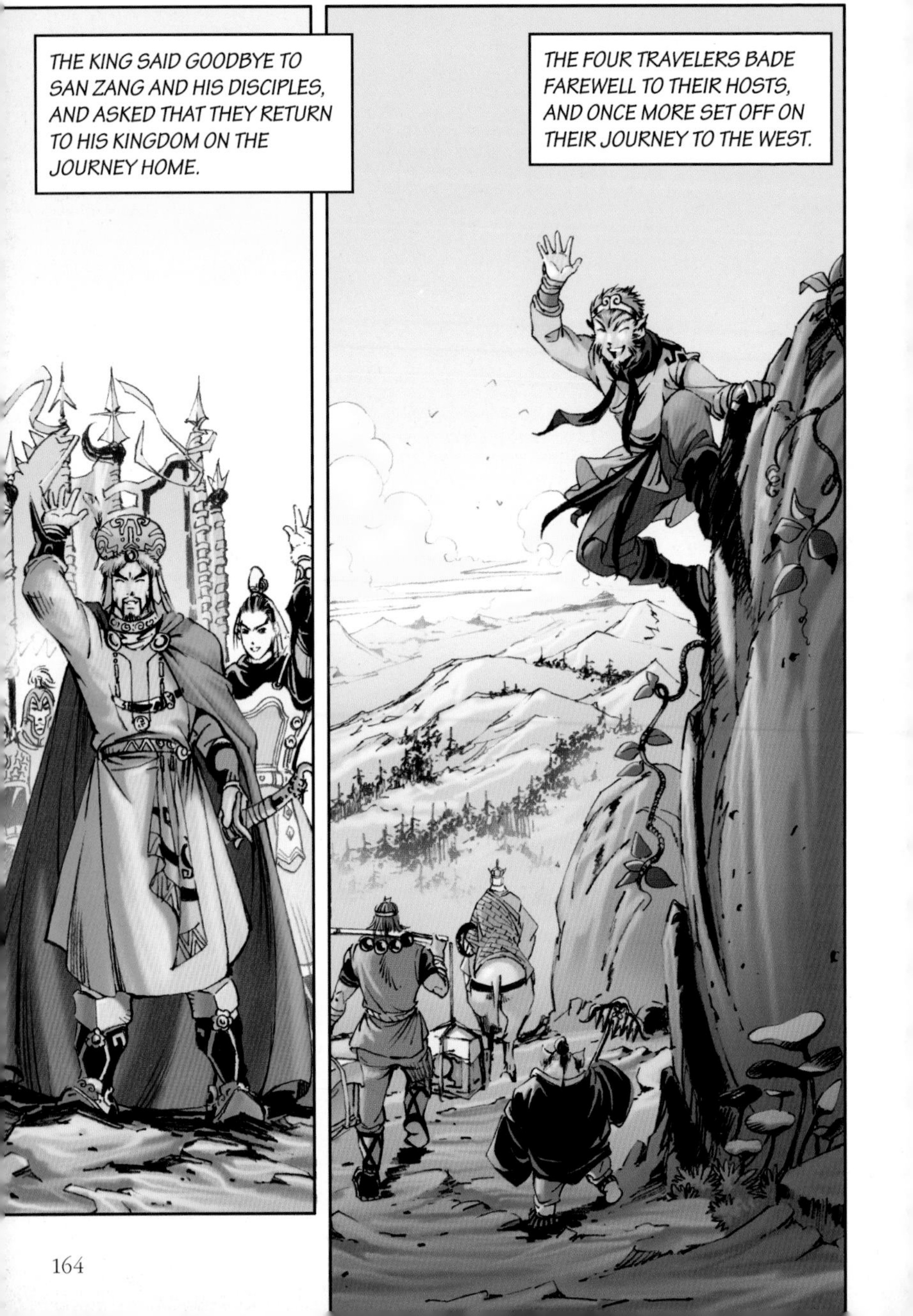
THE KING SAID GOODBYE TO SAN ZANG AND HIS DISCIPLES, AND ASKED THAT THEY RETURN TO HIS KINGDOM ON THE JOURNEY HOME.
THE FOUR TRAVELERS BADE FAREWELL TO THEIR HOSTS, AND ONCE MORE SET OFF ON THEIR JOURNEY TO THE WEST.

MONKEY KING

Appendix

——

THE STOLEN KINGDOM

———

● *San Zang, Sun Wu Kong, Zhu Bajie, and Sha Wu Jing have just come through one of their most difficult tasks yet, confronting and defeating two very powerful monster kings only to find out that the villains were in fact subjects of the Buddhist Goddess of Mercy, who once again has sought to test her subjects' commitment to the journey in the most extreme and dangerous way possible. As they continue along the treacherous path to the West, across rugged and sometimes impassible mountain terrain, they come across Baolin Temple.*

When San Zang asks the monks who occupy Baolin Temple if he and his disciples may spend the night, he is treated with great disrespect and turned away at the door. Enraged by the monks' mistreatment of his master, Sun Wu Kong bursts through the door, destroys a precious statue, and threatens to level the entire temple if the four companions are not offered lodging. The monks cower before the tremendous strength of the monkey king, and quickly offer the priest the best rooms, the best beds, and the best food.

While reading Buddhist scriptures during his first night in the temple, San Zang falls asleep, and in his dream he is approached by a ghost. The ghost was once the King of WuJi, a kingdom that suffered through a period of terrible drought before being rescued by a Taoist hermit named QuanZhen. QuanZhen then overthrew the kingdom by killing the king and taking his appearance, his wife, and his throne. The ghost of the king asks San Zang to avenge his death by recovering his kingdom, but the priest is worried that no one will believe the story. The ghost asks the priest to seek out his son, the Crown Prince of WuJi, and leaves behind a precious piece of white jade as evidence of his story.

San Zang wakes his disciples and tells them what he has seen and been told. At first uncertain of the priest's story, Sun Wu Kong nonetheless agrees to help restore the kingdom, and a plan is devised. Wu Kong disguises himself as a rabbit to lure the crown prince, who is an avid hunter, away from his father's kingdom and toward Baolin Temple. When the prince and his hunting party arrive, San Zang does not acknowledge or bow to him. At first the prince is insulted by the slight, but soon he is intrigued by the priest's words. San Zang tells the prince that he has a precious treasure that can tell the future, and presents a small box out of which jumps Sun Wu Kong. In response to Wu Kong's queries, the prince reveals what he believes to be the truth: that QuanZhen ran away three years ago and stole his father's precious white jade. Wu Kong reveals what actually happened, that the king was murdered and the throne usurped by the hermit imposter, and the prince is outraged. His outrage is quelled when Wu Kong presents him with his father's white jade.

The crown prince returns to the kingdom of WuJi and confronts his mother about the possibility that the king is not who he says he is. At first the queen is suspicious of San Zang's counsel to her son. But her suspicions give way to acceptance when she realizes that her marriage became terrible right about the time the king is said to have been killed. Convinced that the person married to his mother is not his real father, the crown prince returns to Baolin Temple and asks Sun Wu Kong to help him avenge his father.

Wu Kong cons Zhu Bajie into helping him by saying that they are on a quest for treasure, and together the two companions enter the

WuJi Kingdom and attempt to recover the king's body from the bottom of the well. Wu Kong lowers Bajie into the well, and the pig discovers the king's corpse being closely monitored by the King of the Well. Bajie is upset that he has been duped by Wu Kong, but the monkey says that if they can revive the king, the treasures they receive will be endless; but the king has been dead for more than three years, so any plan to revive him will require heavenly assistance. Wu Kong flies to the palace of Lord Tai Shang, whose elixir not only can grant eternal life, but also can restore life to the dead. At first Tai Shang refuses Wu Kong's request, on account of the monkey having eaten all of his elixir five hundred years earlier when he was rampaging through heaven. But when Tai Shang suspects that Wu Kong might be asking for a genuinely selfless reason, he hands over the elixir.

Wu Kong returns to the king's corpse, and Tai Shang's elixir, in combination with Wu Kong's life force, revives the king, who is then reunited with his son. The king, the crown prince, and the four companions then head to WuJi Palace to confront QuanZhen. At first the imposter tries to have his accusers arrested. But he is quickly driven from the palace by Wu Kong, and must resort to impersonating San Zang to attempt an escape. When Wu Kong finds it difficult to determine who is the imposter and who is the real San Zang, he asks his master to utter the spell that causes excruciating pain to emanate from his headband. San Zang does this, and Wu Kong and Bajie chase QuanZhen out of the kingdom and through the skies. Just as they are about to capture QuanZhen, they are intercepted by the Bodhisattva of Wisdom, who explains that QuanZhen is actually the Black Lion Demon, a frequent steed and companion. Apparently, three years earlier the Bodhisattva disguised himself as a priest and asked charity of the King of WuJi, who treated him cruelly and threw him in a well for three days. The Black Lion Demon was sent to WuJi as QuanZhen by Buddha, who sought revenge on the king.

The Bodhisattva and the Black Lion Demon ride off, and the King of WuJi is restored to his throne. At first, the king is humble about his past indiscretions and asks the priest to assume the throne. But the priest refuses, emphasizes to the king the importance of good deeds, and continues to the West with his four loyal friends.

TWIN ODYSSEYS

●   *Previously we have discussed the similarities and differences between The Journey to the West and one of the greatest adventure stories of Western literature, The Lord of the Rings. But if we want to further compare and contrast Journey to the West to the literary traditions of the West, we could do no better than look toward one of the first truly definitive works of the European tradition, an epic adventure that has inspired countless landmark narratives: Homer's epic poem The Odyssey.*

On the surface, the stories bear a remarkable similarity to each other: Both involve an arduous journey, both feature main characters who were forged in the fires of war, both take a considerable amount of time to tell the story of the journey, and both serve as mediations on the struggle between humanity and the world of the gods. Such similarities are striking, because the writing of The Odyssey is thought to have preceded the writing of Journey to the West by several centuries (800–750 B.C. versus 602–664), and because there is little to suggest that the authors of the Chinese novel were aware of Homer's epic poem. But what are even more striking than the similarities between the two works are the differences: while it is not impossible for two stories, written so far apart in terms of time and distance, to feature a long physical journey as the framework of the narrative, the way that the two stories present similar situations in different ways says a great deal about differing attitudes toward storytelling in the East and West.

The Odyssey is set during the aftermath of the Trojan War, as Homer's main character, Odysseus, scarred and cynical from his experience in battle, makes the long journey home to be reunited with his wife, Penelope. During the course of his travels, Odysseus will repeatedly try to reestablish some sense of the innocence that defined his life before he left for the war, and he often enlists the help of Zeus and other deities to achieve this—in the human-centralized world of The Odyssey, gods are powerful, but often act subordinate to people. Such efforts are foolhardy, though, as it is increasingly clear that the Trojan War has compromised humanity in irrevocable ways. When Odysseus returns to Ithaca, he finds it overrun by hundreds of "suitors," who offend him by competing for his wife's hand in marriage. Odysseus enlists the help of various gods—including his guardian, Athena—as well as his son, to kill the suitors and reunite with his wife. In the aftermath of this action, the citizens of Ithaca attempt to kill Odysseus in retribution for his killing the suitors, but Athena intervenes and ends the hostilities. In the end, even though he has succeeded in returning home and reuniting with his wife, Odysseus is left to ponder how the world will never be the same, that there is nothing heavenly worth aspiring to, and that humanity has lost something that can never be regained.

In contrast to the pessimistic tone of The Odyssey, The Journey to the West, while sharing the episodic structure of the journey narrative, presents a more optimistic picture about the outcome of the journey, because it establishes early on that the heavenly world is one to be aspired to and rigorously worked toward. Unlike Odysseus, Sun Wu Kong's experience of war has not scarred him, since he was often the aggressor, trying to fight his way into the ranks of heaven's elite. Rather, Wu Kong's transformation from the Handsome Monkey King to San Zang's loyal disciple on the path to enlightenment is the result of a series of situations that serve to remind Wu Kong that heavenly enlightenment can only be attained through discipline of the spirit, not through declarations of war. Like Odysseus, Wu Kong's journey will take much, much longer than expected, and will be completed only by an otherworldly sense of determination. Unlike Odysseus, Wu Kong is not running away from what the world can be; he is running toward it. Where Odysseus sees a world corrupted beyond repair, observed by often ambivalent gods and left to sink into depravity, Wu Kong sees the potential for synthesis between Earth and Heaven (since he himself is a product of this synthesis) and struggles to find the path of enlightenment that will join the two forever.

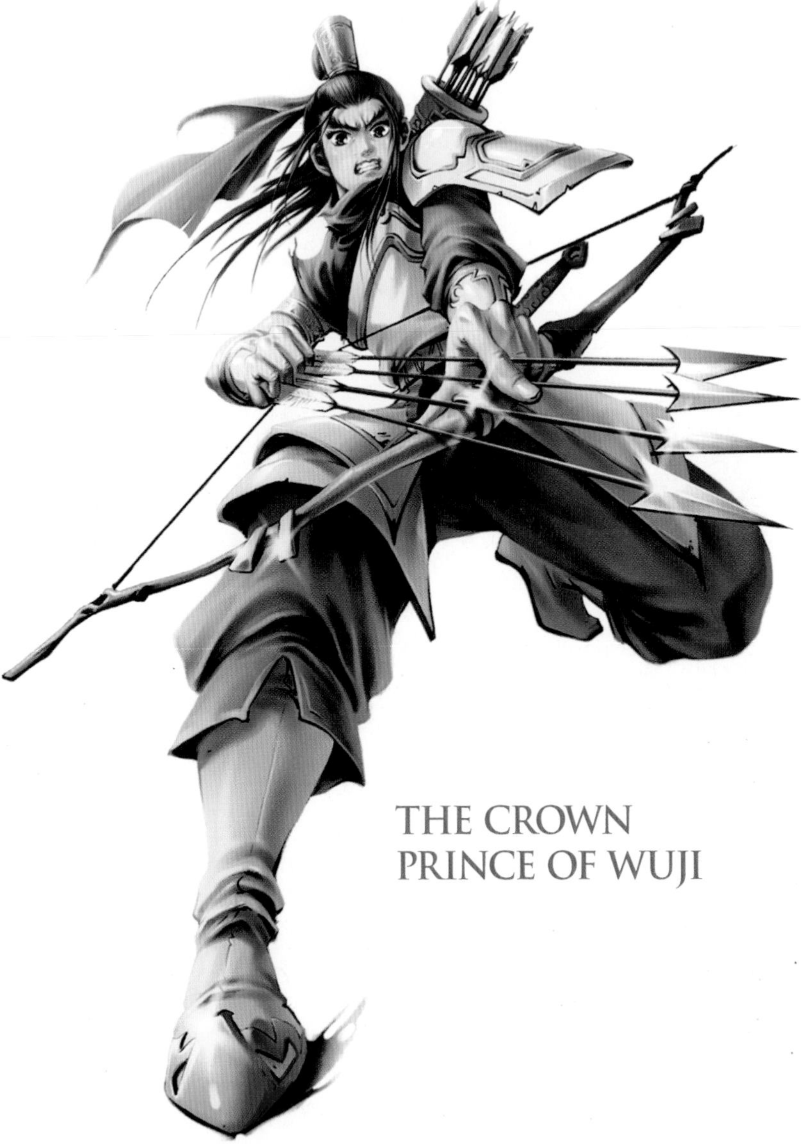

THE CROWN
PRINCE OF WUJI

Adventures from China — MONKEY KING

Vol. 01   **Vol. 02**   **Vol. 03**   **Vol. 04**   **Vol. 05**

Vol. 06   **Vol. 07**   **Vol. 08**   **Vol. 09**   **Vol. 10**

Vol. 11   **Vol. 12**   **Vol. 13**   **Vol. 14**   **Vol. 15**

Vol. 16   **Vol. 17**   **Vol. 18**   **Vol. 19**   **Vol. 20**